PATTI DIENER

Wild Flower

Names: Diener, Patti, author
Title: Wildflower / Patti Diener
Identifiers: ISBN 9781733295420 (paperback) ISBN 9781733295437 (ebook)
Cover Design by Damonza
First Edition: July 2025

For my daughters, Fallon and Emma

*Always stay true to yourself and dream
big. The world needs dreamers.*

CHAPTER ONE

SUMMER 2010
CHARLIE

SUNLIGHT STREAMED THROUGH the sheer curtains of Charlie Kane's bedroom window and pulled at her eyelids. She didn't want to wake and face the reality of what had happened the night before. Sleep was all she wanted. The dark void of nothingness and an escape from feeling and knowing. Still, she knew the sun didn't give two fucks about what she wanted, and it would continue to rise each day whether she craved darkness or not.

If she couldn't control when the August daylight arrived, she could at least control where she chose to be. Today, she wanted to leave the world behind, go to the library, and dive into another book to block out last night and how her mother had failed her once again.

As she lay on her stomach listening to the old creaky house, Charlie squeezed her eyes shut and hoped that the asshole Greg was gone. Her mother, Cece, and Mom's boyfriend, Greg, had been quite drunk and belligerent the night before. When Cece had told him how stupid he was, he'd wacked her across the cheek, leaving Cece in a limp pile on the couch, crying and sporadically laughing all at once like some insane lunatic. But Charlie had made the mistake of getting involved.

When she'd told Greg "to stay the fuck away from her mother," he'd turned his full attention on Charlie, forgetting her crumpled mother, who was hysterical and blabbering on incoherently on the couch.

"Oh, you want some of this, sweetheart? You think you are better than me too? Fuck you, Kane women! You ain't smarter than me, and you ain't better."

Charlie had backed up against the wall of the adjoining small kitchen, as Greg had moved fast to get in her face, greasy skin and fists as big as canned hams. She was taller than him, but her skinny five-foot, ten-inch body was still only a hundred and thirty pounds. He had the upper hand in weight and strength.

Charlie had been against the wall with one hip at the aging Formica countertop. The kitchen wall clock behind her head had ticked so loudly in her ears she'd thought maybe it was the sound of her racing heartbeat that was pounding like a rabbit's. Greg's nose at her chin, he'd looked up into her eyes and snarled at her.

"Not so brave now, are ya, you little slit. You will learn that I don't take no orders from a kid. You backed up now? Say you are sorry."

Staring into his eyes, Charlie reached over slowly with one hand to the counter with the hope of grabbing a knife out of the block sitting there, but she was too far away. Instead, she tried to talk him down.

"I only want you to leave my mom alone. That's all. She didn't mean anything by it. She's just drunk."

He took a step back but kept his eyes glued to her as he crossed his arms over his barrel chest. For a short guy, he was thick as a fire plug, with big hairy forearms. They looked like he could snap her in half. Charlie's mouth was dry, and her long, curly hair was sticking to her face, neck, and back. Sweat dripped between her breasts and drizzled down between her shoulder blades inside her tank top.

"She's weak. That's what she is. But you…I think you are fiery," he said, moving closer now with a smile. "Yeah, maybe I could take a taste of you, and all will be forgiven."

Charlie stiffened at his closeness, sickened by his sour breath. Her head against the wall, she put her hands up to block his sweaty chest from pressing against her, but the next thing she knew, he was running his meaty palm up her thigh to the inside of her shorts.

"Get the fuck off of me, you creep!" she yelled.

He pushed harder against her, and Charlie struggled, wondering why her mother wasn't doing anything to stop him, to pull him off, but Cece sat dazed, having slumped to the floor. As Greg fought Charlie to undo the button of her shorts, she drew her knee up hard and fast, smashing into his groin, and down he went with a groan to the floor.

Charlie ran over to her mother, who just sat watching but doing nothing.

"Now you've done it," her mother mumbled softly. "Shouldn't have done that, Charlotte."

"*Are you fucking kidding me right now?* MOM!" she pleaded.

Greg was coughing and growling words in between. "You… crazy… bitch."

When it was clear Cece was in no condition to help her, Charlie ran to her room, blocked the door with a chair, and flopped on her bed. She'd stayed there watching the door for quite a while before realizing Greg was too drunk and stunned to pursue her or her mother any further that night. Once things got quiet, Charlie decided to leave and went out her bedroom window, propping it open so she could return later the same way she'd left.

Now with the start of a new day, after only about two hours of sleep, Charlie got up and looked outside to see if Greg's truck was still in the driveway. Luckily, it was gone. He must have left during the small amount of time she'd actually slipped into deep, dark slumber. It had still been there when she'd returned just before dawn from a night out with The Guerrillas, the local graffiti artists of Sebastopol and Bodega Bay area of California.

Charlie moved the rickety chair away from her door and cracked it open just enough to sneak out quietly. She found her mother lying on her stomach on the ancient, sagging couch with one arm hanging to the floor. It was still early, and knowing Cece like she did, she'd be out for hours sleeping it off.

Feeling a bit more relaxed with the asshole Greg gone, Charlie brushed her teeth and washed her armpits and chest with a washcloth before going to her room and changing into fresh, comfortable clothes. She raked through her uncontrollable hair with a brush and slapped on some deodorant before walking outside of their shabby 1940s bungalow rental, with its peeling white paint and spongy front steps.

Passing by her steel-gray 1968 Volkswagen Beetle that sat lifeless in the driveway, Charlie gave a heavy sigh. It really would be so much easier if she could take her car instead of walking into town, but with the transmission still needing repairs, she had no choice until she had the money to get it fixed.

Since the library didn't open until ten o'clock, Charlie made her way to Retrograde Coffee for a latte and bagel. She could at least read the paper or scroll on her phone while she waited. Normally, Charlie didn't like to go where she worked on her day off, feeling guilty for not helping, but today she had nowhere else to go. Staying home wasn't an option, and her list of friends to call was nonexistent.

Charlie was a loner, introverted, and liked it that way. She only had acquaintances at school, and The Guerrillas were of all ages, and only went by nicknames so nobody could rat them out. She didn't really know any of them on a personal level.

Street art was one of Charlie's passions, but it was illegal, and nobody wanted to get pinched. Her alias was Star, after her love of the wildflower Star Lily (or its proper name, *Leucocrinum montanum*). No one in the street art community was close to Charlie or knew her real life. She didn't think anyone of them really were friends by day, but everyone in The Guerrillas respected each other and their work. It wasn't vandalism, like the city ordinance claimed.

It was true art, and some of these people would travel around from place to place, just creating the most beautiful and symbolic paintings in one night. Charlie felt alive in their presence. But when daylight threatened, like vampires, they all vanished.

The crisp air in Sebastopol on this August morning was refreshing. The fog hadn't lifted yet, and the dewy streets on that Saturday were still quiet, as the Sonoma County town was just beginning to wake up. While making her way to Main Street, there were shop owners inside their buildings just turning on lights. She passed clothing stores, yoga studios, and rock shops, as well as nail salons, art galleries, and restaurants. A few other people were walking the sidewalks with their dogs and carrying coffees, dressed in leggings and North Face pullovers. It was summer, but with the coastal influence, Sebastopol had a very misty feeling early in the morning.

As she entered Retrograde Coffee, her bosses' familiar faces were at the counter. The husband-and-wife team looked at her and gave smiles. Charlie was a really good barista even at only seventeen years old, and she was often the favorite of many customers. Even though she liked her privacy and didn't allow herself to have close relationships, she was smart enough to understand that polite conversation and smiling a lot gained you more tips. She needed the tips.

When Charlie placed her order for a mocha latte and an everything bagel, Teri and Michael were too swamped to ask her much about why she was out and about so early on a Saturday, or why she was there on her day off. She sat at a window table to watch the town unfold, and before long, it was nearly ten o'clock. Time for the library to open.

Charlie walked a block west and was rounding the corner of Bodega Avenue when a small dog with fluffy hair came flying towards her with a leash and no owner attached to it. The shaggy white-and-tan dog came barreling down the sidewalk and ran right into Charlie's arms as she protectively blocked the critter from going any farther.

She picked up the dog that felt lighter than air and held it in her arms, looking for anyone who might belong to the furball. Then rounding the corner from the Wells Fargo Bank came a stressed-out-looking guy with a large Labrador on a leash. He was in shorts, running shoes, and a sweatshirt. The worried look on his face was cute, then as he saw her holding the small dog, he almost looked apologetic, shaking his head.

"There you are. Holy shit. I'm so sorry he got away. I was trying to use the ATM machine and somehow dropped his leash."

As the man neared Charlie, she felt herself go weak at the sight of this twenty-something hunk with dark facial stubble and blue-green eyes that could melt your heart. He started to smile as he got closer, and he was so good-looking it hurt. A dimple in his right cheek was deep and adorable, and something new stirred inside Charlie. She didn't want to flee.

"What's his name?" she asked. Standing her ground and not turning away from strangers wasn't her norm. Especially when she faced incredibly good-looking strangers who made her heart flutter.

"That escape artist is Henry. I'm not sure he likes taking walks, but obviously, he loves to run."

She didn't want to let the tiny creature go because the longer she had possession of the dog, the longer the guy had to stay with her. He was tall. Taller than her, which was rare for Charlie, and he had broad shoulders. She wondered how they would feel to touch.

"So, you didn't know if he would like a walk, yet you took him out with this big guy? Don't you own him, or are you a dognaper?" she prodded, protectively holding the pup.

"He's actually not mine. He belongs to my uncle who I'm dog-sitting for. House-sitting, too, I guess. This one is George. Thank God he's chill."

He rubbed the top of the head of the large Labrador that looked to be every bit of one hundred and twenty pounds. The look in that dog's eyes though was clear. He was laid-back with no worries in the world.

"Well, we can't all be perfect like George there. Henry might be scared of cars and people," she suggested, gazing into the good-looking guy's dreamy eyes.

"My uncle insisted they go on walks all the time. Maybe Henry's just a runner, and I let my guard down." He smiled that irresistible smile again, with teeth so perfect Charlie thought she might sigh out loud.

As she held Henry close, he started to lick her chin and wiggled wildly. Smiling, she let him down and held on to his leash for good measure, keeping him near her but not offering the leash to the attractive stranger.

"What kind of dog is Henry?"

"I think my uncle said he's a Havanese. Apparently, they don't shed, because they have hair instead of fur. George here seems to shed enough to knit a sweater, so the companion dog he got for him had to have hair. Do you know much about dogs?"

Charlie had never had a pet because her mother was far too self-absorbed and could scarcely take care of herself, much less a pet. A clear example would be their always empty refrigerator. Most of the time Charlie took care of her mother instead of the other way around. Besides, pets required food and vet bills, which they never had the money for with Cece's hairdresser wages, but Charlie had always yearned for something to cuddle and love. It just never worked out. Instead, she read about animals and learned from books, like she learned about everything else that interested her.

"I know enough. I know that you have your hands full with Henry here. He'll require a lot more attention from you while you're visiting. Where are you from anyway? Not around here, that's for sure."

Her antagonistic grilling was a piss-poor attempt at flirting, but what did she know of flirting? Being confrontational was her default. Especially with guys.

Putting his free hand into the pocket of his shorts as he looked at her with an amused smirk, he asked, "What makes you say that?"

"Because I would have known if you were a local."

"Oh, yeah? How so?" He raised his eyebrows as his thick, dark hair fell over one eye.

Charlie looked him up and down as Henry circled her legs and she sidestepped over his leash.

"For one, around here, most people wear long socks and slides. You have no-show socks and running shoes. Also, your sweatshirt says Long Beach. I'm guessing you're a SoCal guy."

He looked at his sweatshirt and laughed. "I guess that was a tell. You got me. So, you are local then, huh?"

"Very." She couldn't believe she was still talking to him, and that her nerves didn't make her clam up. "So, is this house you are staying at enormous to accommodate that dog?" She nodded towards George.

"Um…" He scratched his chin stubble, the motion incredibly sexy, making her want to run her fingers over that strong jaw. "It's fairly large. Yeah, George is plenty comfortable there."

She was running out of things to say to keep him there. When he left, she'd be alone again. Alone with her thoughts. It was far better admiring the tall stranger than thinking.

"Where were you going before you had to rescue my dog?" he asked, turning to walk back up the hill.

Charlie fell into step alongside him, holding Henry's leash herself. The little dog trotted beside her comfortably.

"I was going to the library." She pointed across the street and up the hill.

"Big reader, huh?"

"Yep. Books are always there for you. You can experience anything you want to in books. Do you read?"

He laughed for a second, and she thought maybe he was some jock who only watched sports and never cracked a book in school. But then he surprised her.

"I was actually an English major. I studied creative writing and journalism at UCLA. Honestly, I was working for some tabloid rag in LA and had to leave because, although it paid the bills, it's not what I want to be doing. I want to write something great. I want to be a novelist. So, yeah. I read quite a lot."

Charlie couldn't believe her good fortune. He liked books! But as they were getting closer to the library, she knew he'd go soon. She could walk slower, but it still wasn't going to be enough to stop time, and unlike most guys she'd met, Charlie wanted to get to know him.

"Who do you read?" she asked.

"Oh, well…Um, so many. I love James Patteson, John Grisham, Dean Koontz, the classics, ya know…Fitzgerald, Hemingway. But recently I've been reading Lisa Scottoline. Her thrillers are freakin' unreal."

"I like her too. I was wondering if you were going to list any women, or if you just read male authors. Women are really slaying it in publishing, you know? And Hemingway's third wife, Martha Gellhorn, fought hard to get out from his shadow." She had to nearly bite her tongue to stop herself from rambling.

They looked both ways as they crossed the street to the library. The brick building had two patrons waiting outside of it, and as the doors were unlocked, they went inside, leaving Charlie and the tall stranger alone on the sidewalk.

"Well, I'll have to check her out. I'm not sexist, ya know. I just read whatever interests me." He was smirking, seemingly unaffected by her surly comment.

They leaned against the brick wall of the building as the sun pierced through the tree leaves, sending shards of light into their eyes as they spoke. Charlie shielded her face with one hand to get a better look at this hot guy. Having graduated from college, he was older than her. Possibly too old. Still, he was young enough that they both seemed pulled to continue the conversation, wanting to know more. Charlie drank up everything he said. *He loved books!* Nobody talked about books with her, much less someone she was attracted to.

"Okay, I stand corrected then about my assumption. I read everything too. Fiction, memoir, narrative nonfiction stuff." She stopped and clamped her mouth shut to stop the rambling.

Henry stared up at her with anticipation. She leaned to pick him up and pet him as she continued to talk with SoCal guy. Carrying Henry's light, little body was like holding a bird, even though he looked like he'd weigh much more.

When Charlie looked back at this guy that she'd just met, he, too, was drinking up her every word, eyes locked on hers and fully engaged. Charlie's stomach flipped as he held her gaze. Those eyes shaded by dark lashes. Without him touching her, she had the feeling of being caressed. This sensation of connection was like magic, like nothing she'd ever felt before. It was wonderful and mysterious.

It scared the shit out of her.

"I love that," he said. "Yeah, I read nonfiction too. Have you read *The Warmth of Other Suns* by Isabel Wilkerson? It's a fantastic migration story. You'd like it," he said, stepping closer to her. "See? I read female authors." He smiled as bright as the sun.

Handing Henry's leash over to him, she nodded, looking away and tucking a wild hair behind her ear as the breeze kicked up. "Yeah, I'll look for that one. Listen, I gotta run."

She looked into his eyes one last time, knowing he was out of her league, too busy, too occupied with a future for himself she didn't belong in. He was just a visitor to her town anyway. What was the point of carrying on this conversation? Better to go before it got any harder.

He looked at her, puzzled, and accepted the leash, but not before grabbing her loosely by the wrist. If she wasn't mistaken, he rubbed the inside of her wrist with his thumb. His touch, like tingly velvet, sent a bolt of energy to her heart space that surprised her.

"You in a hurry?" he asked as he held both leashes in one hand.

Gathering every ounce of strength she had to straighten her spine, Charlie snickered in an effort to seem aloof and mysterious.

Reluctantly, she pulled away. "I'm a busy girl. See ya, Dog Man. You really need to watch ole Henry. Don't let him go, or someone will swipe him up and take him home."

She turned and nearly skipped away, telling herself to go. To get! *Don't look back, or you will lose your nerve to walk away from the beautiful man who will just end up breaking your heart. Everyone does eventually. Don't let your guard down.*

As she was nearing the library door, he shouted, "But wait! I don't even know your name."

She turned with a hand on the door and said, "Does it matter?"

Charlie went inside and forced herself to move ahead without turning back.

⁖

CHAPTER TWO

JACK

STANDING OUTSIDE THE Sebastopol Public Library, Jack Connors scratched his head, dumbfounded and confused. He'd thought he'd really hit it off with the beautiful, and somewhat unruly, girl who had saved little Henry. He stood with a furrowed brow and looked around, wondering if he'd maybe said something that turned her off.

"What'd I say, guys?" he asked the dogs.

He turned around and walked back across the street to try his luck again at the ATM machine. He just wanted some cash to go grab a coffee and sit outside on the street to people-watch and get better acquainted with Sebastopol. The city was quite similar to something out of *American Graffiti*, a movie his mother used to watch that she claimed was filmed nearby.

As he took his card from his wallet, this time he looped both leashes on to his left wrist while using his right hand to tap in his pin and grab the cash from the machine.

She seemed so interested and then…what happened?

Jack mulled it over and over like toying with a ball of string, unraveling then rewrapping it again. He and love hadn't been doing so well as of late. It had been six months since his breakup with

Barbie Bianca—as his friends called her—and Jack was beginning to wonder if he'd ever find the right girl. Not the *perfect girl*…just the perfect girl for him.

Now walking down the hill of Bodega Avenue towards Main Street, Jack couldn't get the vision of the mysterious girl out of his mind. Her tall frame was so graceful in how she moved. Although her attire seemed a bit disheveled—with her dark crop top, baggy sweatpants low on her hips, and unzipped sweatshirt showing her navel—he was still very intrigued. Her perfect figure didn't hurt either. More than anything, he was attracted to her soulful, brown eyes. Something about them was dark, troubled, and beautiful. They were large like a doe's but turned down at the outer corners, and they gave her a bit of a sad look, even when she smiled. And that sharp tongue of hers. He loved that she wasn't trying to impress him and had strong opinions. Still… she'd left.

With the dogs trotting alongside him, Jack turned right, and down the sidewalk was a coffee shop called Retrograde Coffee. They had some outdoor tables on the street, just what he was looking for. After he looped the leashes through the chair and took a seat, a woman came out to get his order. When she left, he exhaled and sank deeper into the chair, allowing the tension to drain out of him.

Why was he tense?

With more people cruising the streets and sidewalk now, he considered all he'd been through to get here. The move from LA to Sebastopol, even if it was temporary, was a big change. Being in a smaller community and not knowing a soul was also weird. But at twenty-four years old, he found that his job at the *LA Scoop* had run its course, and he knew it was a dead end for him. Writing fluff over the last year and nosing into celebrities' private business was not something he felt good about. Taking a hiatus and helping out his uncle had been suggested by his mother, Rita, who had been tired of watching him mope around every weekend when they'd meet for Sunday dinner.

"Uncle Rob needs a house and dog sitter, and you have nothing going on. Just take the trip for the month and clear your head. The cooler weather would do you good anyway. Much better than August in LA. Northern California is beautiful. Go get inspired," his mother had said.

Jack had enough in savings to last him several months, and since he hadn't renewed his lease on his apartment in Santa Monica, he either had to move in with his mother, or take the offer to stay at his uncle's. He'd only been there two days and wondered if he'd made the right choice. Looking down at the dogs now, Jack at least felt good he wasn't *completely* alone. The two furballs were growing on him.

Jack's vanilla latte arrived, along with the bill. He paid and sat to enjoy the rich sweetness of the drink while he looked up and down Main Street.

Then the girl from the street popped back into his mind. Maybe he'd be seeing her in the neighborhood while he was here. If he hadn't had the dogs, he'd have followed her right inside the library to try and figure out why she left so abruptly. Still, he didn't want to be pushy.

That long, wild sable hair of hers was also something he'd been compelled to touch and run his fingers through. Wavy and out of control, it hung long down her back and made her thin build seem even smaller in comparison. With full, pouty lips that she kept nibbling the lower corner of. He wondered if it was a nervous tick. The point was, he wanted to know more about her, but she hadn't given him the chance.

His coffee gone, Jack stood and tossed the cup into the trash and unwrapped the leashes. Both dogs stood at attention, ready for their walk back through town and to home for bowls of water and balls to chase.

The three of them kept a good pace along the tree-lined streets, and while they walked, Jack tossed around some ideas for his *great novel* that he would write. Maybe he would write about this town.

Or maybe about a girl like the one he'd met today who had saved Henry from the streets and awakened a twinge of desire in Jack. He kept looking around for her.

As they walked, he took in the scenery of the neighborhood, which included an eclectic assortment of older craftsman houses and a few Tudor styles from the 1940s to the 1950s. Some were kept up really well, with a charming look about them, while just a block away, there were unkept yards and dilapidated porches. On Jewel Avenue, he made his way over to Calder Avenue where his uncle's house was. That block had mostly nice homes with fenced yards.

The trio arrived a bit breathless from walking the hills to the two-story craftsman that was painted navy blue with white trim and had a deep porch with a swing. Jack unlocked the light oak-stained door that had dentil molding and let the dogs into the house, hanging their leashes on the hall tree in the small foyer.

The dogs drank water and settled into their perspective beds in the living room, but Jack was restless. He walked through the newly renovated house and stood at the freshly remodeled kitchen counter to look out the sliding glass door. The patio table on the deck, overlooking the thick foliage of trees, ferns, and hostas in variegated colors, seemed enticing. He took his bottled water outside.

"Now, this would be a great place to write," he said to nobody. Writing had been his passion since he was a kid, and he'd read everything Roald Dahl had ever written. Although he'd played a lot of baseball and basketball in his youth, he'd never been an all-Star, but he could tell a great story.

As Jack was walking back inside to grab his laptop to test the outdoor writing space, the house phone rang. Uncle Rob still had a landline that he refused to let go of, insisting that you couldn't trust cell phone towers in case of emergencies.

"Hello?"

"Jack, my boy! How the hell are ya? How are my dogs?"

Uncle Rob sounded far off because he was. Finding time to call from the Baja in Rosarito was hit or miss. He'd gone down to go fishing with a few buddies, and from there, they were going to stay in San Diego a while before driving home.

"We just got home from a walk. They're exhausted and sleeping in their beds right now."

Jack left out the part about Henry escaping and being rescued by a tall, beautiful girl with captivating brown eyes.

"Sweet! Listen, I forgot to tell ya. I left you a bottle of damn good Kentucky bourbon on the bar cart. If you get a hankering to feel like Hemingway, break it open. I heard he wrote drunk and edited sober. Ha! Anyway, I was just checking in. We will be on the boat most of tomorrow, so I won't be able to be reached. I wrote down our hotel info, and it's all on the tablet by the phone. I'm in room eight."

Jack was nodding as if his uncle could see him. "Okay. I got it. And thanks. Don't worry about anything here. The boys and I will hold down the fort. And thanks for the bourbon. I'll make good use of it."

"See you in a little over three weeks. And Jack?"

"Yeah?"

"If you get laid, don't you dare use my room. You have your own goddamn bed. Haaaa!"

And his uncle disconnected the call. Jack smirked and stood staring at the phone before returning it to the cradle.

"Hardly likely," he said to himself.

Wandering out to the living room, Jack found the bottle sitting on the antique bar cart with a note attached that said, *Drink up! Uncle Rob.* The bourbon was nestled among other expensive bottles of booze, all sparkling like gemstones on the reflective glass-and-brass cart.

For a public high school principal, Jack's uncle had expensive taste and liked to have the best of things. Being a single man in his late forties, Uncle Rob didn't plan on marrying again. He'd warned

Jack that "All women do is want half of what you got and then, in the divorce, take the other half." He'd been divorced when Jack was too young to remember much about Aunt Meg. Since then, Rob lived free and easy. He loved his time off, and public education suited his lifestyle.

His mother's younger brother, Rob, was the only relative Jack was close to. After losing his dad, Jake Connors, to cancer while Jack was still in college, Jack's family unit became very small. Jack was an only child, and since his dad had been estranged from most of his family, Jack's mom and Uncle Rob were all he had left. It was fine though. Really, they were all the family Jack needed. Except… having someone special in his life would be really great. Only Jack never talked to Uncle Rob about how he felt. His uncle would only jade him with his own past experiences with women.

That was one of the reasons Jack loved books so much. The falling in love, the adventure, the chaos, and then the fact that after the shit hit the fan, things would usually get tied up in a neat little bow at the end. Something to count on. He was a romantic, but he wasn't weak. Jack just loved the idea of love, even if it hadn't ever seemed to work out for him. He was still looking for something like his parents had had. So far, no one fit the bill.

He took his laptop outside and sat at the table again. He stared across the backyard with its beauty and found himself wondering about the girl with the shabby clothes and beautiful eyes. *Damn it.* Maybe he should have walked to the library doors and opened them to ask her name again.

But it was a small town, right? Not like LA where you might get swallowed up and never be seen again. No, in this town, he was bound to see her, and when he did, he wasn't going to let her out of his sight until he found out more about her.

With determination, Jack opened his laptop and stared at the blank screen, wondering what to write. He had no idea what his book would be about, but he typed the first words that came to his mind.

On the streets of an unfamiliar place, I met a goddess with wild hair and the face of an angel.

❧

CHAPTER THREE

CHARLIE

ALTHOUGH SHE'D BEEN distracted by his good looks, Charlie really *had* paid attention to what the gorgeous stranger had told her when listing some of the authors he'd read. She hadn't read a John Grisham novel before and found one called *The Confession*. The story was a legal thriller based on the wrong man being convicted of the murder of a high school cheerleader and him being just days away from execution when the real killer decides to come forward. Fascinating and ironic all at the same time. In real life, people got things wrong all the time.

They certainly got things wrong about her. Teachers and the kids at her high school all thought they had her pegged. Most of them assumed Charlie was wild with delinquent tendencies. Because she often dressed in black and gray like a street hooligan, she saw a bit of fear and pity in their eyes. But she didn't give a shit what they thought. Nobody knew her. Nobody ever thought to ask what her deal was or bothered to really get to know her.

Nobody even paid much attention to her, except maybe some of the guys who wanted to get in her pants, and there had been plenty who'd tried. When she'd lost her virginity at fifteen to Tommy Cleary, who was a senior that preyed on freshmen girls, she thought foolishly that he loved her. He'd smooth-talked her for weeks in gym class, and when she'd finally agreed to meet him at the baseball diamond after dark, they'd made out in the dugout when things went too far. She figured if she gave in, he'd love her back. Big mistake. All it got her was a painful crotch and a bad reputation, because the next day at school, she was pointed at and whispered about in the hallway. She'd cut gym class for weeks until her mother got a phone call and told her to go back and get the stupid credits or she'd wind up like her—no college degree, no husband, and no way out.

"Your grandparents won't give you a dime, Charlotte, if you don't do well in school and go to college. You are our only ticket, baby. Our last hope of getting out of this dump. It's too late for me, but you could make somethin' of yourself. Don't screw it up because of fucking gym class!"

So, she'd gone ahead and let the girls think she was a slut and, eventually, didn't care that the guys assumed she was easy. One by one, the girlfriends she'd had in junior high school started playing in band or got involved in sports and had less and less time for her. Besides, with her building reputation, most of them had worried Charlie would steal their boyfriends, so they kept her out of their little cliques. It hurt. It became very lonely. Between being alienated at school and her mother either being inside a bottle or consumed by her latest piece-of-shit boyfriend, Charlie was clearly on her own. All she wanted to do was paint and read. But even that got her into trouble.

During her sophomore year, Charlie had done really well in art class and enjoyed the Art History and Art Composition that Mr. Ingle taught. She was getting pretty good at sketching, and her acrylic painting had improved so much he often let her come in before school to work on some of her pieces while he ate his breakfast and drank coffee, listening to Van Morrison or Steely Dan on the stereo.

One day she came in, and he'd had a very serious tone. No

music played, and he was leaning on his desk with his arms crossed over his chest.

"Charlie, I need to talk to you. Would you sit down please?"

His eyebrows were knitted together, and a frown tugged on his lips. She'd worried she'd done something to upset him as she pulled at the drawstrings of her sweatshirt.

"What's going on?" she asked, taking a seat in one of the chairs in the front of the empty classroom.

"I've been missing a great deal of acrylic paints over the past few weeks, and Kendra Townsend told me she saw you shove some into your backpack yesterday. Is this true?"

Kendra Townsend was a rich, spoiled fucking little lying bitch.

Kendra hated her because, again, of a boy thing. Kendra's football-star boyfriend had flirted with Charlie outside in the quad one day, and when Kendra and her snotty, rich friends saw it, they'd made loud remarks about what a whore Charlie was, and why would he want to talk to her?

"No, sir. I'd never steal anything. Especially not from you. Not after all the help you've given me and letting me paint in the morning."

He shifted his weight and rubbed his chin. "Still, until I get to the bottom of this, I'm going to have to lock up the supply cabinets and only go in them myself. I'm afraid your morning sessions here will have to be suspended until further notice. I have far too much to do in the morning for prep that I can't watch your..."

Charlie knew what he meant. He believed Kendra over her, even though she was a far better art student and took art seriously. Kendra only took it because she thought it would be an easy A, and she produced shit work. Charlie had seen kindergarteners with more talent.

"You mean, you don't have time to supervise my every move and don't want to take a chance that I'm a little thief. Right?" She stood up, adrenaline flooding her body so much she felt lightheaded.

"I'm sorry, Charlie, but it's just for a little while. I'll still see you in class and—"

"Never mind. It's whatever. You believe Kendra over me, and I get it. I mean, she's got great clothes, great hair, comes from a perfect family," she gritted out as she walked away, so angry she wanted to punch a wall.

"That has nothing to do with it, Charlie."

She let out a little laugh instead of the tears she was choking on. "Doesn't it though? I'll see ya around, Mr. Ingle."

She cut his class for a week before her mother heard about it and gave her the same speech she had before.

"What is it with you and these easy classes? You gotta fuck up everything in your life over some simple class you could easily get an A in? Don't be like me, Charlotte."

"I've told you to call me Charlie! Jesus. Nobody has called me Charlotte since the fourth grade but you and your parents. How about I start calling you *Cecelia*? Nice and proper, huh?"

"They are *your grandparents*. And their money is gonna be your goddamned ticket out of here, so you better get smart. Stop screwing around and just get through these last few years of school, for Christ's sake."

Charlie learned to mostly tune her mother out. Still, a part of what her mother was saying was right, even if her mom was a goddamn hypocrite. She really didn't want to be like her mother. Poor, always seeking solace in some lame-ass guy's arms, and getting beaten a lot. Her grandparents' money really was the only way she'd ever get a college degree. But they had high standards and rules in order to receive any financial support from them.

They hadn't given Cece a red cent after she dropped out of high school and gotten pregnant from a guy in a band. Charlie's father had walked out on them before she was even born. At around her eighth month of pregnancy, Cece woke one morning to a note that Dwight Ledger, the attractive lead guitarist of some Bay Area rock band, had left, saying he was going to tour without her and he wasn't coming back. Said he wasn't cut out to be a father and he'd always be on the road. She was better off without him, he'd said. Cece never heard from him again.

When Cece had followed Dwight to California and wound up in Sebastopol because his fellow bandmates had a house here, she'd never thought she'd need to go crawling back to her parents in Virginia. So, when she tried to call them for money to fly home after Dwight left, her parents had declined to help her. Said she'd gotten herself in this mess and would have to prove she was adult enough to get herself out of it.

Now years later, Charlie had only spent a handful of time with her grandparents. They were always telling her how she didn't sit right, used the wrong fork, and her hair wasn't tamed enough…nothing about her seemed good enough, especially to her grandmother.

But they were loaded.

Charlie's grandfather was the managing director of some large bank on the East Coast, and he'd also inherited his father's money that was considered *old money,* handed down from several generations in banking. Charlie's great-grandparents had been friends with the likes of the Roosevelts, Hemingway, and William Randolph Hearst.

Whenever Charlie was screwing up, Cece's only tactic was to threaten her with losing out on inheriting any of her grandparents' money.

After the fiasco with her art teacher and her mother nagging her, Charlie distracted herself and got a work permit so she could save money for a car. Freedom was what motivated her, getting away from her mother and the town that kept letting her down.

Now, in her senior year, she held her longest job working at Retrograde Coffee, where she really liked the vibe. So many artists, musicians, and writers hung out there that the atmosphere as well as the conversations were colorful and enticing. It had been the first place Charlie felt she could be herself and not be judged. Her bosses, Teri and Michael, were both artists and writers themselves.

They had a relaxed view of the world, not uptight like her teachers, and they were always happy to see her. No matter what she wore, how she did her hair, or what her grades were, they just accepted her for who she was.

Charlie checked out the books she'd selected from the library and spent the next few hours walking to the Joe Rodata Trail, a natural wildlife and wetland area that ran from Sebastopol to Santa Rosa with over eight miles of bike and walking trails. She needed to smell the musty earth and feel the breeze on her face. The sun kissed and warmed her enough that she tied her sweatshirt around her waist. A heron flew just over her head and landed in the marshy grass not far from the trail, no doubt to hunt gophers or snakes in the glistening light that reflected off the waters. Dragonflies and birds milled about as Charlie walked past other people enjoying a late summer stroll, languid and peaceful. She breathed deeply and tried to mimic their demeanors.

She'd walked several miles from the town center before her shoulders started to relax. The Dog Man she'd met appeared in a movie in her brain stuck on repeat. *Did she do the right thing running away?* He'd looked almost stricken by her abrupt exit. But what was the point of getting acquainted if he was going to leave town soon? Something about meeting him had frightened her, and after walking and turning the John Grisham book over in her hands along with a book on Havanese dogs, Charlie realized what scared her was how badly she wanted to be with this guy.

Wanting was dangerous. It only left you empty, shattered, and betrayed. She knew this. She'd lived this. That was why she didn't allow herself to get too close to anyone. If she was going to fucking graduate high school and get the hell out of here and away from her mother, she couldn't afford distractions. She had nine months to go. All she needed to do was get good grades, keep her focus, and please her grandparents with proof of her grades and a phone call a week. She almost had enough money to fix her transmission in her Bug, and that would give her enough freedom to head over to the beach in Bodega Bay whenever she wanted, or some night adventures with The Guerrillas. As long as she wasn't caught, she could let loose just enough with them to feel sane. To undo the constraints and chains of daily life that forced her to try and fit into a round hole when she was clearly a square peg.

CHAPTER FOUR

JACK

A WEEK HAD PASSED, and Jack still hadn't seen the fascinating girl from the library who'd rescued little Henry. Normally, time passing by would quell his infatuation for a girl, but this time all it did was agitate him more.

Where the hell was she? Where did she go?

During the week, Jack had settled himself into his uncle's house quite comfortably and even managed to write a few chapters of a very mediocre story. It was shit, but he was just flexing his writer's brain to find his groove. It hadn't kicked in yet, but he was at least writing something.

Days with George and Henry included morning walks then breakfast on the back patio while birds flittered about along the fence line and in the thick row of trees. Jack would write at the outdoor table if the misty fog wasn't too thick, while intermittently throwing tennis balls across the lawn that the boys would run after and wrestle for. On drizzly days, he'd sit at the dining room table, the streaming light from the skylight and sliding glass window making that spot cozy. He wrote until lunch, when the fog would lift, and Jack would eventually break and head into town to look *for her.*

Perusing parks, trendy restaurants, and clothing stores and

milling about in Copperfield's Books all left Jack empty-handed. Regular stops into the library gave him time to establish a library card and check out a few books, even if he had no luck in finding her there either. He looked for some female authors to prove he wasn't sexist, so when he eventually found the elusive girl, they'd have something to talk about.

Kathryn Stockett's *The Help* was one of his favorites in that first week, and Jack found himself reading into the night to finish it. George and Henry had taken to sleeping on the other side of the queen-sized bed in his guest room while Jack turned page after page in bed, nursing a two-finger pour of the Kentucky bourbon from his uncle.

But now, on the sixth day since Jack had seen the girl, he was itchy in his skin and restless. He wasn't used to the slower paced life. He'd planned to pack up the dogs and drive over to Doran Park, in Bodega Bay, for the afternoon, when the house phone rang. He considered letting it go to the machine but sat down his small ice chest and walked to answer it anyway.

"Hello?"

"Hey, Jack! Uncle Rob. What's happening there? You all doing good? How's my house? You haven't burned anything down in the kitchen yet, have ya?"

Jack smirked, looking around the fancy chef's kitchen. Rob knew he wasn't a cook. "No, not yet."

"Listen, Jack, I didn't really call to check up on ya. I'm actually in a bit of a pickle, and I have a business proposition for you. Are you in any big hurry to get back to LA when I return?"

Jack shifted his weight and leaned against the granite kitchen counter near the phone. "What'd you have in mind?"

"I checked in on my emails for the school, and it appears our long-term sub for Senior AP English Lit Class has backed out. The regular teacher is out on maternity leave until the middle of October. You have that fancy degree. How would you feel about being a warm body filling a much-needed space at Analy High?"

"You want *me* to sub? Teach high school students?"

"That's the idea, yes. Look, it would only be temporary, and I'd never ask if I wasn't completely in a bind. I could really use your help."

Jack felt an uncomfortable lurch in his stomach, and he ran his free hand through his thick hair. "Can I at least think about it?"

"Sure. But don't think too long. I'll call you tomorrow after we get back from the boat. We caught the hell out of marlin and grouper the other day. Helluva time landing this one big son of a bitch. Did you get the pictures I texted you?"

He stood scratching his head. How could his uncle be so nonchalant about this? Jack had never taught a day in his life. What the fuck was he thinking, asking him to substitute teach? *Seniors no less!* He'd been a senior himself just six years ago.

"Um...yeah. I got the pictures. Huge fish. Hey, are you sure about this? You really think I'm the best candidate for this? Teaching high school?"

"Nobody ever learned anything by not taking a chance, Jack-o. Anyway, like I said, I'm in a pinch. A real tight spot. Help a guy out, okay? I'll call again tomorrow. And you could use the dough, right? Consider it an adventure. We'll talk soon. Ciao."

And that was it. He'd hung up.

What the hell?

Jack paced back and forth through the kitchen, shaking his head, hearing the word *imposter* on a repeating track in his head. Those kids would see right through him that he had no fucking idea on how to teach an AP English Class.

George and Henry started to become agitated with his pacing, and George was whining now, with Henry right behind his buddy, his ears back.

"Fine, guys, we'll go," Jack said, grabbing up the ice chest again and the leashes. "No sense sticking around here trying to figure this shit out. We'll go to the beach and clear our heads, right?"

No way was he putting the monsters into the back of his late father's '68 Chevy Camaro. Not only was the car too small, but it had been his dad's prized possession, and all Jack had left of him. He loaded up Uncle Rob's Jeep Cherokee, backed it out of the driveway, and headed towards Bodega Avenue and the two-lane highway that would eventually take him to Coastal Highway 1. He rolled the windows down, and the air blew past him and whipped around the dogs in the back seat. Smells of eucalyptus and sea air filled Jack's nose while his uncle's preset radio station played R.E.M.'s "Shiny Happy People." A peaceful feeling washed over him. This was a good idea. Just change the scenery and clear his head.

The fog had lifted to reveal a cerulean sky with puffy white clouds dancing about. He drove all the way to the end of Doran Regional Park to the Jetty Campground. The large rock jetty stretched out like a finger into the bay, and the two-mile beach was filled with sunbathers, sandcastle builders, and kite fliers. The occasional fishing boat would leave the harbor side, heading out in search of their daily catch.

Jack let the boys off their leashes while he spread a large blanket and plopped down the small ice chest filled with water bottles, dog dishes, a couple of beers, and a sandwich. Both dogs ran back and forth between the water's edge and the blanket, their legs sandy and their tongues hanging out, as the calm waves gently lapped the bay's shore.

Breathing deeply, Jack contemplated the idea of what it would be like to sub in a class of seventeen- and eighteen-year-olds. Terrifying. Would he be the cool teacher, or would they prey on him like vultures as most kids did with substitutes? It was a gamble for sure.

Still, like his uncle had said, it would only be temporary. If school started the last week of August, then Jack had approximately six or seven weeks he'd have to endure before the real teacher returned. And it would be a paycheck until he decided what he wanted to do. He really hadn't thought about his next move after house-sitting anyway. Writing the Great American Novel wasn't exactly lucrative. It took time, and in the meanwhile, he had to feed and shelter himself.

One beer down and his sandwich gone, he packed up. With the dogs leashed up, Jack took the boys to the outdoor faucet near the bathrooms, washed each one off, and toweled them as dry as he could before loading them back into the vehicle for the twenty-minute car ride back home.

With a clear head, Jack decided. When Uncle Rob called tomorrow, he'd tell him yes. It scared the living shit out of him, but he could survive a month and a half of teenagers as long as he was getting paid to do it.

Nights were still rough though. That evening, the dogs lay comatose in their beds while Jack paced restlessly, feeling lonely. He pulled open the sliding door to the backyard, and a full moon was peeking through the clouds, eerily hiding and spying. It would shine in a bright beam from the sky, only to slip behind a cloud the next moment and leave the yard in shadows. It was beautiful and disconcerting all at once.

Then he thought of her.

Was she looking up at the same moon tonight and wondering where he was? Or had she completely forgotten about him altogether? Strangely, she'd gotten under his skin. She was nothing like the girls he knew in LA. She didn't dress well, didn't wear a bunch of makeup, *and that hair!* It was wild and untamed, but he loved it. It fit her personality—she didn't really care what flew out of her mouth. She was spunky and challenging. Unpretentious. It was refreshing and made him feel like he could be himself too… if only their conversation had lasted long enough for him to get her name.

The next morning, dog-free, Jack marched down to Retrograde Coffee instead of making himself a pot. He didn't want to wrestle with leashes and decided to walk them later. All he wanted was to

feel the cool morning air on his skin and indulge in something sin-
fully delicious to lift his spirits. He'd run later to burn the calories.

In his hoodie and shorts, Jack walked in the brisk morning fog
that cloaked the town like a veil. Down the hill to the main street of
town, he found Retrograde swamped. The line was about six people
deep, and most of the tables were full. He hadn't realized how busy
it would be at this hour on a Sunday. Chatter from the customers
hummed like a beehive, steadily buzzing. He surveyed the room
as he waited and saw mixed ages of folks like moms with toddlers
meeting with other moms, groggy teenagers, and even writers with
laptops.

He was next in line, and as he turned around to place his order,
the universe screeched to a halt. The girl with the doe eyes and the
tall, lithe build was standing at the register staring at him with mir-
rored disbelief.

CHAPTER FIVE

CHARLIE

"DOG MAN," SHE said without thinking.

"It's you," he said.

Charlie's heart raced, and she couldn't help but stare. Was this happening? There he was. Right there in front of her again. The godlike man with the dark beard stubble and dreamy eyes. She almost gasped at seeing him, but instead, she swallowed and regained her composure. No need *for him* to know how fast her heart was drumming or how her skin prickled with electricity at the sight of him and his perfectly chiseled jaw.

"You wanna coffee?" She fought herself to remain chill like it was no big deal.

He stood with his mouth agape. He blinked a few times then stumbled over his words.

"I'm, I'm...wow. I mean, I didn't...I didn't know you worked here. I've been in a few times, and you weren't here so...but here you are."

"Here I am. You gonna order something, or do I need to read your mind? I'm betting you LA types wanna nonfat or no dairy something or other."

"Oh no. I was dreaming of a full-fat mocha and something really sweet. Do you have cinnamon rolls? I'd die for one today."

He smiled again that irresistible smile and flashed his perfectly white teeth with the dimple in his cheek, and Charlie's knees wobbled. She placed a hand on the counter to support her as she tapped his order into the register. Looking away from him was her only defense.

"Yep. Got those too. You like it hot?"

"What?" he nearly hissed in shock.

Charlie smirked and met his eyes, this time allowing herself to pull at him with a long stare. She saw what she'd hoped to see. He liked her too.

"I mean, do you want the cinnamon roll heated up?"

"Oh. Sure. Yes, that would be great." His perfectly tanned cheeks blushed.

A feeling of satisfaction swelled in her chest. Judging by his stammering, he was infatuated with her, just as she was infatuated with him. Still, starting anything was a risk, and Charlie didn't have time to risk her heart when her future was at stake. Guys always disappointed, and she really wanted to save up enough money to get her car fixed, get money for college from her grandparents, and go as far away from her mother and this life as possible.

He handed her his money, and Charlie felt the tingle of his fingers as they lingered in the palm of her hand. Dog Man gazed at her with such softness she ached. Charlie licked her lips then broke the spell by turning to put the money in the drawer and grabbed the tongs to pull a cinnamon roll from the front case. He stood watching her, the weight of his stare as potent as an actual touch. It was nerve-wracking and exciting to the point that she became flustered. She popped the cinnamon roll into the warming oven then dropped the tongs on the floor.

"Hey, Charlie. You got butterfingers today?" her boss Michael teased her then handed her a fresh pair from the clean utensil holder.

"So that's your name? Charlie?" Dog Man asked her as she

tucked a stray piece of hair behind her ear. She turned sideways and looked at him for a second before continuing to work.

It didn't seem fair that he'd found out her name, and she still didn't know his. As badly as she wanted to know it, Charlie refused to ask. It would only make things harder. Besides, it was more fun to keep him wondering why she wouldn't want to know. Even little things that would give her the upper hand were worth it, and Charlie rarely had the upper hand in anything in life.

"Yep. Now you know."

"I've never heard Charlie for a girl before. It's…unique. I like it."

He moved down the counter while he waited but kept trying to make conversation with her in between her taking other people's orders. She could scarcely keep track of what she was doing as her mind was totally occupied with *him*.

When the timer went off for the cinnamon roll, she wished it hadn't. He would be leaving again. Even though she knew it was for the best, her heart longed for him to stay. To keep talking. To keep staring at her with those dreamy eyes. She turned to face him over the counter again.

"You want this on a plate? For here or to go?"

Her boss had already handed him his mocha that he'd been sipping while waiting for the roll to warm. He lifted his eyebrows at the question.

"I'll have it here. I'm not quite sure where I'm gonna get a table since it's pretty packed, but I'll find a corner somewhere. Maybe wait for you to have a break? I'd like to tell you about the book I just finished."

Jesus Christ, he was too good to be true. More with the book talk. Not about some party, or some great weed he'd scored. Not sports or motorcycles. Books. And he was so fucking tall.

"Where are the dogs today?" She was trying to decide if she would be honest about reading a book on the Havanese dog breed after meeting little Henry.

"They are home. Yeah, I needed a leash-free morning. So, I'll be just over there." He pointed. "I'm gonna wait until you have a break, so I can talk to you some more, if that is okay with you."

She wiped her forehead with the back of her hand, feeling flushed. "I don't think I'll get one." She motioned towards the line of people still coming in.

He just needed to go. It would be too hard. Too much for her to concentrate if they started up something. A distraction if he stuck around. Besides, he was just gonna go back to LA anyway. The voice of reason was battling in her head while her heart kept arguing for the possibility of someone who might really care.

Don't go soft now, Charlie. He'll just leave you.

"Well, I'll just wait and see," he said while standing there at the counter with his drink in one hand and a plate of cinnamon roll in the other. "I love the art in here. Especially that one of the girl walking down the beach at sunset."

"Charlie did that one," her boss said over the noise of the frother.

She wanted to see the look on his face to determine if he was surprised or what, but she was putting in an order for a customer and tried to focus on the register.

"What? You're an artist? That's incredible." Dog Man sounded truly impressed.

Charlie let a tiny smirk of satisfaction pull at her lips, and when she glanced at him, he was staring at her in a way she'd never seen before. In admiration.

He left her to work, but every once in a while, Charlie would look out into the room and find him staring at her. She started laughing and shook her head at one point because it was becoming a game. He'd lick his fingers from the messy dessert and make a face, or he'd pretend to read the paper and hold it up so only his eyes were visible over the edge, like a stalker. She couldn't help but laugh, and it felt good to just relax.

The rush was over, and only a few people were in the small coffee shop now. Dog Man was one of them. He stood and brought her the empty plate. Charlie took it and set it behind the counter then walked around with a wet rag to wipe down all the tables.

He stood in the middle of the room, staying out of her way, but remained close by. "Seeing you again was very unexpected," he said.

"In what way?" She swallowed hard and avoided looking at him when he answered.

"In a good way. I've been wondering where you went. You left so suddenly when I thought we were having a great conversation outside the library."

"It was time to go. Thats all." She continued to wipe the tables, moving from one to the next without stopping.

He made her nervous, and Charlie worried her bosses and coworker Ronnie would be able to tell how much she liked him. She didn't want to be razzed by them. Didn't feel like defending herself or making any explanations.

Dog Man was quiet for a minute then spoke about something entirely different. Something she could at least address.

"You have a tattoo."

Not a question, he just said it as an observation. Charlie turned to face him. In the tank top she wore, the wildflower bouquet on her back left shoulder blade was there for all to see. The one thing she had in common with her mother was their love of nature, so Cece hadn't freaked out when Charlie came home with a tattoo—having used a fake ID to obtain it. The tattoo adequately captured who Charlie felt she was at a soul level. Here she was free to show it. When she was with her grandparents, Charlie had to keep it hidden and out of sight, just like the rest of her true self.

"Yeah, I've got a tattoo. I designed it." She cocked her head to study his expression to see what he thought.

"Do the flowers mean anything in particular to you?"

At least he was curious. There didn't seem to be any judgement in his tone, so Charlie plopped the rag on the table and rested one hand on her hip to explain, watching his face while she did.

"They're wildflowers. Most people consider them weeds. Undesirable. Unruly. But I think they're just as beautiful as any other flower people propagate. And they're super resilient. They grow in places most other flowers won't. They can stand up to all kinds of climates, and some of them thrive in the harshest conditions. They can grow right up in the middle of a cement sidewalk without anyone caring for them or tending them. And they still bloom, even though there is no one telling them how beautiful they are. They don't care. They still seek the sun and grow as tall as they can, sort of giving the world the middle finger, ya know? Like, fuck you, world. I'm gonna grow here and just be me. That's what I love about them."

She waited a second to see if he'd say anything, but he didn't. The look in his eyes changed though, as if he were trying to dig into her soul and learn what storms she'd endured. He didn't ask a single question, but his eyes, with their dark lashes, asked her everything.

Clearing her throat, Charlie grabbed up the rag and started to walk back to the counter, needing to put some distance between her and Dog Man. The flood of emotion bubbling up was becoming too much, and she needed to stay where she was safe.

He didn't follow her this time. Just stood in the center of the room, but his eyes followed her very closely. He spoke loud enough for her to hear while she forced herself to tidy up the back counter from the rush.

"I'll let you get back to work, but I'll be back. It was great to see you again. Maybe we can meet at the library sometime when you are off work, or we could take a walk."

"Maybe," she squeaked out. Charlie's heart pounded. He was leaving, even though it was for the best.

"I'd like to. Anyway, see you around, Charlie."

"Well, now you know where to find me." She struggled to not shut him out entirely. She felt like such a contradiction.

Dog Man opened the glass door and walked outside, looking back over his shoulder through the window at her. A small piece of her heart broke, and a gasp escaped from her mouth as he slipped out of sight.

That day after work, Charlie meandered home in the heat of the day and retraced her steps past the library, hoping to see him walking the dogs. Then she asked herself what the hell she was doing. Continuing on, she found herself home without so much as seeing a single person she recognized, much less the gorgeous stranger. It left her feeling hollow inside.

Her mother's ratty Mazda 626 was gone from the yard. She tried the door, but it was locked. Charlie opened it with her key and went inside to a darkened, abandoned house. At first, she was relieved. Her mom had been such a pain in the ass lately with her drugs and drinking that having the house to herself was a relief. Then she tried to turn on the light, and there was nothing. She walked into the aging kitchen and tried the switch, but the result was the same. The ancient stove's clock numbers weren't illuminated either. It had happened again. The power was off. Her mother hadn't paid the bill.

She flopped down on the worn couch when she saw something on the coffee table. It was a note written on the back of an envelope, just lying there next to an ashtray of cigarette butts and an empty vodka bottle. Charlie leaned forward and held the note up.

Gone to Reno for a few days, baby. I'll be back soon. Don't tell your grandparents when they call.

"What the fuck is she doing now?"

With no power, no way to cook, and the refrigerator thawing what little there was, Charlie grabbed the vodka bottle and threw it across the room. It broke into three pieces and landed in the corner of the kitchen on the yellow linoleum floor.

Charlie ran to her mother's bedroom and found the coffee can she kept their rent money hidden in, on a shelf at the back of the closet. Charlie shook it and didn't hear anything. Opening it, she found it was empty.

She screamed out in anger then punched a wall. The drywall split, and she pulled back a hand that only hurt a little. It almost felt good. To feel. The pain was at least telling her that she was alive. She would continue to survive.

Her mother had gone to Reno with their rent money. The only other money Charlie had was supposed to pay for her transmission to be repaired. That cash was her freedom! If her mom came home empty-handed after a few days of gambling and drinking, then Charlie would either have to forfeit her money, or worry about being evicted and living on the streets.

She stormed to her room near the front of the house and riffled through her closet, looking for her supplies. A tall cylinder with a shoulder strap that held her stencils and a black canvas bag filled with spray paint were the things she'd need when it got dark enough to head into town. She put them both on the kitchen counter then paced the room. She'd leave now except it was too light out. It had to be dark, so nobody would be able to identify her if she was spotted painting.

With no appetite, Charlie returned to her room and lay on her bed. Tears pooled in her eyes before draining down her throat and clogging her nose. So utterly alone, Charlie drew her knees up to her chest and lay on her side crying until sleep took her away. It was the only place she could go where the loneliness and fatigue of fighting the world on her own didn't weigh on her. When she woke four hours later, she slipped into the darkness of night and created something to release her pain, and to prove she was there, that she existed.

స

CHAPTER SIX

JACK

BUZZING WITH ELECTRICITY, Jack was elated, yet confused, at finding the girl. *Charlie!* She was gorgeous and mysterious, and he was impressed that she was an artist too. But Jack wasn't so sure she was as happy to see him as he was to see her. She'd given him such mixed signals he'd felt totally off his game. Her painting of the girl walking down the beach at sunset was just as mysterious as she was. It only showed the dark shape of a girl walking away, her hair blowing in the wind while the ocean roared against the shore and a spectacular purple, fuchsia, and pink sunset blew up the sky. Come to think about it, the girl in the painting looked a lot like her.

He walked the dogs again later in the afternoon towards the coffeehouse in hopes of catching Charlie after her shift. He trudged on with anticipation along the sidewalk in front of Retrograde and glanced in the huge windows, but he didn't see her anywhere.

And so it went for the rest of the week, nearly driving Jack mad. He couldn't seem to catch up with her. Nailing himself to a chair, he tried to keep his mind occupied with writing, but all his ideas wound up being crap. Nothing felt honest or deep enough. At one point, he was so frustrated he started looking into jobs back in LA as a full-time journalist. His mother literally had no advice. She was too laidback, certain things would work out as they should. He wished his dad were here to kick him in the ass.

"What are you so worried about?" his mother asked. "Just take the job as a teacher then reevaluate after that. Stop worrying so much."

Maybe she had a point.

Then one day on a whim, Jack found himself at Retrograde, and even though Charlie wasn't there, he walked up to the older-looking guy who had spoken to him about her painting that day. He had to at least ask about her.

"Excuse me. Um, do you remember me?"

"You're Charlie's friend, right?" The middle-aged guy in a Hawaiian-print shirt smiled kindly at Jack.

"Yeah. Um, we haven't been able to connect, and I was wondering if you knew—"

"Yeah, Charlie has had some problems charging her phone, and it keeps dying. The power was out at her place, so if she's not at work to charge it, it often dies."

This guy thought that he and Charlie were closer than they were. Jack played it off and let him continue to think that.

"Oh. Well, that makes sense. So, when will she be back at work? I'll just pop back over then."

"Tomorrow. Then I'm not sure. We're making a new schedule after that."

Jack nodded his appreciation. "Great. I'll come back then. Thanks."

He headed out and felt lighter. Charlie's power was out. Weird. Jack hadn't noticed any power outages in the area in the past few days, but maybe her house was farther away than he'd imagined and was on a different grid. At any rate, he wouldn't have to speculate anymore on where to find her. Tomorrow he would make it a point to go for coffee first thing in the morning to see her, hopefully before the morning rush.

Later that afternoon, as he was cracking open a beer, Jack powered up his laptop and found an email from the school district office. They wanted him there at eight o'clock sharp tomorrow to fill out paperwork and be fingerprinted. That wouldn't give him a lot of time to see Charlie. He decided he'd stop in after he was done at the district office, so he wouldn't be in a rush to leave. Just thinking about her made him smile.

The phone rang at six that night, and it was his uncle again. He'd made it to San Diego.

"Jack-o. I see my secretary emailed you about your appointment tomorrow. You got it, right?"

"Yeah, I did. I'll be ready. Luckily, I packed a few dress shirts and some slacks from my workdays at the *LA Scoop*. I don't know how English teachers dress these days, but I'm guessing I shouldn't show up in shorts and a sweatshirt."

"Not unless you want them to think you're one of them. In order to get respect, you gotta be nice but firm. Be cool, but more adult than they are. It's a fine line. Don't tell them your age either. Keep them guessing. Anyway, make sure you also get the tour. Someone from the high school will be available to do that for you. Just head to the Analy High School's front office after you leave the district office, and my secretary, Lori, will help you out."

"Lori. At the high school when I'm done at the district office. Okay. I got it." Jack hadn't planned to do that and hoped it wouldn't take too long.

"Yep, and I'll be back next week. By then, all your paperwork will have cleared. Teachers start before the kids do, so you can get settled into your classroom when I go back. I really appreciate this, Jack. It's not forever, and I know you will do great."

His pulse quickened, and a nervous stomach began to agitate him. "I gotta be honest, Uncle Rob. I don't have the first clue what the hell to do."

"Don't worry. I'll hook you up with the English teachers, and they'll get you squared away on curriculum. Plus, the actual teacher for the class is Ellie Pratt. She's going to set up some lesson plans for you, and the two of you will work together through email and phone calls. You're such a bookworm and did so well in college, it will all come back to you. Don't worry. We won't set you up to fail. And if you fuck things up, it will only be a few weeks. Ha!"

"Great. I feel so much better now." Jack rolled his eyes.

"Gotta run. The San Diego nightlife is calling. Catch ya later, kid."

Jack stared at the phone receiver and set it back on the cradle.

"Wow. This already feels like a bad idea," Jack said to the dogs on their overstuffed beds across the room.

The next morning Jack overslept. He threw a bagel down his throat after feeding and letting the dogs out and jumped into his Camaro.

The fingerprinting and paperwork didn't take long. They scanned a copy of his driver's license and had him out the door in no time. Jack was hopeful of getting to see Charlie at the coffee shop as soon as he was done at the high school, but things didn't go as fast there as he'd hoped.

Lori, the administrative secretary, was on the phone when he arrived. He sat in his slacks and burgundy button-down dress shirt, fidgeting with his collar and rubbing his sweaty palms over his thighs. By the time she was able to address him, it had been almost twenty minutes, as each time she'd wrap up one call, another one came in. Once he finally got her attention and explained who he was, she beamed at him.

"Jack! Oh yes, we've been expecting you. Let me radio Sam. He's our campus supervisor and is probably in the staff room. This place is a zoo right now. It's like this just before a new school year."

She put up a finger for him to wait a sec and then spoke on a hand radio for Sam to come to the office. Jack motioned towards the door and walked outside while he waited, pacing around the front of the two-story main building. Sam took forever.

Around the corner, a big fellow with baggy utility pants, a short-sleeved Ben Davis shirt, and a radio hooked to his back waistband appeared. Sam. He swallowed Jack's hand in his as he shook it firmly, then he motioned for Jack to follow. All the while, Jack studied his watch.

They maneuvered around while Sam yammered on and on, showing Jack the staff room, bathrooms, cafeteria, and courtyard. Jack barely got a word in edgewise. Time was being eaten away as Sam showed Jack every square inch of campus except Jack's room.

"So, I'll be subbing in the English department for Ellie Pratt. Can you show me where her room is? I have an appointment I need to get to shortly, but I'd like to know where I'll be working, if that's ok?"

"Oh, sure. I just heard you were Mr. Hill's nephew and thought you'd want the grand tour. The senior English room is down this way."

After being let in with Sam's master key, Jack looked into what seemed to be a typical high school classroom. About thirty desks, all facing a whiteboard, a teacher's desk set at an angle in the front, and a bookcase covering a third of one wall. There were cupboards for supplies against the opposite wall, and suddenly Jack could picture the room full of students. His throat started to close up, and he coughed, shaking off the vision.

"I think I'm good. Room twenty-seven. This is me."

"I don't think anyone from your department is here today, but if you want me to check, we could swing back around to the main office, and I could see."

"NO," Jack blurted out too quickly. He took a deep breath. "Um, I mean, I'd love to, but next time. I have that appointment I was telling you about."

It was almost noon. *Damn!* He didn't know if Charlie worked a full-time shift, or part-time, and maybe she'd be gone. Jack's chest tightened as he hustled to his car.

The Camaro rumbled like a dragon through backed up

lunchtime traffic. The intersection heading to Main Street was like a parking lot, and Jack thrummed his fingers on the steering wheel with impatience. He finally arrived at the coffee shop after having to park about a block away due to the congestion in town.

Pulling the glass door open with great anticipation, Jack looked towards the counter but only saw the large man, a middle-aged woman, and another girl, no Charlie.

People milled about, but it wasn't as packed as that Sunday morning when he'd first run into Charlie here. He waited his turn in line, head down in defeat. Jack decided to order something and maybe get more information from her boss.

The large man with yet another Hawaiian shirt was at the register and smiled upon seeing Jack again.

"Oh man, you missed Charlie. I'm sorry. She went home sick today. I forgot you stopped by yesterday, or I'd have told her. Shoot man. Can I get you anything?"

Exhaustion settled over Jack like the fog that rolled into this town at night. It filled all the spaces inside of him, and he wondered why he was spending so much energy looking for a girl he wasn't even sure was into him. After all, he didn't exactly plan to stay permanently in Sebastopol anyway. Drained, Jack nodded to the guy and looked up at the menu for a lunch option. He decided on the special, his brain too full to make a choice.

The man looked at Jack with sympathy and reached out to shake his hand. "Hey, I'm Michael. That's my wife, Teri, and we own this place. I'll tell Charlie you stopped in. You seem to be a nice guy, and we appreciate new customers."

He shook the offered hand. "I hope Charlie isn't too ill. Whatever it is, I hope she's better soon."

"I'm sure she will be fine. Most likely exhaustion. She looked like she hadn't slept. Anyway, we are glad to see she has a new friend. Take care, and thanks for coming in." The woman smiled kindly at Jack, handing him his bagged order.

Jack was sluggish with disappointment. Being disheartened with the universe for not aligning his path with Charlie's made him realize he had to give up the chase. It seemed futile.

When he returned to the house, he started a new job search with a wider range of options near his mother's place in Los Angeles. He also called his buddy Zane, whom he roomed with at UCLA, to find out what he was up to. Zane was a film school graduate and was always talking to Jack about writing for film or television. With no real prospects, Jack thought he should keep his options open.

"Where the hell are you again?" Zane asked with the sound of waves crashing in the background.

"Sebastopol. I'm at my Uncle Rob's place. Remember my mom's brother who loves to party? Well, he lives in Sonoma County in NorCal. I'm here until mid-October, but after that, I'm fresh out of ideas. I had to leave the *Scoop*. It was sucking the life out of me, man."

Zane continued to talk over the sound of whistling wind and waves. Jack must have caught Zane at the beach, his favorite place and often his office. Zane claimed he got his best creative ideas near the ocean. Also, he played a lot of beach volleyball with bikini-clad women.

"You are better than that shit, Jack. Come home. I'm working on this film with a great new director, and we're about to wrap up. I'd love you to sit in on our next project. Get your feet wet in writing screenplays. I'll email you some info for online classes to get you started. I remember some of the stories you used to write. You are a storyteller, man. Take a leap. Besides, I miss ya. What'd you say you're doing there again?"

"Currently house and dog sitting for Uncle Rob, but he's roped me into being a substitute teacher for the Senior AP English class at his school until October. I don't know what the hell I was thinking saying yes."

Zane's laughter burst through the phone, and Jack had to move it from his ear, it was so loud.

"Are you fucking kidding me, man? You are gonna teach high school seniors? You are either the bravest motherfucker I've ever known or the dumbest. Better lock your dick in a box. Those high school girls are gonna be all over you like flies on shit. Let me know how it goes. And check your email. Start that online screenplay writing course I'm sending you that my buddy teaches. And get writing. You belong here in LA, man. Catch ya later."

After talking with Zane, Jack told himself he was done looking for Charlie. He passed the time over the next few days with writing, researching, and watching videos on teaching English. He stayed laser focused on himself and his next move. Zane was right. He belonged back in LA. Until then, he would do a good job for his uncle and collect a paycheck.

Before he knew it, Uncle Rob returned. He emerged from his buddy's truck with his fishing gear, suitcases, and a bronze tan that showed deep creased white lines around his smiling eyes.

Jack and his uncle got caught up over barbequed steaks, beers, and a few hands of Gin Rummy. It felt good to have someone else in the big house besides the dogs. And George and Henry were thrilled to see their owner again, running around joyfully, barking and tails wagging.

Jack decided not to share with his uncle his momentary infatuation with Charlie. After all, he was trying to let her go. Let go of the idea of touching her, holding her, and kissing those full, perfect lips. Let go of the yearning to run his hands through her out-of-control, sexy hair, or to rub them over her slim porcelain shoulders. To trace his fingertips over the outline of her tattoo of the wildflowers that seemed just like her. Strong, determined, unpredictable, and wild.

෨

CHAPTER SEVEN

CHARLIE

WHEN TERI AND Michael told Charlie about her attractive man friend showing up at work looking for her, she knew it had been Dog Man. Something stirred inside of her. It was just as dangerous as wanting. It was hope. But the days that followed were a disaster, and not seeing him again only made her feel more alone and frustrated than ever.

After four days alone, Charlie received a call from her mother. Charlie was at work and had to ask to leave the register to take the call outside. She hated to ask for any special treatment from her bosses and couldn't stand pity or charity from anyone, but at the same time, it felt good to know at least someone in the world looked out for her. Without second thoughts, they waved her away to take her call.

"Where the hell are you, Mom?" Charlie paced the back of the building by the dumpsters.

"Hey, baby. I'm stuck in Grass Valley. I'm outta gas and crashing at a friend's place. How's it going there? You see Greg lately?"

Charlie's stomach wrenched. "You mean he's still around *here*? I thought he was with you! Who'd you go to Reno with? And Mom, where's our rent money? Please don't tell me you gambled and drank it way. We need that money."

"Hey, get off my back, okay? I needed a little pick-me-up. Greg was getting to be too much of a drag, and I couldn't hang anymore. I drove myself and met up with friends."

"*What friends?* Don't you have hair appointments this week? And the rent, Mom. Where's the rent money? We can't get evicted. You know the landlord threatened us that if we were late one more time, he'd evict us."

"What the fuck is this? The third degree? Kim is covering my chair, and you are the kid. I'm the mom. You don't get to talk to me like that. I was calling you to let you know I was okay because I thought you might worry."

"Jesus! If I'm the kid and you are the mom, then why do I always feel like I'm the one doing the mothering?" Charlie walked farther away from the building because she was talking so loudly and couldn't control her temper any longer. "Please answer the question. Where's the money? Christ, we're out of food, you didn't pay the electric bill, and I've been living in the dark with flashlights and candles for days. If it weren't for my job, I wouldn't have had anything to eat."

"Well, it's a good thing you *do have* that job then, isn't it? Hey, maybe they can give you an advance on your next paycheck, huh?"

"So that's it? You did spend it all, didn't you? Fuck! Can't you think of me for once? It's like you keep getting worse. Just because I'm almost eighteen doesn't mean you get to just check out. I still need you. I need you to hold it together long enough for me to get my car fixed and get into college. Why can't you just do that for me?"

"It's always about you, isn't it? Don't you think I had to give up a lot when I had you? When I chose to *keep you?* Your father ran out on me, my parents disowned me, and they cut me out of their will. I could use a little understanding from you, ya know?"

"Oh shit, not this speech again. I know, I ruined your life. I give up, Mom. Stay away as long as you want. I'll handle things here on my own. I always do."

She disconnected the call and paced with fire inside of her raging out of control. Tears stung the corners of her eyes. She shook her phone like she might throw it across the parking lot but realized she still needed it. Charlie wanted to scream. To hit something. Why couldn't her mother put her first for once?

Between the weird friends, abusive boyfriends, and her partying, Cece never worried about how her actions might affect Charlie. Given all the things she'd seen as a child from drug deals, people snorting lines, sex parties, and fighting, Charlie wondered what life would have been like in a house with normal parents who sat down to dinner and talked about their day. She hated the kids at school who had nice clothes, drove nice cars, and only had to worry about their grades and getting onto sports teams. She hated the girls who had fathers who came home every night, and mothers to go get mani-pedis with. All Charlie had was her art.

With art, Charlie could be anything. She could create a fantasy world, or she could paint her feelings. But ever since her falling out with the art teacher Mr. Ingle, Charlie never felt completely welcome or creative in his class. And art was expensive to make. What little supplies she had were paid for out of the money she earned at Retrograde. Michael and Teri often gifted her supplies, too, because they saw her talent and encouraged her to keep painting, allowing her to sell some of her pieces in the coffee shop. She'd made a few commissions there, and it had helped her to buy her car. Now, she needed transmission work on the Bug, the rent was due soon, and she had to get the power turned back on.

Her head felt like it was going to explode. She took some deep breaths. She needed this job and didn't want to screw it up, so she got herself together and went back inside. No doubt she'd have to explain herself to Teri eventually, but for now, she had to get back in there. The thought also flashed through her head that as therapeutic as it was to lash out at the world with her street art, she might need to focus her energy on more pieces she could actually sell. She was on her own. Like it or not, she was going to have to do something to fix the mess her mother had made.

She returned through the back entrance and tucked her phone into the back pocket of her jeans. As Charlie fixed her hair in her bandana, Teri walked by and rubbed Charlie's shoulder, not saying a word. Charlie walked to the sink to wash her hands before returning to the front and gave a tight-lipped smile of reassurance to her boss.

As Charlie relieved Michael at the register, a sinking feeling hit her. Greg was still in town. He didn't know her mother had left. What if he came by looking for her, and Charlie was all alone? While she rang up the next customer, Charlie made a mental note to barricade the front door at night and sleep with her mom's baseball bat.

◈

Two more days went by. No sign of her mom, no sign of the handsome stranger. She had a day off, and school was going to start soon, so Charlie worked all day on a piece she could sell. She needed money. She hoped the beach girl painting would sell soon at Retrograde and decided to lower the price to get it sold. That would open up space for her to hang more paintings there.

There was an art gallery on Main Street. If she were brave enough to ask, she might be able to sell her art on consignment. Charlie worried they'd laugh her out of the building. Even though both Michael and Teri had suggested it, she was still unsure of herself. One day though…one day Charlie was going to have her own show and sell art all over the world. That was the dream anyway. To study art, travel and paint, and become a huge success in the art world was the only dream she'd ever had. Well, other than belonging. She secretly wanted to just belong, but Charlie rarely allowed herself to even think about that. It was a colossal waste of time and only left her feeling empty and sad. The only truth she'd known was that you couldn't count on anyone but yourself.

So, she'd focus on getting out of the hole her mother had dug and then get back on track with fixing her car and lying to her grandparents about what she wanted to study in college.

Having good grades wasn't something Charlie would have to lie about. She had always been an excellent student. She loved to learn and was probably one of the smartest kids in her school. Most teenagers couldn't see past their social media status, something she didn't even have. Even when she ditched some classes, Charlie could catch up and ace any test a teacher threw out. But regardless of her grades, if Charlie said she wanted to go to art school, her grandparents would say no. They wanted her to get a business degree, or become a doctor, lawyer, engineer, or a banker like her grandfather. *Something worthwhile.* She had to charm them both, and each week when they spoke on the phone, she lied her ass off about her interests, her goals, and what she wanted to do with her life.

The truth was, they didn't even know her, and she was certain they didn't want to. From the picture Cece had painted of her childhood, her grandparents had been just as disconnected from her as they were to Charlie. And when Cece had fallen in love with a musician, they'd reacted as if it was as bad as if she had become a prostitute, a bank robber, or a drug dealer. The sad fact was that Cece eventually kind of became all of those things over time. And although she'd never really robbed a bank, she had stolen from stores and lifted money from boyfriends while they slept. It all felt the same to Charlie.

That morning, as she gathered her easel, canvas, and paints, Charlie moved to the backyard to use the sunlight. The broken fence and overgrown flower beds her mother had long since abandoned sent fragmented memories through Charlie's mind. Once upon a time, Cece had taught Charlie the names of each plant and how to care for them. Now, all that seemed to matter to Cece was her next high. Like sweeping cobwebs, Charlie moved those thoughts aside to set up under the eaves of the house on the cracked concrete patio. She contemplated what to paint.

In the previous two nights out painting with The Guerrillas, Charlie came up with a spectacular vision of busting out from her world into another one of pure wonder. The signature girl she'd created with her stencils and used as the basis for her street art was busting a glass window in a dark space with a hammer. The shards of glass had fractured and fallen away to give a glimpse of a color-ful world of beauty and magic just beyond the broken pane. As she worked on it, a fellow Guerrilla called Dragon asked to help her with the vibrant world beyond the glass. Together they created one of the best pieces she'd ever made, and now, over in the alley of the Asian market off of Gravenstein Highway, you could see the magic they'd made on the side of the building, signed STAR/DRAGON. Only the street artists would know who they were.

Struggling to come up with anything as good as that idea, Char-lie stood before the blank canvas in her run-down backyard and just stared, hoping inspiration would strike. It was easier to come up with ideas when she had adrenaline rushing through her veins and the fear of being caught by the cops or some business owner gnaw-ing on her nerves. Maybe she was addicted to fear. Most everything she did was driven by fear.

Still, it didn't make sense to Charlie that street art was considered vandalism. For the most part, they took a blank and ugly area of the city and made it interesting. It became a place to ponder and offered beauty where there had been none before. And yet, people still con-sidered it defacing property, and there was a huge fine or even jail time as a consequence. Then again, if there was no element of danger to doing it, Charlie wondered if she'd even bother. Probably not. It was knowing she could get caught that gave her the rush she loved.

Because she couldn't come up with an idea, she decided to start with just color and see where it went. On her palette, the yellow was screaming out to her, so using a large brush, Charlie started sweeping the upper left corner of the canvas with sunny yellow. Back and forth, the brush made smooth strokes of golden streaks until her hand had a mind of its own. She grabbed orange, then red, and made streaks of white. Her hand flew faster, and after several hours with her acrylic paints, a blazing sun evolved from nothing. It burned and sent rays of powerful light down to a meadow where the back of a small girl stretched, her arms reaching towards the sun, beckoning it to encompass her. Charlie could feel the girl's yearning to be devoured by the rays, to fill her with so much light that the darkness would be cast out forever.

When she finished, the actual sun of her reality had moved clear across the yard to the other side of the house, and she'd lost the light. Tears streamed down her face. She'd painted herself again. It never started out that way, but it always wound up being so. Just like most everything she painted, there was an element of her own desire somewhere in there. Whether she added a girl to it or not, her paintings were always about her feelings. What she craved the most.

Wiping her nose on the back of her wrist, Charlie packed up her materials and put them into her bedroom. As she went back to grab the easel with the painting, she heard a truck so loud that it sounded like it was in her driveway. And then she knew.

As fast as she could, Charlie moved to secure the easel and canvas safely in her bedroom then ran to the front door. She was about to flip the deadbolt when Greg came in. She stood there with her hand up. She'd missed her opportunity by a second.

"Where's your mother?"

Charlie moved back as his stocky frame pushed through the entryway, reeking of booze and sweat. Greg's scratchy, booming voice sent chills throughout her body. He stumbled around with darting eyes and rumpled, dirty clothes.

"Ah, she's not here. She went out." Charlie moved over by the sofa and crossed her arms over her chest, trying to act as normal as she could with her heart beating like a jackhammer.

"With who? She hasn't answered my calls in days, she's not at the salon, and I drove by here twice and her car has been gone. Where is she?"

"Like I said, she's out. I don't know where she goes. It's not like she asks my permission or anything. She'll be back soon."

He turned and stared her straight in the eyes, laser focused on her. She was the deer, and he was the lion. One false move, and he'd be upon her.

"How do you know she'll be back soon if you don't know who she's with or where she went? What the fuck kinda game are you playin'?" He glared at her and stepped closer.

Charlie moved away from the sofa and tried to be casual, stepping into the kitchen and opening a cupboard for a glass to drink some water. She wanted to show no fear, even though she thought she might vomit from anxiety. Her mother's boyfriends were always weird, but Greg was a predator. He was a bully, and the worst abuser of any of the guys Cece had brought around. She reached up for the glass, her hand shaking so badly she almost dropped it before it reached the faucet. As she filled the glass, Charlie saw Greg approach from the side in her peripheral view but didn't want to look directly at him.

"She seeing someone, huh? She fucking around on me, kid?"

Charlie stood facing the sink and continued to swallow water when Greg grabbed her by the arm and swung her around so fast she dropped the glass in the sink, and it shattered. He pushed her up against the counter and grabbed her face, pinching her cheeks with his meaty hand, pressing them into her teeth until she tasted blood. She moaned in pain while he pinned her there, unable to move.

"Not so fucking tough now, are you, little girl? You thought you were pretty smart kicking me in the balls, but I won't make that mistake twice. You Kane women think you are better than me. If

Cece thinks I'm that easily replaced, she's got another thing coming. I'll teach her a lesson. Teach you both!"

He moved his hand from her face to her neck and held her there, just tight enough to hurt, but she could breathe. Gasping and panicked, Charlie searched for a way out. She pushed at his arms, his chest, and then seized the counter by her sides to keep from being shoved so hard into it. Greg's free hand grabbed the waistband of her sweatpants, and he started to yank them down. Charlie squirmed and pulled them up again, but his grip on her throat tightened, and he crushed his body into hers.

"You little bitch. Think I'm leaving without some of this? I'll teach Cece to cheat on me!"

"NO! No, no, no."

Charlie murmured through spittle and gasps, fighting to breathe. He pressed his boots over her feet, so she couldn't knee him. Her feet only protected by flip-flops, the crushing of skin and bone shot bolts of pain through her like lightning. The glass in the sink was just behind her, and she tried to grab a chunk, but with only one hand pushing back on Greg, he got her sweatpants pulled down and was fumbling for her panties. He groped her crotch and ripped her underwear down, tearing the fabric. Charlie shrieked out as his mouth came down on her collarbone and a finger scratched into her vagina, sending her mind into a frenzy of hysteria.

"You'll get what you got comin' to ya," he said as he let go of her throat to unbutton his pants.

That was her chance.

Charlie took a chunk of glass from the sink and slashed it across Greg's neck, just above his collarbone. He stumbled backwards as he grabbed his neck. She lunged away, but he seized her arm again and was on her fast. The cut wasn't deadly, but still, his blood came quickly. The slash was deep enough to make a mess of his shirt. The hand he had pressed against the wound was now covered in blood, and because he'd grabbed Charlie, she, too, had the red mess all over her. She yanked up her sweats.

"YOU! I can't believe you fucking cut me!"

"LET ME GO!" Charlie screamed and kicked him, making contact with his shin. He hopped back but continued to lunge towards her. She slipped away from one hand, and he grabbed her with the other. They tumbled to the floor. Greg reached for her arm, then a leg, as Charlie kept fighting to escape from him. She pulled herself up and, in a final blow, stomped Greg in the ribs and then the face. He yelled out in pain, and she made it to the front door.

Bloody, now barefoot, and terrified, Charlie ran feverishly to the neighbor's house and stumbled up the front steps. She pounded on their door and yelled for help at the residence of an older couple she often saw working in their yard but didn't know. The woman had lovely roses.

"HELP! Please help me. He's trying to rape me. He'll kill me. Help!"

The door opened, and the alarming sight of Charlie made the old man's eyes pop. She threw herself into his arms and begged him to help her. The woman came to them then, and a shrieking Charlie tried desperately to tell them to call the police, that Greg was going to rape and kill her.

As the man passed Charlie off to his wife, he bravely walked down the steps from his porch to look over into Charlie's yard. Fearing for the older man, Charlie ran after him and begged the wife to call the police. The truck rumbled to life, and Greg backed the thing up, threw it into gear, and spit gravel from the back tires as he barreled away.

But the old man got the license plate number with his cell phone and told his wife, who was on the phone. The police arrived, and together, over cups of chamomile tea, they gave their statements. The kind couple had Charlie stay with them through the questioning, and when the police needed to go investigate the scene at her house, they went with her.

She walked back into her house. With the broken glass and all the blood around, it looked like a murder scene.

"His name for the record again, miss?"

"Greg White. He works construction or as a mechanic or something. I'm not really sure."

"And where is your mother?"

Charlie didn't want them to possibly put her into some kind of foster care since she wasn't eighteen yet, so she lied.

"She's visiting her friend overnight and will be back tomorrow. She forgot her charger though and called me this morning to say she won't be able to be reached since her phone was dying."

"You don't have any power here?" The officer kept trying the lights.

"It's getting turned back on tomorrow. My mom was late paying the bill, but we've paid up now."

The officers took pictures of her injuries. They suggested she go to the hospital because of the bruising around her neck and the fact that she was limping pretty badly because of her feet. Fear wrapped around Charlie like a boa constrictor that they'd somehow take her away from her mother. Cece might be a shitty mom, but Charlie didn't want to be with anyone else either.

"I'll be ok. I just need you to find that son of a bitch. I'll press charges."

"You're a minor, so it's not necessary. He'll be charged. We ran his plates, and it checks out. And with his cut as you described, we'll know it's him. We took samples of his blood that's around the kitchen too. We can clearly see the bruising around your neck and scratches you have all over. We can haul him in and start an investigation on your behalf without you or your mom. We will be in touch. It would help if you got checked out by a doctor though."

She thought of the doctor's bills and having to explain everything to her grandparents. Charlie shook her head. "I just want to go to bed. I don't want to see anyone right now."

The officers gave her their cards, and the older couple promised they'd keep an eye on her.

After the officers left, the elderly neighbors, Joan and Randy Taylor, offered to stay and help her clean up, but she said she was fine, so they went home. Charlie looked around the house and started to shake. The trembling started in her legs and worked its way up into her chest and arms. She couldn't clean this now. Instead, she showered then curled up in bed, bundled tight around her pillows, and began to sob. She cried for her innocence that was lost long ago. She cried for her mother who clearly didn't love her enough, and she cried for the life she wished she had.

When the trembling subsided, Charlie vowed she was never going to let anyone control her or take anything away from her again. She was going to have that life she deserved. And as the determination sunk in, she was able to slip away into the quiet of slumber that was the only place where nightmares didn't lurk. When you lived in a nightmare, sleep was the only peace you knew.

CHAPTER EIGHT

JACK

THE MORNING THAT Jack walked onto campus with his uncle to his first staff meeting to get acquainted with the other English teachers, he felt like a fish out of water. He continually asked himself what the hell he was doing, thinking he couldn't pull this off. But once he was introduced, people were kind and helpful. Especially Emily Wellington.

Emily taught ninth grade English, was a second-year teacher, and was extremely cute. Her pert little nose, bouncy blonde hair and soft blue eyes made her look like some kind of doll. She laughed at everything, her smile a permanent fixture on her face, and she kept touching him with her slender fingers and manicured nails.

After the meeting, Jack followed his uncle into his principal's office, and once the door was shut, Rob was elbowing him about Emily.

"See! I told ya you'd do fine here. Not bad, that Emily, huh? I saw how helpful she was. She's single and obviously into you. This substitute teaching gig might work out pretty well for you, huh?"

"Oh Christ, Uncle Rob. It's my first day. I can't even go there. But yeah, she's very nice."

"Keep your options open, Jack-o. Anyway, go see Lori about

time sheets and then head over to room twenty-five for your first department meeting. Emily will be there to be sure you are *very comfortable.*" He winked at Jack as he opened the door for Jack to leave.

The morning went by fast with one meeting after another. When they broke for lunch, Emily accompanied him, and then the entire afternoon was in the auditorium for a pep talk from their superintendent. At the end of the day, the sun was high, and Jack was walking to his father's black Camaro far more confident than when he'd arrived.

"Jack! Wait up." Emily nearly ran after him, giggling as she did.

He turned her way just before opening his car door. She was definitely cute, but something in his chest caught as he admitted to himself that she wasn't Charlie. He didn't feel a flutter in his chest or that pull from his solar plexus when he looked at Emily.

"This is yours? Nice car!" Emily ran her hand across the fender. "Hey, we're all going to grab a drink over at HopMonk, if you wanna join us. It's a tradition for the first day back, and everyone is going. You should come."

She batted her eyes and popped her hip out, studying him as she waited for his answer. The truth was, Jack was really tired of his routine of just hanging out alone at the house writing. Grabbing a few beers with a group of people sounded pretty good. If he were in LA, he'd be at some beach bar with Zane or listening to live music somewhere. Although he didn't miss chasing celebrities, this slower pace of life was getting him down.

He smiled at her. "Sure. Where is this place?"

She grabbed his phone and entered the name and address of the bar and told him to meet them there. Emily bounced away like a little sprite, and Jack hopped into his car.

HopMonk was pretty amazing, with an outdoor beer garden and stage. The rustic tavern made of stone and timber was like the Old West meets upscale contemporary. Most of the high school staff started pouring in, and with all the lively conversations flowing,

Jack's energy rose. Maybe his uncle was right. Maybe taking this job was just the shot in the arm he needed.

Wednesday to Friday flew by, and school was going to start that following Monday with actual kids. Jack had his curriculum, his room was set and ready for students, and Emily made sure he knew she was just two doors down. His anxiety started to build again, and she must have been able to see it in his eyes.

"Look, Jack, I had the worst first few days last year in my first-year teaching, but after you get to know the kids, it's like riding a bike. You get into a groove, and all your own high school years will serve to help you know what to do. Remember who your favorite teacher was and emulate them. Just follow the lesson plan and relax. Before you know it, teaching will feel like second nature. And I'll be here to help if you need anything."

She looked up at him with such infatuation that he felt himself blush. The last thing Jack wanted to do was become entangled in a workplace relationship, and he quickly ducked out for the weekend, declining another offer for drinks, saying he and Rob had plans.

But Uncle Rob had plans of his own.

"I'm headed to Sacramento for the weekend to see a lady friend. You don't mind staying with the boys, do ya? I might not get a chance to see Angela again for a while after school starts with our schedules being so different. She's a flight attendant for American Airlines, and she's gone a lot. Smokin' hot, this gal. Great legs."

"Sure, go have fun. The dogs and I are well acquainted. I'm gonna write as much as I can before school starts anyway. I can tell once I'm in the thick of things I probably won't get much of a chance to write until the other teacher returns."

Uncle Rob grabbed a duffel bag from the hall closet and threw it over his shoulder. "Have you given any thought to what you are gonna do when this sub job is over? I mean, no rush. You can stay as long as you'd like."

"As much as I love hanging with you and the boys here, I think I'm gonna head back to LA and room with Zane. He's been on me about it and has some job opportunities I might be interested in. I think I'm gonna try my hand at screenplays or writing a pilot for television."

Rob's eyes widened. "Wow. Ambitious. Well, if you've got connections, then I say go for it. Anyway, I'm gonna pack. And thanks for hanging with the dogs."

After Rob packed and drove away, Jack settled in for a writing marathon. No more mad drafts to the *Scoop's* editor about Brittany Spears buying groceries. He was determined to focus on writing a great story. And although he ached to go searching for Charlie again, he let her go.

But his subconscious was clearly still focused on her. The novel he started that weekend, where he got over eight thousand words written, was about a struggling writer who lived at the beach in Southern California and fell in love with a mystery girl he met at an underground nightclub. Jack described her exactly like Charlie with smoldering eyes, uncontrollable hair, and a long, lean body. By Sunday evening, Jack was sorry he'd have to put the story on the back burner. For the next six weeks he was committed to being an English teacher for Analy High.

On Monday morning, Jack was up before the sun. With buzzing nerves, he went for a run as the sky was just turning pink and the last of the evening's stars were fading in the light. He showered and dressed in tan slacks, a gold short-sleeved button-down, and brown Italian loafers. He looked like he was either going to church or a wedding. It was normal business attire in LA, but here in Sebastopol, he felt like a total poser. After living in shorts, T-shirts, and pullovers for weeks, Jack looked at himself in the mirror and almost didn't recognize the reflection.

"There you are, man. I knew you were in there somewhere. You are gonna be alright."

The self-talk surprisingly made him feel better, and he worried if he might be going nuts.

Being the principal, Rob had to get to school even earlier than he did, so Jack was the last at home. He put the dogs in the backyard and left them water, then off to school he went. The nearer Jack got to campus, the more chaos ensued. Congested traffic and school buses piled up. The staff parking lot was loaded, and when Jack came rolling in with his deep rumbling muscle car, people took notice. He made his way over to the main building through the swarms of kids, all whispering after him.

He filled out his time card for the day and walked to his room with flocks of students in cliques everywhere, clad in new shoes and backpacks. He shakily opened the room with his key and hid behind the locked door.

Safely inside, Jack took deep breaths to calm himself. He jumped when his cell phone buzzed. The screen showed it was Emily. *Was she stalking him?* He fumbled to answer it.

"Hey, Emily."

"Open your door. I'm right outside."

Christ, there's going to be no stopping this train now. His day had begun, and he'd need to get on board with it.

Jack opened the door to the noisy eruption of kids talking and stepped aside so Emily could come in. As he shut his door and locked it, the room fell quiet again. His nerves ebbed and flowed like waves crashing against the shore.

"How you holding up? Here." She thrust a coffee into his hands from Retrograde, and his heart sank as he thought of Charlie.

Had she made this coffee today? Maybe her hands had been on this very cup just a little while ago.

"I'm a bit nervous, but mostly fine. Thanks for this."

He sipped the too-sweet pumpkin latte that he never would have ordered. Still, he nodded his appreciation and crossed the room to set it on his very organized desk.

"I just wanted to remind you of my extension. Call if you need anything at all. We have first break at 10:10. Just holler if you have questions."

Emily pressed herself around him in her tight pink dress to write her phone extension on a sticky pad, then she smiled up at him as she stood dangerously close. Jack could almost feel the heat of her body when the bell sounded loudly outside, startling him so much he jumped. Emily laughed.

"Ok, break a leg. You'll be great," she said as she headed out the door.

Kids started to pour in. Jack walked to the whiteboard and began writing to keep himself occupied while they settled in for first period. He wrote his name, JACK CONNORS, then grabbed the eraser to wipe out his first name and replace it with Mr. After the second bell rang, he went to his computer to bring up the roster for first period. He printed it out and stood in front of the kids, smiling as they continued to talk quietly amongst themselves with perplexed looks on their faces.

"You are right in your assumption that I am not Mrs. Pratt. I know on your class schedule it says she's your teacher, but I'm Ja...I'm Mr. Connors and will be with you for your first six weeks of school this year, until Mrs. Pratt returns from maternity leave. So welcome to your senior year of AP English. Please quiet down while I take roll call. When you hear your name, please just say *here*, and we can get going."

The kids were putting backpacks on the backs of their chairs, on the floor next to them, or on their desktops to use like pillows. They got quiet while Jack read off the names from the list.

"Jason Baker – Keanu Dyer – Krystal Gage – Jose Hernandez – Jamie Ingles." The kids kept saying *here* after each name was called.

"Charlotte Kane...Charlotte Kane?" Jack looked up from the paper when nobody had answered. "Is there a Charlotte Kane here?"

The door flew open, and Jack thought his heart stopped. Standing in the doorway, wearing a pullover sweatshirt and tight ripped jeans stood the object of his desire these past few weeks. Her hair sprang out everywhere in haphazard curls that spilled down like an untamed waterfall, and she looked at him with the same amazement that he had.

"Dog Man?"

"Charlie?"

The class turned around and stared at Charlie, then slowly turned back to look at him.

Holy shit! This was NOT happening.

CHAPTER NINE

CHARLIE

*O*H NO! NO, no, no...*he was NOT her teacher. But how was this possible? Wasn't he leaving to go back to LA? Or did she just make that up in her head? This wasn't happening. The one guy she actually thought she could fall for, that was different than the rest, was a fucking teacher?*

Charlie froze in the back of the room with her backpack hanging off one shoulder when she realized all eyes were on her. She had to blow it off and take a seat even though the shock of seeing him at the front of the room dressed in...*what the hell was he wearing?* Teacher clothes. He was cleaned up all pretty like he just stepped out of a fucking country club. But God...he was still completely gorgeous, and his eyes were boring right through her. They stayed connected to hers as she slowly moved to take the back corner desk. Charlie broke the spell and let her eyes move to her desk as she flopped her backpack onto the ground.

"You two know each other or what?" Danny Rogers, who was sitting across the room, asked in an apprehensive voice.

Charlie looked up to see Dog Man's expression and let him do the talking. She wanted to know how he would handle knowing her. Would he be embarrassed to be associated with her or tell the truth how they'd spent time having deep conversations during the summer? She crossed her arms over her chest, and again, their eyes met across the room.

"Uh, yes. I met Charlie over at Retrograde Coffee this summer where she works. She makes a mean latte." He ran a hand through his perfectly combed hair, mussing it, and pulled at his collar before dropping his eyes to look at a piece of paper. "Let's finish roll, shall we?"

As Dog Man rambled off names of students in the class, she twisted her head around and rubbed her mouth with her hand, staring at the back corner of the room. She tried to catch her breath. He hadn't told the class the whole truth. Actually, he left out the best parts. But Charlie wouldn't have shared about their talks either. She wouldn't tell anyone about how he kept looking for her and waiting for her at work just to continue their conversation. How it became clear to her that he liked her too. How the fuck would *that* look?

But now, *shit!* It was so unbelievable that he was here. And what the hell was he thinking of her now? He'd figured out she was a high school student, and she still had no idea how old he was. It felt totally unfair that he knew her name, *her real name*, and how old she was, and yet, she had virtually nothing on him. *Fuck!*

After roll call, Charlie looked back at him, and he lasered in on her once more but then tried to avoid making eye contact after that. He explained what could be expected from the class this year, and specifically what they'd cover while he was there.

"As I've said, I'm only here for six weeks until Mrs. Pratt returns, but that's still a long enough time to get to know each other. I want to be sure you all get off to a strong start for your senior year."

Charlie started to bite the skin around her thumbnail while she studied his movements. He was pacing. Was it teaching that made him nervous? Or was it her? She couldn't tell. Then she looked up at what he'd written on the board. *Mr. Connors.* But the blue ink was smudged across his name on the whiteboard. He'd written something else before. What was it?

He was rambling on about something she hadn't heard because inside her head it was pretty noisy. Her mind drifted to the past few days when she had gathered her strength to recover from nearly being raped. That she had to clean up her house from the bloody mess Greg left all over her floor, walls, and front door. How the police had called her to say they'd arrested Greg and that he was being held with bail set at one hundred thousand dollars, and that the hearing would take a while. What would Dog Man think of all that? If he was still just a guy and she were just a girl, and not his student, would he still be interested in her, or would he run?

The clock on the wall said she'd been in here fifteen minutes, but she couldn't remember much of what had happened during that time. She'd been studying him and stressing about what he must be thinking, without truly listening.

Mr. Connors handed some papers to the people in the front rows to pass back, and when he stood at the front of her row, he looked at her and their eyes locked again.

"This is your reading list for the first semester. I collaborated with Mrs. Pratt on this, and I hope you will all enjoy these books we've chosen. The suggested list allowed for many choices, but these are the ones we thought were best to start off with."

She grabbed the paper handed to her. There were three books listed with a summary of each. The first was *East of Eden* by John Steinbeck. The second title was *The Great Gatsby* by F. Scott Fitzgerald—one of Dog Man's favorites, if Charlie recalled correctly from their conversation. And the final one was *Wuthering Heights* by Emily Bronte, one of Charlie's favorites of all time. The only book of the three she hadn't read was *East of Eden*. A retelling of a biblical story didn't interest her, but she was required to read it now. She wondered which of them chose the book. Had it been him or Mrs. Pratt?

As the class was coming to a close, Charlie felt the familiar pang of dread she got whenever she left him. But now she'd be seeing

Mr. Connors every day for at least the next six weeks. Still, it was different now. She wasn't the mysterious girl she wanted to be anymore. Now she was his student. She'd lost the upper hand.

The bell rang, and kids were up and gathering their things. Charlie slowly started to stand when, to her surprise, she heard his voice ring out above the noise of the bustling class.

"Charlie, could you please come up to my desk for a minute?"

Her heart leapt at his request. She looked around though, feeling conspicuous and wanting to see if anyone thought it strange that the teacher asked to see her. But everyone seemed occupied with leaving class. Charlie made her way against the wake of kids moving the opposite direction and approached Dog Man's desk. He ran his hand through his hair again and looked at her with raised eyebrows.

"Charlotte?"

A nervous laugh escaped from her. "Yeah. Nobody's called me that since I was a kid. Except my uppity grandparents. So, you didn't tell me you were a teacher."

He looked around cautiously before he quietly responded, "Well, it wasn't my plan. Mr. Hill, your principal, is my uncle. The one with the dogs? Anyway, they needed a sub, so here I am."

He let out a big exhale and blew his cheeks out in exasperation before shaking his head and laughing nervously.

"I suppose you won't be coming to get coffee from me anymore now that I'm a student, huh?" She tested the waters and waited for his reply, shoving her hands into her sweatshirt pockets.

"I mean...I still drink coffee. That hasn't changed. But with this strange situation, I hope we can be...friends."

Friends.

Charlie felt a fissure form within her heart at being demoted to the friend category when the last time he'd been with her, he'd acted like he wanted to be more. There was nothing she could do about it though, and she refused to look like some lovesick puppy that was needy and clingy. The air of confidence was her only leverage.

"Sure. We're friends." Charlie looked away with disappointment, biting her lower lip to keep from saying more.

Kids were spilling in for second period. She looked at him and waited for his response, but all he did was stare at her with apologetically gorgeous eyes that seemed to change color every time she saw him. Were they gray, blue, green, or hazel? He started to reach a hand towards her arm then pulled it back and put it into his pocket. "It's just...I'm..."

She didn't want to stick around for his excuses and explanations. It hurt too much, and she understood clearly. She was a student. He was an adult. But how old could he be? He had to be in his twenties. Either way, it sucked, and once again, disappointment weighed down her stomach like a lead brick.

"It's all good. But to even things up, *Mr. Connors.*" Charlie gave him her best smile and paused for effect. "You know my name. *My real name.* I don't know yours."

He shined that brilliant smile at her, and his devastatingly cute dimple appeared. "It's Jack. Jack Connors."

Charlie adjusted her backpack over her shoulder and raised one eyebrow at him as she turned to leave. "See you around, Jack. Tell George and Henry I said hello."

Rounding the corner from Jack's classroom, Charlie became overwhelmed and started to hyperventilate. Her breathing became rapid and short. She ducked into the girl's bathroom and took a stall just as the bell rang for second period. She was late for American Government. The bathroom got quiet, and she knew she was alone. Tears spilled over her eyelashes, and she took huge gulping breaths, forcing herself to slow her breathing down.

Why? Why did it seem like everything Charlie wanted and strived for became so incredibly hard?

After a few minutes, she was able to compose herself again, and she emerged from the stall to give her reflection a look. Wiping her face and blowing her nose, Charlie threw her shoulders back and stared herself in the eyes.

You can do this. Stay the course. It's no different than when you reminded yourself he was just going to leave and go back to LA. You have to stay focused no matter how much of a distraction Jack Connors is. You only have until graduation, and then you are leaving anyway. This isn't your life. Your life is out there somewhere, and you don't need anyone holding your hand to get it. Suck it up, baby. You've got this.

Her mental conversation in the mirror calmed her, and late as she was, Charlie decided to go to class instead of giving in to her initial instinct to cut school and run. She only had nine months until she was free. Nine months until she had that diploma in her hand and the freedom to change her life.

CHAPTER TEN

JACK

H E MADE IT through his first day. With his mind completely rattled by seeing Charlie and discovering she was a high school student, it was by far the longest day of Jack's life. Staying focused for all his other classes once she left his room had been nearly impossible.

At lunch, he went to grab his food from the staff room refrigerator and avoided eating with Emily by stating he had a lot of phone calls he needed to make and was just going to eat in his room. He didn't stick around to see if she had a hurt look on her face.

When he finished his last class, Jack opted to work alone in his classroom instead of going to the staff room for cake and conversation. Emily had called his extension only a minute after the last bell rang to tell him about it—yet another tradition the staff had of gathering around a huge sheet cake and commiserating about the first day back. His whole body ragged with frayed nerves, Jack was emotionally spent and had no ability to socialize.

Heading to his car, he found himself scanning the campus for Charlie, his eyes darting this way and that like a skittish bird. But of course, she wouldn't still be there. School had let out an hour before, and it wasn't likely she'd be waiting around for him.

Had he hoped she'd be waiting?

With the realization of how incredibly inappropriate his attraction to her was, he felt like he'd committed some horrible crime. And although he had some guilt over it, Jack still desired her in a way he'd never felt before. No other girl he'd known had had the same effect on him as Charlie, with butterflies and curiosity…but she was off limits.

And there was no way in hell he could tell anyone about her! *Christ*, he was glad he hadn't mentioned meeting Charlie to his Uncle Rob, his mother, or even Zane! The only person who might have the slightest idea of his interest in her was her boss at Retrograde, and because of that, he'd have to be very careful not to show any interest like that again.

Jack agonized over the situation the whole night. He played off being jittery to his uncle by claiming his mind was on the new job. Which it actually was. He was trying to figure out how the hell he was going to see Charlie every single day and hide how he felt about her.

"So, Emily Wellington has the hots for you. She asked me a lot of questions about you in the staff room after school." His uncle handed Jack another beer over the kitchen counter as he sauteed some vegetables for their dinner.

"I'm *so* not going to get involved with a coworker. Especially when I'm only gonna be there for six weeks."

Jack took a long pull from his second bottle of Pacifico beer and started to feel some of his anxiety melting away. Emily was cute, but she was giving him the full-court press, and it wasn't exactly attractive. His skin crawled at the thought of a needy girlfriend, always asking him where he was, what he was doing, and who he was doing it with. He'd had one of those before. *Barbie Bianca*. Bad idea.

"Nobody said you needed to get involved," Rob said, "but you might loosen up a bit if you got laid. Christ, you are wound tighter than an eight-day clock."

His uncle Rob laughed at his own comment as he popped the seared filet mignon from the stovetop into the oven with some potatoes he was baking. His skillful maneuvers in the kitchen were like those of a professional chef.

"Thanks," Jack said. "I'll take that under advisement."

❧

The next day, and for the remainder of the week, Charlie arrived in class on time, but she never talked to him before or after class. She acted like any other kid in the classroom except that she was quieter than the rest. She avoided making eye contact with him. After a few days, it wasn't as hard to have her so near and not be able to approach her like he wanted to. He did find it sort of soothing though knowing she'd be there every day, even if she didn't speak to him.

The voice of his buddy Zane was ringing in his ear though as the high school female population began to flirt with him, from girls in the hallway to the parking lot before school. But with them, he had no temptation at all. It was only Charlie he yearned for, and every day he had to suppress it.

His days were filled with teaching, and his evenings involved grading papers, writing, and online screenplay classes. After his first disastrous day of school, things smoothed out, and he thought he might actually be able to do this. It was only six weeks. After that, who knew?

But Friday, when the kids were spilling in for first period, Charlie entered the room with some boy who didn't belong in his class. He was talking to her aggressively, and he followed her into the room all the way to her desk. The hairs on Jack's arms prickled, and his blood pressure rose. The look on Charlie's face was agitated and uncomfortable.

Jack moved past the students taking their seats and approached the kid who was almost as tall as he was. The kid wore gauges in his ears, was dressed in black, baggy clothes, and had tatts on his hands.

"Can I help you?" Jack said too loudly.

"It's fine, Jack," Charlie said, trying to call him off but not very convincingly.

Jack looked at Charlie with raised eyebrows.

"Settle down, player. I ain't here for you," the kid said with a mocking sneer.

"Who are you, and what the hell are you doing in my classroom harassing my students?" Jack demanded.

Adrenaline pulsed through Jack, and he wanted to slam that kid against a wall and tell him to stay the fuck away from Charlie, but he had to remain calm. It took all his strength to not grab the kid and throw him out. Instead, he got very close to him and looked him right in the eye as a warning.

"Whoa, step off, teach. I'm just havin' a conversation here with, uh…with Charlie here. She and I got business to talk about."

"We've got nothing to talk about, and you need to stay away from me." Charlie shrunk into her desk. She spoke a tough game, but her eyes were wide, and she was skittish.

Jack set his jaw. "Where are you supposed to be? Because you don't belong in my classroom!"

The kids all fell silent, staring at Jack and this hoodlum that nobody seemed to know. Nobody except Charlie.

"He doesn't go here. He's not a student at Analy High at all. Isn't that right?" Charlie glared up at the kid while he and Jack stood side by side at her desk.

"What the…? Get out before I call the cops. NOW!" Jack yelled, and a student in the back desk nearest to the door ran out. Jack had no idea what the hell was happening now.

The street hood in black smirked at Jack and backed away slowly. "You ain't gotta get so uptight. Like I said, I ain't here for you. I just need to talk to Charlie here. But that's alright. I'll just wait, and we can continue our little chat when you are done here. I'll catch up with you later."

"You won't be *catching up* with anyone! Get off this campus and back to wherever the hell you came from, or I'll escort you off myself."

"Jack…" Charlie tried to reach up and put her hand on his arm, but he moved towards the kid, threateningly, and puffed out his chest as a warning. Jack was seeing red.

What the hell is going on around here? Who is this kid, and why does he know Charlie?

Jack's mind was spinning. The scumbag kid looked at all the faces that were glued on him, watching his every move. As the derelict moved for the door, Jack's uncle, Principal Hill, came in with the football coach, Dan Weeks, a man with a huge barrel chest who stood at least six feet three, with a no-nonsense face. Trailing them was the kid who had run out of the room. Jack then realized he'd run for the calvary.

"What are you doing on my campus, young man?" Rob and the coach sandwiched the kid between them.

"Hey, I'm just here to have a chat with uh—"

"You don't belong here. Let's take a walk to the office until the police arrive. You have some explaining to do." Coach Weeks grabbed the kid by the arm, and he tried to pull it away, but he was no match for the enormous strength of the powerhouse football coach.

As they were leaving, Jack's uncle leaned back into the room and addressed Charlie. "I'll need you to come with me, Charlie. We need to straighten this out. And thanks, Trevor, for coming to the office to get me."

Charlie's eyes met Jack's. He stood at the back of the room, holding back questions for her he couldn't ask, his mouth open in confusion. She threw her backpack over her shoulder, and as she passed him, he started to reach out for her hand. She pulled away, reminding him of his station. Jack swallowed as she left, the door slowly closing behind her.

He turned around, and the entire classroom was staring at him.

He moved back to the front of the room, rubbing his forehead, then refolded his collar. Jack cleared his throat.

"Well, thank you, Trevor, for helping us get that under control."

"Looks like you almost had that under control yourself, Mister C," another one of his boys said, smiling and looking at him with admiration.

Jack laughed a little, and they all shook some of the tension off. "Well, I can't just have anyone off the streets come and harass my kids, now can I? Anyway, it was a good thing your coach Weeks showed up. Let's get to work, shall we?"

They started the class without Charlie, and it ended without her return. Jack's stomach was in knots. How the hell had she been wrapped up with that crazy street urchin? And who was he to her? So many questions. Somehow he got through the two classes before his morning break, then he went to his uncle's office and closed the door behind him. "*What the hell?* Who was that kid?"

"Take a seat, Jack." Uncle Rob nodded to the chair.

"You guys have this sort of thing happen often?"

Rob smiled and shook his head. "No, actually. It's fairly calm usually. Looks like this scumbag was the nephew of a man Charlie had arrested for assault. The kid might be looking for some kind of retaliation against her. His uncle is in the pen, and it looks like the bail is set pretty high, so he won't be getting out for a while. Charlie was pretty shaken up but embarrassed more than anything. Poor kid. She didn't want to go back to class afterwards, so she hung out with Lori in the office until it was time for second period. Police are charging the shithead with harassment, and since he's over eighteen, he's headed to jail. He gets to see his uncle. Nice little family reunion."

Jack's mouth went dry. He could hardly swallow. "Charlie was *assaulted*. When?"

"I guess a week or more ago. Not one hundred percent sure, but anyway, she says she's fine now. The kid was waiting for her outside the school gates today and walked right up to her. She claims to have never met him before, but he told her he knew her from pictures his uncle had. Creepy, right? Besides, it's not like Charlie Kane is hard to forget. The kid is tall as a stork and gorgeous to boot. She said she walked straight to class to keep him from getting her. Smart move on Charlie's part. She showed me bruises on her neck. Helluva mess. Anyway, I think she's okay now."

"Jesus." Jack sat there stunned. He ached to find her and hold her. To protect her and take her away somewhere that no one could get to her ever again. But he had to remain professional, and he couldn't let on just how badly this shook him.

"Right," Rob said. "You hear lots of stories from the kids over the years that you have to learn to compartmentalize. It's hard, but you can't let it get to you, otherwise you'll fall apart all the time. Shit happens in these kids' lives, and we are only here with them for a short period of time. Gotta advise them the best we can, keep them safe while they are here, and hope the rest of the time they will be okay."

Jack mumbled mostly to himself, "I guess so."

"You gonna be alright, Jack-o?"

He tried to hide the sting of worry and helplessness. "Sure. I gotta go. Thanks for telling me."

He finished his day with a cloud over his head. Everyone was talking about the incident and how Jack wasn't taking any shit from this crazy kid, but after learning about the situation, Jack was sick with worry about Charlie. What happened when this kid was let out? They'd probably only hold him until a hearing, if that. And what had happened to Charlie when she was assaulted? Jack could hardly bear it.

His last period ended, and Emily walked through his door with concerned eyes.

"You could use a drink, huh?"

He gave a half smile. "Yeah. I'm thinking I probably could. Guess I'm not as seasoned as you all. What a day."

"I'm headed to pizza with friends and some beers. Wanna join us?"

"I think I'll take a rain check, if it's okay. I'm probably gonna go for a run and work off this extra stress."

She followed him to the door and nodded her understanding. "Maybe you'd like to come out with me tomorrow night then?" She batted her eyes at him. "Look, Jack, I'm gonna be open here and tell you I really like you and would like to see more of you outside of school."

He peered down at her sweet smile and kind face. She really was being very nice, and he was running out of excuses. He couldn't use Charlie as a reason he didn't want to go out because how would that look?

"That sounds fun. But you have to know, I'm leaving in five weeks to move back to LA, and I don't think it would be smart to get anything started here relationship-wise. So, if you are good with that, maybe we can do something tomorrow."

She beamed up at him. "Great! I'll text you tomorrow, and we can go from there. Go for your run and relax. I'll talk to you later."

Emily walked towards the parking lot as Jack was turning to lock his door. He was headed to his car when he remembered he left his lunch bag inside and didn't want to leave it over the weekend to stink. He went back inside and headed for his desk. Grabbing his insulated bag, he heard someone walk in behind him. He hoped Emily wasn't back to press the pizza thing, but when he turned around, it wasn't Emily.

Charlie stood with the door shut behind her, backpack at her side, and eyes as wide as saucers. She said nothing and neither did he. Jack moved towards her, and she stood still, waiting and not saying a word. When he reached her, his heart leapt, and instinctively, he pulled her into a hug, holding her against him as his heart raced. He breathed in the lemon and sage scent of her hair. Knowing he had to let go, he ran his hands down her arms and held her wrists.

"My God, are you okay?"

She looked up at him with tired eyes that held so many secrets. He wanted to drown in those eyes and have her share everything she was thinking.

"I'm better now."

He had to correct his behavior and move away from her, but his body wouldn't do what his mind was telling it to.

"I was sick with worry all day. Rob said you were assaulted by that creep's uncle. Are you hurt? What happened to you?"

She shook her head. "It's over now. My mother's boyfriend. I hope he rots in jail. But anyway, by the time it all gets settled, I'll be gone anyway. When I graduate, I'm leaving Sebastopol. I'm never coming back here."

"Where will you go?"

Charlie smiled up at him, and his heart broke wide open.

"I was thinking LA sounds pretty good for college. I'm going to study art."

She was making plans. As much as he wanted her in his life, he was worried he'd give her false hope that he could offer something more sooner than he actually could. Jack dropped her wrists and put his hands into his pockets.

"LA is a great place for that. You're really talented too." He rubbed his neck. "I'm sorry I shouldn't have…we can't…I was just so worried today. Charlie, this summer when I thought you were older, I felt something for you. More than I guess I was willing to admit, but now…Look, I have to be smart here. But we are friends, right? You said so. And I'd like to continue to be friends. It's just…that's all I can offer right now. But if you ever need help, Charlie, I want you to come to me. My God… I can't believe someone hurt you."

She looked wounded hearing his words, and she stood perfectly still. He wanted to brush her hair off her face. Not touching her was agonizing.

"You can't have it both ways, Dog Man." She gave a half-hearted smile. "And a moment ago, you didn't act like we were *just* friends."

"I was wrong to do that. Like I said, I was worried." He swallowed again, trying to move out of her gravity, but he found himself being pulled towards her.

"Well, I can take care of myself. Been doing that all my life," she whispered, tilting her head up towards his, biting the corner of her full lower lip as she stared at him.

Jack felt drugged and allowed his eyes to droop nearly closed, anticipating a kiss when his mind suddenly kicked in and he woke up, moving back.

"We can't. I'm too old for you. It's not right. I'm so sorry. Um...I think you should go. We can't be seen leaving at the same time, so I'll say how very sorry I am and that I am truly glad you are okay."

Crossing his arms over his chest, he stepped back some more, wishing like hell things could be different.

Charlie gave him an understanding tight-lipped smile and nodded her head. "Sure. I understand. I mean, how old are you anyway?"

He shifted his weight from one foot to the other, feeling awkward. "I'm twenty-four."

She sighed then smiled a big grin and pulled her backpack up over her shoulder again, one hand on the door. "Today, you think I'm too young, but next year when I'm in college, you won't. It's crazy. But yeah, sure. You are too fucking old for me, Jack. Have a great weekend."

He winced as she turned and walked out, letting the door slowly swing back until it clicked shut behind her. He stood there in the room, looking at the empty space where they had both just been. He could still feel the warmth of her body against his. This whole thing was completely unfair. He'd waited to feel something for someone like this his whole life, and when he'd found her, she was his student.

CHAPTER ELEVEN

CHARLIE

IT SUCKED! NOTHING seemed to be going right, and after the whole ordeal with Greg's freaky nephew, who she learned was Justin White, Charlie felt her whole life would forever be in chaos.

When the school tried to contact her mother, Charlie lied again and said Cece was out of town visiting her sister and didn't have a cell phone. If she'd told them the truth, that her mother had been gone nearly two weeks and soon they might be evicted from their home, Charlie was certain the school would have called social services. It looked far better to think she was a girl nearly eighteen whose mom left for an overnighter. Nobody would suspect anything wrong with that. And as frightened as she'd been when Justin had followed her onto campus, it was the first time in all her years of high school that anyone ever acted like she mattered. It felt kinda good that Principal Hill and Coach Weeks actually gave a damn.

One positive thing was that Charlie had gotten the power turned back on at home. She was no longer living in darkness, but it had cost her. She'd taken the bill her mother hadn't paid and some of the cash she'd saved for her transmission down to the PG&E office. The power was restored the next day. In the meantime, the sweet neighbors who had saved her from Greg had provided her with a hot meal every night. It turned out Joan Taylor cooked like Julia Child. Chicken Kiev, pot roast with potatoes, and spaghetti and meatballs were just some of the delicious cuisines Charlie had experienced since the incident. A far cry from her mother's slop, which usually resulted in opening a can and heating it up.

The constant look of concern in Joan's eyes though was almost not worth it. Almost. If Charlie hadn't salivated so much over the wonderful meals, she definitely would have declined her generosity because it was unnerving having the woman pity her so much.

"Mrs. Taylor, it is so nice of you to worry, but honestly, I'm better off with my mother gone since she always seems to bring around the worst kind of company. I have my job at the coffeehouse, so I have money, and I'm back in school. I do appreciate your cooking though. Just please don't feel obligated. I'm fine."

"Oh, my dear, it is my pleasure. I haven't had anyone to cook for besides Randy and me for years. It's never a bother. A girl your age shouldn't be all alone."

Joan came over every evening at five o'clock sharp without fail, which was perfect timing for Charlie to eat, do her homework, and, if she felt up to it, slip out for a night with The Guerrillas.

She'd only gone out a few times though since the Greg incident and hadn't even painted. It was as if her creativity had been lost along with more of her innocence. Charlie wasn't able to come up with an idea to paint on the fly. Maybe she'd try a collaboration.

That night, Charlie was still pissed about Jack and his stupid boundaries. That hug he'd given her had been, down to her bones, true comfort and the safest place she'd ever felt. Her body had literally seemed as if it had melted into his, forging the two of them into one. How could he be like that one minute and withdraw his intentions in the next. She knew he felt the same way about her as she did about him, but he wasn't willing to fight for her. So weak. She was beyond hurt. She was annoyed. Her disappointment had turned to anger, and without any place to put those pent-up feelings, she decided to slip out into the darkness and try to paint again.

Her mother was still gone, and after devouring a helping of chicken pot pie, Charlie stashed the peach cobbler Joan made into the fridge for later and grabbed her gear. She met up with another Guerrilla that went by Stix, who was answering another artist's piece by adding some scenery around it. Charlie asked if she could join him.

When you answered an existing piece of street art, you had to be careful not to disturb the original artwork. It was only acceptable if you added nuance and expression that would enhance the original art. If you painted over the original, or changed the message, it was considered disrespectful. Some assholes who were just looking to be mean would tag a piece, and that was how wars in the street art community were started. Charlie was always very careful if she helped to answer a piece.

The one she helped Stix answer was originally a wizard with light blazing out at all angles from his staff. It was on the back wall of an antique mall just outside of town on Highway 116. There was enough light coming from the streets' intersection to work well, but quiet and deserted enough at that time of night to not be seen. Stix had the idea of adding a flying dragon. He started spraying the outline, and Charlie was quick behind him filling it in with red, pink, and orange. Shaking his paint can, Stix worked after her with black to add scales, and an open mouth with huge teeth and a forked tongue. Their synchronicity was like a fine-tuned machine.

They contemplated adding flames when they heard a car pull up to the front of the building. Frantically, they stashed their supplies into their totes and fled to a field behind the building, running in the damp, inky night through brush, tall grass, and trees. With her heart in her throat and her pulse thumping like a stampede of horses, Charlie slipped and cut her knee on a huge boulder. The pain was blinding, making her stomach sick. As they hid behind the big rock, a beam of light sliced through the night over their heads in the darkness.

Holding her breath in the wet grass, Charlie sat, wondering if it was all worth it. Maybe she'd outgrown the need to prove she was brave. A rebel. It was an exhausting way to express yourself, and sitting in the dark with Stix, both of them trying to catch their breath, Charlie had a brand-new feeling. It was something she didn't recognize, and it surprised her. She was bored with the whole scene.

The three years she'd spent making street art had given her purpose and allowed her to feel like she was part of something, but it wasn't enough anymore. In the street art community, she was Star, but other than the occasional other street artist, nobody knew who Star was. She was hiding, and she knew it. Just as sure as she was sitting in the fucking wet grass in the middle of the night, hiding out with Stix, she was also hiding her art from the world out of fear of criticism and judgement. She wasn't brave enough! And all the pieces she'd ever painted and sold, she only ever initialed them C.K. Here she thought she was this badass artist, painting on the streets and making a statement, but she was really just a chickenshit.

All the years she'd felt alive, living dangerously and risking being caught, pushed her to do more and become bolder, but it wasn't sustainable. A shift inside of her happened right then and there, in the darkness hiding with Stix, and Charlie knew it was her last night as a Guerrilla.

When the car left, she limped back through the murkiness of night with Stix and took the side roads, avoiding the main streetlights. They parted ways as he went to wherever he lived on the north side of Sebastopol. For a few more miles, Charlie hobbled with her cylinder of stencils slung over one shoulder and her canvas bag of paints on her other. She thought about Dog Man...*Jack*. What would he think of her as this ghostly artist, painting in the night? When he'd complimented her art in Retrograde, he hadn't even known it was hers. Had he meant it when he'd said how much he liked it, or had he just been trying to make conversation? She wasn't sure. But the painting with the girl on the beach had sold recently, so there was more room for other paintings she could hang. She was grateful, too, because she needed the money, and selling her work meant that at least some people actually thought she was talented.

As Charlie neared her house, the lights were on inside. *She'd left them off.* Then she saw her mother's car in the driveway. Instantly, a pit formed in her stomach. Her phone said it was one fifteen in the morning. Tensing her jaw, Charlie braced herself for what she might walk into. After two weeks of Cece being away, Charlie was getting used to being on her own. The chaos her mother always created made Charlie's chest tighten. Before she even reached the door, she felt like a cornered animal.

Counting to three, Charlie flung open the door and found her mother calmly sitting on the sofa in a sheer nighty, eating the peach cobbler Charlie was saving for later.

"Well, look what the cat dragged in. Where ya been, sugar? I was worried." Her mother smiled at her like everything in the world was right as rain.

"That was mine. Glad you think you can just come back here like nothing happened."

Charlie stormed to her room to drop her things into her closet. The anger inside of her was building like a volcano. Squeezing her eyes shut, Charlie dug the heels of her palms into her eyes. She took a few deep breaths before going to face her infuriating mother.

Walking slowly, Charlie entered the living room and stood behind an old wing-backed chair that faced the sofa. Her mother sat there staring at her with a strange, yet peaceful, sort of expression. She lit up a cigarette, taking Charlie in like she was seeing her for the first time.

"What's with you? You look different."

"I am different, Mom. That's what happens to a person when they've been abandoned, left to fend for themselves, and nearly raped. You become stronger and stop giving a shit about anyone else's opinion anymore. The only thing I care about right now is getting through school and getting the fuck out of here. Unless of course we can't make rent, and then, I guess I'll be on my own even sooner."

She stared daggers into her mother. Charlie had been saving this anger that was building up inside of her, and it was threatening to boil over like an unwatched pot. It started to bubble and soon would be spitting and spilling out. If she was unable to stop it, the entire flow of bitterness she harbored would be unleashed upon her mom, and it all depended on what Cece said next.

"You really should watch your anger, Charlotte. It's not good for your complexion. Besides, cranky pants, I don't think we need to worry about the rent. It's not due until Monday, and look…"

Cece pulled a wad of cash from her purse and fanned it in front of her, smiling like the Joker in a Batman movie. Charlie's eyes popped wide, and her mouth dropped.

"What the fuck? Did you knock over a bank or something? Where in the hell did you get that kind of money? How much is that?"

Charlie rushed to her mother and tried to snatch the money from her to count it, but Cece pulled it away and folded it in half, holding it close.

"It's five thousand dollars. Didn't I tell you your momma had everything under control? Look, I have enough to pay rent, fix your little Bug out there, and buy a little something for Mommy. I think I'll go shopping this weekend for clothes, or a nice piece of jewelry." She tucked the wad of cash back into her purse and hugged the bag to her chest.

Charlie got caught up in the moment and laughed at her mother as Cece casually took a long drag off her cigarette with smiling eyes. She plopped down in the chair in front of her mom before more questions started to register in her brain.

"Mom, seriously, where did you get that money?"

Cece's smile fell, and she pinched her face with annoyance. "Really, Charlotte, I swear you can suck the joy out of any celebration. *I made this money* in Grass Valley. As a matter of fact, I think we should consider moving there. The rent at the salons is cheaper there too. You'd like it. Very artsy community. By the way, I covered for you with your grandparents. They called you while I was gone, but you didn't answer. I told them you were working a lot, and I lied and said I was here," she laughed.

Charlie narrowed her eyes again at her mother. "Yeah, not buying it. You didn't make five thousand dollars in less than two weeks doing hair, especially without a chair at a salon. And didn't you go to Reno first? What really happened?"

Cece set the purse down and leaned to smash out her cigarette in the ashtray. She picked up the bowl of peach cobbler and started eating from it again. "Are you guys selling this at Retrograde? It's amazing."

"MOM? Where'd the money come from?"

She slapped the bowl hard onto the coffee table and, like a child, gave Charlie an eye roll. Cece threw her hands in the air in exaggerated surrender.

"Fine. I might have sold a little weed on my way back. But it's going to be made legal soon, so you can just get off your high-and-mighty horse. I'm fixing your Bug, aren't I? And you said the power was out. What was that about? A ploy to get Mommy to feel sorry for you and come home sooner?"

Tension nearly locked Charlie's jaw as she leaned forward in the chair, a hand on her throbbing knee. She spoke to her mother through clenched teeth, and the muscles of her neck strained.

"Mother…the power *was* out. That's why I didn't get the grandparents' call, because I couldn't charge my phone. I used *my* money that I was saving to fix my car to turn it back on. And while we are at it, didn't you hear me say I was nearly raped while you were away?

DID YOU HEAR THAT? Because it's your doing. The choices that you make and the friends that you keep got me into that fucking mess. Greg came here, madder than a wet cat, looking for you, and he took it out on me. He ripped my clothes and tried to strangle me. I cut him and got him arrested. That cobbler you just finished was made by the neighbor lady who's been feeding me since you left because she was worried about me after I went screaming to them, all bloody, the night Greg tried to rape and kill me. He's in jail now, in case you are wondering, and we will probably be called to testify against him if it goes to trial."

Slowly, she leaned back against the chair again, rubbing her knee, as her mother's face went slack with shock. Cece looked at Charlie while her hands went to cover her mouth, and she shook her head in disbelief. Tears filled the corners of her eyes, and Charlie saw true regret in them as she looked upon her from across the room. The disdain Charlie had felt for her mother was waning again, and she came to the realization that she'd never be able to fully hate her mother. As much as she deserved to be shut out, Cece always had a way of inching back into Charlie's heart, usually out of pity.

"Oh, baby. Oh, my baby. I am so sorry. Oh fuck, I am so glad he's in jail, or I might kill him myself."

Highly unlikely.

Cece got up and walked over to Charlie. Cece kneeled on the floor in front of her and begged her forgiveness. She cried and buried her head in Charlie's lap. Cece's tears chipped away at Charlie's anger, and she found herself stroking her mother's head, as if she'd been the one who had gone through the terrible ordeal instead of Charlie. It was harder to stay angry than it was to just forgive her and move on. Cece was home now. However her mother had gotten the money, it was going to come in handy, and getting her car fixed would restore the freedom Charlie was counting on.

In the following days, Cece turned things around, cutting way back on her alcohol and not using any drugs. She even met the neighbors and didn't embarrass Charlie by showing up drunk or high to greet them. For the next few weeks, things got better, but Charlie remained skeptical. Cece went back to work doing hair and, as promised, had Charlie's car repaired. The day Charlie was able to go pick it up, she drove it to the beach.

She sat on Pinnacle Gulch Beach in Bodega Bay for hours, just watching the waves crash against the shore and the birds diving around the shoreline looking for scraps of food. The smell of the salty ocean eased some of the tension she'd been carrying and opened up the floodgates within her. As the sun set and the sky turned fire orange, her shoulders began to shake, and her chest heaved. All the bottled-up pain she'd held inside was finally too much. Grasping sand in both hands, Charlie threw it towards the ocean, releasing the inferno of anger.

Although her mother was showing signs of change for the better, Charlie cried for the years of suffering and sadness she'd carried. She cried for the loneliness she had in not knowing her father or having him in her life. She cried for the lack of a mentor to direct her creativity, and the struggles she'd gone through in being mostly on her own. She also cried for Jack.

In the past weeks since the Justin White incident and the lingering hug Jack had given her, he'd been true to his word. Jack showed interest in her as a student and nothing more.

Sitting on the beach and letting all her emotions flow out of her allowed Charlie to see things from a new perspective and take a different look at Jack. She respected and understood his decision, even if she hated it. Plus, Charlie would be hated even more at school if people found out she was with her teacher, and she'd lose what little understanding she was getting from some of the staff since Justin had been arrested. She'd be labeled a slut again.

As she drove home that night with the soft humming of the Bug's engine, Charlie felt drained but lighter. She wanted to start fresh and keep her eye on the prize. She still had her weekend job, she had her art, and she was building a better relationship with her mother. Michael and Teri had sold another of her paintings, leaving yet more space at Retrograde for her to hang new pieces. She was also considering having that talk with the local art gallery, if she could muster up the courage.

And with fall in the air, Charlie felt change coming. She wasn't scared anymore. It wasn't so much because things were slightly better, even though they were. It was more that Charlie realized she didn't have much to lose. When she looked at it like that, she was much braver in an optimistic sort of way. Not like her past self who gathered courage from a bad attitude. Instead, she was ready to place her hopes in some *otherly cosmos*. If she failed now, at least she didn't have far to fall. She made a deal with herself that she was going to pursue art, she was going to ace her tests and get good grades, she'd impress her grandparents and tell them whatever they wanted to hear, and she'd release the idea of having Jack…for now. Who knew what the future would bring?

CHAPTER TWELVE

FALL 2010

JACK

HE ONLY HAD three weeks left of subbing at Analy High School. The job had turned out to be surprisingly fulfilling. The kids were mostly respectful, and he didn't give much energy to the ones who weren't, because after all, he was leaving soon anyway.

After telling Charlie they couldn't get involved, he'd worried she would retaliate or become an emotional teenage mess around him, but she didn't. Jack wasn't sure if he should be offended, that maybe he didn't mean that much to her after all, or if he should be impressed by how mature she was. Either way, it was extraordinarily hard seeing her every day.

Initially, a fresh wound ripped open when she'd entered his room and he'd see her delicate face haloed by that wild, mahogany hair. He would sometimes watch her from the safety of his position at the front of the room, giving the illusion that he was just teaching and looking around the room at everyone. Yet, Jack would always look the longest in her direction even though she rarely looked at him.

She'd done exactly as he asked, being ever the student, making things easy for him so there was nothing to lie about. She'd let him off the hook, but inside, he still struggled. After a few weeks, most of the tension released into a dull ache of wanting what he couldn't have.

And he'd gone on a couple of dates with Emily. While he was with her, his brain was occupied, and it offered the kind of distraction necessary for him to move forward. Her upbeat personality was infectious, and she was easy on the eyes. Even though their conversations didn't stimulate him much, Emily filled a space that would otherwise be full of loneliness.

The cool fall air was damp and earthy. When he moved back to Southern California, he'd miss this. Sebastopol was growing on him, but the real reason he'd miss this place wasn't because of the weather.

Having finished the screenplay writing course, Jack had scrapped the book idea he'd started for a different one that he was going to adapt into a proposal for a movie. He was so excited about it that he wanted to share it with someone. The problem was, the person he most wanted to talk to about it, that would fully understand the art of creating something from nothing, wasn't exactly talking to him.

Then one day, Jack got brave enough to approach Charlie. They said they were friends after all, so after class one day, he started to follow her outside. He called out her name and smiled at her when she turned around. Her expressionless face only had one raised questioning eyebrow, but he took that as an invitation to carry on.

Charlie stood just outside the door and turned to wait, but when Jack stepped outside, Emily slammed into him. She was walking fast, and as they collided, she laughed and put her hands on his chest, very familiar. The way Emily looked up at Jack, he knew instantly that Charlie would see in the situation more than he wanted her to know. He snapped his head towards Charlie, his eyes wide with fear, then he stepped back from Emily and smoothed the front of his shirt as if to wipe off her touch.

Instantly, Charlie wrinkled her brow and pinched her face with disapproval, and she walked away. Jack reached for her arm and turned her around.

"Wait! I have something to talk with you about. Would you excuse us please, Miss Wellington?"

Now it was Emily's turn to give him a disapproving eye, but she stepped back and said, "Oh, of course. We'll catch up later."

It was a bad idea, but he had to clarify with Charlie that nothing important was going on with Emily, even though that wasn't at all what he'd intended to speak with her about.

"I'm going to be late, Jack." Charlie tried to turn around again.

"Please. I just had… Damn, I really had something I wanted to share with you about what I've been writing, but now…"

"What? Now your *girlfriend* interrupted? I get it. She's a passable age. Why don't you go tell her what you're writing."

Jack was freaking out inside, but he had to be careful. He couldn't make a scene and appear as if he was forcing Charlie to talk to him. He stood there, wanting to touch her, but whispered, "*Please.* Won't you listen for just a sec? I can't make you, but there are things I'd like to say."

She stopped and turned to look at him, doe eyes bright and beautiful even with the anger she had brewing in them. She shrugged her shoulders, giving him the go-ahead.

"I know you have class soon, so I don't have time to tell you much, but I'm writing a screenplay. I'm hoping to pitch it to some studios when I get back to LA, but what you just saw with Emily… it's nothing."

Charlie chuffed in disbelief. "Oh, sure. Emily Wellington looks like a real *chummy friend.* Not that I care. It's not my business. Anyway, I hope you're writing something real. Something that will make people feel things on a deeper level. Not just some lame-ass Hollywood crap. Maybe I'll see it on the screen someday, Dog Man." She turned to leave again but then spun around while he stood there with his tongue tied.

"Oh, and Jack..."—she looked around before continuing—"maybe ask yourself why you wanted to share that information with me and not your girlfriend. See ya around."

Then she was gone. Jack looked both ways outside of his room and saw a throng of kids headed in his direction for second period. No one seemed to notice or care about his conversation with Charlie. Emily had entered her own room, and he realized now he had to give her an explanation as to why he'd had to talk privately with a student. *A beautiful female student.* His nerves were buzzing again as he headed into his room with a tight throat.

So much for things going smoothly. He'd fucked that all up and was now back to being on pins and needles.

Way to go, Jack-o.

But when he saw Emily again, she didn't seem to remember, or even care about him speaking with Charlie. She chatted on and on about some weekend retreat that the English class was going to attend—the Shakespeare Festival in Ashland, Oregon, and Emily was heading up the committee to fundraise. As she rambled on about the trip they'd take in the spring, she flirted about how much she wished he were still going to be there and how much more fun he'd be than Ellie Pratt.

Having dodged a bullet, Jack felt a sense of relief, but a nagging ache still settled in the back of his mind and heart, knowing that now Charlie had figured out he was seeing Emily. Even though he didn't have a commitment with Charlie, he still felt terrible guilt, and it gnawed at him for days afterwards. She continued to not make eye contact with him but turned in perfect paper after paper in his class.

The question she'd posed to him was a valid one. *Why hadn't he shared with Emily what he was writing?* She was an English teacher, after all. But something about Emily felt hollow, and superficial. Charlie, from the very first time they met, had depth. She was complex and complicated in a way that intrigued him so much he couldn't compare her to anyone else.

With a little over two weeks to go, Jack happened upon something in the hallway of the main building that upended him and left him shaken. He was coming from the main office, having just seen his uncle, and headed down the hallway past all the interior classrooms. He saw the back of a tall, muscular kid leaning up against the wall with his forearm, facing a girl with long, curly hair.

He knew that hair.

As he passed the couple, Jack nearly twisted his neck off trying to see if his assumption was true, and it was. Charlie had her back against the wall, while lover boy, Leo Lombardi, made time with her, standing way too close. Just like in a movie, time seemed to move in slow motion. Charlie's eyes slowly lifted and locked with Jack's. She leisurely tucked a piece of hair behind her ear and laughed at something Leo said, while staring at Jack, almost mockingly.

What the fuck is this?

Jack's forward motion stopped abruptly as he slammed hard into an open door from a classroom. The teacher who had opened it came to his aid apologetically, asking if he was alright. The only injuries were his pride and the bump on his cheekbone that felt hot and stung, but all Jack wanted to do now was hide.

That afternoon, while he stepped outside for some fresh air after the last bell, he looked towards the student parking lot and saw Charlie with Leo. They climbed into a gray Volkswagen Bug, and she drove off with the windows down. He'd never seen her drive that car before and wondered how long she'd had it. And where was she going with Leo? Wasn't he a wrestler, and didn't he have practice soon? The questions mounted and fried Jack's brain. The thought of Charlie with Leo kicked him in the stomach. Leo was a clown, a player. Even Jack had figured that out in the short period of time he'd been at Analy High.

His distraction over Charlie that evening came out in his writing. His uncle Rob had a school board meeting to go to, so he was alone in the house with the dogs. When Emily called, he declined it, sending it to voice mail to stay focused on his writing. It seemed to flow out of him effortlessly now, and like Charlie had told him to, he began a story of meaning that would make people feel something. His other story idea was good, but once he got going, this became something he had to write. It was pressing from inside of him and needed to find a way out, or he might explode. The writing helped calm that sour spot inside him. Without it, he might have gone crazy.

In class the next day, they were discussing *Wuthering Heights*. Jack could quickly tell who was reading it and who was not. What surprised him though was Charlie's contribution to the conversation. She'd never been one to speak up in class. This day of all days though, right after she'd succeeded in pulling the rug out from under him, she decided to talk. He had no right to be upset with Charlie, but he was, nonetheless. Keeping his anger and frustration out of the tone in his voice was a huge challenge too.

"Why do you suppose Cathy chose to be with Edgar Linton instead of Heathcliff?" Jack asked the class as he paced the front of the room.

Without raising a hand or being called upon, Charlie said, "Cathy was embarrassed to be seen with the likes of Heathcliff, and she was a selfish, spoiled brat. She led Heathcliff on, making him believe it didn't matter that he was without status in the community, but what she really wanted was to be rich and show off. Cathy chose status over love, because she truly was in love with Heathcliff, but she screwed that up and broke his heart. She couldn't undo what she'd already done, and he went mad and became hardened against her. Can you blame him?"

Many in the room turned slightly to look at Charlie as she sat there with her arms crossed over her chest, a smug look on her face. Jack swallowed hard. He wondered if she associated herself as the *Heathcliff* in their situation. If she saw herself as a Heathcliff, then was he *Catherine?*

"That's an interesting observation. But don't forget that Cathy described her love for Heathcliff and how it was eternal and necessary as the rocks beneath the trees. Maybe if Heathcliff had stuck around long enough to hear the rest of her speech, he would have understood how very much she loved him instead of jumping to such devastating conclusions."

The class looked back and forth between the two of them like a tennis match.

"All I know is that if she had never been distracted by shiny, pretty things offered over on the other side of the moors, none of the problems they had between them would have happened," Charlie spat.

Jack conceded and nodded. "Yes, but isn't it human nature to make mistakes? And Heathcliff's anger destroyed them both."

"Whoa, Mister C! Don't give it all away. We still have more of the book to read," Linda Tallman protested with a laugh.

"Quite right, Linda. We will continue this debate after we've finished the book. You all will be writing an essay about this with some writing prompts once we're done. Be aware that it will be imperative you read the book to be able to properly complete the essay using one of the three prompts I will give you. Charlie, great participation today. Class dismissed." He nodded towards the clock just as the bell rang.

She left his room without speaking, but she did give him one last glance over her shoulder at the door. Her expression wasn't a welcoming smile or a look of admiration but one of contempt. Jack stood by his desk. It wasn't safe to approach her, lest they stir up rumors. Instead, he straightened papers while he watched her leave.

So, did Charlie believe he thought she wasn't worthy of pursuing? She couldn't possibly think that, could she?

Having Emily Wellington practically throw herself at him in front of Charlie probably hadn't helped his case, but what could he do? Charlie was off-limits to him, and no amount of explaining to her was going to change their circumstances. He was twenty-four! She was seventeen, and his student. That was that.

But the image he still had in his mind of that weasel-dick Leo Lombardi touching her made him sick. The infatuation and desire Jack still had for Charlie, even though he clearly understood he had to keep his distance, was so consuming he just wished he could run from his feelings. He wished he could get her out of his head and heart for just a little while. He wanted to complete a thought that didn't revolve around Charlie. In a few weeks, he wouldn't have to see her every day, and maybe that would cure him.

So, he stayed busy. Passing the time over that weekend, Jack went to a dinner party with Emily, and afterwards, she invited him to her house. He knew what that meant, but after a few drinks, he felt weakened by her continuous advances and agreed to go.

She lived alone in a small white cottage. He only glimpsed the outside of the house, but inside, it was very feminine. A mix and match of furniture had fluffy pillows in green, pink, and white, and there was a floral throw blanket over the back of the sofa. Her home had a small adjoining kitchen and a cute little front porch, but Jack knew they wouldn't spend any time at all in those places.

Without wasting time, Emily started pulling his shirt off, and Jack didn't resist. He needed to be swallowed up into a place where his thoughts could no longer hold him hostage. Where he could go numb and allow himself to be devoured by the touch of another. Needing to release his primal desire for Charlie, Jack took Emily instead.

They lay on her bed. Jack kissed her deeply as she arched her back, pressing herself against him. Emily's half-naked body beneath him, Jack closed his eyes and envisioned the person he longed for most. He battled to see Emily, but his mind's eye kept taking him to Charlie. Between kisses, Emily gasped, whispering his name. Over-whelmed with guilt, Jack sat up. It wasn't going to happen. With a heavy sigh of exhaustion and pent-up sexual energy, he made his excuses and left Emily's house. He gave her half-truths, and a weak apology, reminding her again of his impending departure.

Home again, Jack was sheepish around his Uncle Rob who figured out why he'd snuck in so late at night. The dogs hadn't barked, because they knew him so well now, but they did stir.

"Late night, huh, buddy?" Rob was scrambling eggs in a pan as Jack descended the stairs, rubbing his head.

"Hmm, yeah."

"Emily finally captured ya, huh? I told you she had the hots for you. Want some eggs?"

"No, I'll just make toast. And it doesn't matter. I'm done there in two weeks. I warned her I couldn't handle a relationship, but she's very persistent."

His uncle threw his head back, laughing, "They always are, Jack-o. They always are."

On Monday, it rained. Jack was wringing his hands like a little girl about how Emily would handle herself at school. He'd nearly made himself sick with worry. If he hadn't been so fucking torn up over Charlie with Leo, and the stupid Heathcliff and Cathy conversation, he might have avoided going to Emily's house. And if Emily acted like they were a couple in front of people at school, he swore he'd set her straight, no matter how much it hurt her. But Jack hated the thought of hurting her too. None of this was Emily's fault. It was all Jack's. He'd made a mess of things for sure.

It turned out that his concern about Emily wasn't going to be the greatest issue of the day. Not even close.

The weather got windier and wetter as the morning progressed. Walking outside the house, Jack stepped into a pile of dog shit. Turned out that Henry was scared of the rain and pooped right outside of the door instead of his usual place in the yard. Then Jack had a low tire, but luckily Rob was still home and pulled out his air compressor to fill it up with him. His foul mood didn't get any better at the realization that he was now running late and had no time to swing by and grab a coffee.

With his windshield wipers on high and the grayness of the day, it was hard to make things out. Two blocks from the school, he had a stop sign. Next to his car, someone walked by wearing a sweatshirt and jeans. They didn't have an umbrella to keep them from being soaked. But there were two things that alerted him to this person. One was the tufts of unmanageable hair blowing out of both sides of the drawn hood, and the other was the unmistakable white backpack that had peace signs and flowers drawn all over it in colorful ink. His dad had installed aftermarket power windows on the Camaro, so Jack rolled down the passenger window to get a better look and to be sure he wasn't just seeing things.

"Charlie!" he yelled above the noise of his rumbling car and the storm.

The person in the gray hooded sweatshirt twisted around quickly to look in his direction.

It was her.

Without thinking, without asking questions, without considering the ramifications of what could happen because of his choice, Jack pulled up alongside of her and yelled to her.

"Get in."

CHAPTER THIRTEEN

CHARLIE

WHEN MISS WELLINGTON had rubbed Jack's chest, eyes all googly, Charlie had been slammed with the rude awakening that Jack had a girlfriend.

So, what? He could do what he wanted, and he'd made himself clear that she was too young for him. Emily Wellington was scarcely older than her, but whatever. What really infuriated Charlie though, was that Jack kept sending her mixed signals, and it was really messing with her head.

Why the fuck had he told her about his writing? Why had he asked to talk to her like they were friends? Maybe she didn't want to be Jack's goddamned friend anymore. It was all too much, and he was taking up valuable space in her head when she needed to focus on the SAT test. She needed to look at colleges and apply for financial aid. She needed to get the hell out of this town.

Sebastopol would have been lovely if seen through a different lens. If Charlie had had a different experience, if her mother didn't need mothering, and if the majority of the people here didn't look down their noses at her, maybe she'd like it better. But the truth was that Charlie needed a fresh start with new people and without the trauma of seeing her troubled past around every corner.

Jack was just another complication to her already crazy life.

Leo Lombardi, who she had in her biology class, needed some tutoring, or his coach wasn't going to let him wrestle this season. Charlie might not be popular, but she was known for being really smart. Leo was the first jock who didn't treat her like a leper or a quick piece of ass. He'd said he could pay her to tutor him. Having Leo flirt with her without suggesting they hit the sack made Charlie feel worthy, and pretty. He was asking for her help in his charismatic way when Jack had plowed into the door in the hall. It served him right. But again, it sent her mixed messages.

Why would he care if Leo was coming on to her? Leo was her age! Age being something Jack kept making a big deal about. But clearly, it bothered him, and he was making her crazy with the mixed messages it sent.

The *Wuthering Heights* conversation in class had been just her firing pent-up anger towards Jack and the unfairness of his hot-and-cold reaction to her. She wasn't a fucking mind reader. It felt like she was most certainly the Heathcliff of this relationship. Whenever it suited him, Jack loved her company, but when it looked bad, then he turned away from her. If timing was the issue, then he needed to stand by his decision to stay away. But he yo-yoed back and forth, and Charlie just wished she could be done with him.

But her heart ached for one touch, one word, one more moment...and it was killing her.

Monday's rain was unexpected. The bitch of it was that after getting the transmission working properly again, her Bug's clutch went out over the weekend, and she was left on foot once again until she could get it fixed. She was definitely going to need that tutoring money now. Her mother, as per usual, was back on the bottle and claimed it was just because it was the weekend. But Cece was hungover, and Charlie hadn't been able to wake her mother up to drive her to school. Searching for Cece's car keys left Charlie empty-handed, and it had gotten late. Charlie had an appointment with the career counselor that day, so as bad as the weather was, she'd walked.

The wind was spitting rain sideways, and trees sent falling debris in the streets. With each car that passed by, more water splashed against her legs and shoes. She was soaked to the bone.

Two blocks from school, she passed a dark classic Camaro that had stopped at the intersection. As she walked by, she thought she heard her name being called above the growl of the engine and the sound of the wind. As the car pulled up alongside her, she peered into the open window, and her heart stopped.

"Get in!"

Jack's beautiful, concerned face was inside that car. She only hesitated a moment, then seeing his penetrating eyes staring at her, she was defenseless to say no. How could she resist the close proximity of him in his warm, dry car over being alone, wet, and frustrated on the street?

She hopped in. He rolled her electric window up using his controls as she adjusted her backpack between her feet. The car was impeccably kept. *Of course he'd have a muscle car.* Jack sat staring at her a moment. She must look a mess. Charlie quickly pulled off her drenched hood and scratched her hair out to make it full around her face. Wet and scraggly ends dripped onto the car's bucket seat.

She shivered and sat looking at him. "Nice car," she said barely above a whisper.

"It was my dad's," he said, but turned away from her, steering back onto the road, saying nothing more.

She wanted to ask him more about it, but Jack set his jaw, and Charlie's blood began to boil. She dug her nails into her palms. Getting into his car had been a mistake. She didn't want his goddamn charity. "You know, just because you rescued me from the storm doesn't mean I'm not still pissed at you."

"So, you are pissed at me?" he spat back.

"Of course, Jack! Anyone would be. You are hot and cold,

fucking self-righteous, then a hypocrite. What's with you? You tell me you aren't interested, you get a girlfriend, but then when you see me with someone, you act like you're so surprised! What did you think I was going to do, Jack? Sit around and cry my eyes out pining for you? I don't work that way. I've had far worse things happen to me in my life than having some guy ghost me. Anyway, it's not like we ever dated or anything. Hell, we never even started, but you… YOU kept coming around, and then when you got my hopes all up, you put on the brakes."

He made a fast turn down a wrong road and accelerated quickly through a potholed street, sending water flying. Charlie stared at his face, his eyes narrowed into a glare and his mouth pinched into a deep frown with nostrils flaring. She'd hit a nerve.

Calmly, Charlie said, "You're going the wrong way."

"I'm not going to the school!" he barked.

He had her attention. Charlie didn't say anything more but put her hands together in her lap and watched to see where he was taking her. He maneuvered the car down an alley, to the back lot of a grocery store, and cut the engine then turned off the lights. The dark morning encapsulated the car. He pulled at the collar of his jacket and ripped the buttons open then turned to face her with sparks flying from his eyes.

"*So that's it? That's how you see things?* Do you have any fucking idea how hard it is for me seeing you every day? Every single day I struggle to keep my shit together. To be the responsible person I'm supposed to be. *I could get arrested for being with you!* And I don't want to be that guy who takes advantage of you either. So, I battle with myself every fucking day to keep my distance. And yeah, maybe I've sent you mixed signals sometimes, but it's because the truth keeps sneaking out and surfacing until I can shove it back down again. I try so hard every single day to keep people from seeing the truth…and that is that I'm completely consumed with thoughts of you. I can't get you out of my mind. You've taken over me, and I wish I could make it stop, because we can't be together. We can't be together, Charlie, and it's killing me. So don't sit there and judge me, thinking I'm this asshole who is toying with your emotions, because this…YOU…are the hardest thing I've ever had to resist."

Every cell in her body was alive and on fire. Jack's eyes were wild and bright with such turmoil and passion that she was at a loss. His words pierced her soul, and Charlie knew that this was it. This moment was probably the only opportunity she'd ever have to be alone with Jack Connors. He was right, and it felt like something inside her was tearing apart. He was right, and he was going to leave. All they had was that very moment, and she refused to waste it.

Charlie reached up and touched Jack's exposed collarbone. He closed his eyes with her touch and took a gasping breath. She rubbed her thumb over his bristly cheek then gently pulled him by the neck and leaned in to kiss him. Jack slipped his arm around her, too, and lowered his hot mouth on hers. The kiss was deep and wet, desperate and searching. Something inside of Charlie cracked open, as if Jack's kiss allowed her to feel beauty in this world in a way she'd never experienced before. Tears spilled from her eyes as he explored her neck and earlobes, then went back to her waiting mouth. Clutching him, she rode the wave of this feeling for as long as she could, until he was finally the one to pull away and stared deeply into her eyes.

"I want you, Charlie. You have to know I do. But we met at the completely wrong time. As badly as I'd love to be with you, it's just not possible. Not now. What can I do? Tell me what to do! Because if I pursue you, I'm this creep that's preying on a young woman who hasn't even come into her own yet. If I let you go, I might be losing out on one of the greatest things to ever happen to me. But I can't be selfish. You need time to figure out what you want and where you are going with your life. I can't be what makes you decide."

He searched her eyes, and Charlie just sat there completely paralyzed with her mouth open and unable to speak. It was goodbye before it even started, and her heart was being ripped from her chest.

Fresh tears started to spill over her lashes, and she was frozen in time, just staring at him. She worried if she blinked, he'd disappear.

"Please...say something," Jack pleaded.

"I...I know...you are right." She held his hands in hers, shaking. Not from the cold, but from the shock her system was feeling at a core level. "I'll be eighteen in January, but still, I'm in school, and you're leaving."

Jack rested his forehead against hers. "I'm so sorry. I don't ever want to be the reason you cry. I wish things could be different."

Would it have been easier staying mad at Jack or having this honest and private farewell? She wasn't sure. Either way, she suffered. At least now she knew the truth about how he felt.

They agreed it was over. She vowed to let it all go, so he wouldn't have to feel guilty in the last two weeks he would be there. Inside, Charlie felt empty. She went numb, like a shell of a person. Her mind went blank, and she knew this entire day she would be undone, so as they drove towards the school, she knew what she needed to do.

"Please stop the car."

"What? It's pouring."

Charlie kept looking forward and whispered, "Please just stop the car, Jack."

He pulled the car over just a few streets from the school. He looked at her, and she felt his eyes. It killed her to turn to see them, sad and filled with trouble.

"I can't be there today." She tried to suppress a fresh wave of tears. "I'll be back, but when I go, things will be different. I need time."

Charlie mustered up the courage to give him a weak smile. She wanted to leave letting Jack know she was strong and unbroken... even if it was a lie. She wanted to release him from any guilt, so that years later, when he thought of her, he'd have no regrets.

"I'll just be late. I'll drive you home. Let me take you home, Charlie."

She just shook her head. "I'm fine, Jack. I need this walk. When

I see you tomorrow, if I don't speak to you or look you in the eyes, don't take offense. I'm just going to be protecting myself. I'll be okay though."

"I can't believe this is happening," Jack said under his breath. "Okay. I understand. But when I do the same, remember everything I told you today. And on my last day, I want to meet you to say goodbye."

Charlie shook her head, and a fresh batch of tears welled up. "No. No, Jack, I don't think…"

"YES! Charlie, I'm not moving back to LA without saying goodbye to you. Agree to meet me at the public library on Saturday after my last day, or I won't let you walk home." He reached over and grabbed her hand. "I swear, if you don't agree, I'll just drive around until I run out of gas."

He was smiling his gorgeous smile at her, and that dimple she loved creased his cheek. His thick, dark hair hung over his forehead above his shining eyes. She imprinted this sight of him to her memory, so she'd never forget this moment. Charlie let a laugh escape her throat, and she wiped her tears with her shirtsleeve, nodding in agreement.

"Fine. You win. I'll meet you at the library after your last day. But now I work the morning shift on Saturdays at Retrograde. Meet me at two-thirty at the library, and I'll be there."

His smiling face turned dark again. He pulled her by the arm and leaned over to kiss her cheek.

"Be safe. Again, I'm so—"

"Don't say you're sorry, Jack. I'm not." She grabbed her backpack and opened the door, the wind at her back already spitting rain. "Better hurry up, Dog Man. First period starts in fifteen minutes."

She shut the door before he could respond, and Charlie turned away from the car, holding herself together as best she could until he slowly pulled away. As she walked, Charlie's chest and throat tightened until she could barely breathe. Like stiff balloons, her lungs wouldn't expand, and each breath she took was nearly a gasp. With the rain pummeling her and her clothes completely soaked, it felt fitting to her that the outside world looked as dim as she felt.

Once home, she stripped off her wet clothes and jumped into a hot shower. The steamy water washed over her body like a baptism of sorts, like she was being washed clean of the grief she felt from losing something she never really had in the first place. She stayed in the shower until the hot water ran cool, and during that time, she allowed herself to cry as hard as she wanted, vowing not to do it again.

When something comes into your life that you never even knew you wanted or needed, it can be alarming and disruptive. The life she had before Jack arrived, Charlie was familiar with, and she never allowed herself to crave or want for so much. Now everything had changed.

Now she wanted it all!

Since Jack's arrival, Charlie lost the urge to do street art and suddenly became more driven to do canvas paintings. Her confidence had built, and she wasn't quite sure exactly why. She could envision a successful future more surely than ever, and she knew someday she'd have it all. Charlie promised herself that one day she wouldn't need her mother, her grandparents, or the father who left her. She'd have admiration in the art community, and she'd have love too.

Perhaps it was in the discovery that a man like Jack could see true beauty within her that had made the difference in how she viewed herself. Whatever it was, she was stronger, even with a shattered heart.

Jack's last day subbing for Senior English AP Class in room twenty-seven had arrived, just as she'd dreaded. During those final days, Charlie was tutoring Leo and got her car running again, and she'd stayed clear of any conversation with Jack. He had only looked at her from afar. He'd smile at her, and sometimes she saw darkness or maybe remorse in his eyes, but he never approached her. She, too, would smile when their eyes met, but Charlie wouldn't stare too long.

The whole class was sorry to see him go, as Jack had turned out to be a great teacher with a quirky sense of humor. She'd miss his stupid jokes and adorable dimple, but mostly Charlie knew there was going to be a huge void inside her from his absence for a long time.

Jack Connors took up quite a lot of space.

After first period on his last day, he was standing at the door to say goodbye, receiving high fives, hugs, fist bumps, and handshakes. When it was Charlie's turn in line, she was the last to leave. Her stomach knotted up, but she kept her promise to herself not to cry. He smiled down at her and threw his arms open, laughing and keeping things light.

"Charlotte Kane? Is there a Charlotte Kane here?" He joked about his first day and his shocking discovery of who she was.

"Dog Man! Is that you?" she laughed back.

When he wrapped his arms around her, they were both trying hard to keep up the appearance of teacher and student, but he grabbed on tight and held her just a few seconds longer than any of the others. She squeezed her eyes shut, inhaling his scent of cologne and peppermint gum, then she pulled away and looked him dead in the eyes.

"See you around, Dog Man. Try to stay out of trouble. Maybe one day I'll find your book in some store or see your name on the credits of a movie."

"Or maybe I'll stumble into some art gallery and see a collection of Charlotte Kane paintings."

They were staring again, and Charlie broke the spell. She tucked a piece of hair behind her ear and smiled at the ground. It was time to go.

"Maybe. Well…see ya…Mister Connors."

He reached out as she walked away, and he rubbed his hand across her back as she left, sending shivers of desire through her body.

"Bye, Charlie."

The next day after work, Charlie broke her promise. When her shift ended, she couldn't face seeing him again, fearing she'd come completely undone. Instead, she left town and escaped. She went to Bodega Bay and sat on the beach with a Pepsi and threw rocks and shells towards the surf, feeling hollow. She struggled knowing that right at that very minute Jack would be waiting inside the library, maybe flipping nervously through a book.

Was he watching the door every time it opened? Or maybe he'd stood her up, too, afraid of making things harder? She'd never know.

It was the hardest thing she'd ever done, and it wrecked her. But she had to move on. Charlie let Jack go with a deep-seated hope that someday, when things were different, their paths would cross again.

CHAPTER FOURTEEN

JACK

SHE DIDN'T SHOW.

After waiting for over an hour, Jack left the library, having returned the last of the books he'd borrowed. His sorrow at not being able to see her one last time burned his insides. He only planned to be in Sebastopol until Monday, and then he'd drive south. There really was little chance he'd ever see her again.

He could hardly blame her for not showing up, but it left too many questions open in his head. *Was she okay? Was she hurt or stranded somewhere?* By not going to look for her was he being a shit, or was he just respecting her decision? It was enough to drive him a little mad.

But LA was waiting, and Jack's mother was eager for him to return and have weekly dinners again. Zane said his room was prepared in their bachelor pad. If only his heart were in it. He tried to get himself excited for this new direction, but all he could think about was Charlie.

He supposed now he'd be wondering about her for quite a long while. He hoped time would ease his pain. They'd never exchanged phone numbers, although he'd meant to. He didn't know where she lived, but he *did know* where she worked. Jack contemplated that.

Then there was the Emily debacle. He'd been ghosting her since they'd nearly had sex. When he finally answered her call, she'd made it clear she felt shunned. Even though he reminded her from the start that he'd said a relationship wasn't in his best interests, she sulked over the phone enough to leave him feeling guilty. Almost sleeping with her had been a huge mistake, but she was an adult and knew the situation. He refused to shoulder all the blame.

"So, you have lots of plans that will be keeping you busy in LA," his Uncle Rob said. "I suppose I'll have to take a trip south around the holidays to see you and my sister. I'm happy for you, Jack-o. You have your whole life ahead of you. Do something interesting with it."

After a weekend with Uncle Rob, some drinking, great food, and playing with George and Henry, it was time for Jack to go. He'd packed up his suitcases and laptop, along with loads of notes he'd taken on story ideas. When he got back to LA, Jack wanted to try his hand at developing his screenplay, but the pull to stay because of Charlie weighed heavy on him.

There was absolutely no way he could though, and worse, Jack couldn't even share what he was feeling with anyone! He hadn't even gone into Retrograde on Sunday to see if she was there, although now it haunted him that he hadn't tried to see her. Still, what would he have said? It would only have made things worse. Jack was more than six years older than Charlie. Soon, that wouldn't be an issue, but right now it clearly was. The only thought that kept him from becoming completely unhinged was that if they were truly meant to give it a go, she might find him someday in Los Angeles when their timing was better. Still, that was a long shot, and he couldn't hold his breath and wait. Charlie was young and gorgeous, and very talented. He figured she'd forget about him, and he couldn't blame her if she did.

With his car packed and a full tank of gas, Jack said good-bye to his uncle and the dogs, bending to pick up Henry one last time. Jack smothered the dog with snuggles and buried his face near Henry's ear.

"It was because of you, you little escape artist, that I met Charlie," he whispered. "I'll always be grateful for that."

Putting Henry down, Jack took one last look around at the place he considered his home away from home. It had brought a great source of comfort to Jack, this house, this town. To his surprise, a lump formed in his throat.

Rubbing the top of George's large head, Jack turned to hug his uncle goodbye.

"I appreciate the time you spent here, kid. You really bailed us out at the school, too, and I think you got something out of it, even if you aren't willing to tell me about it."

Jack's heart lurched into his throat. *Did Rob know about Charlie after all?*

He held his breath. "What do you mean?"

Rob laughed his huge belly laugh. "About you hooking up with Emily Wellington. Well, that, and of course, I think you actually *liked* teaching. You were good at it."

Jack smiled at the thought. It hadn't been such a bad job. "Yeah, I guess I did kinda like teaching. But I wouldn't want to do it full-time. It was a good experience though, as you said." He clapped his hands together. "Okay. You gotta get to work. I'm off."

Rob walked Jack out to the car and said he'd always have a room there. As he drove away, something inside of Jack splintered. Pieces of him were breaking apart at not seeing Charlie once more before he left. Right now, she'd be headed to school, and he had a lot of miles ahead to contemplate how he was going to be able to leave her behind and let her go.

❦

What he didn't miss was the bumper-to-bumper LA traffic at three o'clock in the afternoon. In northern California, there was traffic, but Los Angeles had suffocating traffic nearly all the time. Sitting on the I-5 with his windows down, listening to the growl of the Camaro, and with the music turned up, Jack immersed himself in the familiar smogginess of home.

Inching his way onto the I-10 Santa Monica Freeway, he became increasingly curious about his new residence with Zane. Agreeing to live somewhere sight unseen wasn't usually Jack's style, but he'd been desperate for a change. Moving back in with his mother, Rita, wasn't an option for Jack, but he planned to stay with her for the night since it had been a long day, and all his belongings were at her house in Westdale. Zane was going to meet him the next day with a truck to help him haul his loot to their pad in Culver City, just a twenty-minute drive away.

Culver City was closer to the film action, and as much as Jack loved living in Santa Monica by the beach, Zane assured him that if he wanted to get into writing for film and television, being closer to the city was smart.

His mind was swimming in a stew of emotions as he pulled into his mother's driveway around four thirty in the afternoon. Nine and a half hours after leaving Sebastopol, Jack felt like he'd arrived on another planet.

He was barely out of the car, legs feeling like rubber and a body on autopilot, when Jack's mother was already upon him. She threw open the front door of her single-story tract home to run and hug him hello, laughing and talking his ear off before he could focus. Switching gears was going to require a lot of effort.

She fed him pot roast with all the fixings, and after he threw back a couple of beers and heard all about his mother's fundraiser for Breast Cancer Awareness Month, Jack just wanted to go to bed.

"I have your room all made up, so go ahead and get some sleep.

I'm glad you're home. You can fill me in on what it was like living with Uncle Rob tomorrow. Then you can tell me about the girl too."

Jack's head popped up at attention. "What girl?"

She laughed at him. "The girl I'm sure you met, and whose heart you broke when you had to leave. You are always breaking hearts wherever you go, son. With that face, how can you not?"

He shook his head and blew out a huge exhale. "Goodnight, Ma. You are really funny."

The pale golden light cast shadows as he lay in his old room with the nightlight his mother insisted he needed as if he were still ten.

He twisted in the sheets. His mind wouldn't shut off. He thought of Charlie. How was he going to forget her full, warm lips on his? How he wanted to drown in the feeling of the wetness of her mouth. He remembered how she tasted, both sweet and metallic. Their bodies had been musty from the heat of the car and the dampness of the rain, and his desire had built until he'd become rock hard with yearning. They'd given and taken from each other, wanting more forbidden pleasures but unable to fully satisfy each other's urges.

He groaned and pulled a pillow over his head. Fantasizing about it and reliving the scene over and over in his mind like a movie was not helping. Pulling the pillow back down, Jack did the only thing he could in order to get some sleep. He jerked off into some Kleenex, thinking of Charlie, then nearly passed out from emotional exhaustion. He slept so deeply that he didn't wake during the night.

In the morning, after his mother fussed over him and Zane, serving them a hearty breakfast of pancakes and bacon, they were full as ticks, and Jack feared they'd fall into a food coma.

"Thanks, Mom, but if we eat any more, we'll never get any work done today."

"I know, I know, but I don't get to spoil you boys enough. Now that you're home, Sunday dinners are back on. Zane, that means you too. You are always welcome."

They loaded their vehicles and drove to their new place. It was small but clean. In their upstairs apartment, Jack had his own bathroom. Even though it wasn't an en suite, he didn't really care. Zane took the master bedroom, which meant he paid more rent, so that was fine with Jack. The main living area was an open kitchen and living room with a place for a small dinette table. His bedroom and the living room both had windows overlooking a beautiful garden of tropical plants, palm trees, and the huge turquoise pool for the complex. It might not be the beach, but they could have done worse.

In Culver City, you could smell money in the air. This city was basically headquarters for film and television, and opportunities were everywhere. The nightlife was bustling with nightclubs and bars, all briming with beautiful people either chasing or living a dream. The women were rail thin, overpainted, and scantily dressed, waiting to be discovered by some agent, or hoping to break into the industry somehow. The sharply dressed men were either waiting to pitch an idea, looking for an investment, or trying to get laid. But everyone was always out for a good time.

There were dance parties, cocktail parties, and pool parties. Every night, Zane took Jack to some swanky event and introduced him to film directors, screenwriters, models, and television producers. Jack enjoyed warm nights with poolside champagne and caviar under twinkling lights, and bourbon and cigars in the dark paneled rooms of men's clubs. Jack couldn't keep anyone's name straight, but he collected a lot of cards, and people either engaged him in conversation or smiled and moved on, but they were all generally kind.

When he'd worked for the *LA Scoop*, Jack had been invited to a lot of parties, but most of the time they felt immoral and sleezy. The people Zane hung out with were serious about their craft, and even though they were drinking and socializing a lot, it was important networking.

After a few months of writing during the day and staying out most of the night, Jack became melancholy and was beginning to miss the slower paced life of Sebastopol. The holidays were upon them, and his uncle Rob would be coming soon for a visit. Just thinking about the morning fog, the smell of the salt air, and Charlie waltzing into his classroom first thing in the morning with her beautiful mane of hair made Jack feel homesick.

Would he ever be able to feel like this was home again? The LA life that he'd always known now felt like the place where he was on vacation. And even with all of the people he'd come into contact with, no one had drawn him in like Charlie.

Declining yet another night out to yet another party, Jack stayed in while Zane disappeared into the city of soirees. Lying in his bed, Jack picked up his copy of the third book in Suzanne Collins's Hunger Games series. *Mockingjay* was so good he almost didn't want the story to end. Jack wished he could talk to Charlie about Katniss Everdeen, the heroine of the series, and tell her how much he thought she was like the popular character. Strong, determined, fiercely independent, and gorgeous, Charlie could easily be Katniss.

Setting the book aside, Jack looked out the window at the ambient lights around the pool area at night. Then an idea struck. Standing to stare outside, he scratched his head, and his pulse quickened.

Sitting down at his desk that faced the window in his cramped bedroom, Jack pulled open his laptop and began banging away at the keys. He typed all night, fully energized.

After only two hours of sleep, Jack sat sipping a cup of coffee and wished he could pop into Retrograde and see Charlie. She'd stand at the register and give him shit about not knowing what to order. Exhaling, he looked up at the painting on his wall in the small apartment and smiled. He wondered if she'd ever asked who bought the painting of the girl on the beach.

When Jack purchased it, Charlie hadn't been there. It was just as well. He didn't ever want her to think he'd bought it out of some kind of charity or disingenuous support of her work. He really loved it. The brilliant colors of the sunset, the crashing waves, and the wind blowing the hair of the girl in shadow as she slipped down the beach in a sort of haunting, sad way had completely captured Jack's heart. He'd been enthralled by it before he'd known who the artist was, and after discovering it was hers, Jack had realized she'd painted herself.

And now it was giving him a great twist for his screenplay. Better than his idea in Sebastopol. Once again, Charlie's spirit, her passion and mysterious essence…she was inside of him, and now Jack would carry her with him to fulfill this dream of telling an epic story that he hoped the world would fall in love with. Or at least Hollywood.

CHAPTER FIFTEEN

WINTER 2010-2011
CHARLIE

DECEMBER WINDS BLEW in, creating an ache that settled into Charlie's bones, but not a drop of rain fell that month in Sebastopol. The town was just shrouded in bleak grayness, and it did nothing to boost Charlie's spirits.

With winter break approaching, Charlie was anxious to get all her college applications sent. Because she had a 4.2 GPA, and she'd tested in the top twenty-fifth percentile of the nation on her SATs, Charlie was hoping to get into one of her top three picks for schools. UCLA was her first choice. Los Angeles, and hopes of someday seeing Jack.

Her FAFSA, completed with help from the high school counselor, showed she was eligible for financial aid, as it only required she list her parent's income. It seemed she wouldn't really need a whole lot of help from her wealthy, uptight grandparents. Still, Cece insisted that living expenses were going to far exceed what financial aid would give and said *it wouldn't kill her to put on a dog and pony show to impress her moneybags grandparents.*

"Seriously, Mom, I'd just as soon get a part-time job than ask them for money. They don't even like me."

"Who said they have to like you? They're your grandparents, aren't they? They sure as hell didn't give me one damn red cent when I needed help raising you, and I didn't get any fancy college education because I dropped out of high school and *shamed the family!*'" Cece used air quotes with her hands and pinched up her face as a cigarette dangled from her mouth. "So, get all the money out of those tight-asses as you can, baby, and throw some your momma's way too."

The whole experience of preparing and applying to colleges was like juggling anvils. Charlie was constantly exhausted, overloaded with school, tutoring Leo, and work. She worried she'd be stuck attending some dumpy junior college in a ghost town. The worst part of applying was asking teachers for letters of recommendation. It wasn't like Charlie had ever been *Miss Congeniality*. In truth, she barely spoke, but most of the teachers had their minds made up about her. Regardless of her good grades, they could never see past her reputation and her clothes. But the one person she really needed to get a letter from she had blown off for far too long, and she worried that by doing so she'd shot herself in the foot.

Making her way to Mr. Ingle's art room, Charlie almost changed her mind several times and nearly bolted to her car, but she forced herself, one painful step at a time, to proceed. If Jack were here, he'd be telling her to go for her dreams and accept nothing less, to push on until she succeeded. But he wasn't around anymore, and now all Charlie had of him was the sound of his voice in her head.

Knocking on the doorjamb of Mr. Ingle's art room, Charlie saw him seated at his desk, tweed jacket open to a Doors T-shirt and his shaggy hair hanging over his eyes. He typed away on his computer, the Eagles playing in the background. With her knock, he looked up over cheater glasses and gave a smirk upon seeing her.

"Charlie Kane. Come in." He removed the glasses and stood to walk around his desk.

"Hey, Mr. Ingle." She approached cautiously and stopped midroom, not getting too close. She fidgeted with the strap of her backpack that was slung over her shoulder as she looked around aimlessly.

"What brings you by? I haven't seen you in my class this semester."

"Yeah, I have a heavy class load right now. Senior year and all. Maybe next semester."

She was making small talk, procrastinating. *So fucking lame.* The need to ask anyone for anything simply put Charlie on edge. It was like peeling back layers of skin.

"Well, it's good to see you anyway. I hope you're painting. Anything you'd like to share with me? I'd love to see what you're working on."

He cocked his head to the side in question, but she only met his eyes for a split second before smiling and looking away.

"Um...yeah, I have been painting a lot actually. I'm selling my pieces over at Retrograde Coffee and even have a few over in the Sebastopol Gallery." She'd finally worked up the nerve to ask and was surprised at the owner's enthusiasm to put her pieces up on consignment.

"That's wonderful. Really, Charlie. I'll have to stop in and check it out. Good for you."

Jesus. Just fucking ask!

She swallowed hard. "So, I am applying for colleges, and I'd like to get into a school that has a great art program, ya know? And...I was wondering if...I mean I know I haven't been in here for a while, but..."

"Would you like me to write you a letter of recommendation?" He smiled at her with shining eyes.

Feeling the tension leave her body, Charlie exhaled. "Yes. I would love that, Mr. Ingle. Thank you. I really would appreciate it."

He came closer to her and met her in the middle of the room where she'd first gained confidence that she had real talent. The place that felt like magic to her before Kendra Townsend had ruined it with her mean accusations. The place where every morning she'd had somewhere safe to go for a while. Since her sophomore year and the fallout they'd had, Charlie had only taken a semester during her junior year with Mr. Ingle, but it had never been the same. She'd barely spoken to him and only worked during class, never coming in to see him outside that time. But now, she was returning after almost a year of not seeing him and asking for something that could change her life. A lump in her throat threatened to choke her as the emotions of being in this place and with this once-trusted teacher began to overwhelm her.

"It would be my privilege and honor to write you a letter for college, Charlie. I've never had such a talented student as you, and I know one day you will blow the doors off the art world."

A single tear escaped her eye, and she choked out a small laugh and nodded her appreciation, wiping her cheek with her hand. Mr. Ingle approached her slowly, like you would a wild horse, with caution and care. He reached for one of her hands and then her other, squeezing his reassurance.

"And I know I was wrong in listening to Kendra Townsend. I kept waiting for you to let me tell you how sorry I was, but you didn't give me the chance. You deserve great things, Charlie."

Embarrassed and relieved all at once, Charlie felt the tension from ages of putting up her walls start to dissolve. It wasn't easy for her to trust, and being vulnerable was going against the grain. But she needed his support, and now, Charlie felt she was one step closer to realizing her dream.

In January 2011, Charlie turned eighteen on a very anticlimactic day. No fanfare, just a single piece of store-bought cake. It was gift enough to her that she was finally an adult.

By February, her college letters started arriving a few at a time. With the opening of each envelope, Charlie felt such trepidation that it might be bad news. Her stomach lurched, and she would shake uncontrollably. She was declined at the University of California, Berkley, but that didn't break her heart. The others, however, gave her the green light to the University of California, San Diego, and NYU, which would make her grandparents happy, as they'd told her over and over how easily it would be for them to see her regularly. Then, her heart leapt into her throat when she received an acceptance letter from UCLA.

Los Angeles…Jack.

It was going to happen. Charlie was going to move away from her mother and start a whole new life. It seemed like a dream. The fantasy of living on her own without the looming responsibility of caring for Cece was so close she could taste it! It was so beautiful that Charlie didn't even want to share the news with her mother, for fear her mother would ruin it. This high Charlie was on would most definitely be squelched once Cece got news of Charlie's impending departure from Sebastopol and their little house together. So, she decided to savor the news a bit longer, keeping it locked in her mind and the envelopes locked in her sweater drawer in a little box where she'd kept her money before she started her checking account.

She did share the news though with Mr. Ingle. He was thrilled by her choice, UCLA being his alma mater. There was absolutely no dilemma on her part which school to choose. Charlie had made up her mind months ago where she wanted to be. Sharing the news with her grandparents would be tricky, and she needed to convince them why it was the best school. Either way, she would be living in LA, and the sheer excitement of it all danced through her like a pulsing light show. Charlie could scarcely contain herself.

Then she got a phone call from the district attorney's office. They wanted to confirm Cece's phone number. They said there was news about the case with Greg.

"I'm eighteen now. You can share anything you need to tell my mother with me," Charlie said, her voice wavering as she tried to sound firm and reassuring.

"Okay, Miss Kane." The secretary transferred her to the district attorney.

"Hello, Charlotte," Charles Waterford greeted her then took a breath. "This is District Attorney Waterford. I'll get right to it. Looks like Greg wants a plea bargain. This changes things. I'd like to set up an appointment for both you and your mother to come in."

"What umm…what exactly does that mean?" Charlie sat and held her stomach.

"It means that if he pleads guilty to a lesser charge, he will still most likely go to prison but for a shorter period of time and have a smaller fine, but no trial that could possibly exonerate him. This is a guarantee of his punishment. Also, you wouldn't have to testify, nor would your mom or neighbors. Can you both come for an appointment this week? I'll go over everything then."

Charlie's mind raced, and the walls in her room started to look like they were melting in front of her. Her throat constricted as her mouth went completely dry.

"Um…Yeah. I…I think so." She rocked back and forth, sitting on her bed.

"How about Thursday at three thirty? Can you both come then?"

Charlie rubbed her eyes and pulled at her sweatshirt that was suddenly too hot to wear. "Thursday. Three thirty. I'll tell her."

"Thank you, Charlotte. We will see you both then. Bye now."

All the good feelings about college dissipated from her brain like a hard drive that was wiped clean. She was reliving that horrible day. What if he got out right away? Would he come after her? Would he hurt her mom? Kill them both? Charlie's mind was in a whirlpool of anxiety, twisting like a tornado.

Later, once Cece was home, Charlie had to tell her mother about the district attorney's office appointment, and strangely enough, her mother was very calm about the whole thing. She simply nodded her understanding without much of a reaction.

"Okay. I'll be sure to reschedule my last client, and we'll go together." Cece lit a cigarette and walked to the couch, rubbing Charlie's arm as she left her standing in the middle of the room.

"Mom…what if…when he gets out, he comes back? He almost killed me. I'm serious. I would have been raped at the very least if I hadn't gotten away from him. He had his hand in my pants. He strangled me. He said…he was going to teach you a lesson."

Charlie stayed in the space between the small kitchen and living room, holding onto the back of the ratty chair that faced her mom on the sofa. Cece took a hard drag off her cigarette, pulling her cheeks in as she did. After a long exhale, her mother nodded then looked Charlie in the eyes, holding her gaze with the most intent look she'd ever seen.

"He's not getting away with it, baby. I promise you that. Mark my words. He will pay."

Charlie heard something in Cece's words she couldn't quite put a finger on. The conviction and determination in her voice made the hair stand up on the back of Charlie's neck.

That Thursday, Charlie went with her mother to Santa Rosa to the District Attorney's Office for Sonoma County. They sat nervously in the office where a sweet-looking receptionist sat behind a large, crescent-shaped desk, taking call after call. Soon, another woman in a skirt suit appeared to escort them down a long hallway of doors all dark-stained wood. She opened the door on the left near the end, and they entered a posh office. There were floor-to-ceiling windows in one corner, while the other walls were painted in a warm sandy tone. Several certificates were displayed behind the desk of Charles Waterford, District Attorney, and a comfy blue couch was placed in the middle of the room with two beige armchairs facing it. The coffee table between them had a pitcher of water and cups sitting on top. Mr. Waterford hung up his phone and motioned for them to sit down.

Charlie sat in an armchair, not wanting to have her mother too close or clingy during the conversation. Cece sat in the chair next to her. Charlie shrank into her chair, like Alice in Wonderland growing smaller and smaller.

"Hello, Mrs. Kane, Miss Kane. I'm glad to have you both here." He was a large, middle-aged, balding man in a dark-blue suit. He took a seat on the couch in front of them.

"We are both just *Miss*. I've never been married." Her mother smiled. "You can call me Cece. Can I smoke in here?"

Charlie shot her mother a look, and the DA shifted uncomfortably in his seat. "Uh, no, I'm sorry. This is a nonsmoking building. We shouldn't be too long though." He smiled and set a bunch of papers on the coffee table.

"Fine. What can you tell us is going to happen?"

"Okay then, I'll get right to it. Charlotte, I have here some photos of the bright red marks on your neck and the subsequent bruising from the following days that you sent to our office. Thank you for that. I also have photos taken by the officers of the scratch marks on your inner thigh and the blood all over your clothes and the kitchen floor of your house. We have lab results of your skin found under Mr. Gregory White's fingernails as well. We have statements from your neighbors the Taylors, and from the officers who arrived on scene. The pictures shared by your neighbor Randal Taylor were of Greg White's truck leaving your property, and luckily enough, he also got a great shot of the license plate, which was how the officers were able to ascertain Mr. White's whereabouts to arrest him.

"All this is a great start. I'd like a charge of aggravated sexual assault, but since you didn't go to the hospital for an exam, all we have are the photographs to go by. As I told you, his attorney is interested in a plea bargain. He might plead no contest or guilty, but the blood at the scene was all his. I know you were defending yourself, but his attorney will spin it that you were assaulting him.

That's why I believe making a deal would be in our best interests instead of a trial."

"Are you fucking kidding me right now! My daughter was nearly raped and killed, and you are going to sit there and tell me he might get away with this?"

Cece was on the edge of her seat, and Charlie put her hands to her face in horror, not believing what the DA just said.

"Miss Kane...Cece, that's not what I'm saying. I'm merely saying we have to hammer this guy with everything we have evidence for, but if you want a guarantee of prison time, a plea bargain is the best way. They will most likely agree to it if we offer a lesser charge. Instead of a third-degree felony, we can drop it to a first-degree misdemeanor, and with his lengthy record, he'll go to prison for at least a year."

"And the fine? Will he have to pay?"

"Probably in the range of around two grand."

Charlie shook her head, saying nothing but looking out the large windows at the swaying oak tree. She felt like she was in a tunnel, and her ears started to ring.

"I wanna see that bastard rot for what he did. That's all. I'll do whatever it takes to see to it that son of a bitch never comes near my daughter or me again." Cece sat back in her chair.

The large, well-groomed man adjusted his tie and straighten his papers. "I understand, Cece. I have daughters too. I'd feel exactly like you do if anything like this were to happen to them. So, I promise you I'll do what I can to keep Greg White behind bars as long as possible. I'll just need your cooperation. I believe this is the best we can hope for under the circumstances. Are we in agreeance?"

"It's fine. You good with this, Charlotte?" Her mother glanced at her expectantly.

Charlie looked at her mother, who had that weird gleam in her eyes again. She turned to look at the DA who was sitting forward on the couch with his hands pressed together between his knees.

Her heartbeat was in her ears, but she really had no other choice than to agree. She worried the odds were that Greg would eventually get out and come looking for her. But the DA made it sound like no matter what, he'd spend some kind of time behind bars, and maybe by the time he was released, she'd be long gone. Moving forward, she understood this was the best outcome she could get.

Charlie nodded her approval and looked at her mother's determined face before giving her answer.

"Okay. Let's do it."

CHAPTER SIXTEEN

JACK

FTER EIGHT WEEKS of living in *the city of dreams and beautiful people*, Jack was burning through his savings at what seemed to be the speed of light. It was a good thing he'd taken that job at the high school after all because the money he'd saved up before he'd left the *LA Scoop* was nearly gone. At this rate, if Jack didn't sell some writing, he'd be moving back in with his mother. He couldn't think of a better incentive to bust his ass.

Culver City was draped in the holiday spirit. The sounds of Christmas carols blared out from every store, restaurant, and business in the Los Angeles area, each decorated in glitzy winter wonderland decorations despite the near seventy-degree weather. With holiday parties in full swing, there were more opportunities than ever to meet movie execs and producers.

Jack was nearly finished with the first draft of his screenplay, and Zane was itching to see pages. The thing was, Jack didn't think Zane would be interested in the kind of story this screenplay would tell. Zane was more of a political, big message kind of filmmaker. He focused on stuff like human trafficking, drug smuggling, and the dangers of losing freedom of speech. Jack's story was nothing like that, but he thought it was turning out to be pretty amazing.

A secret desire to *go big or go home* was swelling inside of Jack. The dream of being a famous novelist had changed into being a big screenwriter. It was starting to consume him, this deep-seated yearning to see his creations come to life on the big screen. He knew it was a long shot, but since he was so near the Big Five of Paramount Pictures, Universal Studios, Warner Bros. Pictures, Walt Disney Studios, and Sony Pictures, he figured why not? Jack wanted to pitch to a producer in one of the biggest companies in film.

He realized it might bring laughs at his expense, this pipe dream of fame and fortune, but every great movie started with a great story, and Jack knew he had it in him. Sometimes this desire to create and have his stories reach the world became so gripping that he could think of little else. The only other thing he thought about was Charlie.

When he couldn't get her out of his mind, Jack would go a little nuts. He drank too much, he ran a lot, and he wrote sometimes all night long. Jack was possessed with desire for something he could never have, and some days he thought he was going a bit mad. When he was out with Zane at a party, he compared every woman to her, and it was beginning to become ridiculous. Anger would sometimes replace his otherwise upbeat temperament, then he'd wallow in self-loathing for a few days. The good thing was it made for great writing sessions.

With just the ending to finish, Jack hit a wall. He couldn't decide on which ending to write. So instead, he submitted some articles to *LA Weekly* and *Variety Magazine* to get a bit of cash flow going.

Christmas came and went without much fanfare, and it was just as well. Jack was so detached that even seeing Uncle Rob at his mom's house for a few days didn't lift his spirits. All it did was bring back memories of Charlie that he tried to disguise as preoccupation for his latest work. Then just before New Year's, something shifted. Something struck a nerve in Jack that felt curious, compelling, and intriguing. It gave him hope where he thought there might not be hope for him again. He met a woman.

They were walking up the elegant, sweeping staircase at the mansion of actress Christina Applegate when both Jack and Zane's heads nearly twisted off as they stared at a gorgeous blonde that passed them as she descended. She was wearing a daring red satin gown with a crisscross back, showing off her perfectly sculpted shoulders and flawless shape. Her tiny waist and exemplary ass made Jack's mouth drop open. She turned and looked back up the stairs, catching them both staring at her, when she locked eyes with Jack and gave a devilish smile. The scent of her perfume as she'd passed had triggered pheromones that could wake a dead man. Her crystal-blue eyes and cherry-red lips grabbed his attention, and he forgot where he was for a moment.

A jab into his rib cage awakened Jack to his surroundings again, then Zane cleared his throat loudly and continued to walk upstairs. Jack turned around and followed the platinum goddess. She might look *very* LA, but she had an air of intelligence as well as confidence that created a powerful pull.

Her name was Giselle Baker. She was twenty-three, single, and a secretary for Richie Lamont, a studio exec at Paramount Pictures. *BINGO!*

They sat at the outdoor pool bar under a clear sky, twinkling lights, and a full moon. She was sexy and smart, and she flirted shamelessly with Jack over pink cosmopolitans while he threw back Manhattans on the rocks. Zane raised his glass from across the patio behind her, and Jack nodded in return. With Giselle's inside connections and drop-dead gorgeous looks, she was definitely someone he wanted to spend time with.

"What do you do, Jack?"

Swirling the brown liquid in his glass, he smiled confidently and said, "I'm a screenwriter."

"Hmm. Nice. What do you write?"

He swallowed a sip of encouragement. "Romantic suspense at the moment."

A half smile crawled upon her scarlet lips. "Are we talking like a *Fatal Attraction* thing?"

"More like *Sweet November* with Keanu Reeves meets *Autumn in New York*. You know the one with Winona Ryder and Richard Gere? I suppose it's more melodrama than suspense. There's a lot of suspicion… evasiveness, but wild connections. Things get weird."

He bit the cherry off the tiny skewer in his drink, and her eyes watched his mouth intently. When she licked her glossy lips, a twinge in his groin had him shifting in his chair.

"How's the sex?" She uncrossed then crossed her legs, the slit in her dress opening nearly to her crotch.

Jack cleared his throat. "Um…it gets pretty extreme. He's wild about her."

"You said things get weird. Maybe like *Basic Instinct?*"

He laughed. "Somewhat. Only I don't see my protagonist as a killer. She's more or less hiding some dark secret, and they only just met. It all happens over about a week's time. Fast-paced."

"He's already doing her after only a few days? Naughty boy." Giselle threw back the rest of her drink and stood.

"You aren't leaving, are you?" Disappointment flooded him. He'd thought he was getting somewhere with her. An unwelcome reminder of Charlie leaving him outside of the library flashed in his mind, and his chest tightened.

"I thought it might be time to go. Shall we?" Giselle ran a finger around the rim of his glass, then up his hand, and circled his wrist.

Holy fuck!

Taking her lead, Jack threw back what was left in his glass and then stood, smoothing the front of his designer shirt and adjusting his jacket. He nervously looked around the room for Zane, but when he didn't see him, Jack pushed in his barstool and put a hand on the small of Giselle's back to lead her out towards the front door.

⌁

He woke up hungover and naked on a bed of pink satin. Giselle was sprawled inside the twisted comforter with her shiny hair draped across the pillow. She looked like a passed-out princess. Groggy and bleary-eyed, Jack peered around at the room with daylight spilling through the sheer curtains. A crystal chandelier hung from the ceiling, and there was so much pink in the room it looked like the inside of a Pepto Bismol bottle. Jack squinted his eyes and covered his face.

The urge to pee made him move, so Jack searched for his boxers and found them on a nearby chair. Her en suite bathroom was marble and all white. The high ceilings and cold surfaces seemed sterile and, in comparison to the Barbie Townhouse bedroom, were stark. It was impossible to take a leak in there quietly. Everything echoed. He flushed the pristine toilet and washed his hands, drying them on a fluffy white towel before returning to her bedroom.

When Giselle rolled over, her pouty lips and pink cheeks were still glowing. How could she possibly wake up so damn cute? From what Jack saw in the mirror, he looked like an alligator that had been run over. He was dehydrated and scaly, with pillow lines and hair that looked like he'd recently been electrocuted.

"Mmm, good morning," she purred.

"Hi." He sat on the edge of the bed awkwardly, feeling the morning-after guilt.

Patting the bed, Giselle pulled back the silky comforter. He ran a hand through his mop of hair and slipped in beside her shyly. He still wasn't sure what he was doing here.

"Last night was amaaazing," she groaned, drawing out the word as she arched her neck back.

Too bad he couldn't remember much. Jack smiled. "Yeah, pretty great."

He remembered they'd been drunk, fast, and furious. She'd sat on the edge of her bed and had nearly ripped his belt off his pants. Her small, firm breasts had been exposed, and Jack recalled cupping them as she pulled him out of his jockeys and put him into her mouth. They hadn't stayed that way for long. She'd leaped back onto her bed and flung off her underwear, offering herself up. He didn't recall it lasting very long, and then they both had passed out. Still, a vague memory of seeing Charlie came to mind.

"Wanna go for round two?" Giselle lay on her side, propped up on her elbow, and stared at him with those piercing blue eyes.

"I mean…you might have to twist my arm." He wiggled back out of his boxers and kicked them to the bottom of the bed, suppressing thoughts of Charlie, realizing he'd probably never see her again anyway.

Focusing on making a more lasting impression, Jack took his time. Giselle was petite, firm, and sexy as hell. He kissed her neck and used a finger on her first, working her up to a breathless frenzy before stopping for a condom and moving on top of her. He entered slowly, inching his way into her wetness, feeling her arch and wrap her legs around his.

"Yes, Jack! More."

They found a rhythm and stayed with it until Giselle began to moan louder, and her body tightened around him in a shudder. She grabbed his ass, pushing him deeper and deeper into her until their bodies were forged in sweat. Jack came hard, and when he was spent, he collapsed in satisfaction.

This, he could get used to.

After a shower in her fancy bathroom, they were toweling off, and Jack's curiosity got the better of him.

"So, is this your house alone, or do you have a roommate?"

"It's my parents' house."

Jack nearly shit. He stopped drying his hair and stared at Giselle in shock. "And we've been having sex here? *Twice!*"

She laughed and threw her towel at him, walking back to her bedroom naked. She had the best ass. He really hoped she was truly twenty-three like she'd said.

"Relax, Jack. They're out of town. Gone to Belize. Do you really think I'd have brought you here if Daddy was home? He'd kill you."

Great! Just what Jack wanted. More entanglements. His head hurt behind his eyes.

"Exactly what does your father do?" Jack was pulling on his slacks, looking out a window at meticulously manicured gardens and an enormous pool.

"Well, I didn't want to say last night because…well, I wanted you to like me for me. He's Thomas J. Baker."

Thomas J. Baker. Thomas J. Baker. Who the fuck was Thomas J. Baker?

She laughed and put her hand on her hip, standing in just her bra and panties. "You really don't know, do you? Thomas J. Baker, the movie trailer producer. He works for Paramount, and that's how I got the job right out of college working for Richie Lamont. Anyway, I can see you really didn't know."

"No, I had no idea." He said it out loud, but he was talking to himself.

"Relax, Jack." Giselle started pulling on a pair of jeans. "I said he'd kill you, but he'd really only blackball you in the industry. Not *actually* murder you."

Adrenaline rushed to his extremities, and suddenly he felt queasy. "That's wonderful. Just great, Giselle." He rubbed his forehead and sat down on her bed, buttoning his shirt.

She laughed, throwing her head back in hysterics. "I'm just fucking with you, Jack. He's not that bad. My father is a bit protective of me, but he's not a prude. He's okay with me working in this industry knowing it can be cutthroat and that his little girl might be hit on by a whole host of men. I can handle myself. I make my own decisions. I just don't bring guys home to fuck them in my parents' house…*usually.*"

The smirk on her adorable face lifted the weight within his chest.

Jack was severely dehydrated, he was lightheaded, and in dire need of food. Maybe he'd feel better after some coffee.

She was buttoning a white blouse over her perky breasts when she came to straddle him on the bed. "I think it's cute how you're scared of my father."

Jack grabbed her hips and moved her off of him then stood and grabbed his shoes. Not wanting to be emasculated, he straightened up.

"Not scared. I never said I was scared. I just don't like to seem disrespectful. That's all."

She narrowed her eyes and retained her smirk. "I can see that. A man of integrity. I like it."

Fully dressed now, Jack stood in front of Giselle in the sickeningly pink room and struggled to come up with a way to exit this situation while still keeping his relationship moving forward with her.

"Giselle…I would love to see you again. Maybe we could go out on a real date or something. What do you think?" Even to him that sounded mechanical.

She put her hands up onto his chest and looked deeply into his eyes. "Really? That's your line? Where do you have to be this morning that's so pressing you're gonna ditch me after we just…ya know." She nodded towards the unmade bed.

He heaved an exhale. "Honestly? I'm hung over as shit, and this is not me at my best. I think if I don't get some coffee, food, and ample amounts of water, I might shrivel up like a dry sponge."

Giselle laughed at him. "Why didn't you say so? Let's sneak out before the housekeeper shows up, and we can go grab breakfast. I know this fantastic little place not far from here that makes the best huevos rancheros you've ever had, and the coffee is strong."

Coffee. A flash of Charlie swept across Jack's mind before he wiped her away like a cobweb. Giselle deserved his full attention. Even as lousy as he was feeling, getting to know Giselle might be really good for him. He had to move on, and Jack couldn't afford to pass up a great opportunity.

"Yeah, okay. But I'm warning you that I'm kind of a crab ass when I'm feeling like this. I'll do my best to shake it off. Consider yourself warned though."

Grabbing her purse, Giselle reached for Jack's hand and started pulling him out the door. "I'll take my chances."

CHAPTER SEVENTEEN

CHARLIE

IN HER FINAL semester at Analy High, Charlie was enrolled in Mr. Ingle's advanced art class. She tried to stay focused on the positive things for her future, like saving money for summer classes in Paris, a dream she'd had for years. With the money she earned the previous semester tutoring Leo, the sale of a few paintings, and her job at Retrograde, she was hopeful she could swing it. It was all that kept her from going crazy worrying about the Greg issue, and her only incentive to get out of bed.

Mr. Ingle and Charlie were great friends again, and he spun amazing stories of his adventures in Paris, strolling down the Rue Saint-Dominique, sketching the luminous Eiffel Tower, and savoring patisseries filled with rich chocolate. About stepping through time on Rue Saint-Rustique and feeling the spirits of Van Gogh, Picasso, and Monet as he painted the scenes of bustling people in the village. The sophistication of eating alfresco at historic cafés and walking down the cobblestone street near La Bonne Franquette, a famous centuries-old bistro. Charlie could feel herself there. She could taste the food, smell the café crème, and feel the sumptuous sunlight of a perfect Parisian summer upon her shoulders. But mostly, she wanted to feel enthusiasm for life and put it into her paintings.

She'd researched a summer program for drawing and painting at *Mosavitra – cours de dessin `a Paris*. Charlie was saving every penny and hiding her savings from her mother, depositing them into her secret bank account. She just had to find a way to tell her grandparents about her studying art and hope they didn't find it frivolous. Maybe they'd invest in her opportunity.

The best part was many of the sessions for Mosavitra would take place at the Louvre, but the cost of entrance into the museum was additional to the class fee, so Charlie was still working out a budget in case she had to spring for it on her own.

The excitement of having her whole life about to begin in mere months was both exhilarating as well as terrifying. She was too scared to believe it could be true. So afraid of it being sucked away from her in the vacuum of universal disappointments where most of the wants and dreams of her life had gone that she almost didn't allow herself to think about it.

And the situation with Greg was enough to paralyze Charlie with fear, but she was leaving everything to the district attorney, and all she could do was wait.

Just a week after meeting with the DA about her case against Greg, Charlie arrived at work after school. Teri smiled at her as she moved behind the counter to grab an apron, then Teri pointed to the back room.

"I put something in your box. Some guy came by this morning and left it for you." Teri continued to stay at her post at the register while Charlie stepped around the corner to the staff's boxes where they received their paychecks and any notifications.

The plain white envelope had rudimentary writing on it that simply said, *Charlie*. She didn't recognize the handwriting and couldn't imagine who it was from. When she opened it, her knees became weak, and her gut felt like she'd just dropped several stories on a roller coaster. Michael came around the corner and saw her.

"Whoa…Take it easy, my friend." He caught hold of her shoulders and pulled her up then rubbed the sides of her arms.

She put the single piece of paper face down on the counter, her hands shaking so badly they trembled. Charlie tried to swallow, but a lump the size of a baseball blocked her throat, making it hard to breathe.

"I…I…Christ. It's him again."

"Who, him?" Michael asked. He tried to pull her chin up to make her look at him, but her eyes were glued to the piece of paper.

Slowly, Charlie turned the paper over to show her boss the elementary-looking writing that was the cause of her panic. She knew exactly who had sent it. She also understood that this situation with Greg was far from over. He was still terrorizing her from behind bars.

Michael turned his attention to read the paper.

Be careful. Remember, I know where you live.

"What the hell? Do you know who this is, Charlie?" Michael asked, taking the paper and looking at it closer.

"Yeah. I think it's the crazy guy who came to my school a few months back to scare me. His uncle is the guy I pressed charges against."

"Holy shit. We need to call the police. I'll go grab Teri and see if she can give a description of the guy who came to drop this off for you. We've also got video footage I'm sure, so no worries, honey." Michael pulled her to a chair near a small break table and helped her to sit down. He left to go get Teri.

As she sat there, Charlie wondered if she was ever going to be okay again. She hadn't been able to paint and couldn't even read. Her focus was all over the place. When she wasn't in school or at work, she'd sleep. Now that asshole was coming to her workplace. *How the hell did Justin White know where she worked?*

In a moment, Teri was back with her, and Michael was on the phone. They'd left the shop with Frank up front, a new employee that was just learning the ropes, and Charlie couldn't help but feel like a burden.

"I'll be okay. I just need a minute. I'm sorry. I just—"

"No way. Honey, *I'm* sorry. If I'd known that idiot was a bad guy, I'd have kept this from you and called the cops myself right away. You're going to be alright. This guy screwed up. We've got him on video, and he was dumb enough to write you a threat." Teri kneeled in front of Charlie as she sat in the chair shaking her head in disbelief.

Charlie could hear Michael on the phone with the Sebastopol City Police Department. It was like a fucking circus, all the chaos that seemed to follow her around. Charlie wanted to run away, to drive to Los Angeles and into Jack's arms. To get a start on her life right now. Fuck high school! Fuck college! Fuck Greg and his fucking nephew! And fuck her mom, too, for bringing Greg and his nephew into their lives. She just wanted out.

Michael hung up the phone. "They're on their way. I gotta get back out there and help Frank. Teri, can you pull up the video from this morning when you think that guy came by? Make a copy for the police, okay?" He reached down to rub Charlie's shoulder. "Charlie, this was probably the best thing that could have happened, honey. I know it doesn't feel that way, but he just shot himself in the foot. This will look bad not only for the asshole who wrote it, but for his uncle's case too. They've just given you more evidence. Hang in there, kiddo. It's all going to be over soon."

When the police came to take their statement, and the note into evidence, Charlie was starting to calm down again. Maybe Michael was right. Maybe Greg and his nephew were just too stupid to realize they'd made things worse for themselves. But the fiasco continued when she got home. In her mailbox was yet another envelope with the same writing on it. When she opened it, there were pictures of her inside. Shots of her getting into her VW Bug at home, of her walking across campus at school, even pictures of her entering Retrograde Coffee. The creep had been stalking her. She looked up from the mailbox, searching the neighborhood for Justin White lurking behind a bush or in a tree. She got goose bumps at the thought that he might be watching her right now. Charlie went inside, deadbolted the door, and called the police.

It took about half an hour to speak with the two officers about the ongoing situation, but luckily they were the same two who had been at the coffeehouse, so things went pretty quickly. They promised they were going to haul Justin in as soon as they located him, and that it was going to be their top priority.

As the officers were leaving, Charlie walked outside to see the Taylors at their fence, looking over at Charlie's house with concern. Before the patrol car could leave, Cece pulled into the driveway and hopped out like her hair was on fire.

"What the hell's going on now?" she demanded.

It took the officers a few minutes to explain the situation to Cece, but as each moment passed, as she listened, Charlie became more and more angry. The tension built inside of her as she looked at her mother. *How dare she have the fucking nerve to be appalled.* She didn't have the right to be upset, to be surprised, or to act annoyed in any way. She'd brought this into their life and continued to bring Greg around, just like all the other filth that Cece had welcomed into their world.

Charlie turned around as the officers were backing their car out, and she walked into the house without acknowledging her mother at all. Cece followed her in and started her questioning, but Charlie had no patience for it. She was tired and angry, and it was all she could do to keep herself from fleeing to her car and leaving her mother forever.

"Will you please turn around and tell me what the hell happened at work, and why you didn't call me. What the hell, Charlotte?"

That was it. Charlie couldn't take it anymore, and the pressure inside of her spit out like venom. She didn't yell, because she was too tired, but her words were like acid, tasting bad as they left her mouth and burned into her mother like fire.

"Why would I call you? What the hell would you do about it anyway? You never fix a fucking thing. You are like a natural disaster, all on your own. You bring about chaos and turmoil everywhere you go. It wasn't enough that you had to ruin your own life with fucked-up friends, drugs, and drinking, but you had to fuck up mine too. I got into this mess trying to save my own life from some guy that YOU brought into our lives. You weren't here to be my mom and protect me, because you were off gallivanting around doing whatever the fuck you wanted. Anything but be responsible. You didn't pay the power bill, you left me with no food, and you left me to be raped by that asshole, and NOW…I gotta be stalked and terrorized by his lunatic nephew too. All because of you. So why the hell would I ever think to call you for help? I'm done lying for you, making excuses for you. I'm just done. I've made it to eighteen, and I'll be leaving as soon as I possibly can. Until then, let's just try and stay out of each other's way. Okay?"

Cece stood near the door, looking stricken, with tears threatening to spill over the corners of her eyes. Charlie had hit a nerve, but she was too mad to care. She loved her mother but hated her all at the same time. She was about to go into her room when Cece turned and headed for the door.

"I've got somethin' to do."

Without another word, her mother left and closed the door softly behind her. Where she was going Charlie didn't know or care. She was just glad to be away from her at that moment.

After she heard her mother drive away, Charlie locked the door and turned the deadbolt. She stepped into her room and closed that door too. She had no idea of her mother's intentions. If she knew, she might have refrained from being so hard on her. She might have thought it through and decided she only had a few more months left to endure living with her, so why make such a fuss now?

When her cell phone rang a few hours later, the sun had gone down, and Cece hadn't returned. Lying on her bed, unable to stop thinking, Charlie answered it on the third ring. She didn't recognize the number. "Hello?"

"Charlotte? This is District Attorney Charles Waterford. It seems we have a problem."

She sat up, a bit disoriented. What more could possibly go wrong? "What's happened?"

"Seems your mother is in jail. She went to visit someone at the county jail and solicited him to rough up Greg on the inside. They have her in custody now."

Charlie was speechless. She sat holding the phone but was unable to process what he'd told her. How could this be?

"Charlotte?…Miss Kane? Do you understand what I've just said? Your mother is being held in the Sonoma County jail on charges of solicitation to commit a crime. It's too late today for bail to be set, so unfortunately, you won't be able to get her out right now. Also, I'm not a defense attorney, so I cannot help her. It's quite a mess. Do you have an attorney you'd like to contact? Your mother called me when they booked her. Said she had my card in her purse and didn't know who else to call. She told me to let you know."

Charlie stood looking out the window at the soft pinks and oranges of the sky through the ornamental plumb tree limbs. Its flowers, just starting to bloom, were dark in the twilight. Her heart was heavy, and her spirit was drained. *What had her mother done?*

"We have no money for an attorney, Mr. Waterford. There's nothing I can do."

"She'll be assigned a public defender then. I just thought you ought to know what is happening. It's late, so I'll leave you to your evening. Do you have someone you can call? A friend or family member maybe? I'm sorry to have added to your burden. But I've learned about the new evidence against Greg and his nephew Justin. I'll be looking it all over tomorrow. At least I can say I'm fairly confident Greg's sentence will be a bit longer now. Justin's gonna serve a bit of time too. I hear he's just been apprehended. I'm truly sorry for your troubles. Try to stay positive."

Charlie was too tired to talk. She had nothing left and just wanted to disappear. "Fine. I appreciate your call. I'll get in touch with you tomorrow."

"Goodbye then, Charlotte, and again…I'm sorry."

She clicked off the phone and tossed it onto her bed. Charlie opened her bedroom door and turned on the living room light. The quiet was mocking her. This time it was her fault. If she'd just left her mother alone, maybe she wouldn't have gone to the jail. *Who the hell did she go see?* It didn't matter now. What was done was done. The only thing she could do was move forward on her own. *But what the hell had her mother been thinking?*

Getting her mother out of jail would require money. Money, they didn't have. It didn't matter how low the bail was set, they simply had nothing to spare. Another debacle to contend with.

Charlie went to the refrigerator and looked inside. Her choices were few with the nearly empty shelves. She grabbed her mother's half-full bottle of wine from the door and took a glass from the cupboard. She almost never drank. Only occasionally, she had a sip or two from someone's beer when she painted with the Guerrillas. She'd also had some champagne on a few New Year's Eves with her mother, but tonight, she would try what some said *took the edge off.* It helped, and she was able to sleep, but in the morning, she had a headache and decided it hadn't been worth it.

Anticipating a shitty day, Charlie skipped school. The last thing in the world she wanted to do was deal with her mother's bullshit, but she needed to go to the jail and see her and find out what to do.

After being processed and scanned for weapons and such, then filling out the paperwork to go in, Charlie was escorted to a room where she sat at a table for the women's population and waited for her mom to arrive. After the sound of a buzzer, the door opened, and a guard let her mother in. In her orange jumpsuit, Cece walked over to take her seat across from Charlie.

"I'm sorry you have to see me like this." Cece stared at Charlie with swollen red eyes. "I could really use a damn cigarette." She laughed nervously before her face went slack again.

"I don't know what to do about this, Mom."

Cece shifted in her chair and nodded. "I know. I just wanted to hurt him like he hurt you, that's all. I had a plan. I guess I wasn't thinking."

Charlie sighed. "Yeah…again. What the hell did you do? Mr. Waterford said you're being charged with solicitation to commit a crime. What happened?"

Cece took a deep breath and looked over at the guard by the door, but he didn't seem to acknowledge them. "My friend's boyfriend is in here waiting to go to trial on drug charges. I came here to visit him and slipped him a piece of paper offering him money if he roughed up Greg while they were in together. The guard saw me and confiscated the note. They held me and then…well, you know the rest."

Charlie dropped her head into her hands and slowly shook it in disbelief. Nothing her mother did should surprise her at this point. Yet again, she'd managed to make a bigger mess than ever.

"Listen, Charlotte…you are gonna have to call your grandparents. Tell them what's happened. You are gonna have to tell them *everything.*"

They hadn't told her grandparents anything about the situation with Greg. They'd hoped to let it come and go undetected, but now, there was no more hiding it. They were in trouble.

"Great. I really didn't want them to come here on top of everything else, Mom. They'll make me nervous. Probably force me to stay with them until the mess with Greg is over. I'm gonna feel trapped! They barely know me, Mom. I just want to stay at the house on my own. I can't believe this is happening." She put her elbow on the table and her forehead in her hand, shaking her head from side to side.

Cece sat back in her chair and looked at the wall behind Charlie. "I really know how to fuck things up, and for that, I'm sorry. I'm really good at it. I fucked up my relationship with my parents until they disowned me and then drove your dad away too. If he'd known I was pregnant, I'm sure he wouldn't have let you live like this."

Charlie sat up slowly, her eyebrows knitting together. She stared at her mother, who was still in another world, looking at the back wall. The simmering blood was starting to race through Charlie again as she bore daggers into her mother with her eyes.

"*What did you say?*"

"Hmm?" Cece barely heard the question. She finally met Charlie's eyes and raised her eyebrows in surprise at the look on Charlie's face.

"Does my father even know about me? You said *if* he knew you were pregnant. You told me he left us. *US*...Mother. Like he knew about me and discarded us when you were eight months pregnant. That's the story you've always told me. Does Dwight Ledger even know I exist?"

Fearing rejection, Charlie had never even considered looking for her father. Cece had made a great case for being cast away, and Charlie never wanted to subject herself to more pain and heartache by finding out that he didn't want her. But it was all a lie!

Cece's eyes were spilling tears, and she reached for Charlie's hands. "Oh, God. I didn't mean it. I mean...I'm so sorry. It's just that you were all I had. I didn't want him to leave if he found out I was pregnant, but then he did leave before I could tell him, and I didn't want him to take you away. You were mine! Someone all mine, to love and be with. Someone who would never leave me. And... well, I didn't mean for you to find out this way."

Charlie pulled away and stood up. "You mean you didn't want me to find out at all! Answer the question, Mother. Does Dwight Ledger know about me?"

Cece put her hands to her mouth and looked pleadingly up at Charlie. She waited for her mother to answer as Cece slowly shook her head no then dropped her hands to her neck.

"No. I never told him."

The floor dropped out, and her world spun on its axis in a different direction. Charlie asked to be let out. The man opened the door, and Charlie left her mother sitting in tears.

Breathing heavily, she left the jail. Charlie drove her Volkswagen to the ocean, stood on the beach, and screamed. The wind was howling so much in her face that it nearly drowned out her voice. She screamed with rage until her throat was on fire, while the gusts and gales of the sea air blew her hair into a frenzy. She hurled her emotions out into the Pacific in the hopes the gods would hear her cries and the angels would weep along with her. She wanted everyone to hurt. She wanted the injustice of all she'd endured to be paid for, and to be seen and understood for once. Charlie wanted her wounds to be right in their faces so they could see what they'd done to her. Taken from her.

When she was spent and finally drove home, she sat in the living room of her silent house. She stared at her phone, thinking of calling her grandparents, but her hand just wouldn't do it. Instead, she found herself looking up Dwight Ledger online. Turned out that he was still in a rock band called Warning Signs and producing music at a studio called Midnight Madness Productions. The last thing it said gave her reason to hope.

He is currently living in the hills near Los Angeles, California.

⋙

CHAPTER EIGHTEEN

JACK

WHEN GISELLE'S PARENTS arrived back from Belize, Giselle expected Jack to meet them. Without using the word *exclusive*, he and Giselle had been inseparable for a few weeks. Although he felt the pressure of a vise upon him when he walked into the famous Musso & Frank Grill on Hollywood Boulevard, her suntanned parents were surprisingly lighthearted and jovial about meeting their youngest daughter's new beau.

Jack's palms were sweating as he ushered Giselle through the rich, dark oak-paneled room of the restaurant that had served the likes of Charlie Chaplin, Bogart, and most of Hollywood's elite. His nerves were as jittery as if he'd consumed a triple shot of espresso.

When he'd met his ex's mother, they'd been together for a few months first. He didn't know how he'd gotten roped into *meeting the parents* so quickly with Giselle. But if he were being honest with himself, he knew why. He could use the connections her father could bring to him. That and the great sex. Of course, the main reason he allowed himself to be shanghaied was his absolute denial of the biggest problem of all. He missed Charlie. Giselle was a good distraction.

He was feeling like a schmuck as they neared her parents' table.

Jack's stomach tightened upon seeing them, and he discreetly wiped his palms on the hips of his slacks. Four people stood to welcome Giselle and meet Jack, her new mystery boyfriend.

Thomas J. Baker was a formidable man. He was tall, pleasantly handsome with silver at his temples. He stood to shake Jack's hand in his firm but friendly grip. It was his smile that put Jack at ease, letting him know he was welcome and not being scrutinized.

While Giselle was making the rounds hugging everyone, she introduced him to the rest. Her mother, Jennifer, was a lovely woman who easily could have passed for Giselle's older sister, possibly due to a little nip and tuck. Her sister, Simone, was a taller version of Giselle, with light-brown hair like their father but the same incredible piercing blue eyes that Giselle and their mother shared. Lastly was the brother-in-law, Leo. The name reminding Jack of the jock back in Sebastopol that Charlie had tutored, and a pang of grief shot through him momentarily. This Leo was quite fit like the kid in Sebastopol. Jack tried not to hold it against him. Hugs, handshakes, and cocktails started the evening off.

At some point that night, Giselle started talking to her father about Jack's screenplay and asked if he thought he could set up a general meeting with one of the producers over at Paramount for him. Immediately, Jack's heart rate increased, his blood coursing through his extremities in a rush of nervous excitement.

"Is it ready to pitch yet, Jack? When it is, I'd be happy to help you get an informal meeting set up to discuss your project. I have connections pretty much all over this town, but Paramount is my home."

Jack smiled, shaking off the gnawing feeling in his gut. "Mr. Baker, I would be thrilled with any sort of connections you could help me with. It's not easy getting your foot in the door. I've met a lot of people since I got back to town but haven't been able to land any solid leads yet. As soon as it's ready, I'll give you a call."

"Listen, you should come to our company New Year's Eve party. Almost everyone from Paramount will be there. I'll introduce you."

Jack took a swig of his Manhattan, nodding. "I'd be honored. Thank you."

Jack smiled in amazement. He couldn't believe his great fortune. Timing was everything.

❦

Uncle Rob swung by Jack's mom's house on his way home from San Diego. He was planning to spend New Year's with his flight attendant girlfriend up in Sacramento, so his stay would be abbreviated. Giselle went to Scottsdale, Arizona, to a spa with her sister, so Jack hung out at his mother's for some much-needed family time. But like before, seeing Uncle Rob brought thoughts of Charlie, and he so desperately wanted to ask about her but didn't know how to without creating suspicion.

Then he just bit the bullet. "Remember the tall girl with the wild hair who had the crazy encounter with that hoodlum you had to haul off to the office and have arrested?"

"Hell, yes. That punk-ass kid went to jail alongside his screwed-up uncle who had assaulted poor Charlie Kane. What about her?"

His mother brought them a couple of beers and sat down to join them in the living room, eyeing the two with curiosity.

"I was just wondering how she was doing after all that. Did she ever have problems with that weirdo coming back on campus? Did he get released and stalk her more, or is she doing okay?"

Jack saw a flash in his mother's eyes. Concern maybe or curiosity, but either way, he tried not to indulge her by looking too long in her direction for fear that she'd be able to read his mind.

"Charlie seems to be doing pretty well. I heard she's been tutoring some athlete, but I haven't heard anything more about her. She's a quiet kid, keeps to herself. But to answer your question, no, I haven't heard anything else about that creepy kid who was bugging her."

"Sounds like you were a really good teacher, Jack, to take such an interest in your students like that." His mother cocked her head at him while she sipped her wine.

He'd need to change the subject quickly before *mother's intuition*, or whatever that shit was moms had, kicked in.

"Yeah, well it was an interesting day. Anyway, Uncle Rob, I have a huge opportunity coming for New Year's Eve."

Jack told him about Giselle's father and how everyone who was anyone would be at this shindig for New Year's Eve, and he was hoping for the best. It did the trick in changing the subject like he'd hoped, and no more talk of Charlie came up the rest of the evening.

But back at his apartment, when he went to bed, Jack whipped out his phone and tried, as he had multiple times, to look for Charlie online. No Facebook account. Nothing on Twitter. Then he tried a brand-new platform that had just opened in October called Instagram. He had set up an account for business reasons to get into the film and writing industries.

He searched for her name, Charlie Kane. None of the people that came up were her. Then he tried Charlotte Kane, and he immediately had to sit up in bed.

There she was!

She only had three posts, and they were of her paintings, but it was her in the profile picture. In her bio, she just said, *"Art is forever"* *Quote from Thomas Kinkade.*

He stared at her picture. She had that half smirk she'd give. He felt as if she were looking at him in particular with her soulful eyes. Or was she thinking about someone else? Was she seeing someone? *Did she think about him?*

But Charlie was still in high school, and he had Giselle to think about now.

When Giselle returned from Scottsdale, she was immediately all over him. She arrived at his apartment the day before New Year's Eve, straight from the airport. She dropped her bags in his room, and they went straight away to tearing off each other's clothes. He ran his hands over her deeply tanned skin, and the eagerness she had to please him was insatiable. Just as he was about to climax, Jack squeezed his eyes shut for a split second, as thoughts of Charlie flashed into his mind.

By the time they came up for air, it was dark outside. Jack shoved aside the guilt he had about thinking of Charlie once again while having sex with Giselle. He forced himself to focus on the present and not the past. But since finding her online, Jack found his mind drifted to Charlie more and more.

Later at dinner, he and Giselle sat staring at each other over gnocchi and wine. The Italian restaurant was small, but dark and romantic, with just the right amount of space to give privacy. He hadn't realized that he'd missed Giselle until she was in his apartment. As he sat looking deeply into her impossibly blue eyes, Jack wondered why that was. More guilt piled on as he wondered if what he truly missed was the great sex.

"Miss me?" she asked as if she could read his mind.

"Occasionally." He smirked.

"Yes, you did. I could tell by the way you couldn't get enough of my body. I missed you too."

He poured them more wine as she leaned on her elbows and set her face on her palms. Her eyes followed his every move. It was adorable how she was smitten with him, and although Jack wondered if he was as smitten with her as she was with him, he did realize how incredible it felt to have someone truly care about him. And clearly Giselle Baker could have any guy she wanted. Of that, Jack was sure. He was extremely lucky.

"Daddy's having a limo take us all to the New Year's party, so don't be late. A lot of important people will be there. It's a great time to network and make connections. Only don't seem too eager either."

He nodded, contemplating how he'd handle shaking hands with the likes of Richie Lamont, a studio executive for Paramount

Pictures. He was a god. A genius. The Gatekeeper. If Jack could get in with Richie Lamont, it would be a dream come true. "So be interested but not eager. Is that right?"

"Well, a little eager but not desperate. You'll do fine." She smiled and ran a foot up the side of his leg from under the table.

⌁

Zane had his own plans with an A&E Indie Films soiree for New Year's Eve, so he wished Jack good luck on making connections at the party. They could both benefit from Jack meeting folks from Paramount.

Jack paced with a flute of champagne in the huge two-story contemporary living room at the Baker home, waiting for Giselle. The place was like a palace, all glass, polished stone, and brass. The living room had floor-to-ceiling, sixteen-foot-high windows on two sides, and in the middle of the room was a two-sided gas fireplace that splashed a dance of colors within the rectangular glass walls. All the furniture was white with overstuffed pillows in teal, taupe, and gold. Jack pulled at the bow tie of his tuxedo, afraid to touch anything. Everyone else was ready and waiting.

"Here comes my babygirl," Thomas said of Giselle descending the wide, shiny stairs. They all looked up in unison.

Like Scarlotte O'Hara, in *Gone with the Wind*, she commanded full attention. Her ice-blue dress was a high-necked halter, floor-length with a side slit, and as she turned on the landing, Jack saw it was backless, open all the way down to the top of her ass. It clung to her exquisite body like a glove. Jack swallowed hard.

"Dang," he whispered.

A sudden burst of laughter came from her family as he realized they were all watching him watch Giselle.

Laughter was good.

The Beverly Wilshire Hotel ballroom was a dazzling display

of glitz and glamour. The white and gold decorations were overflowing with iridescent crystal, shiny vases, and enormous floral arrangements. The high-top cocktail tables were draped in white with gold bows tied around the middle of the bases. The waitstaff milled about in black and white, carrying trays of delicious tidbits and flutes of shimmering champagne. Two full bars were situated on either side of the expansive ballroom, which was a two-level floor plan with Italian crystal chandeliers. The live band played on the stage in the center of the far end of the room, and flashing lights streamed across the musicians. This was the Hollywood most people only saw in the movies.

Draped on his arm, looking like a movie star, Giselle was Jack's security blanket. He was working on his second drink, so the confinement of his bow tie made him warm, and he tugged slightly at his collar. Giselle gently pulled his hand away from his throat and spoke through her smiling teeth for him to stop fidgeting.

"I'm not. It's just a bit warm in here. Isn't it warm?" He looked around and spotted Leonardo DiCaprio talking with Martin Scorsese. The last time he'd seen Leonardo was when he'd been working at the *Scoop.* Suddenly Jack felt like an imposter. "I think I'll hit the bathroom and meet you back here in five. That okay?"

Giselle looked at Jack with a smirk. "You're nervous, aren't you? Look, these people are just people. They need to make a living, too, ya know. Go…I'll be here. But when you get back, just relax. And you might need to eat something, so you don't get drunk before you meet Richie. I think I see him walking in now." She pointed across the room at the doorway.

Richie Lamont was a striking man with long, dark, slicked-back hair and a woman on his arm wearing a candy-apple-red dress. Jack swallowed and leaned over to kiss Giselle on the cheek.

"I'll just be a minute. Promise."

In the restroom, Jack stared at himself in the mirror. He washed his hands and straightened his tie, looking deeply into his own eyes, taking deep breaths.

He's just a guy. Only one of the biggest movie executives in the world, but just a guy.

On his way back to Giselle, Jack grabbed three hors d'oeuvres off a tray and began eating, trying to walk slowly and finish them before he returned. He gazed over the crowded room, looking for his beautiful date in the ice-blue dress. He spotted Scarlett Johansson and Gwyneth Paltrow speaking to a group of people whose backs were to him, when just to their left, he saw Giselle talking with her father…*and Richie Lamont!*

The gorgonzola tartlet he'd just swallowed stuck in his throat. A waiter walked by with another tray of champagne flutes, and Jack grabbed one. Heading towards his group, Jack began licking his teeth with closed lips to be sure there was nothing left of the appetizer. As he neared, Giselle spotted him and smiled. Jack put on his best confident smile in return. It was showtime.

CHAPTER NINETEEN

CHARLIE

AFTER CECE WAS put in jail, everything in Charlie's world was flipped upside down. If it were only the problem of her making enough money to pay the rent and bills by herself, she might have attempted to do it on her own. Although Teri and Michael offered immediately to have her move in with them, which would have given her options, there was still the little problem of getting her mother out of jail and hiring an attorney.

Part of her felt she didn't owe her mother shit! After all the woman had put her through, she should just be grateful to be rid of her mother. To start her life on her own right now. But the part of her that loved her mother despite all her flaws and shortcomings knew she'd never be able to sleep again knowing she'd abandoned her. That wasn't who Charlie was, and it made her angry that she couldn't just walk away. Also, she knew she couldn't deal with this by herself. She had to call her grandparents. The next day, her grandfather Felix Kane arrived at her door.

Her grandfather was strikingly handsome, even for his age—very tall, a thin build, and a full head of gray hair. Even after traveling across the country, the man wore a perfectly pressed button-down shirt, slacks, and a blazer like he was fresh and ready for a board meeting instead of aiding his incarcerated daughter in the county pen.

Charlie assumed he'd bail her mom out, but Felix wouldn't hear of it. In fact, he told Charlie she'd be wise not to say a thing about her wealthy grandparents to anyone, lest Greg tell his attorney and they twist the charges against her and sue for money.

"She hasn't got a record, does she? Please tell me this is her first offense," her six-foot-four grandfather asked over blueberry scones and coffees at Retrograde. Even in a casual atmosphere, the man sat tall and proper, but he wasn't as uptight as she'd expected.

Being unfamiliar with her grandfather, Charlie wanted to be in safe territory and near the support of her bosses, who were more like surrogate parents lately. Her grandfather was all too happy to meet her employers, and strangely enough, Felix Kane was a lot more relaxed without his wife around than Charlie thought he'd be. She hadn't seen her grandparents in person in several years, but it would seem Elsa Kane, her uppity grandmother, was the stuffier of the two, constantly badgering her with questions each week on the phone about what she was up to. The old woman had refused to fly out and be subjected to the unthinkable mayhem her daughter had created.

"Well, Mom hasn't always made the best decisions, but no, she's never been arrested," she said after taking a deep sip of her mocha. Charlie didn't say a thing about her mother failing to tell Dwight Ledger he was a father, but that was another issue she had to deal with on her own.

"Good. That should help. I'll allow her to use the help of the public defender then, and in the meantime, we need to get you settled. As soon as this mess is handled with that Gregory White, you will go on independent study to finish out the last few months of the year and move to Virginia with your grandmother and me. Until, of course, you go to college. I do wish you'd accepted the offer from NYU though. It would have been much nicer to have you close by, but I suppose Los Angeles is just a plane ride away."

Charlie's heart immediately jumped into her throat. Change of any kind, that wasn't *her choice*, never sat well with her, and not having any time to digest the idea of leaving made her panic. After spilling the beans on one of their weekly phone calls about her going to UCLA, and reluctantly agreeing to a month's long visit with them during the summer as a way of getting in their good graces, Charlie thought that would be all that she'd have to endure. But moving in with her grandparents all of spring and summer was extreme. She turned to look over at Teri for help, but she was talking with a customer and didn't see the pleading in Charlie's eyes.

"Charlotte? You realize you cannot stay in that house without the income necessary to keep it going, and frankly, I'm not feeling good about you living here alone should your mother wind up being incarcerated longer than a few weeks. It's high time you were able to see there are other ways of living and a better course for your life. Cecelia has made her own bed. She will have to learn to turn her life around."

"But she can't find herself homeless when she's released either! I feel this is partially my fault. I was angry with her, and I told her off. If I'd have kept my mouth shut, she'd never have gone to the jail and tried to get back at that son of…that monster."

Her grandfather set his cup of black coffee down and put a hand over both of hers that were sitting on the table in a twisted mess. Charlie looked up at him with tears in her eyes, wrestling with her guilt at the thought that she'd abandon her mother. Crazy as she was, Cece was all Charlie had ever had, and when she left her, she envisioned being able to say it was because of college. She never meant to just walk out and abandon her mother, even though she'd wanted to a thousand times.

"My darling girl, I see your fierce protectiveness for your mother, and it speaks volumes of your character. No, we won't allow Cecelia to become homeless. She is your mother, but after all, she's also my daughter. Once upon a time, she was the light of my life. I'll see to it that her rent is paid in advance for several months. Misguided as she was, she was still trying in her own way to be your mother when she went after that maniac. In the meantime, you'll come live with us in Virginia and start your new life. We see great potential in you, Charlotte. Don't throw away your incredible mind trying to get your mother to stay afloat. I believe Cecelia will find her way once she no longer leans on you for support."

Charlie sniffed back the tears and dabbed at her nose and eyes. He was right that Cece depended on her far too much. But this amount of change made Charlie feel a panic rise up inside of her that threatened to strangle her. They didn't even know her, yet part of that was her own fault for always listening to what her mom said. Were they as awful as Cece made them out to be?

Months before, when asked what she was planning to study at college, Charlie had told her grandparents she was applying to specific schools to study business and the arts, and that she'd like to study both. As always, her grandfather had had his phone on speaker, so both he and her grandmother could hear and reply.

Felix had said, "I have quite a lot of connections on the East Coast. What sort of business are you interested in?"

Charlie had avoided making eye contact with her mother, who had been sitting on the couch chain-smoking as she always did during these weekly calls.

"Sole proprietorship and personal finances interest me most," Charlie had said as she'd rehearsed multiple times. "I'd like to run my own business eventually. I'll need accounting and management skills, so a business degree sounds like my best bet."

They'd loved what they'd heard, and even her judgmental grandmother hadn't had anything to criticize. But now that her grandfather was here and was making plans to alter the course of her life, Charlie needed to tell him everything. But first, there was a burning question she wanted the answer to.

"Granddad, what you said…about Mom being the light of your

life. What happened? I mean, she told me her version of it, but I know she's left key things out."

Like never telling her father she existed.

He took a deep breath, narrowing his eyes at her thoughtfully. "I'm not sure this is the time or place, but I will at least tell you that it broke my heart the day your mother left. I had high hopes for Cecelia, and looking back, I realize maybe your grandmother and I had pressed too hard to get her to do what *we wanted* instead of asking her what it was that *she wanted* to do with her life. But she was wild and rebellious, not finishing high school and running off with that rock-n-roll musician...Well, it just wasn't acceptable. I would have liked to patch things up, but your grandmother thought it best Cecelia go it alone until she could agree to come home and be the daughter we raised her to be. Maybe I allowed outward appearances to be more important than they should have been."

Charlie crossed her arms over her chest. "So, Mom didn't fit in with the country-club friends grandmother had, and she was an embarrassment because she got pregnant out of wedlock. Is that right?"

He sat back and twisted his mouth in a disapproving pout. "I'm not sure I like your tone, but...I cannot disagree. In hindsight, I'd have handled many things differently."

What Charlie was coming to understand was that Felix probably wished he'd handled *his wife* differently. She was about to tell him about her father living in Los Angeles, then thought better of it. Instead, she steadied herself to reveal another truth.

"I think there are a few things you need to know about me, Granddad, before you move me across the country. This outfit... this is me." She had on her normal jeans and sweatshirt. "I'm not the fancy socialite that Grandmother wants me to be. Granted, I'd be happy to wear nicer clothes"—she extended her arm up and down over her body like a wand—"but this is what I've been comfortable in and what we could afford." She knew her worn-out jeans and sweatshirt weren't up to Elsa's standards.

He wrinkled his forehead for a moment and nodded his understanding.

"Also, I am probably the smartest kid in my class, so moving away before I'd have to write a valedictorian speech is fine with me, but I'm more than smart. I'm incredibly independent and extremely creative. Painting is my passion. I told you I wanted a business degree, and that's true. But I'll double major in art."

She stood and walked to the wall where three of her paintings were hung, one large canvas and two smaller ones. Each depicted great emotion. One was of a girl running through tall grass in a field at sunset, another was her running on a darkened, rainy city street, and in the last one, she was standing on a beach at sunset, yelling out towards the raging sea, arms stretched and the sun sinking low. In all of them, the girl had her back to the viewer, never showing her face.

"These are my paintings. My bosses let me sell them here, and I have some at the local gallery as well. I'm starting to sell more and more. I'd love to have a gallery of my own one day. I know I could do it, too, but I just need the right education and the time and money to do it."

He stood and walked slowly over to see her work. Charlie felt her body trembling and wondered why the hell the opinion of an old man she barely knew mattered so much to her, but somehow it did. Could it be possible that she really wanted Felix's approval? This man who allowed his wife to keep him from his daughter for nearly two decades?

Charlie studied his face to try to decipher what he was thinking. She wanted him to say something, but he just stood, considering the pieces that hung on the wall before him, rubbing his clean-shaven face with a manicured hand. Then her grandfather turned to look her in the eyes, and a corner of his mouth turned up approvingly.

"You have great talent. Why haven't you told us? There is depth and passion in what you paint. With proper training, you could be the next Mary Cassatt. You know her work, don't you?"

Charlie smiled back, and her chest relaxed with relief that she wasn't going to have to fight him on this. "Yes, of course. I've taken art at school for several years, studied books from the public library whenever possible, and gone to museums. I love her paintings. *Portrait of the Artist* and *Lady at the Tea Table* are my favorites because of how she captures a certain look on the women's faces. You wonder what it is that they're thinking. She makes these women so interesting."

Teri had come over to join them then, as there were no customers standing at the counter. "She's very good, Mr. Kane. We are so proud of her here."

Nodding and smiling at Charlie, her grandfather agreed, "Yes, I am very proud of her too."

⁂

Charlie began the laborious task of packing. Her grandfather remained in town, staying at the Sonoma Coast Villa, just fifteen minutes away. Charlie was allowed to stay in the house until Greg's hearing, so she could go through her belongings to get ready to move. Cece remained in custody, since she hadn't been bailed out.

Charlie felt fairly safe, knowing the Taylors were just next door and that the only two people who wanted to hurt her were behind bars. The biggest reason she declined her grandfather's generous offer to have her own room at the Sonoma Coast Villa was that this would probably be the last opportunity for her to be in the house that she'd shared with her mother. Even if Cece wasn't there, it was the space they'd built together, run down as it was. It wasn't much, but it was always clean and was home. Charlie had thought the prospect of leaving would be a relief, but now that it was happening, it was like peeling Velcro for her to walk away.

Her meager possessions only filled two suitcases and one small duffel bag. Charlie's entire life, packed into a space smaller than a closet, and most of what she was taking were art supplies. It seemed sort of pitiful.

But a light in the otherwise total darkness emerged. That night after telling her grandfather everything, Charlie flipped onto her belly in her rickety old bed and opened her phone to Instagram, the online space she never checked. She'd created an account a while back because Teri and Michael thought it would be good for her to create a *Charlotte Kane* art brand to showcase her work and start to claim her name online.

She saw the red dot that indicated she had a message.

It was him.

Adrenaline rushed through her body so rapidly that tingling sensations pulsed from her core to her fingertips and toes. The account handle was simply *Jack Connors*, but his bio said he was a writer, and his quote said, *"All you have to do is write one true sentence. Write the truest sentence that you know." Hemingway.*

She rolled over and sat up, hugging her knees to her chest, then pulled the blankets up tight as she paused before going back to Messages to read what he'd written to her. Once she'd read it, there could be no unreading it or unknowing what he'd said. It might be good, but it also could be the final nail in their shortest-relationship-ever coffin, and she just didn't think she could handle one more heartbreak.

With her heart hammering in her chest, she tapped the message dated January 1. It was now March 4.

> Hey, Charlie. I'm hoping it's okay that I send you this message. I just was thinking of you and looked you up. I see you are still painting. That's wonderful. I'm still writing. Made a really great contact with a studio exec on New Year's Eve. I've nearly finished a screenplay I hope to pitch to him. Nothing much else to report except to say that I wish you well and hope all your dreams come true. You deserve it. Happy New Year. J

He was thinking of her.

Her heart swelled like it might burst through her chest. She sat there a minute just hugging the phone to her, wondering what she should write back. She scrolled his pictures, just a few posts of him in different locations in Los Angeles. His eyes staring back at her pierced her soul.

Jack wasn't her teacher anymore. It was innocent enough writing him, and he was worlds away from Sebastopol, so nobody could judge. And it wasn't like she had any girlfriends to talk to. Charlie wouldn't ask anything of Jack, just text through Instagram Messenger. He wasn't even in her contacts on her phone, so there'd be no temptation to call. This was more like a pen pal. After convincing herself that it was a good idea, she wrote him back.

> *Hey there. It's good to hear from you. Yeah, I'm still painting. Quite a lot more than usual actually, and I've sold some pieces. I'm glad you are writing. I'll be hoping the studio exec wants to work with you. Who knows? Maybe in a year or two, I'll go to the movies and see something you dreamed up on the big screen. I've been thinking about you too. C*

There was so much more she wanted to say. To tell him about her mom in jail, the scare with Justin White...and her moving to Virginia. She didn't want to burden him with too much drama and scare him away. This messaging over Instagram was the only contact she would have with Jack, and she couldn't jeopardize it. It was her only thread of hope.

Setting her phone on the wooden crate she'd placed on its side as a nightstand, Charlie went to turn off her light to try to sleep. But the place she usually loved to slip away to didn't come easy. Sleep was normally her best friend that hid her away from the ravages of life, but tonight her mind was too full. Jack took up all the space in her head and didn't allow slumber to block out her thoughts. For nearly two more hours, Charlie lay in the dark with visions of Jack's face and his shining eyes. She longed to feel his hands on her and be wrapped in his embrace, which was the safest place she'd ever felt. The last thing she remembered before drifting off was hearing his voice his last day at school when she'd turned to go after saying goodbye. His voice was like an echo in her mind, and she hoped she'd always be able to remember how it sounded. He'd reached out his hand and ran it across her back as she was walking away, and she could still faintly hear him as she transitioned into sleep.

"Goodbye, Charlie."

CHAPTER TWENTY

JACK

FOR DAYS AFTER messaging Charlie, Jack looked at his Instagram account multiple times a day to see if she'd responded. Nothing. He was dying to talk with her, but waiting to hear from her felt like he was walking through the scorching desert without water. The only thing that gave him hope that she wasn't ignoring him was that she hadn't added any new posts since he'd messaged her. He hoped she simply hadn't been on to see it.

Then there was the guilt he felt for even reaching out to Charlie. *He had a girlfriend, for fuck's sake!* Giselle was wonderful in her own right, and he did enjoy being with her. She was what any sane man would want. Gorgeous, sophisticated, warm, and funny. What the hell was he looking in the rearview mirror for? Why was he haunted by Charlie when he knew damn well a relationship with her wasn't a good idea? She was far away and still in high school.

So instead, Jack stopped looking at Instagram and focused on editing his screenplay to prepare for pitching it to Paramount. He'd rewritten the ending three times before he settled on what he knew in his heart he wanted it to be, but he kept second-guessing himself for fear it would be rejected.

Richie Lamont was an enigma. His exotic appearance with his

long, slicked-back hair and chiseled good looks was so Hollywood. Upon meeting him that night at the party, Jack had been greeted with a warm smile and a firm handshake, but it was hard to read whether or not Lamont truly was interested in Jack, or if he was just being polite for the sake of his friend Thomas J. Baker. Either way, just getting to meet Richie in person had been a foot in the door.

"If you are ready and you have something original, I'd be glad to take a look," Richie had said, but the comment had been a bit offhanded.

Still Jack wasn't discouraged. In fact, the evening had turned out to be very surreal, rubbing elbows with the royalty of Tinseltown and actually being invited. In his past line of work, Jack had always felt like an irritant to these celebrities. This time, he hadn't had to lurk around a restaurant, questioning the waitstaff who Tom Cruise was eating with, or sneak into an event just to get the story about a congressman who was sleeping with a starlet. His days of skulking about for the *LA Scoop* were over, and he had Giselle to thank.

That was why in mid-February, when Jack was sitting at the dinette table in his apartment, he felt like shit when Zane caught him looking at the message he'd sent to Charlie over a month ago without getting a response. Jack read the message three times before he felt Zane behind him.

"Who's the chick you're messaging?"

Jack startled, bumping the table and sloshing his coffee. "*Jesus!* Why the fuck are you sneaking up behind me, Zane?"

He laughed at Jack, putting a hand on Jack's shoulder but not moving from his perch. He loomed over Jack and read the text. Jack pulled the phone to his chest defensively and twisted his head around to glare up at his friend.

"Is nothing sacred with you? Why are you being so nosey?"

Zane walked around and took a seat in the chair opposite Jack. He set his cup of coffee down, placed his elbows on the table, and rested his chin on top of his folded hands. After a moment of Zane staring at Jack and not saying a word, Jack raised his eyebrows questioningly and lifted his palms upward to coax Zane into saying whatever was on his mind.

"So, what are you doing? You gonna mess up your best chance at hitting the big time because you wanna play the field? If I'd known you were gonna do that, I'd have gone after Giselle myself."

Jack set his phone on the table screen side down and grabbed his coffee. "I'm not playing the field. It's just a friendly thing. I met a girl in Sebastopol, and she's an artist. I encourage her, and she encourages me with my writing. That's it. Besides, who are you preachin' to, *Player?*"

Jack sipped his coffee, trying to keep things light, but guilt gnawed at him as he set the cup back down and stared into it, rubbing the handle with his thumb.

"For women, it's never just a friendly thing," Zane continued. "I oughta know. They always want more. All I'm sayin' is, be careful not to fuck this up with Giselle. She's your ticket, man. You piss her off, you can say bye-bye to her daddy's connections. She'll castrate you in this town, man. Think about it."

Zane pushed his chair back and stood up with his coffee, leaving Jack to contemplate his words alone.

It was true. Zane was right. But even as fantastic as Giselle seemed, Charlie continued to infiltrate his mind and heart, snaking through his veins so much that he worried he might never be able to completely let her go.

After a month went by and Jack had tormented himself with worry about whether his story was good enough or not, he decided he was ready to pitch it to Paramount. It was as ready as it was going to be, and anymore manipulation of the story would only screw it up. It was time.

He and Giselle hiked up the Baldwin Hills Scenic Overlook. They reached the top and gazed upon one of the best views of downtown Los Angeles. That sunny day in March, the high-rise concrete jungle in the distance was a huge contrast to the nature they'd just walked through. The steep trail through the state park rolled along, covered in grasses, early wildflowers, and huge oaks.

"Let me read your story," Giselle said.

"Sure…If you want to. You'd be the first, other than Zane's editor friend who helped me a bit. Getting your eyes on it would be helpful."

Jack rubbed the back of his neck and kicked at a rock on the ground, fidgeting. Giselle laughed.

"You're nervous for me to read it, aren't you? Relax. It's just me. I won't be too hard on you. I mean, I'll be honest, but not ruthless. That's what you want though, Jack. You need honest feedback. How thick is your skin?"

She squinted up at him as the sun shone brightly on her face, dancing off her platinum hair. He looked in her aqua eyes. She was all business now, coaching him. She knew his history of working at the *LA Scoop*, and his ambitions of writing the *Great American Novel* before this. She also knew this was the first screenplay he'd written, but his writing skills were pretty sharp.

"I can take criticism, if that's what you mean. I'm used to that. I just don't want to hear a hard no. Changes, yes. Edits, I can handle. But a flat out no…no writer wants to hear that."

"So, you'll let me read it." It was more of a statement than a question.

He didn't want her to know the real reason he was nervous about her reading it. It had nothing to do with his ability to write. Still, he let her believe he was being shy about it.

"Fine. I'll give it to you tomorrow."

Jack turned away from Giselle to look out at the famous skyline of the city where dreams of grandeur and show business culture attracted creative minds as well as plastic people. Los Angeles was the microcosm of a fantasy world derived from the desperation of people who so badly wanted to be discovered and loved into fame. He was one of them. But more than anything, Jack just wanted to be respected for his craft, and he loved writing so much he'd do it for free if he could live that way.

Giselle took his hand, and Jack looked down at the woman who was changing his life for the better on so many levels. But he was still waiting for that feeling to swell up inside of him that Charlie had evoked. That feeling that no other woman had brought out until her. For all her beauty and brilliance, Giselle still fell short in his heart, and Jack couldn't understand why.

It didn't help that for a few days now, Jack and Charlie had been trading messages through Instagram. She'd finally gotten back to him. This way of communicating was more private than general texts using their phone numbers. She wasn't even in his contacts. There was no risk of a loud chime going off to alert Giselle that he'd received a text. Which might be dishonest, but he justified it because neither he nor Charlie had said anything to each other that was romantic. Without setting parameters, their conversations were short and friendly. More like checking in. But those small sentences he'd get every so often were like a lifeline to him, even though he told no one about them.

Then what Jack feared would happen did. After he let her read the script, Jack found himself in a conversation with Giselle where he had to lie.

"The story is great, Jack. Who is she?"

"Excuse me?" His heart rate accelerated.

"The girl in the story. Who is she? You must have come up with her from some experience or other. Who was your muse?" Giselle cocked her head, studying him.

"I don't know. I mean, I just saw someone with wild hair and a tattoo in a coffeehouse one day, and I dreamed up her life. I thought about what it would be like and created her story." Okay, not a *total* lie.

"*Wildflower*, that's a great title too. I think you really have something here. The love story is so tragic though. You really have a great imagination. There were a few spots I made notes about where you could pick up the pacing because it dragged a bit, but other than that, I think Richie will love it. Are you sure about the ending?"

Jack took a deep breath. Truth was he wasn't at first, but his gut told him it would have the most impact. Some would leave the theater pissed off, but he hoped most folks would be so wrecked with emotion that the roller-coaster ride would give him points. Life wasn't always a fairy tale. After all, Nicholas Sparks's film adaptations for *Message in a Bottle* and *The Notebook* didn't exactly end with happily ever afters. They were more honest and portrayed real life instead, which was what Jack was after.

Zane's editor buddy, Tito Parks, got ahold of it, and there were many more hours of edits. But now, after both he and Giselle had read the screenplay, Jack felt he could turn it over to Richie. He asked Giselle to set up a general meeting for him at the studio.

"Have you memorized your elevator pitch and your log line?" Giselle was back to being his coach, but she was a solid shoulder as well as a no-nonsense mentor.

"Yeah, I've got it down." He ran a hand through his thick mop and looked at her across the table at Fifty One, a Chinese restaurant they loved. Giselle popped the last bite of a lettuce wrap into her mouth, eyeing him. Jack just pushed his food around the plate while he polished off their bottle of wine.

"Whatever happens, Jack, know that you are a really great writer. I love the story, even if I am a little jealous of this girl, Corina, you've created. The way Jeremy loves her…it's like Dante with Beatrice. He is destroyed for all others after only meeting her a few times in his life. Women are going to fall in love with you, Jack. If this gets picked up, it'll be a hard one to follow."

Nodding his understanding, Jack stared directly at Giselle, wondering what she'd do if she knew Corina was Charlie Kane, the wide-eyed, complicated siren who'd won his heart in a single conversation. He'd written nothing else but about her since they'd met. This story though was the best work of his life thus far, and he owed it to Charlie. He knew he owed so much to Giselle for her support and connections, that without them he'd never have this chance. But wrong as it was, Jack would always feel connected to Charlie, and God help him, he just couldn't get himself to sever ties with her. He couldn't explain it if he tried, but their bond was simply undeniable.

CHAPTER TWENTY-ONE

SPRING 2011
CHARLIE

THE DAY DISTRICT Attorney Waterford would be negotiating the plea bargain with Greg's attorney and the judge, it felt as if Charlie's nerves were outside of her body, prickly and exposed. With money her grandfather had given her, Teri had taken Charlie shopping for clothes that were more suited to the occasion of showing up in court should she be required to go. It was surprisingly comforting knowing she wouldn't look like some hood rat in court, and in her new clothes, she held her head a bit higher.

The first day started late and dragged on. Nerve-rackingly, nothing was decided. After two days, they had their answer. Greg pleaded guilty to a first-degree misdemeanor of assault and got a year and a half in prison with a two-thousand-dollar fine. This, the DA insisted, was far more lenient than if they'd pushed for a trial, for which they'd have pressed for felony aggravated sexual assault and many more years in prison with a heftier fine. But taking out the risk of him being exonerated altogether gave Charlie the satisfaction that he was at least put away. Also, neither she nor her mom had to testify, and never having to see Greg again was worth it.

As for Justin, his case wouldn't be heard for months, and by then, Charlie would be long gone. If she needed to fly back to testify for some reason, her grandfather promised that it wouldn't be an issue. Mr. Waterford said that with his extensive record, like that of his uncle Greg, Justin would no doubt plea bargain too.

Cece was still waiting for her own arraignment, since the courts were backed up. The stress was heavy to carry, and Charlie had to look away, chin quivering as she heard the news from her grandfather over dinner that they'd be leaving before Cece was released.

Having to say goodbye to Teri and Michael brought about tears and heartfelt gratitude. They took her out to lunch in Santa Rosa, where Charlie wore one of her new outfits that Teri had helped her pick out. They were her only true friends, and she loved them more than she could express.

"You always have a place here with us, kid," Michael said, bear-hugging her as they dropped her off at home.

All Charlie could do was nod through her tears, and she laughed occasionally at herself then cried some more. Teri was next to hug her with tears of her own, both holding on tight to one another. Then Teri leaned in, whispering in her ear, "And don't think I don't know about a certain guy you will be looking up once you're in LA."

Pulling away from Teri, Charlie looked at her with wide, surprised eyes. Was she talking about Jack or Dwight Ledger?

Teri laughed, teasing her. "You know who I'm talking about. That sweet-looking prince of a guy with the dimple who hung around so much. We know he moved to LA because he came to the shop and talked about having to go back. Anyway, whatever happens, know we are just a phone call away."

Charlie smiled, feeling good that at least *someone* else knew about Jack. She already missed Teri and Michael. Knowing she wouldn't see them regularly hurt in places she didn't know could hurt.

There were two more conversations to have, and one was at her school. The hardest conversation was something Charlie saved for last, as she was trying to avoid it as long as possible.

First, she got everything settled with the school, and since she was eighteen, she handled all the paperwork herself for independent study. It was spring, and tulips had sprouted up in the front planters of the campus. Mr. Hill, her principal, got wind of her leaving from both Mr. Ingle and the office staff where she'd filled out her paperwork. He caught her as she was leaving the building.

"Charlie, I heard you are going on independent study these last weeks. I also heard of your difficult time in court with that crazy guy who hurt you, but I'm happy to see you moving on, even if we'll miss you here at Analy High."

He must be joking. She didn't have any real friends in the entire place, except maybe Leo from tutoring him, and Mr. Ingle. Clearly not a tribe of friends.

"Well thanks, Mr. Hill. I appreciate you saying that."

He nodded. "Yes, and you made quite an impression on my nephew, Mr. Connors, who taught those first few weeks here when all that went down with Justin White. Jack, uh...*Mr. Connors* asked about you when I saw him over Christmas break. He was worried about how you were doing."

Heat rushed to her cheeks as she tucked a piece of hair behind her ear. "Really? Well, I grew fond of him too. It wasn't the same after he left. For all of us, I mean. He was a great teacher. Please tell him...uh, tell him for me that I'm doing well. That I'm painting again. He used to encourage me."

Charlie smiled to herself all the way through town and felt warm inside knowing Jack was talking to his family about her. The tingly feeling subsided though as she drove into the parking lot of the Sonoma County Jail to see her mother and have the conversation she was dreading most.

As Charlie waited at the steel, cold table in the visiting room, the queasiness of dread built inside of her. Saying goodbye to her mother in this manner, in this place, felt like some cruel ending to an already difficult movie. It wasn't at all how she'd thought it would play out. Yet here she was, and the next thing she knew, the door opened, and her mother walked in looking ten years older than when she'd left the house that day she was arrested.

"Hey, baby, we did it. Greg won't get out for quite a while. I'm so damn proud of you." Cece reached across the table, offering up her hands.

Charlie allowed her hands to drift over to hold her mother's shaking ones. They were cold as ice and holding onto hers tight as a lifeline. A lump rose to choke Charlie's throat as she swallowed back tears. "I'm glad it's over."

They sat a few seconds in silence before Charlie could continue. "Mom, the rent is paid up for the next six months. Granddad made sure of it, and he promised to put money into your account when you get out of here. The thing is…he wants me to go to Virginia early. I'll be on independent study."

"Shhh. I know. Daddy came by already and told me everything. See, I told you that your grandparents would come through for you. My plan worked." Cece winked and smiled bravely at her, but Charlie knew she was scared shitless and putting up a brave front for her sake. No guilt trip like normal. The most selfless thing her mother ever did for her, and she chose to do it now, *when Charlie was fucking leaving.*

"I didn't want to leave like this, Mom. I just don't know what else to do." Tears spilled down her cheeks as a wave of grief choked her. She already missed her mother, and she hadn't even left yet. Stored anguish came gushing out. All Charlie ever wanted was for her mother to love and protect her. To guide her and support her without Charlie having to worry constantly *as if she were the parent.* But even with all her flaws, Cece was the only person who'd been a constant in her life, so screwed up or not, she was her mother, and God help her, but Charlie loved her. The woman would occupy parts of Charlie's soul no matter how much she tried to prevent it. Their lives would be intertwined like the stubborn vines of ivy encroaching in unexpected places.

"Hey, this is temporary. I'll get out and go back to doing hair. You were going to leave anyway, babygirl. So, fly! Fly so fuckin' high that you touch the sky, and use those wings to make your mark on the world. You are an artist. You get that from me, by the way." Cece laughed and squeezed Charlie's hands, making Charlie laugh a little too.

"Of course, Mother. You've told me." She pulled her hands away to wipe her tears and cleared her throat.

"Okay…you might have gotten some of that from your father too." Cece looked away for a moment. "Dwight was always making music, but he painted and drew a lot too. It was wrong of me to keep him from you. Look him up. When you find him, tell him… I'm sorry," she choked.

When Charlie left her mother that day, she drove back to the house they'd shared with a lighter heart. Cece had accepted her mistakes and was going to pay for them, but it wasn't Charlie's debt to pay. She closed up the house, leaving one light on in the window for when Cece would return and dropping spare keys with the Taylors next door for them to check on the place. She said goodbye to the only life she'd ever known and left for San Francisco International Airport with her grandfather, scared and uncertain, to a new life she hoped would open doors.

❦

That first day that Charlie arrived in Virginia, exhaustion had set in, and all she wanted to do was sleep. Between the stress of leaving behind her mother, her bosses and a job she loved, as well as everything else that was familiar to her, not to mention the general stress of air travel, Charlie felt fatigue all the way to her bones. By the time they landed at Dulles International Airport, gathered their luggage, and were picked up by her grandfather's driver, it was after six o'clock in the evening, eastern time. When they arrived in Great Falls, the sun was low in the sky as they drove through an iron gate, down a long driveway to a monstrosity of a house with multiple rooflines and huge glass windows.

Although she was weary, heavy-headed, and her body ached, the house was such a sight that she couldn't help but be impressed and the slightest bit intimidated. She couldn't remember being here as a small child, the one and only time she and Cece visited. Charlie had been told she'd been only four, and even though her memories of the large staircase and a nice lady in the kitchen giving her a piece of cake were fuzzy, she remembered next to nothing else.

Seeing it now, it was a formidable place, yet elegant, and she couldn't believe she was going to actually live in such opulence. Outside, the warm air was sticky, but a rush of coolness from the air conditioner hit her as she and her grandfather entered through the enormous double doorway.

Her eyes darted everywhere. The house looked like a museum, complete with a formal marble-floored foyer, art on the walls, and a gigantic staircase front and center. Soft lights were positioned just so to showcase individual sculptures or paintings, and the walls were painted a warm tan or were wood paneled and polished to a shine.

After being greeted by Gerty, the middle-aged housekeeper with the kindest eyes and smile she'd ever seen, Charlie was starting to let her shoulders relax. But then, from around the corner of the impressive staircase, her grandmother Elsa emerged. She wore a light-blue pantsuit with pearls, and her nails were polished shiny pink. Elsa stood with her hands folded in front of her and looked Charlie up and down, making her feel as if she were being put through another airport scanner. No smile. No hug. Just acknowledgement of her arrival.

"I see you've made it. Clearly, you're worn out. Gerty has some dinner made, and once you get settled in your room and washed up, please come down to join us. I'm sure you'll want to turn in early tonight since you've spent all day traveling."

Her grandmother's voice was unenthusiastic to say the least, but then again, Charlie wasn't overly thrilled herself, and it had been a long day. So, she just nodded her understanding towards her rather short grandmother and then looked to her grandfather Felix for his reaction. He at least smiled warmly down at her, then he nodded towards the stairs for her to go up and follow Gerty.

"Come, my dear. I'll get you all settled in your room. I have everything prepared for you."

Gerty climbed the wide staircase that had shiny, dark wood steps, a cream carpet runner up the center, and wrought iron and polished wood banisters. Charlie grabbed her other two bags and followed the lady, ascending slowly as her grandparents' voices began to fade below.

There were so many doors! "This place is huge," Charlie said under her breath. They continued down a long hallway that had hardwood flooring and expensive area rugs, with an occasional side table holding a vase of flowers or an art sculpture. They passed walls hung with tapestries and paintings, and…*was that an actual Renoir?* Charlie's head nearly spun off before she realized Gerty was continuing without her.

"Five bedrooms, seven baths, a formal living room, sitting room, formal dining room, chef's kitchen, and dinette area, and your grandfather's office, of course. There is also an atrium with a sitting area and a small library, and more plants out there than I know the names of. That's your grandmother's expertise." Gerty smiled, finally placing her hand on a doorknob. "Here we are."

Gerty opened the door. Her bedroom was bigger than the living room and kitchen space of her house in Sebastopol combined. It had high ceilings and hardwood flooring—the same as throughout the house—and a four-poster bed with a billowy duvet and large pillows in crisp white. A rich sapphire-blue throw blanket at the foot and accent pillows in jewel tones of ruby, emerald, and gold gave warmth and texture. The furnishings were feminine with both a dresser and vanity, complete with an ornate mirror and a stool with a white cushion. There was a wingback chair in the same sapphire-blue color as the throw blanket, and a plush floral rug under and surrounding the bed in the same jewel tones tied it all together. The windows were layered with heavy gold velvet outer curtains and sheer white inside ones that allowed the light to filter through. Charlie peered out to see the pool and backyard below. It was like a park. Charlie shook her head in disbelief, too tired for words.

"The closet has hangers for your things, love, and the bathroom is here." Gerty opened a door to a bathroom that had a white-tiled floor and both a soaking tub and a shower. The single sink was surrounded by a marble countertop and a white cabinet. Her bedroom was nicer than any place Charlie could remember ever staying in.

"This is my room?" Charlie asked in disbelief. She set her suitcases down in front of the closet near her duffel that Gerty had brought up. Her eyes took it all in, but her brain couldn't conceive of it. She'd known her grandparents' house would be nice, but this was beyond anything she'd dreamed up!

"Of course, dear." Gerty smiled brightly at her.

Charlie walked slowly to the wingback chair, running her hand across the back. A small bookshelf nearby had a few books, a box of tissues, and a table clock. It was mostly sparse though.

"We weren't certain of what books you like to read, but I assure you, there is a whole host of them in the atrium library to choose from as well as in the sitting room downstairs. I hear you love books. The public library is also quite beautiful, so I recommend visiting there as well." Gerty turned to leave. "Alright then. Please get settled and come downstairs as soon as you are washed up and ready. I've prepared a lovely *coq au vin*, your grandfather's favorite. A nice homecoming meal. See you downstairs, Charlotte.

And please, let me know if there is anything I can do to make you more comfortable."

More comfortable? It wasn't the place that was making her uncomfortable. It was the company. The way her grandmother looked at her made her feel like shedding her skin, but she had to try and make this new life work.

Fatigue settled in again. Charlie went to lay down on the bed, and it was as she'd suspected. Heavenly. Like a cloud, the puffy white duvet cradled her as she sank into it like a bird in a nest. If she wasn't careful, she'd fall right to sleep. Forcing herself to get up and wash her face was like prying plaster off a wall, but if she missed this first dinner, it would set the tone with her grandmother that she was ungrateful and put an even bigger wedge between them. The last thing Charlie needed right now was more tension in her life.

After washing her face and tying back her hair, Charlie descended the staircase to the quiet house below, feeling the anxiety of a trespasser. Something smelled wonderful though, and the cozy feeling of anticipating a good meal warmed her insides. She tried to relax. Golden light from the large windows drenched the front sitting room like fairy dust. Maybe it wouldn't be so bad living here, if she could relax and give it a chance. Charlie followed the soft voices to the back of the house, savoring the smells of what promised a full belly. She'd get through this evening and turn off the world with sleep. This was not her home, but she could do worse. If getting to Paris this summer, then eventually to Los Angeles and to Jack, meant she had to endure her grandmother for a few months, it would all be worth it.

CHAPTER TWENTY-TWO

JACK

NOT ONLY DID Richie love Jack's story, he wanted to buy it from him. Jack didn't have an agent, so he had the editor that Zane had hooked him up with give him the number of an attorney to handle the negotiations for him. After going back and forth a few times, they settled on two percent of the film's budget. It was more money than Jack had ever made.

"For a first-time screenwriter, you got a sweet deal, my friend. I'm fucking jealous." Zane was pumped for him, and the whole thing seemed unreal. "I mean, writing isn't my deal, and I wish you'd written something I could use, but I'm so happy for you. Still, I *cannot believe* you fuckin' got in with Richie Lamont. I'd say it's because you must be keeping Giselle happy, but I know Richie only works with the best. Congratulations, man. We need to celebrate."

They rented a beachfront house near their old neighborhood in Santa Monica for a long weekend and got together with some of the guys they used to hang out with. Zane invited a date, but he still didn't have a girlfriend, since he loved his freedom with no strings attached. Jack invited Giselle, and it was three beautiful days of beach volleyball, street basketball, beers, and fish tacos. Jack worried Giselle would be put off by the rowdiness of the guys and the no-frills living for the weekend, but she surprisingly fit right in. She befriended Zane's date with ease and drank beers, ate hot dogs and tacos, and never complained once. His appreciation for her deepened.

After their three-day weekend of playing at the beach, Giselle was back to work. She called him from her car during her drive home. "Richie handed your story off to casting now. These things take time, but aren't you excited to see who is going to play Corina and Jeremy?"

"I still can't believe this is happening. I feel like it's somebody else's life."

Jack sat at his desk in his bedroom, scrolling through his phone while Giselle was on speaker. They weren't planning to get together that night because she hadn't been home in days. As much as he loved her company, Jack found himself feeling relieved for a night apart.

"Well, it *is* your life now, Jack. You will have red carpet events coming soon too. I think it's time you actually bought a tux. Also, you should start brainstorming for your next screenplay. Once you get your foot in the door, producers will ask you for what's next."

Nice, Giselle. No pressure. Jack rolled his eyes at her comment and continued to scroll on his phone after opening up the Instagram app. The weekend had been great, but now she was right back to pushing.

"I know, Giselle, but this whole deal for *Wildflower* sort of took all my brainpower. I'll get back in the saddle here soon."

He had a message on Instagram.

"I know you'll come up with something brilliant. Maybe you can write a love story based on us."

Jack stopped cold. He looked out the window at the blowing banana and palm trees on the walkway leading to the pool. It was blustery outside like the sudden tension he felt in his body. A storm was coming. He said nothing.

"Helloooo? You still there?" Her voice sounded tinny as she spoke through her car speakers of her fancy BMW.

"Yep. Still here." How was he supposed to respond? They'd never even said *the words*.

"I suppose in order for it to be a blockbuster though we'd have to have some sort of tragedy, terrible conflict, or a love triangle," she teased.

"Something like that." It was all he could think to say. He wanted to read the message but waited.

"Well, it sounds like you're busy, so I'll let you go. Have a good evening, Jack. I'm gonna do laundry and watch TV until I fall asleep. Talk to you in the morning. Don't miss me too much."

"Sleep well."

They hung up. *No, I love you.* Neither had said it yet. They were both very independent, and Giselle certainly wasn't a clingy girlfriend. She was a woman who didn't need a man. She'd learned of her power early. Jack hadn't said those three words yet because it would feel disingenuous. He was a terrible liar too. *Did he love her?* He'd thought long about it, how if Giselle said it first, could he say it back to keep things going? If she said it, and he didn't say it back, it would be over. For now, he was just grateful it hadn't come up.

He eagerly opened the message from Charlie, and his heart nearly stopped when he read her text.

Well, I'm in Virginia. Greg plea-bargained, but he's in prison. My mother is in the pen now, too, because she tried to pay an inmate to beat him up on the inside. Justin is still waiting for his preliminary hearing as far as I know. I'm living with my grandparents in a hoity-toity mansion until college. I haven't told you, but I'll be at UCLA. It's a lot to take in, I know, but just wanted you to know I'm alright. What's new with you? C.

Jack's mind spun. *She moved to Virginia?* At least she wasn't in any danger now. His blood began to boil at the thought of what *that Greg* and his fucked-up nephew had put her through. He wanted to see her. To protect her. Her mother was in jail! He couldn't imagine what she was feeling, but it was just like Charlie to downplay things. She must be wrung out from it all, and not being able to see her to know for sure that she was okay just made his heart ache and his stomach sink.

Then it hit him. Chalie said she'd be attending UCLA. *She'd be here.* What was he going to do with that information? Honestly, part of him was thrilled, but the other part of him was terrified. The temptation to meet up with her was going to be such a struggle. She was like a magnet for him. Their attraction was more powerful than he'd be able to resist. He needed to address the first issue though and at least respond to her with support.

> *Hey there. I'm sorry you're going through this terrible ordeal. I know how strong you are though. Soon it will be behind you, and you'll be able to move forward with your life. Don't let this incident hold you hostage to the past. Deal with it and keep your eyes on the prize. You will be moving on soon. Maybe paint some of your emotions out. When I can't let something go, I write about it. I hope it works for you in the same way. Let me know how it goes. As for me, I'll be fine as long as I know you are alright. I'll be waiting to hear from you. All the best, J.*

He purposefully didn't address the fact that she'd be moving to Los Angeles. It would be better if they didn't discuss it just now. He also didn't tell her about selling the screenplay yet. They hadn't messaged each other since his meeting with Richie, and now he knew why she'd been preoccupied too. He didn't feel good about sharing his happy news when she was in the midst of a problem. It could wait.

Weeks went by before Jack heard more about *Wildflower*. His attorney, Daniel West, drew up in his contract that Jack would be privy to information about the film, such as casting, locations, and release dates, but it didn't matter, because when Giselle found out first, she came to his apartment.

"You aren't going to believe who is playing Jeremy!" she nearly squealed, flitting about the apartment with wild energy. "I mean, it's not one hundred percent, but it's looking good if filming can take place between his projects, and since a great deal of it will be filmed here in Los Angeles, then…"

"Giselle! Calm down and tell me who." Jack laughed at her.

"Robert Pattinson! The star of *Twilight*. He's perfect for the role. My God, Jack, you must be so excited."

"Clearly not as excited as you are." He pulled her into his arms and laid a long, wet kiss on her to bring her back to reality. "Now, who is this Robert Pattinson?"

She swatted at him playfully. "Don't toy. You know who I'm talking about. Aren't you excited?"

"Yeah, I am. This is amazing. I'm just too scared to get wound up about it until filming starts. It's like I'm afraid the other shoe will drop, ya know?"

"They've given you your first installment check though, so it's a done deal. Oh, Jack…you've made it."

Her enthusiasm contagious, Jack began kissing her neck, feeling amorous. "Come into my bedroom, and I'll show you what I've got that Robert Pattinson hasn't," he joked.

Jack hardly had to do any work in the bedroom because Giselle was so worked up she practically mauled him. She was savage and wild as she drove herself over the edge just before he climaxed. Giselle flopped over on top of him like a wet rag doll, exhausted and pleased with herself.

They chatted in his bed for a while about some options she heard flying around the office for who might play Corina.

"There is so much buzz about *Wildflower* in the office it's like everyone's baby. I hope you've started writing something new, Jack.

You could have a home at Paramount. Won't it be great? We can work together... *and play together."*

He knew she was teasing, but there was an underlying truth to what she was saying. Giselle enjoyed the fact that she had something to do with his success. He was grateful but leery of being owned. Giselle never behaved in that way, but her words somehow made him feel like he was a bought man. He'd have to deal with it though for now. What other choice did he have? He was suddenly more successful than he'd ever been.

As Giselle buttoned her blouse, she stood in front of the painting Charlie had made, staring at it. Then with the tip of her finger, she traced the bottom of the frame Jack had put around it. "Nice painting. Very unusual."

Pulling on a T-shirt, Jack felt his insides lurch, and he kept his eyes downcast. "Yep."

"Is she your muse? The girl in this painting? She also has wild hair like Corina."

"I don't know," Jack lied as he walked to the door and opened it. "Maybe."

Ever since he'd found out Charlie would be coming to LA in the fall, he'd become jumpy around Giselle. He'd done nothing wrong, except maybe have a few innocent conversations through texts that she was unaware of. Okay, he'd also omitted the truth about his inspiration for writing the screenplay as well as his feelings for a girl who wasn't quite out of high school, but those were small things, weren't they? It wasn't like he'd had sex with anyone or been seeing someone on the side. Jack had been an attentive boyfriend and included Giselle in nearly everything in his life. So why did he feel like a son of a bitch?

He knew why. It was no use trying to justify his actions. Jack was in love with someone else and trying desperately to fall in love with Giselle. He just hoped that, in time, his feelings would strengthen into true love for her, and somehow Charlie wouldn't take up so much of his heart. That if he could just hold on long enough, Giselle would be the one he had dreams about instead of the passionate, wild-hearted girl with the flowing, untamed locks he'd met in Sebastopol. Charlie was under his skin, but she was still in high school and too young. He needed to find a way to let Giselle take up residency in his heart instead.

⤚

By mid-May, temperatures in Los Angeles were in the high eighties during the day, and the spirit of the city was chaotic. Santa Ana winds blew through for weeks, stirring up havoc, making everyone annoyed. This contagion filtered into Jack's relationship with Giselle as well.

Most nights, Jack felt like writing or spending time with Zane and his cohorts in lieu of seeing Giselle or having *family time* at the Baker house. This clearly upset her, as she was starting to press Jack that he was expected to come for a weekly family dinner. It didn't even conflict with his Sunday night dinners at his mother Rita's, because at the Thomas J. Baker house, they gathered on Thursday nights. He just didn't want to go.

"Are you getting nervous because we keep asking about your next project? I mean, you have been writing, but you never seem to want to talk about it. Or are you feeling like we're getting too close to something else?" Giselle pressed when she called him on her break on Thursday morning.

Sitting at his desk in the very confined space of his bedroom, Jack felt like the walls were closing in on him. Giselle was pressing, the apartment with Zane was pressing, and what felt most aggravating was that he hadn't heard a thing from Charlie in over three weeks, and it was starting to make him a bit nuts.

"I'm just feeling oddly constricted. Like I'm being squeezed somehow, and I need to clear my head. Does that make sense?"

There was a pause on the line. Giselle didn't answer him right away. Then with an eerily calm voice she spoke. "I do understand. Maybe you need a change, hmm? Some time? I don't know what you're going through, but I'm going to assume it's some creative genius thing that I can't understand. Let me know when you want to see me."

She disconnected the call, and Jack immediately felt like shit. Although she had a right to feel shunned, he couldn't help how he felt. Since the casting was set for *Wildflower*, with Australian actress Alice Englert as Corina, and they were working out dates and locations for filming within the year, it was all Giselle wanted to talk about. Jack's career and where it would take them next. As grateful to her as he was, it felt more and more like they were a package deal. That without Giselle, he wouldn't be able to take a piss. She wasn't emotionally clingy, but she was suffocating him with her business ideas for him. It was like she'd become his agent without his permission, and this left no room for him to breathe.

Because of his frustration at not hearing back from Charlie, and his uneasiness with Giselle, Jack's writing was crap. He tried to come up with a new idea, but his brain was jumbled. What he needed was fresh scenery. To go somewhere that would give him a jolt.

"Let's take a trip to New York. I have a little business to handle, and then we can cut loose. What do you say?" Zane was meeting with a new potential investor for his next film and didn't want to take a girl along.

"Maybe that's what I need. A new perspective. I'm in," Jack said. "Let's get out of here and grab some dinner. I'm starved."

The next week, Jack was on a flight with Zane to New York City, and Giselle acted like she couldn't care less. He went to her house before leaving to try to explain his writer's block and his need to stir things up for inspiration, but she was playing hard to get. No tears or pleading on her part, just indifference. At least he made an effort. She gave him a kiss goodbye that felt like something his mother would have given him—quick, cool, and dry. He left feeling drained and decided to address his relationship issues when he returned. For now, he needed to let his hair down.

In the Big Apple, Jack was grateful for the energy, the anonymity, and the endless parties. For four days, it was a kaleidoscope of lights and color with sumptuous cuisine and penthouse fantasies. Jack had money now that he'd never had before, so he decided to live a little and, for once, spared no expense. They hired a driver for their entire trip, and the limo was stocked with all their favorite drinks and snacks. They had a suite at the Ritz-Carlton Central Park and never went to bed before four in the morning. It was invigorating and liberating to not have to check in with anyone.

The entire time Jack was gone, he never missed Giselle, but when it was late at night and he'd been drunk for hours, the one person he wanted to reach out to was Charlie. Each time he checked his Instagram though, there were no new messages. He hadn't heard from her in over a month now and wondered if he'd said something upsetting to her in his last message. After rereading it, he decided it was nothing but encouraging. Maybe it was because he hadn't addressed her coming to LA for school. Rubbing his face with both palms, Jack was at a loss.

The last night he was there, Jack was feeling particularly vulnerable. Zane had hooked up with a flavor of the week from a party they'd attended at Edward Burn's penthouse apartment, the actor from *Saving Private Ryan* and the writer and director of *Sidewalks of New York*. In a twist of fate, it was Jack's connections—through his writing *Wildflower*—and not Zane, that got them the invite, even if no one else knew who he was. Ed had been considered for the role of Jeremy in *Wildflower* even though he was a decade too old for the part. His youthful appearance had put him on the list of casting possibilities, but he'd turned it down because of a conflict with filming another project. Still, Ed liked the screenplay so much he'd reached out to Jack personally and said that in the future he'd be interested in seeing more of Jack's work. As a fellow screenwriter and director, Ed thought Jack had great vision and told him to give him a call if he were ever in New York.

But now, with Zane off to some woman's hotel room getting lucky, Jack wound up back in the very large suite overlooking the city lights alone. His sense of virtue, or whatever the hell it was, wouldn't allow Jack to cheat on Giselle. He could, however, manage to make excuses to himself as to why it was okay to message Charlie. Staring at his phone, he had no idea what to write, so instead, he went back downstairs to the bustling hotel bar and continued to drink until dawn.

❦

Their flight home was quiet, as both Zane and Jack were hungover. Somewhere over the Rockies in their first-class seats, Zane turned to Jack, a Bloody Mary in his hand.

"Did you get any writing inspiration from our long weekend in the city that never sleeps?"

Jack gave a half smile as he poured a shot of tomato juice into his beer. "Actually, I did."

Zane nodded silently, pulling out a sad piece of celery from his drink. "If it's not going to be another one of your Nora Ephron-esque stories, I might be interested. I could use something meaty with violence and shit," he teased.

"We'll see." Jack smirked. He was just happy to have something to write about again. Still, he didn't plan on sharing this idea with anyone yet. Especially not Giselle.

When they landed and got stuck on the tarmac due to a problem at their gate, Jack didn't call Giselle. Instead, he opened his Insta-gram account and saw the red dot indicating he had a message from Charlie. He couldn't help but feel energized, smiling from ear to ear.

❦

CHAPTER TWENTY-THREE

SUMMER 2011
CHARLIE

THE FIRST FEW days of getting adjusted to living with Felix and Elsa Kane seemed like some melodramatic movie. Felix played the ever charismatic and doting grandfather to Elsa's judgmental, strict, and uptight grandmother. Charlie was constantly walking on eggshells.

The theme of this imaginary movie was set with that first dinner after her long day of travel, when she was exhausted, homesick, and, oddly enough, missing her mother.

She came down the stairs quiet as a mouse, reaching the foyer. At the front of the house, Charlie found the sitting room. The fireplace was unlit, as it was late spring and the muggy heat of the East Coast didn't require it now, but she imagined it would be nice in the colder months. The room drew her in and on either side of the hearth were shelves filled floor to ceiling with books, just as Gerty had said. There was only one lamp lit, since everyone was in the back of the house, but the windows offered light from the fading sun. Framed photographs were on a table. Picking one up, Charlie saw her mother as a child. As a teenager. Then she found some of herself in school pictures. One was from second grade when she'd been missing a tooth, and another one was from her eighth-grade graduation wearing that itchy dress with her hair pinned back on one side.

"That one is my favorite."

Charlie startled and turned around, still holding her picture. Her grandmother stood near the thick, arched casing that framed the room.

"I was excited to get the picture, even if your mother didn't invite us to the ceremony."

"Maybe she didn't think you'd come." Charlie tried to not sound defensive, but it came out that way anyway.

"Well, guess we'll never know now, will we?" Elsa remained there and stared challengingly at Charlie, and they stayed that way for a few moments in silence. Charlie still clung to the picture, and Elsa continued to look her dead in the eyes. "Shall we? Gerty has dinner ready." Her grandmother turned to leave, and it was clear she was to follow.

The table was set in the formal dining room, and it seemed odd that only three of them were at this gigantic table. It was long enough to host a dozen people. There was shiny flatware, crystal glasses, and Charlie was sure the plates were fine China. *Fucking China on a Tuesday.*

"Here, Charlotte. Gerty has set this place for you." Felix sat at the head of the table, and he motioned to the seat next to him.

Her grandmother was at the far end of the table, sitting like a queen on the other side of a candelabra that reminded Charlie of a murder mystery weapon. She tentatively sat in her chair that had a high back and was sturdy, like everything else in this place. She looked down at her place setting and took a deep breath. So many utensils.

Gerty came out with a champagne flute filled with golden, bubbly liquid. "I think some bubbles are in order to celebrate your arrival. A little sparkling cider, love." The woman winked at her, and dinner was served immediately after as they sat in the eerily lit room that felt strangely like the set of a play. Unreal. It felt like she was in Wonderland or something. Everything was upside down and strange. She was making friends with Gerty, had a seemingly upbeat grandfather, but maybe The Queen of Hearts was her grandmother.

Off with her head!

Each subsequent evening was the same, her grandfather and her at one end, the grandmother at the other, him with a bourbon, Charlie with sparkling cider, and Elsa drinking her double martinis. She always had two.

Days went by, and she turned in schoolwork through email, read books from the massive home library, and explored the property, which had a swimming pool, a gazebo, a forest of trees, and lush flower gardens. The flowers reminded Charlie of when she was a little girl and her mom taught her about perennials and annuals, back when Cece cared about such things. Her chest ached at the memory.

She was living in a magazine, something from *The Martha Stewart Show*. Then just when she thought her grandparents might not be as stuffy as she'd imagined, her grandmother, over dinner, started trying to groom her.

"Charlotte, this Thursday I have a luncheon in town with the Great Falls League of Women. I'd like you to join me. I think it would be good for you to understand how enriching volunteerism can be. Of course, you will have to find something more suitable to wear than jeans. I assume you have other clothes than jeans, don't you?"

Just as Charlie was about to respond with a smart-ass remark, Felix spoke up. "Dear, Charlotte has a lot of new clothes I bought for her in California that will be more than suitable, but let's not bombard the poor girl on her first week here, shall we? There will be plenty of time for her to learn all about your charitable organizations. In the meantime, I thought maybe we could take her over to DC to the Smithsonian American Art Museum."

Their gazes clashed with one another in a duel. Charlie's dark eyes locked onto Elsa's steely-blue ones. Charlie was getting quite good at biting holes in her tongue while faking a smile.

For weeks, her grandfather had run interference between Charlie and Elsa. Snarky remarks were traded between her and her grandmother, but then, out of the blue, Elsa would offer to do something nice for her, like take her to a salon for a day of pampering. The mixed signals her grandmother sent baffled Charlie. Mostly, she knew her grandmother just wanted to tame Charlie's feral looks.

By June, she'd finished her independent studies, was awaiting her diploma in the mail from Analy High, and had visited most of the museums in DC. A corner of the atrium had been set up as her art studio, her grandparents giving her all the supplies she needed, and the light was exquisite there, like golden honey.

Right after she graduated, her grandfather called her into his office. He handed her an envelope, and she opened it up. Inside was a letter of enrollment to the Art League, and a list of summer classes available for the next four weeks. Her eyes popped out, and she put one hand to her chest. "The Art League? Oh my gosh, this is such a prestigious school!"

"Yes, well, it's over in Alexandria, and we've paid for you to have two classes a week. It should prepare you nicely before leaving in July for art school in Paris. A little graduation gift from both your grandmother and me. And Gerty, of course." He beamed his perfect smile at her, and the walls around her heart started to crumble.

Still, she was nowhere near making friends with her grandmother, and she missed her mom terribly, only getting to talk to her once a week. Cece had been sentenced to six months in jail with a thousand-dollar fine. Charlie tried to put thoughts of her mother behind bars out of her mind.

One day after returning from art class, Charlie was walking down the hall upstairs when she heard her grandmother's voice coming from their master bedroom. Although she spoke in hushed tones, her irritation was unmistakable, and it was apparent her grandparents were arguing. *Arguing about her.*

"Felix, you are far too doting and spoil that girl. I swear, it's just like how you were with Cecilia, and look how she turned out! The moment Cecelia was born, it was as if I no longer existed, and you ruined that girl. Now, since Charlotte arrived, it's been the same. Whatever she wishes, you grant, and my words mean nothing. You've got to be stern with her and stop giving in to her every whim. She'll become lazy and feel entitled. And this Paris trip! All that will do is encourage disorderly conduct and promiscuity. Frankly, Felix, I'm surprised at you."

Charlie crept up closer to their door, leaning into the nearby bathroom doorway for cover, holding her breath in order to hear.

"Elsa, you speak to me as if I'm a child. Charlotte hasn't asked anything of us that is even remotely indulgent. She's our granddaughter, for Christ's sake! I would think you'd be happy to invest in her education and encourage her talents. Don't you remember how it felt when you first came into my family? Penniless, and my mother complaining you weren't cultured enough and lacked discipline and poise. I recall you being mortified. I stood up for you, and we were married. Somehow, you've forgotten yourself, and now it's *you* who I fear lacks compassion."

There was silence for a moment, and Charlie thought maybe it was over, but then her grandmother spoke up again, so she darted back into the doorway of the bathroom to listen.

"Oh, I recall more than you think, Felix. I fought long and hard to be accepted in your family, and even harder to make something of myself in this community. I wasn't about to let Cecelia shame us with her distasteful behavior and be a misrepresentation of this family. You agreed to let Cecelia fight her own battles after becoming pregnant by that guitar player, but now you're making the same mistakes with Charlotte, and if you aren't careful, she'll end up exactly like her mother."

Steam rolled out of Charlie's ears, and heat rose from her chest to her neck with fury. The urge to run in and defend her mother nearly moved her feet, but her grandfather spoke up.

"Maybe I shouldn't have agreed with you back then, Elsa. Alienating our only daughter and, by association, our only granddaughter has cost us years! Time we will never get back! If I had stood up to you all those years ago and brought Cecelia home, things would have turned out very differently. We aren't young anymore, and if you aren't careful, Elsa, you will miss an opportunity to know your only grandchild! How much time do you really think we have left?" he wheezed.

"Clearly, you won't see reason. I am well aware of my years, *thank you very much*. And in the time I have left, I feel it's my duty to mold Charlotte into a well-groomed, respectable, and admirable young woman. The girl has a *tattoo,* for Christ's sake!"

"Oh, let it alone, Elsa," Felix spat. "And what makes you think she's *not* respectable and admirable? It's as if you've forgotten all about growing up poor and wearing hand-me-downs. You went to community college, drank and smoked, and never set foot in a debutant school. I loved you just as you were when we met. It was you who felt the need to change just because some narrow-minded people judged you. It was never me. Maybe my mother gave you a hard time, but I loved your fire! I loved how you stood up for yourself, and that's why I did, too, and married you regardless of her wishes. Why can't you accept the girls for who they are instead of trying to mold them?" Charlie heard him breathing harder, nearly panting. "I've already lost one child, Elsa. I'll be damned if I'll lose another."

Then there was a sickening thump, and her grandmother let out a shocking yelp. Charlie moved just outside their door before she heard her grandmother yell.

"FELIX!"

Barreling into the room, Charlie threw the door all the way open to find her grandfather on the floor in the middle of their bedroom. She ran to him and skidded to her knees, feeling his carotid artery on the side of his neck. His pulse was weak but beating.

"Charlotte, what are you doing? Oh, Felix!" Elsa stood over them with her hands near her mouth.

"You've given him a heart attack! Don't just stand there, call 911!" Charlie barked at the old woman. Elsa looked horrified, eyes darting around the room, but she failed to do anything.

"Oh, for crying out loud…" Charlie pulled her own phone out of her back pocket and called, leaning down with her cheek to her grandfather's mouth to feel if he was breathing. The CPR training from school was kicking in, but her emotions remained numb. She couldn't handle losing her grandfather right now. She shoved the fear in the back of her mind and pushed herself to stay on autopilot. She needed to help the man without thinking of herself and what it would mean if she lost him and was stuck alone with Elsa.

"Yes, this is Charlotte Kane at 500 Seneca Knolls Court. We need an ambulance. I believe my grandfather is having a heart attack."

∞

Throughout the entire event, Charlie could only feel seething anger for what Elsa had done, pushing and pushing him. Her grandmother's callous remarks burned into Charlie's memory. Gerty arrived upstairs moments later, but Charlie barely acknowledged her because she was on the phone with the dispatcher giving information about her grandfather's condition.

Gerty went downstairs to open the gate and escort the paramedics upstairs. The whole time she was gone, and even after she came back with the paramedics, Elsa sat on the bed, rocking back and forth, moaning, "Oh, Felix. Oh, Felix." She was as useless as a handbrake on a canoe.

"He's still breathing on his own, but his pulse is weak, and he's in tachycardia. Did he speak to you at all?" one of the paramedics asked.

"No, but he was in the middle of having an argument with his wife just before he fell," Charlie explained, avoiding looking at her grandmother.

They administered something through an IV and loaded him up on the gurney. Charlie stood to follow them downstairs, but Elsa still remained on the bed, whining and rocking. When they had him on the staircase, Charlie returned to Elsa with all the fire of an angry dragon.

"Snap out of it, Grandmother! Your husband is being hauled to the hospital, and it's your fucking fault. So, get up and get your shit together. We're following them to the hospital. Let's go!" Charlie shoved Elsa's purse into her arms and grabbed her by the arm, assisting her up and onto her feet.

She looked into Charlie's eyes, blankly at first, then a realization awakened in her expression, and she nodded. They rushed downstairs, and Gerty put them both into her car and drove behind the ambulance to the hospital.

In the waiting room, Charlie left Elsa with Gerty and found the bathroom. She locked the door, leaned her back against the wall, and slowly slid down as tears erupted from her eyes. Grief and fear bubbled up and spilled out of her like thick lava, scorching and hot. "Not now. Please, not now." She whispered a quiet prayer to the cosmos. The anguish was so intense her face, throat, chest, and stomach contracted until the muscles ached. She doubled over in both physical and emotional pain.

What was she going to do?

After Charlie had released the worst of her anxiety, she collected herself by splashing some cold water on her face and blew her nose. Looking into the mirror, Charlie knew she couldn't call her mom. She needed her and couldn't call. Then she thought about Dwight Ledger, the father who didn't even know she existed. What would it feel like to know you had someone to lean on and call whenever you needed them? She thought of Jack, but if she called him, the words would freeze in her throat.

If her grandfather died, Charlie would feel like an orphan in this world. He was becoming someone she felt connected to and could count on to have her back. This was why letting people in just wasn't worth it. She pulled herself together and went to face whatever was next, letting the bathroom door swing softly closed behind her.

꙳

Felix lived.

When the doctors shared the news that her grandfather was expected to recover nicely because of the quick actions taken in getting him to the hospital, Charlie melted into the waiting room chair. She took big gulping inhalations as discreetly as possible, but Gerty saw. The sweet woman sat between Charlie and Elsa and wrapped a supportive arm around her, rubbing her shoulder as the doctor explained the situation. Elsa was back in control of her emotions, but Charlie could hardly look in her direction.

"Felix will remain in the hospital for a few days. We'd like to continue to monitor him, be certain his blood pressure is stable. He has to be able to walk himself to the bathroom and dress himself. If his sinus rhythm stays stable and the stint I put in continues to work well, then Felix can be released."

All three women let out audible sighs of relief. They were able to see him one at a time for just a few minutes. The doctor said he needed his rest.

Her grandmother went first. Charlie stared daggers at the back of the woman's head as she walked through the motorized door of the ICU Cardiac Ward. *They wouldn't even be here if it wasn't for that fucking awful woman! No wonder Cece had run as far away as she could.*

When it was her turn, Charlie was assaulted with the visual of this otherwise big man turned much older and smaller in his bed. Tubes, wires, and machines hooked to her grandfather looked alien. His nurse finished charting his blood pressure and checked his monitors. When the nurse left the room, Charlie walked slowly to his bedside, reaching for his hand then snapping hers back quickly as he rolled his head to the side, facing her and peeling his eyes open one at a time to see her.

"Ah, Charlotte. I'm fine, my dear. Sorry to worry you all." He reached for her hand with his bruised one. The back of it was all veins and bone bandaged with an IV. She didn't know what was safe to hold but managed to loop her fingers around his. They were cold, and a sudden gasp of emotion burst from her mouth as she tried to choke back her anguish.

"Don't worry, my dear. I know this looks bad, but the doctors insist I'm going to be just fine."

She mustered her strength to speak. "You are going to have to follow his orders to a T once we get you home. No more chocolate cake for dessert and no bacon sandwiches for lunch. And we will have to get you walking each day as well. Less checking the stock market on your computer and more exercise." Charlie forced a smile and tried not to show the fear that was gripping her from within.

He managed a smile and squinted his eyes closed as he did. "Fussing over me like your grandmother. I guess I'm outnumbered."

She didn't say so, but in her head, Charlie was thinking that she was nothing at all like her grandmother. *He wouldn't be in this hospital if not for the pushy bitch.* Instead, Charlie just kissed his cheek and left to let him sleep.

∽

CHAPTER TWENTY-FOUR

JACK

WHEN JACK RETURNED from New York, Giselle had asked "for a break." By June, little had progressed with filming of *Wildflower*, but Jack was assured things were moving forward. That information came from Giselle, but she'd called him on a professional basis rather than personal.

For over a month, they barely spoke, even when Jack tried to explain himself once more that he was just going through a creative roadblock. She had zero sympathy and said maybe time apart would give him a little clarity. Her demeanor was icy and callous, but the truth was, Jack felt a bit of relief in having more time to himself. With the separation being her idea, it also let him off the hook.

Other than the celibacy part, Jack was happy without Giselle. Her constantly pressing him to write *the next blockbuster* had made it hard to breathe, let alone be creative. Since his return from New York with Zane, and his newfound freedom, the writing was pouring out of him.

The other thing that had him smiling constantly was his regular chats through messaging on Instagram with Charlie. He let go of the worries about her age. There wasn't anyone looking over their shoulders, and nobody knew or cared now anyway. She was of age, out of high school, and he was single. Not that anything was really going on. They simply encouraged each other, talked about their day, and what they were reading. Still, neither made promises they couldn't keep, and Jack had no business asking anything of her anyway. But talks with Charlie, even just texting, were more captivating than any conversation he'd had with Giselle.

He did miss the sex though. Sometimes he wondered if he should just give in and call Giselle to say he was sorry and ready to share his work with her as well as his bed. But when he got his mind off his demanding loins, he realized that would be a mistake, as well as selfish. So, he spent most of his time writing, going to the gym, running to get rid of most of his pent-up energy, and jacked off when that didn't work.

With his new work in progress about his time in New York, Jack thought about another trip out. When he pondered making the trip alone, a sudden realization of what he could possibly pull off made his pulse quicken. *Was it even a good idea or not?* He struggled with it for two days before booking his airline ticket…and a rental car.

By the end of June, he was thirty-two thousand feet in the air and flying coach because he was back to being frugal. The anticipation for what he was planning to do while on the East Coast both scared and delighted him. One minute he was giddy, and the next, he was thinking he might be crazy.

He planned to get settled in his hotel in Manhattan for a few days for some research and writing, then he'd pick up his rental car. The question was, would he be a welcome surprise, or would this trip be a disaster?

He needed to see Charlie.

Although he hadn't heard from her for about a week, and he had no intention of telling her in advance that he was coming for a visit, Jack surged with anticipation of surprising Charlie. Sure, he was being impulsive and slightly arrogant in believing she would not only want to see him but she'd be available. From all she'd messaged him over the past few months, Charlie had gone through quite an adjustment, moving from California to Virginia to live with her grandparents. It hadn't sounded easy.

More importantly, it sounded like she was a bit frustrated about her relationship with her grandmother Elsa Kane, and Jack wasn't one hundred percent sure he would be welcome. It sounded like Charlie was being scrutinized with her every move, and he didn't want to make her situation harder.

All that in consideration, Jack knew he had to try. He had to at least see if there was anything real between them, and he would never know unless they were face-to-face. He needed to see if the electricity flowed like a vibrating current between them as it once had when they'd first met. Back then, their attraction had been palpable even when she stood across a room. Jack had been able to *feel* Charlie in a room before he looked up to see that she was there. Now that he and Giselle were through, and the timing was better, he needed to know if the magic still existed with Charlie.

Jack spent three nights immersing himself in the New York nightlife. One was spent with Ed Burns at the home of his famous playwright friend, where Jack met numerous new connections and added more fuel to his already fiery work in progress. He shot one drunken text through Instagram to Charlie though and spilled the beans that he was in New York. Still, he said nothing of his plans to see her. By day four, he'd written a few articles for *Vanity Fair* and had added to his screenplay outline. He then packed up his laptop, grabbed the rental car, and headed for Virginia, still having gotten zero response from Charlie.

He already had a room reserved in Arlington at the Holiday Inn Rosslyn at Key Bridge. It was conveniently across the river from Georgetown and DC, where he hoped to do a little more research. But more to the point, he would be less than a half hour from Great Falls, where Charlie now lived.

The drive from New York was arduous, and traffic was a tangled ball of yarn with congested freeways and angry commuters. He could have taken the train, but then he'd be at the mercy of getting a cab everywhere, which would hamper his seeing Charlie privately. If the weather was crappy, he'd want his own car to at least have a conversation with her.

By the time Jack checked into his hotel room, he was ready for a meal and a stiff drink. While sitting in the high-rise bar overlooking the golden lights of Georgetown across the Potomac, Jack messaged Charlie of his whereabouts.

> *I wasn't sure of my timing, and I didn't know for sure that I could squeeze it in, but I wanted you to know that I'm here in Virginia only about 25 minutes away from Great Falls. What's the possibility of getting to see you while I'm here?*

His finger lingered over his phone screen, hesitating to send off the message. It wasn't completely honest. He didn't tell her that his entire reason for coming to Virginia was solely to see her.

He tapped the screen and sent his message.

Setting his phone on the small corner table, Jack picked up his drink in the quiet barroom with its ambient blue lighting and floor-to-ceiling windows facing the river and the Francis Scott Key Bridge below. It was a weeknight, and only a few guests were quietly talking. He stared at the never-ending parade of cars and people crossing the bridge. With nothing but glass in front of him, historic Georgetown held his gaze with its twinkling lights shining across the water.

He drank half of his bourbon before looking at his phone. There was a new message.

It was a text from Giselle.

A sinking feeling of dread took hold of him. *Why now?* They'd only spoken through texts and only about business in the last several weeks. His curiosity nagged him, so eventually, he opened the text to see what she wanted.

I hear you're in NYC. What took you there? I'm sorry I've been salty. The truth is, I miss you. Give me a call if you have time. There are things to say.

What the hell? How did she know? Then Jack remembered he'd taken pictures of him and Ed Burns in the swanky Cobble Hill apartment and posted them to his Facebook and Instagram accounts. The scene in the photos was bougie and an obvious party. He'd also used the hashtag #NYC. Oh, well.

Irritated, he had nothing to say to Giselle. After polishing off his drink, Jack checked again for a reply from Charlie on Instagram and got what he was waiting for.

I can't believe you are here, Dog Man! Honestly, I'm a bit shocked. A lot has gone down since I last messaged you. Things are tricky here, but I really want to see you. Also, timing is sort of tight for me. I leave in two days for Paris. Tomorrow afternoon might be my only chance to slip away. You'll have to endure some interrogation first. Are you brave enough to come to the house? I'll share the address. Let me know.

He couldn't help but smile. The waitress appeared at his side, asking if he'd like another. He nodded yes, then began energetically responding to Charlie.

I'm not afraid. Send the address. Promise not to embarrass you. BTW, can we please just exchange phone numbers now? This, going through IG isn't necessary anymore. Don't you agree?

He waited a few seconds and saw the bubbles indicating she was typing.

You mean we don't have anything to hide? That feels

good, doesn't it? Can't wait to see you. I only wish you had
George and Henry with you. I miss them. Come at 2:00 p.m.
My number is: 703-555-1616. Text me, and I'll send you
the address.

Jack's drink arrived, and he didn't bother looking up as he said thank you. He was busy putting Charlie's phone number in his contacts with buzzing excitement pulsing through him. He'd be seeing her tomorrow! The last time he'd been alone with Charlie, she'd left his car and tore his heart out, and the last time he'd seen her was their public goodbye at the school. But tomorrow he'd be with her again. He ached in anticipation.

He stared out the windows. The night had become inky, and the river sparkled like stars from the city lights. Jack took a deep breath, steadying himself. It was finally going to happen. He didn't know if what he was doing was a good idea or not, only that he couldn't stop thinking about Charlie, no matter how hard he tried. Even a beautiful, rich, sophisticated woman like Giselle couldn't keep Jack from thinking of Charlie.

Giselle. He hadn't responded to her text.

He thought about what he'd say. He owed Giselle a lot. He didn't want to burn bridges but was careful not to offer too much. After all, she was the one who'd wanted some space. He opened her text and made a simple reply.

I'll call when I get back.

The next day, with excited trepidation, Jack was barreling northwest on Interstate 66 towards Great Falls in his rented Chevy Malibu. It wasn't the sexiest car, but the shiny black exterior at least gave the illusion of sleek style. It had been either that or a red Mazda, and he'd thought Charlie's grandparents would scoff at the sight of a guy pulling up in a red car.

He was nervous Charlie's grandparents would notice the age difference between him and Charlie, so Jack took care to have a clean-shaven face before he left the hotel in hopes of taking a few years off his looks.

Great Falls was charming. Jack drove past the Village Center with its town green and gazebo. The brick-faced shops and parks with lush foliage gave a friendly welcome to any traveler. He drove using his GPS, and his directions took him into old residential neighborhoods with varying styles of houses. From Tudor to Craftsmen, Colonial or Victorian, there didn't seem to be any rules. The one thing they all had in common was that they were all impeccably kept, despite the fact that some were almost two hundred years old.

He turned onto Seneca Knolls Court and discovered a significant difference. These were mansions. Looking at each passing home with their gated and brick-lined driveways, Jack swallowed hard and pulled at the collar of his short-sleeved Armani shirt. It was one of a few that Giselle had insisted he buy, and now he was glad he had it.

Arriving at 500 Seneca Knolls Court, Jack pulled to a stop in front of the gate, and his heart raced at the sight of the enormous tan brick house that lay beyond. It was like a fairytale home, forested in the back and sides by tall evergreens, dogwoods, and oaks. The front was wide open and had a view of the majestic roofline, huge windows, and a bridge walkway leading to a backyard side pool that was barely visible from the road.

It was showtime, and all that was left to do was pull forward so he could reach the intercom box, but he struggled with what to say. Jack sat looking at the house and pulled out his phone to alert Charlie that he had arrived. He hoped by doing so she'd answer the intercom herself.

Go ahead and pull forward. I'll have Gerty buzz you in.

He read her text and did as instructed. *Gerty?* It dawned on him then that they had help. Of course they did.

"Jesus, I hope this was a good idea."

He drove the car forward, and slowly the bronze-colored ornate gate slid sideways on a track to allow him in. He accelerated and followed the brick drive that was lined with a short hedge of boxwood and flanked by lawn on either side. Jack parked off to the far-right side of the house, careful not to block the three-car garage doors. He turned off the engine and sat.

No going back now.

The walkway had a three-step incline leading up to the huge double front doors. The porch wrapped around the left side of the house, and Jack caught a glimpse of a grand glass atrium and deck filled with potted plants. Standing at the doors that were dressed with two floral-and-ivy wreaths, Jack rang the doorbell. It echoed throughout the interior, and then steps softly approached him. He stood up straight.

A middle-aged woman with short brown hair answered the door in slacks and a green blouse. She smiled at him pleasantly. *This must be Gerty.*

"Hello, ma'am. I'm Jack Connors, and I'm here to see Charlie. Uh…Charlotte."

She let out a small laugh. "Yes, of course. She's expecting you, Jack. Do come in." She stepped aside and motioned with her arm for him to proceed.

So far so good.

From the front door, he entered a foyer containing a large round antique mahogany table with a marble top dressed with a tall arrangement of flowers. Just beyond it to the right was a sitting room with a fireplace, and on the left was a hallway with light coming from the back of the house. Right in the middle was a fantastic staircase, and as he looked up, there she was.

It had been over eight months since he'd seen Charlie, but just looking at her now felt like it must have been an eternity. He didn't know how it was possible, but in that short period of time, she'd become even more beautiful than before. Gliding down the stairs in a blousy white top and soft-gray linen pants that flowed around her with each step came a goddess with hair that spilled down and around her shoulders and back. Her eyes lit up, and then came the showstopper smile that beamed at him, causing his heart to skip a beat as he held his breath. For the rest of his life, Jack would remember this moment—the way she looked coming down those stairs, and how their eyes locked on one another with pinpoint precision, the moment he knew he was in serious trouble. She would always be the one he longed for.

"It's good to see you, Jack."

∾

CHAPTER TWENTY-FIVE

CHARLIE

TENSION BETWEEN CHARLIE and her grandmother continued, but at least Elsa stopped her nagging and criticizing her. She simply avoided Charlie altogether. Armed now with the knowledge that her grandmother had once been poor and not always this proper, moneybags socialite, Charlie couldn't help but wonder why Elsa was such a judgmental witch. But for now, she had more important things to worry about.

Charlie helped get her grandfather settled in once he returned, fussing over a menu with Gerty that would be healthier for him, researching low cholesterol treats he would enjoy instead of his favorite butter-laden chocolate cake.

But she promised him she'd keep up the classes that she loved at the Art League. Twice a week, Charlie was immersed in the art world. It was the one reprieve she had from worry, even if her grandfather seemed perfectly fine now. His heart attack had scared her so much that she had a hard time treating him normally. She always seemed to have one eye on him and kept a keen ear tuned into her grandmother's comments, fearing she could set the man off again. But she was grateful for the distraction. She was learning not just composition, but about narrative, color, and technique.

Charlie felt herself growing with each class, enjoying the praise of her instructors.

She was so busy she didn't bother Jack. Her every waking moment at home was spent making Felix laugh, going on sun-filled walks just the two of them, or taking twilight evening swims in the pool for exercise while fireflies darted about the yard. He insisted on teaching her about the stock market though, so they compromised with some time in his book-filled office with its leather scents and dark-green walls. Over the next few weeks, Charlie grew closer to this man whom she'd never known until recently and felt a bond that not only filled her heart, but scared her to death, knowing one day she'd lose him.

With only a few days until her departure to Paris, and her school at *Mosavitra – cours de dessin,* Charlie had been so preoccupied that the only time she was tempted to contact Jack was late at night when everything was so still she could almost hear her heart beating. She didn't want to bother him with her fears and drama though, so she kept her thoughts to herself.

She was also haunted with thoughts of her father, Dwight. She'd study his face online, seeing her own eyes and dark, curly hair. She listened to some of his music, but Charlie wasn't in a hurry to be rejected by him. She promised herself that when she was settled at UCLA, she'd contact Dwight Ledger and break the news that he was a father. Until then, she spied on him online, stalking him from the safety of her brand-new laptop that her grandfather had bought her to keep track of the stocks while she was in Paris.

Then an unexpected message appeared in her DMs on Instagram. Jack was in Virginia and wanted to see her. An overwhelming yearning was reawakened inside of her, and Charlie's heart ached so badly for Jack that regardless of what her grandparents thought, she knew she'd see him. She had to break this to Felix gently though, so as not to upset him.

With her stomach in knots, Charlie waited until he was alone at the breakfast table eating his oatmeal with berries and toast and drinking black, French-pressed coffee. Her grandmother had gone to a fundraising meeting for the children's hospital, and Gerty was busy doing laundry.

Charlie slid in opposite of him at the banquette table. The nearby large window showcased morning sunlight spilling over the flower boxes outside and ash, dogwood, and oak trees swaying in the breeze.

"Good morning, my dear. What is on your agenda today?" Felix's smile was warm and easy.

"Granddad? I have something interesting to share that's pretty unexpected." She laughed nervously. "Very…unexpected actually." She took a sec to gauge his expression before continuing.

Her grandfather cocked his head to the side inquisitively.

"Um…I have a friend from California who happens to be here in Virginia doing some research for a writing project, and he'd like to stop by and visit me. I was hoping he could meet you…and…grandmother, of course." She knew she had to add the irritating woman to the equation even though she'd personally like to shove her off a cliff.

Felix swallowed a sip of coffee and carefully placed the cup back on the table before speaking. "This gentleman friend of yours, is he a *special friend*?"

She swallowed hard and started picking the cuticle of her thumb. "We're just friends, Granddad. We can't have a relationship *like that* when we live clear across the country from each other. But yes, he's special. I think you'll like him very much." Her voice was quivering a bit, and she cleared her throat. "He'd like to stop by this afternoon since I'm leaving the day after tomorrow."

A slow, knowing smile curled one corner of her grandfather's mouth as he looked her in the eyes. "Alright then. If he's a friend of yours, then your grandmother and I would be delighted to meet him."

Charlie couldn't mask her elation, and her smile broke open

wide. "Thank you, Granddad. You will love Jack!" She placed both of her hands on top of his and squeezed.

Jack was coming!

Life felt so good Charlie didn't want to tempt fate with worries of how it could all be swept away at a moment's notice. She held on to the moment of joy, but deep within the recesses of her mind, Charlie feared it was all too good to be true.

The rest of the day, Charlie was filled with electric energy, anticipating Jack's arrival. Even her grandmother's surly attitude couldn't ruin her happiness. The woman wasn't too pleased when she returned from her meeting to learn her granddaughter had a suitor coming to meet the family, even if Charlie insisted they were just friends. To Elsa, everything was a tawdry affair. But no matter. Jack was coming!

When she got the text right at two o'clock that he had arrived and was waiting at the gate, she called out to Gerty to open it while she quickly went to her room to double-check her appearance. Her grandparents were already perched on the sofa in the sitting room downstairs.

Wearing only a tinted moisturizer and a hint of gloss on her lips, Charlie looked into the mirror for one last inspection before blazing down the hallway. At the top of the stairs, Charlie heard Gerty let Jack in, and muffled voices echoed up to her, the familiar reverb of his deep husky voice floating to her ears. She felt a tug from her insides, acknowledging that this man was definitely more than *just a friend*. After all her efforts to be careful not to allow herself to want too much, Jack was the one person she let her guard down for again and again.

Listening to his voice, Charlie slipped down the stairs as if she were locked in to the gravity of him, pulling her effortlessly towards him. And there he was.

He was unusually clean-shaven, sparkly eyed with that dimple, and that first look after all this time was just as Charlie had imagined it to be. Magic.

∽

CHAPTER TWENTY-SIX

JACK

ORGETTING GERTY WAS standing nearby, Jack couldn't help but put his arms around Charlie and embraced her in a long hug. He felt like he was dreaming, holding her at the base of that incredible staircase. It was like a movie set of some long-ago black-and-white film, and he could almost hear the musical score in a crescendo as the two lovers finally came together after much difficulty and adversity.

The clearing of someone's throat came from the opposite side of the staircase. Jack quickly pulled away from Charlie to smooth his shirt. Her grandfather stood ramrod straight with his hands folded in front of him, his wife at his side. Neither smiled.

"Charlotte, won't you introduce us to your gentleman friend?" The old man stood tall and thin, wearing a dark-blue button-down shirt with slacks, and had perfectly combed gray hair. His wife wore a pantsuit in gray with a pink blouse and pearls. They looked like they were headed to a business meeting.

"Sir." Jack reached out to shake his hand first. "I'm Jack Connors, a good friend of Charlie's...sorry, Charlotte's."

Her grandfather took his hand, and Jack caught a twitch at the corner of his mouth, holding back what Jack hoped was a smile.

"Jack, my grandparents Felix and Elsa Kane," Charlie said, standing next to him. "As I told you, Jack and I met in Sebastopol while he was house-sitting for his uncle."

"Yes...the dog person," the old woman said, raising one eyebrow at Jack.

"Ma'am," he said, talking her hand into both of his. "It is a pleasure to finally meet you both. Charlotte has told me so much about you."

"Yes, well, we have heard little about you until now," the old woman replied. He recognized what Charlie had been telling him about her grandmother's rigidity.

"Let's come sit down. Gerty is busy making us all a snack. In the meanwhile, she has iced tea set up here in the sitting room for us." Felix motioned with his hand to the plush room adjacent to the foyer. There was a sofa in front of the fireplace the grandparents sat on, facing the floor-to-ceiling windows. Felix motioned to the two chairs that faced them Jack and Charlie were to sit in. Clearly, they wanted to keep them separated. The coffee table between them was set up with a tray and pitcher of tea with four glasses filled with ice. "I hope you like iced tea, Jack. If not, we can offer you coffee, or a soft drink."

"Iced tea is great." He cleared his throat and tried not to pull at his collar.

They conversed in idle chitchat about what Jack did for a living and where he lived now, and when the conversation got too uncomfortable, Jack managed to ask Felix about his work and his time in the banking industry. Jack was smart enough to know that people often liked to talk about themselves. Before long, Gerty arrived with a tray of fresh vegetables, crackers, nuts, and assorted cheeses, with small plates. The older couple ate while Jack and Charlie picked at a few bites here and there.

It was a great deal of work deciphering what to, and what *not to,* say. Periodically, Jack would look to Charlie for clues, and she'd pick things up in the conversation, talking of her grandmother's charity work. Knowing how Charlie felt about the woman, he realized she was trying to keep Elsa calm and happy by buttering her up in front of him. And it worked. All Jack had to do was keep smiling at the woman and remain interested.

"So, I gather you two are going on an outing then? Charlotte mentioned something about dinner in the city after she shows you some sights," Elsa said, smiling and softening her mood towards him. Charming older women was never difficult for Jack. It worked on all his mother's friends anyway, and it appeared it also worked on Charlie's curmudgeon grandmother.

Just when Jack was feeling the noose loosen up, her grandfather asked a pointed question. "And just how old are you again, young man?" he asked, his eyes so fixated on Jack's that he couldn't look away.

"I'm twenty-four, sir. I'll be twenty-five in July." He swallowed some tea and looked over at Charlie.

"I see. Well, Charlotte is technically an adult now, but I'll remind you both that schooling is very important to having a successful career. You earned your degree already, Jack, and are already on your way to great success. Charlotte is just embarking on her educational journey. This trip to Paris is part of that. I gather you know long-distance relationships can be quite difficult." Felix folded his hands in front of him.

"Granddad, Jack and I are just friends. He's well aware I won't settle down until my career is underway. Isn't that right, Jack?" She looked at him with one corner of her mouth turned up in her teasing way that made his blood run hot.

"Of course. Yes. We are both far too busy right now to worry about a deeper relationship," Jack said to Felix, then turned to look at Charlie while he finished. "I just find that there isn't anyone that piques my interest quite like Charlie. She's intelligent, honest, funny. Her love of books and art... She's a great talent with her painting.

Charlie has more strength than most people I know. I admire her. And she's very beautiful."

He hadn't planned on saying all that, but it came spilling out. Charlie looked at him from her chair with her mouth slightly open, processing. Her eyes were glued to his, and if they were alone at that moment, he wouldn't be able to resist kissing her.

But they weren't.

Elsa brought them back to earth. "That's a lovely speech, Jack. So long as you both keep in mind that we fully expect Charlotte to graduate from college without any... *complications.*"

Swallowing hard and jutting his jaw, Jack took a beat before responding, but Charlie did not.

"Grandmother, we just told you we're planning to focus on our careers. The lecture isn't necessary." Then, Charlie seemed to catch herself, swallowed and looked at her grandfather. Remembering Charlie told him the man was recovering from a heart attack, Jack wanted to be careful not to upset him.

Charlie's face softened, and she smiled. "Jack and I only have today to visit before he heads back to California and I get on a plane to Paris, so if it's alright with you both, I'm going to show him around Georgetown, and we'll have dinner in the city tonight. I'll be late but will check in."

A reassuring nod from Felix with a warm smile gave the go-ahead, and Jack was relieved to have his approval. Elsa said little else before they were all standing at the doorway in the magnificent two-story foyer.

"Call no matter the time, darling, to alert us you are heading home. Remember, the alarm will be set, so you'll need to disarm it once you get inside," her grandfather reminded Charlie.

Handshakes and hugs were exchanged, and Gerty gave Jack a quick wink. He understood why Charlie liked her so much. Nothing pretentious about that woman.

❦

When they were seated in the rental car, Jack looked over at Charlie, and they both let out an exhale of relief while beaming smiles. The scrutiny was over, and they were free to leave and be alone.

Alone with Charlie.

He drove down the driveway and past the iron gate. His pulse quickened as they circled the park and drove in silence to a side street and out of town towards some open fields of tobacco. Jack's pulse thudding like a drum, he pulled the car over and threw it in park. With no other cars around, Jack undid his seat belt and turned to Charlie. His mouth landed on hers with fierce urgency, and she welcomed it. Grabbing at the front of his shirt, pulling him closer to her, Charlie allowed him to explore her mouth—warm, wet, and eager. She tasted like he'd remembered, only better, and without the fear he'd harbored from before that they were doing something wrong. Now all his desires were spilling out of him without reservation. They were finally together.

Charlie was the first to slow things down. They put their foreheads together, slowing their breathing, catching their breath.

"Wow. It's been a long time," Charlie laughed.

"Yeah. Very long."

They pulled apart, and she looked so deeply into his eyes he felt like she was crawling into his psyche. They were one in the silence of that moment. He'd never felt so connected to another human being before in his life.

"I've never seen you so clean-shaven." She stroked his face with her soft hand.

"Your hair is different. Your curls are so defined. It's always been beautiful, but it's so shiny." Jack gently touched her hair, soft and bouncy, shining like polished cherrywood.

"Well, it's amazing what money can do."

They searched each other's eyes again, cars passing periodically.

"Where do you want to go? I'll drive you anywhere. I only wish we had more than this one day. I know you have to leave the day after tomorrow. God, I'm so glad I didn't miss you!"

She sat there quietly for a moment, just stroking his cheek. Then she surprised him.

"You have a hotel room, don't you?"

He raised his eyebrows in question. "Are you sure about that?"

"Only if you are."

They drove to his hotel and left the car with the valet. Silently, Jack held her hand through the lobby and into the elevator. When they arrived at his room, Jack fumbled with the entry card. After the third try, the green light beeped, and the door unlocked. They walked in, and his curtains were open, showing the great view of Georgetown and the bridge below.

"Wow. Nice view."

"Yeah, it's not bad." He walked up behind her and wrapped his arms around her. She felt firm, thin, and shapely in the right places, which aroused Jack instantaneously.

He pushed his groin near her ass and held her that way, swaying back and forth for a moment. She turned in his arms, wrapping hers around his neck, pulling him into a deep, slow kiss. When they parted, her lips were shiny and plump, looking so erotic he couldn't help but imagine other places for her to put them on his body.

"God, I wish I'd have come sooner so we'd have more time."

"Let's just be grateful for the time we have now," she said, ever the reasonable one.

They closed the curtains and moved to the bed, kissing the whole way. She set her cell phone on the night table, and Jack did the same. They started to peel off clothes, first his shirt then hers. Lying there in her bra and drawstring linen pants, she was extremely sexy, and he tried to commit every moment to memory. He didn't want to miss a single thing. In fact, these moments felt like they were already going way too fast.

"Let's slow down. Is that okay? I don't want to rush through this. We've waited far too long." He tucked a curl behind her ear and ran his thumb down the side of her face.

Charlie propped herself up on both elbows behind her and arched forward towards him with a questioning look. "You are full of surprises, Dog Man. Okay. Slow is good."

One thing was for sure, Jack had fallen hard for Charlie. And all the months he spent with Giselle, he'd never wanted or even thought to say the words that were on the tip of his tongue now, but he was in love with Charlie. He loved her. It was completely undeniable to him now, and the only question left was what he was going to do about it.

◈

CHAPTER TWENTY-SEVEN

CHARLIE

BEING WITH JACK was all she'd thought about for so long, and now she was with him…in his hotel room. It was like a dream. With everything she'd been through, it felt like it was all worth it if she could finally find love. Someone who really loved her.

They were stripped down to their underwear and lying on the bed. Jack kept tracing her body with his fingers, talking about how beautiful she was. He kissed her neck, her collarbone, her belly button. It made her stomach quiver, and she grew wet between her legs in anticipation.

"I want to make sure you enjoy this as much as I do. I never want to hurt you, Charlie."

What did he think?

Charlie propped herself up on one elbow and faced him, running one hand through his hair. "Jack, I'm not a virgin, if that's what you're worried about."

"Huh? Oh. Okay."

He looked away for a second and seemed to be a bit flustered. Then he nodded and returned his eyes to hers, softening his gaze.

"You aren't disappointed, I hope."

"Oh, no. Not at all. I just didn't know, and…well, I wanted to do the right thing by you." He smiled at her and pulled her closer, rolling on top of her.

"I appreciate that, but you don't have to worry. I won't break. If it makes you feel any better though, I've never been with anyone I really cared about. It's never meant this much to me before."

That seemed to rev his engine, and this time when he kissed her, it was as if he was a freight train set on a destination. He was rock-hard against her thigh, and she couldn't wait any longer to feel him inside of her. She pushed him aside a minute to unfasten her bra and slip her panties off, kicking them to the side of the bed. She pulled at his briefs, and he willfully removed them. He moved into position between her legs when he hesitated, his breathing laborious.

"What about birth control? Are you taking anything?"

"No. Do you have anything?"

He nodded, grabbed his wallet from his jeans, and pulled out a condom. She was relieved because stopping now would not only have been incredibly disappointing, it would have taken superhero strength to deny their urges.

When he pushed into her, Charlie let out a whimper of ecstasy. She'd yearned for this moment for so long. Fantasized about Jack making love to her, and now he was here. His muscular body moved on top of her with such skill she felt like she was having an out-of-body experience, yet she'd never felt more *in her body* than she did at that very moment.

Her legs wrapped around his, pulling him deeper into her, and they moved in a rhythm she'd never experienced. Sex with Jack was magical, passionate, and just as she climaxed, tears spilled from her eyes. That had never happened for her before either. Sex had just been mechanical before Jack, not that she'd done it many times. Two times, to be exact, and she'd never reached orgasm. Being with Jack was like tasting food she'd never eaten. Like traveling to a land she'd never seen. He was an adventure she'd never expected.

When it was over, he lay with her, staring like he was seeing her for the first time.

"What? What it is?" Charlie propped on her side, watching his wheels turn through his eyes.

Jack smiled at her, playing with her hair. "I knew it would be great, but I can't tell you how happy I am being with you. I've wanted this for so long."

She couldn't hide her smile if she tried. "Me too. Although, I have to admit, I never really thought it would happen like this. I mean, I hoped that maybe when I got to LA we'd find each other, but…"

"But what?" He grabbed both of her hands in his, wrapped a leg around hers, and pulled her closer.

"But I figured you'd have moved on by now. Found someone, ya know?"

His body tensed, and he looked away.

"There was someone for a while. It's over now. It was never serious though."

Charlie tried to read him, but he kept darting his gaze away from hers, looking at their tangled fingers, and back again.

Was he lying?

"Are you sure? Jack?" Her stomach tensed. What if Jack had feelings for someone else? She couldn't handle lies. Honesty, no matter how painful, maybe. But lies would kill her.

He looked at her, and this time he peered deeply into her eyes. "I assure you. I'm only interested in one girl, and she's lying in this bed with me right now." Then his killer smile melted away any insecurity she had.

❧

They were famished by the time they showered. Charlie couldn't get her hair wet because the fancy product and diffuser she used to manage her insanely curly hair wasn't with her, so she highjacked the complimentary hotel shower cap, and Jack teased her the entire time. She looked ridiculous. He lathered her up, clearly enjoying rubbing bodywash all over her breasts and making them come alive beneath his hands.

"There's a great restaurant just over the bridge in Georgetown. Wanna get Italian? I hear it's amazing," Jack said, buttoning his shirt.

Charlie loved watching him dress. She could do this forever. Be with Jack. It felt so natural.

"Yessss. I'm starving. I hope I'm dressed for it though. I still hate to dress up."

"I was going to say that I love your new look, but I'd have taken you in sweats and a T-shirt any day. Do you know how incredibly beautiful you are?" Jack pulled her to him again and kissed her.

They decided to walk to dinner because it wasn't that far, and parking would be murderous. Besides, Jack said it would be romantic to walk the Francis Scott Key Bridge.

Charlie hadn't had many experiences in her life outside of Sebastopol. She visited the ocean and painted the streets at night, but beyond that, she rarely had adventures. On a few school field trips when she was younger and actually had friends, she'd gone to Alcatraz, and once to Sacramento to Sutter's Fort. Her mom had only taken her once to San Francisco. It had been a nightmare of a trip—they'd crashed at her mom's friend's house in the Haight, and Charlie had basically stayed in a corner coloring the whole time while her mother and friends did drugs and drank. She'd never even seen the sights.

Since living with her grandparents, it felt like she was living someone else's life. She hated to admit it, but they had opened doors for her, just as her grandparents had said they would. If she hadn't moved to Virginia, would she be having this experience with Jack now? And even though she was constantly at odds with her grandmother, it was tolerable because Charlie had only a short time to endure it. She'd miss her grandfather terribly once she left, but thinking about her poor mother now, Charlie could understand how that constant pressure and ridicule could have driven her to leave and follow a rock band across the country. Especially if she were in love, as Charlie suspected she was with Jack.

She was in love with Jack.

They walked across the bridge as the sun melted behind the skyline. All the lights of Georgetown were beginning to glow that amber gold, reflecting off the water of the Potomac. Once in the city, they walked a few blocks, with warm breezes caressing their skin, to Filomena's Italian Restaurant.

From the street, it looked small, but inside, a stairway took them below to a large and elaborately decorated dining space. The lamps on each table cast a reddish glow, and gold and floral decorations hung from the ceiling and on the walls. It was like being in an Italian grandmother's dining room. Waitstaff in professional black and white were at their service immediately. They asked if the two of them were celebrating anything special, and Jack immediately said yes.

"We are celebrating our anniversary."

Charlie nearly spit with laughter but managed to play along as the waiter pulled out her chair for her before Jack could. She sat and took the leather-bound menu the server offered, thanking him.

"Splendid! Would you enjoy some champagne?"

"Sure. We'd love a glass. Not a bottle though, because we have a long drive tonight," Jack explained.

"Certainly. I'll be right back."

Charlie was afraid they'd ask for her ID, but when the champagne arrived, he said nothing and gave them a minute to decide on food. The entire day was like a dream. Her life was beginning to feel like a dream. She worried that it was too good to be true and that surely something was going to screw it up any minute. The urge to go down that spiral of dread pushed at her chest, but she suppressed it with a sip of champagne and bites of calamari fritti, her new favorite food.

Through dinner, Charlie asked about Jack's life in LA since he'd left Sebastopol and teaching. He shared about shenanigans that he and his best friend, Zane, took part in at fancy parties, dune buggy races at the beach, and about his mom and how happy she was he was close by again.

"I mostly write though, every day. I work really hard and put in long hours, but I play just as hard. Here, look at this picture of me and Zane at the beach volleyball tournament a few weeks ago."

Jack leaned over and showed Charlie his buddy with blond hair all mussed from wind and sand. The two of them were all sweaty and tanned. She took his phone and started swiping sideways through his pictures. He reached across their lobster raviolis to get it back, but Charlie held it close to her chest.

"Just a second. I want to see the life and times of Jack Connors, LA style." she smirked as she scanned the pictures.

Two more were of Jack and Zane posing for the camera, but then a blonde girl with insanely blue eyes popped up, Jack next to her with his arm around her. Charlie's throat tightened as she tried to swallow her feelings.

"Well, this one doesn't look like Zane." She turned the phone around for him to see, and Jack sank in his chair, a defeated look on his face. "I take it this is the one you said you were involved with, huh?" She turned the phone around again as Jack tried once more to reach for it. "She's pretty. In a very predictable sort of LA way. What's her name?"

Jack let out an exaggerated exhale. "Giselle. Her name is Giselle, and she's total history. Like I said, it's over. Can I please have my phone back? It's not gonna do either of us any good rehashing the past."

"True…" she said but continued to swipe through more of his pictures. Giselle making a pouty face with bright, glossy lips. Giselle in a bikini. Giselle and Jack in formal wear. In between, there were some pictures of him with an older lady that had to be his mom, a few selfies he'd taken with palm trees and an outdoor bar, but...a... lot...of...pictures...of...Giselle.

She handed the phone back over the table to him. "Lots of pictures of someone you claim you weren't serious about." Her heart hurt. He had a right to have a life, and she and Jack weren't even a thing when he was seeing Giselle, so he'd been free to date whomever he pleased. Still, Charlie was seething inside and tried desperately to remain cool.

"Like I said, it was nothing really. We dated. I liked her. But she and I have a different idea of what being a couple should look like, so we ended it. Anyway, I was happier as soon as it was over. Then when I was honest with myself and realized I couldn't get you out of my mind, I came out here to find you."

He was looking at her with so much pleading in his eyes she had to give him a break. The knot forming in her stomach was loosening, and he reached for her hand, so she took it.

"I thought you said you were in New York and came to the DC area for research on another project."

He squeezed her hand. "Yeah, but what I didn't say was that the trip was a ruse just to get to see you. I'd planned the entire time to see you. I just didn't want to freak you out by saying I was obsessed with you and had to come across the country to see if there was anything still between us. I'm glad I did."

"And? What's your hypothesis on the situation?" Charlie smiled, the tension leaving her. She tickled the inside of his palm.

"There are definitely still sparks between us. I think we could have burned the whole hotel down earlier with those sparks," he admitted and laughed, making her laugh with him.

❧

They walked back, passing Federal-style brick buildings along cobble-stone streets. Holding hands, they were guided by the lights of the town and the boisterous sounds from taverns and college students living it up. On the bridge, Jack took their picture with the waterfront buildings and Potomac River behind them. He sent it to Charlie's phone then kissed her as they leaned against the railing of the walkway.

She felt like she was in some lovers' scene from a romance novel. This couldn't be her life. The life of Charlie Kane was filled with drama and pain. It almost made her feel guilty that her mom was still wading through crap back home, but as her grandparents had reminded her, Cece had to figure out what was important to her.

At the hotel, the valet brought around Jack's car. It was nine thirty. Charlie sent a text to her granddad as promised, and they started the half-hour drive back to Great Falls. When they got to the 193 in Langley, Jack pulled over to get gas.

"I'll be right back."

He ran inside to pay the attendant. Charlie pulled down the visor to look at herself in the lighted mirror when, on the center console, Jack's phone started to ring. She looked down at the screen as the phone buzzed and rang persistently. Her heart leaped into her throat when she saw the name on the screen in bold letters that burned into her retinas. GISELLE.

Holy fuck! Why was she calling him if they had broken up?

Charlie looked out the window and saw that two people were ahead of Jack in line inside the gas station store. Her hand trembled as she picked up the ringing phone. She slouched down in the seat and tapped the phone to answer the call.

"Hello?" Charlie spoke soft but clear.

At first there was no sound. Maybe Giselle had hung up before she answered the call. But then, after a second, she spoke.

"Who is this? Is this Jack Connor's phone?"

Charlie swallowed and narrowed her eyes as she stared at the dashboard. "Yes, it is. Who is this?"

"This is his girlfriend!"

Her heart slammed against her chest wall so hard the reverberation traveled up into her skull. Charlie slapped the screen with her finger to end the call and threw the phone into the cubby of the center console of the dash. Jack was standing at the pump now, selecting his fuel, when a wave of nausea rolled through her.

He'd lied!

When he got into the car, she averted her gaze, looking out her window. *He'd fucking lied!* Jack started the engine and turned to her, but Charlie couldn't look at his face. She felt like such an idiot for believing this could be real between them. That she really was special. But all of those texts between them for months…had that been real? Did he really care? She was so confused. Rage built inside of her like fire, and when he reached to touch her shoulder, Charlie snapped like a wounded animal.

"You missed a call while you were out there." Her words bit like ice.

"Huh? Who? What do you mean?" Jack reached for his phone and reviewed his recent calls. His eyes bulged out of his head when a horn beeped behind them.

"Oh shit," he mumbled and set down the phone before putting the car into drive. He steered it away from the pumps but pulled over into a parking spot on the side of the building. "What happened, Charlie?"

"Nothing except that *your girlfriend* called and wanted to chat."

"I told you, she's not my girlfriend, and what…did you *answer* my phone? You actually talked to Giselle?"

"Yeah, and she was pretty upset that a girl answered your phone. Said she was your *girlfriend* and wanted to know who the hell I was."

"Jesus Christ. What the fuck? I don't understand, but she is *not my girlfriend*, okay? And I'd appreciate it if you would just ask me and not listen to her. But…why the hell would you answer my phone anyway?"

"I was curious, okay! Your fucking ex-girlfriend calls right after we…ya know, had SEX…and I thought, if she's nothing to you, then why the fuck is she calling you at almost ten o'clock at night?"

"Well, technically, it's only nearing seven o'clock on the West Coast and—"

"Oh, cut the shit, Jack! Are you still seeing her? What exactly are we? You and me? What are we? I'd really like to know because I'm a little confused right now."

"I DON'T KNOW! I thought this was us picking things up and starting something really good. I know I only want to be with *you*, but I have to fucking work with Giselle because she works at Paramount. And I don't know why she was calling me. Maybe because she's got something to tell me about the film, or maybe because, I don't know, maybe it's not over for her, but IT IS FOR ME! Okay? I don't want to be with her. I want to be with you."

Adrenaline flooded her veins, and she grabbed him by the shoulders and made him face her in the soft glow of the parking lot lights.

"WHY? Why do you want me? My life is a mess and…what? *You work with her?* Really, Jack? Tell me why you want to be with me."

"Because…"

"Because why?" She was shaking him by the shoulders, and tears were filling her eyes.

"Because…I'm in love with you, Charlie."

CHAPTER TWENTY-EIGHT

JACK

H E'D SAID IT. It was out. He'd never said those words to a woman before, and now she knew. He wouldn't take it back if he could, but looking into her wounded eyes, Jack wasn't sure the magnitude of what those words meant to him registered with her.

"I mean it, baby. I am one hundred percent completely, utterly, madly in love with you and only you."

Her fingers that were digging into the sides of his shoulders loosened then. She pinched her lips together and turned her face away, her chin trembling. God, she was stubborn! Always had to be so damn tough.

"Jesus, say something to me, Charlie. I'm pouring my heart out to you here, and I can see that you don't believe me."

She looked at him, but her expression was threatening. He didn't know if she was going to slug him, yell at him, or kiss him.

"I can handle most anything, Jack, but lying. I have been lied to, and promised shit that never works out, my whole life. There is so much about my past you have no fucking idea about. I don't go plastering my personal shit on billboards, but I'll assure you, I've had my fair share of crap go on. I won't be lied to, so I'll give you one last chance to come clean and tell me the truth, and I'll believe you. I can handle it now, but if we continue on, and I find out you're lying, it's over. Okay?"

"Okay, what? I told you." He pulled her to him, kissing her nose then her lips. "I'm in love with you, and that's that. I'm serious. I don't know why Giselle called, and if she said she's my girlfriend, then she is lying. She was just probably upset someone else answered my phone, and she's being jealous and petty. Now, can we please stop talking about this? I don't want to ruin what's been a perfectly wonderful night."

She went slack on the passenger seat and nodded in agreement. "Fine. Let's just go."

But he knew she wasn't alright, and it was killing him. *Fucking Giselle had to call tonight?* He couldn't believe her timing after giving him the cold shoulder for so long.

"I can't drive and take you home before I know we're okay. Are we okay? Because I've never said that to anyone before, Charlie. I'm not fishing for you to say it back if you aren't ready, but you have to understand that this is a big deal for me. And yeah, I've dated some girls over the years, but I've never felt as connected with anyone as I have with you."

He was praying she believed him, but he couldn't pull her beautiful head apart to see what was going on inside. All he could do was continue to stay open and hope she'd come around.

"I believe you, Jack." She sounded exhausted, sad. "I've known some crazy jealous girls who would pull something like that. It's just… I don't know. I'm leaving for Paris. You live in Los Angeles. Maybe we got ahead of ourselves. Maybe we should have waited until we are at least in the same state, ya know?"

His heart fell. What was she saying?

"You don't want to wait for me? For us?" Jack tried to stay calm, but inside, he was freakin' out. The thought of her not being his, being with someone else, would surely destroy him. Not now, after he'd had her. Made love to her. Felt her body so intimately and tasted her. He'd go mad thinking of her not being his.

"I don't know what I'm saying. I'm confused now, and it's late. I know I care more for you than probably anyone else in the world. It's not like I have a huge fan base of people lining up wanting to be in my life. You mean everything to me, Jack, but that's why I have to protect myself. I don't think you could possibly understand."

He was getting so frustrated he was afraid he'd punch the windshield or something, but he held it together. "Understand what?" he spat.

She turned to look at him, her eyes wells of darkness pooled with anger and tears. "That I wouldn't survive the fallout of you and me if I let myself be completely consumed by you. I've only ever belonged to myself. Nobody has ever put me first. Shit, not even me until recently. I need time to trust whatever this is. Can you give me that? See how we do over these next few months. If we can handle being apart after tonight, then I'll know it's real."

"So, this is a test then? These next few months?" He wasn't sure he liked that, but what other choice did he have? "If that's what you need, then fine. It makes no difference to me. I'll still feel this way when you get back. Hell, I've felt this way for you since Sebastopol."

"Yes, but you were seeing *Giselle*. Obviously, you weren't that sure, or you weren't yet."

He ran his hands through his hair and tried not to pull it out. "Yes, but when I left, you didn't even come say goodbye at the library like we'd planned. I had no cell number for you, and you weren't on social media until months later when I found you on Instagram. If I hadn't searched for you, we wouldn't be here now! Don't you see? Even then, when I was seeing Giselle, I couldn't get you out of my mind. That should count for something."

She sat looking out the window as if contemplating what he'd said. Charlie raised one eyebrow and smirked. "You're right. And I'm probably being overly cautious about this, but please, humor me." She turned to look at him. "Let's just see where this goes and not label it until I'm living in LA. You focus on your writing, and I'll focus on my painting, until we can be together again."

He had no choice but to agree. Something inside of Jack cracked. A fissure, like the beginning of a chip in a windshield that you knew with enough bumps and jarring would grow and eventually split.

The drive back to Great Falls was excruciating. He needed more time with her. Jack drove as slowly as he possibly could, and yet time was going too fast. He held her hand the entire way back, but even then, he felt her pulling away.

Far too soon, they arrived at her grandparents' house. He was about to pull up to the gate but stopped just short of the entrance, turning off his lights.

"I can't do it. I can't let you leave like this." He squeezed both of her hands in his. "See me tomorrow. I'll come in the morning and not stay long. I know you have plans with your grandparents and packing to do, but we just didn't get enough time." It felt like he was begging, and he hated even hearing his own voice, whiny and desperate. But he *was* desperate.

Her smile was sweet in the glow of the dashboard. "It won't make it any easier." She touched his face, and he leaned into the feel of her, closing his eyes.

"It will go by fast. I'm supposed to arrive on August twenty-ninth for orientation as a freshman. I'll only be in Paris six weeks. As soon as I get to California, I'm seeing my mom, grabbing my car, and driving to LA. You will be the first person I contact. We'll stay in touch."

She leaned over and kissed him softly. He grabbed her and pulled her closer, plunging into her mouth and planting the most desperate kiss on her he'd ever given. Jack knew he had to let her fly and do her thing, or he'd regret it later when she'd grown tired of him and felt suffocated. He had to give her space, but he was dying inside.

"Okay. I understand." He pulled forward and pushed in the gate code Charlie gave him.

Parked in front of the house, they sat staring at one another, feeling the weight of the moment without speaking a word. He hoped she could see in his eyes all he was holding back. There was really nothing more he could do to convey how he felt. The ball was one hundred percent in her court now, and it was an unusual place for Jack to be in.

"I have a lot of material now to work with from this trip," he joked. "I suppose separation from the one person you desire most is what all the epic love songs and famous movies were built on."

"Yep, that was my diabolical plan all along. To make you a better writer. Glad I could help. Now, if I can only channel the same feelings into my paintings."

There still wasn't the same lightness in her that he'd felt when he'd first arrived, when they'd been at the hotel, or walking through Georgetown. The call from Giselle had put a wall between them he had to break down. Charlie's guard was up, no matter how she felt about him. Being patient wasn't Jack's strong suit, but he was determined to build her confidence in them once again. He had to.

He forced a charming smile. "This has been the best day of my life, Charlotte Kane."

She smiled a real smile for the first time since the blasted phone call. They stared at one another. She kissed him softly, then before he could protest or procrastinate any further, she got out of the car and walked away. Heartsick, he waited until he saw her safely inside, turned the car lights back on, and drove away, leaving pieces of his heart along the highway between himself and Charlie.

⁓

At the hotel bar, Jack ordered a Manhattan and stared forlornly out the window. He pulled out his phone and, without thinking it through, sent Giselle a text message, releasing his fury on her.

> *I don't know what the fuck you were thinking! You were the one who broke things off, and you had no right calling my phone and saying you are my girlfriend. Not cool, Giselle. I don't get involved in your personal business, and it sure as shit is no longer your business who I see or what I do. So, unless you have actual business to talk to me about, don't call me. You made your choice. I've been more than patient. Move on. I did.*

He sent it, and when his drink arrived, Jack downed more than half of it straightaway. He stared at his phone, waiting for retaliation to come, preparing for a fight, but Giselle didn't respond at all. No bubbles to indicate she was trying, and no return fire. Just silence.

⌇

Back in LA, he didn't have long to wait for the other shoe to drop. When Jack returned, he opened up his laptop to an email from Paramount, Corporate. The filming for *Wildflower*, scheduled for late 2011-2012, was being delayed…possibly indefinitely.

Jack looked out his bedroom window, glad he'd already cashed his check for the purchase of the literary rights to his screenplay. But he wouldn't receive any residual checks if filming didn't happen. No fanfare, no red-carpet event, and worse, unless Paramount made the film, the world would never see *Wildflower*. They owned the rights! Then, Zane's words came back to haunt him.

You piss her off, you can say bye-bye to her daddy's connections. She'll castrate you in this town, man.

He slammed the laptop closed. Maybe he had it coming, but he didn't' think so. Giselle liked power, and she was pushy and controlling about his work, but he'd never expected her to pull the rug out from under him. Was what Zane said true? Would she blackball him in the industry? Did she have that kind of power? Maybe Giselle didn't, but if she was a real daddy's girl and asked Thomas J. Baker to, he might. Jack's entire future could just have been screwed because he broke it off with the wrong girl.

CHAPTER TWENTY-NINE

CHARLIE

ARRIVING IN PARIS was like landing on another planet. The lights, the traffic, the architecture, and the language were all so hypnotic. Charlie started to understand the poetry of this place just as her teacher Mr. Ingle had described. But for all its elegance and beauty, Charlie found herself missing Jack.

After the whole debauchery of his ex-girlfriend calling, and Charlie telling Jack their relationship should be put on hold, she became more confused about him than ever. But she vowed to herself that this opportunity to study art in Paris wasn't going to be wasted on the preoccupation of her heart. She wanted to be fully immersed in this once-in-a-lifetime experience.

Her first week, she was staying at the five-star hotel Regina Louvre. It was walking distance to the Louvre and a quick taxi ride to her school, *Mosavitra – cours de dessin `a Paris*. The hotel was like a fairy tale, from the revolving door encased in highly polished wood and brass to the diamond-patterned marble floors. Elegance started in the lobby and spilled into every room. From there, Charlie had reserved an apartment she found on the Home Away website. She insisted on paying for the apartment with her own savings since her granddad had been so generous booking her the fancy hotel and paying for her tuition and other expenditures for the trip. He understood her pride in needing to pay for at least something. That one week at the hotel cost more than the entire month at the apartment.

The first day, she had nothing on her agenda, as she arrived on Saturday jet-lagged with brain fog. Still, she was in awe of the lavishness of her taupe-and-cream, high-ceilinged room, with its heavy draperies and extravagant gold-and-crystal chandelier. Champagne chilled in a crystal bucket, making her feel like royalty. She slept like a princess.

On Sunday, she was free to get acclimated. Charlie felt out of place among these Parisians, but she reminded herself that she'd likely never see any of them again. If she fumbled over her words or felt stupid with her English-to-French dictionary, she didn't care. Luckily all the hotel staff spoke English.

She started the day with a recommendation from the concierge and went to a nearby café that served chocolate croissants and rich caffe crema, just like Mr. Ingle had talked about. Charlie found out this coffee drink was actually Italian, but who was keeping score? Not Charlie. It was like black silk, smooth and rich, with clouds of creamy heaven, and although she'd never tell Michael and Teri, it was easily the best coffee she'd ever had.

July sunlight in Paris was like a party mixed with fairy dust and splashed with the lightest scented perfume. She strolled without a timetable to the nearby Place de la Concorde, one of the most famous city squares in Paris. She marveled at its fountains, statues, and magnificent Ferris wheel. She was fascinated to learn this was also where the French Revolution's guillotine executions had taken place. YIKES! She walked cobblestoned roads, past colorful flower beds of larkspur, tulips, and water lilies in Jardin des Tuileries. Charlie could almost hear her own personal themed French music as birds sang above like something from out of a Disney movie. While indulging in ice cream, she walked the Champs-Élysées, a long avenue famous for its shops, cafés, and theaters. She hadn't even had lunch yet, but there were no rules. Shamelessly devouring the blackberry cream, Charlie wondered how anyone ever left this place. And she was just getting started.

She stopped for a late lunch at a little red-and-white restaurant called Café Dalayrac, where she sat outside in a courtyard sheltered by a wrought iron awning. Charlie chose a familiar dish, Caesar salad, but it was more delicious than any salad in America, then she headed back to her hotel. Exhausted, but elated from her day, she kicked off her shoes and flopped onto the expensive duvet on her perfectly soft, yet supportive, bed and fell asleep.

She woke almost three hours later and looked at the time. Cece would be phoning shortly for her weekly Sunday call. It was almost six o'clock in Paris, so in California, it would be ten o'clock in the morning. Charlie hopped up and walked to the balcony doors. She threw them wide open, revealing her spectacular view of the Eiffle Tower and the twinkling lights of the Place de la Concorde Ferris wheel. She headed outside just as her phone began to buzz. The breeze blew Charlie's hair back, and sounds from the street below floated up to her like notes of a flute.

Cece would be blown away by all this.

"Mom?" Charlie leaned against the railing.

"Hey, babygirl! Momma's only got four more months to go, not that I'm counting. Tell me everything. What's Paris like? Don't forget to send me a postcard of the Eiffle Tower," she laughed.

A lump formed in Charlie's throat, and tears sprang to her eyes, her chest tight.

"Mom, it's…" She gasped over the sob that threatened to erupt into an emotional spillway. "It's amazing! More than I ever dreamed. I'm actually here."

Cece stayed silent for a moment then quietly said, "I knew it would be, baby. You are living your dream, just like I told you to. I'm so proud of you."

❧

Sitting in her first sketching class at *Mosavitra – cours de dessin `a Paris,* Charlie looked around the room at the other students. Some were old, some middle-aged, and some were as young as their thirties. Charlie was the youngest. She was one of ten sitting in wait, facing an empty chair in a room with white-tiled floors and plain, cream-plastered walls. They were waiting for their subject. This was a figure drawing class, and the instructor, Madame Dubois, had just informed them that today they were doing a life drawing exercise. Their subject was Jean-Claude.

Jean-Claude? Really?

Charlie kept telling herself this was Paris, and this was art. She swallowed her discomfort, knowing the guy would be nude, and began checking her pencils. She had graphite, non-graphite, and charcoal all ready to go. Someone opened one of the interior doors, and Charlie glanced up. A godlike creature in a white robe stood before them. He was tall, like Jack, but he had blond, shaggy hair, a clean-shaven face, and when he looked at her, his eyes were jade green. His chiseled jawline and high cheekbones were bronzed from the sun, and when he dropped his robe, she took a deep breath that was noticed by Madame Dubois.

"You will be capturing the lines, contours, shapes, and angles." Madame circled around Charlie and placed one hand on her shoulder as if to steady her before walking towards the next student.

Jean-Claude stood, staring beyond them at the back wall, while Madame continued to talk. As Charlie was admiring his sculped chest, carved abs, muscular thighs, and impressive... *Oh my God...* She looked back to his face, and to her embarrassment, he was staring directly at her. Jean-Claude kept a straight face, but in that very moment, she saw a small twitch in the corner of his mouth and one eyebrow raise slightly.

He took a seat in the padded chair and hooked one heel to the underside rung, leaning into the back of the chair with one arm draped across his raised thigh. His other hand was on his hip, elbow bent. For the remaining seventy-five minutes, Jean-Claude didn't look at Charlie. Once she got over the shock of his model good looks, Charlie found her pencil gliding and tried to listen to the thickly accented words Madame uttered throughout the seemingly lightning-fast class.

"You can use an overhand grip. Use the whole arm while sketching," Madame reminded them.

When the class was over, Charlie ducked out quickly, grabbing an iced tea before heading to her digital drawing class. It was amazing what technology could do, and she tried so hard to focus on what Monsieur Moreau was saying, but she found herself giggling about the absurdity that her first nude model was both male and ridiculously perfect. Her mother would have said something highly inappropriate for sure.

A few days passed, and Charlie had attended all five of her courses over three days. She had class Monday through Wednesday, and the rest of the week off. One of the girls in her watercolor class was chatty, buddying up to Charlie, and made her laugh a lot. Her name was Daphne. She was twenty-two, from London, and her only agenda was having fun.

Daphne was staying in an apartment with two sisters that she claimed were boring as hell. They didn't drink, didn't smoke, were very studious, and never went out dancing. She said they were like watching paint dry.

"I just need someone to cut loose with once in a while. Shit, we are in *Paris* for God's sake! Not some bloody boarding school. Wanna come to a club with me tonight, Chuck?" Daphne had taken to calling her Chuck right away. She said all her friends eventually got nicknames from her, and she liked Charlie.

With nothing else to do, Charlie agreed. The drinking age in

Paris was eighteen, but even if she wasn't a big drinker, it made her happy that she was old enough to go wherever Daphne wanted to hang. It felt really good to have an actual girlfriend to talk with for a change. It had been a really long time since she'd had one, and Charlie was in desperate need of real fun.

Like polar opposites, Daphne was small, about five-foot-two, and had short, pixie strawberry-blonde hair with blue-dyed tips. Next to Charlie's five-ten stature and long dark hair, Daphne seemed like a sprite. They hit it off immediately, Daphne talking nonstop like one of the Gilmore Girls from television. Her energy was infectious.

They met in the lobby of Charlie's hotel. "Jesus-H-Christ, Chuck! You are staying in the freakin' Taj Mahal of Paris here. Fancy shit." Daphne plucked a complimentary buttermint out of a bowl that sat on a table of flowers and bottled waters before they walked outside into the warm Parisian evening.

The dazzling lights of the Ferris wheel, the Eiffel Tower, and city streetlights, and the hum of the traffic, peppered them with excitement. Daphne looped an arm through Charlie's, and off they strolled along the inky-dark Seine, giggling with anticipation.

They danced in tight quarters at The Velvet Bar, with neon lights and the pulsing beats of hip-hop. Charlie's hair stuck to her neck and face as she sweated in her tank top and jeans. They wandered outside for air, and Daphne dragged Charlie, laughing and giddy, to another spot called Le Klub. They dipped into the underground stone cellar below the city for blazing rock music, and Charlie tried a cosmopolitan for the first time. The liquor went straight to her head. She could barely see the band because of the crowd, but as the sea of bobbing bodies parted, Charlie got a glimpse of the guitar player and almost tripped over her own feet.

It was Naked God Man. Jean-Claude, the model from her figure sketching class.

"Holy shit!" She quickly looked away from the band, and Daphne caught on that something was up.

Looking around Charlie to the stage, Daphne smiled like the Joker. "You know that guy? He's fucking hot, Chuck! I'd shag the hell outta that for sure."

"No! I don't know him. I sketched him though. He's the model from my class," Charlie shouted over the wailing music.

"You've seen the guitar player naked?" Daphne yelled just as the song was finishing, and heads snapped towards them.

Charlie's face grew hot as she nodded yes to Daphne, and they both burst out laughing as they made a beeline to the bar. Her throat parched, Charlie ordered water just as the band took a break. She was throwing back the ice water when Daphne's breath caught and she pulled at Charlie's arm, her head motioning behind her. Charlie spun around, and Hot Model Guy was standing right there with a toothy smile. His sexy jade eyes stared at her with a familiar look.

"We meet again," he said in a thick French accent. "Although we didn't actually meet, maybe we should since you've already seen me naked." That same eyebrow raised at her like it had momentarily in class, and Charlie just knew she was turning a dark shade of red.

"Um…Charlie. My name is Charlie."

She didn't offer him her hand, but he arrogantly took it anyway and pulled it up to his mouth, kissing it with his full, warm lips. "*Bonjour*, Charlie. America, yes?"

She felt a tug in her solar plexus then gently pulled her hand away, wrapping it safely around her glass. Not even in Paris for one week, and already she felt the beginning of an enormous complication.

His bandmate handed him a beer and pointed towards the stage.

"I must leave, but it was lovely to meet you, Charlie. I'll be seeing you Monday, I suppose." Jean-Claude looked so intently into her eyes she felt hypnotized by him. "Anyway, I know *you* will be seeing *me*," he added then winked at her. "*Au revoir*, America." He left her standing next to Daphne, who immediately started to squeal like a mouse.

As the music started up again, she could feel Jean-Claude's stare from across the crowded room, and it made Charlie laugh out loud. The nerve of this guy. She reminded herself she couldn't afford a distraction like Hercules, The Guitar Player. She told Daphne it was time to go. It was all fun and games until someone got hurt, so while they were all still having fun, Charlie decided to call it a night.

Later in her room with the sounds of the city below, Charlie thought of Jack. She loved him, but she wasn't so sure he wasn't going to break her heart. Then she lay worrying about her mother in jail and her grandfather and his health, and with all the preoccupation, her precious sleep eluded her. She got up and turned on a lamp, pulled out her sketch pad, and before she knew what she was drawing, a perfect likeness of Jack materialized on the paper, completely from memory. It pulled at her heart. He'd kept his promise not to pressure her and only sent texts every other day, ending each by saying he loved her. His texts lifted her spirits, but she still hadn't said it back, even though it was true. When sleep finally arrived, she dreamed of painting, sitting overlooking the ocean from a house on a bluff. It felt safe and familiar, like somewhere she truly belonged.

❧

That Sunday, Charlie was getting prepared to check out of Hotel Regina Louvre and move over to her apartment near the Seine. Daphne was more than happy to accompany her, and after she saw the view of the water from Charlie's apartment, the streaming light from the huge windows, and the fantastic little French bakeries, restaurants, and shops just downstairs, she half-jokingly said, "Christ, Chuck, you're bloody brilliant to find this place. I could move right in and never leave here."

Charlie invited Daphne to stay a few nights a week. Daphne could sleep on the couch. The apartment was small but had everything she needed, and the convenience of its location near the school was perfect. Daphne started staying over on nights they didn't have class the next morning. They bought takeout, went to some parties, and Jean-Claude stopped pressing to get to know Charlie better when she lied and said she was gay and in a relationship with Daphne. This baffled Daphne, and she questioned why Charlie wouldn't want to go after such a hot piece of ass, but when she explained that obstacles and barriers like Jean-Claude would only keep her from following her own heart, it seemed Daphne understood. They were becoming great friends, and it was a relief to finally have someone who truly liked her for who she was. No expectations, no pressure, just acceptance of exactly who she was. Charlie had never felt so comfortable in a friendship as she did with Daphne. It was just easy.

Then her luck ran out.

In her second week in the apartment, Charlie got a phone call that fulfilled the dreaded prophecy of her never sustaining good fortune. On a Wednesday, as she was returning from her Art Appreciation Class at The Louvre where her instructor Madame Girard hosted their weekly education on the great artists during different periods in history, Charlie was on a high. She floated upstairs to her perfect Parisian apartment after the perfect summer day when her phone rang.

It was Gerty.

Like a heavy stone thrown to the bottom of a well, Charlie's stomach sank. Her throat constricted as she sat down slowly on the overstuffed sofa. The light spilled in through the row of huge windows overlooking the Seine. She knew the moment she answered this call she'd have to say goodbye to all of this. The phone buzzed loudly in her hand. She answered.

"Gerty?"

A small exhale came through the phone before Gerty spoke. "My darling girl, I'm so sorry, but you are needed back home. It's your grandfather. He's passed."

⚘

CHAPTER THIRTY

CHARLIE

DAPHNE OFFERED TO fly home with her.

"You have quickly become more like family to me than my actual family," Daphne choked out. "I want to be there for you."

Charlie didn't see the use in both of them missing out on the last few weeks of art school, and since the apartment was already paid for, she turned it over to Daphne to enjoy. "No. You have to finish what you started here."

"I won't feel good about this, Chuck, knowin' that you are back in the States grieving your granddad and dealing with a funeral. It's just too generous."

Pressing the big skeleton keys into Daphne's hand and rolling it shut with her own, Charlie looked teary eyed into her sweet friend's cornflower-blue eyes. "I need you to do this for me, Daph. I need to know one of us is still here finishing our courses and loving every minute of being in Paris."

They hugged and wiped their eyes, sniffling and smiling weakly through the discomfort. Charlie didn't know what she'd have done if she were all alone to receive the news that her beloved grandfather had left this world, and she hadn't even gotten to say goodbye.

Daphne had arrived at the apartment shortly after Charlie got the news, finding her sitting almost comatose on the sofa, still holding her phone and staring out the windows at boats on the Seine. Now hours later, Daphne had gotten her fed, gave her a couple of shots of tequila, and helped her pack her bags. She had a flight the next day.

"What should I do with those?" Charlie asked. Propped against the brick wall were canvases that Charlie had painted during her stay.

"I'll get it sorted. I'll ship them to you." Daphne gave her arm a squeeze and motioned for them to sit down together. "You know, I wasn't looking for a relationship when I came here, Chuck. I got online and booked a room with those depressing sisters who wouldn't know a good time if it bit them on the ass, but I found you. Who needs a man when you can find your soulmate in a sister from another mister? I love ya, Chuck. I hit the bloody jackpot when you walked into my watercolor class. We've had some fucking great times, you and me. And even though you totally botched that opportunity to sleep with Prince Long-Dong, depriving me of living vicariously through you, I still respect your values."

Charlie was laughing now, her nose running and tears streaming from sadness and such gratitude for her quirky, funny friend. Daphne put one arm around Charlie, and they flopped back against the sofa, Daphne's head resting on Charlie's shoulder. "That Jack must really be something," Daphne said.

The next morning, Charlie took a taxi to the airport, saying goodbye to the best and only friend she felt she had in the world. Somewhere over the Atlantic, the crushing reality of her immense loss and life without her grandfather hit her. She locked herself in the airplane bathroom until she could breathe again.

❧

The service was held in the historic Saint Catherine of Siena Church. The white arched columns of the cathedral with its high polished floors were as impeccably refined and aesthetically pleasing as her grandfather Felix had been. People showed up in droves, a sea of suits and ties and designer dresses, with hats, pearls, and diamonds galore. Charlie sat in the front row, fidgeting with the buttons on her black Anne Taylor dress, feeling slightly nauseated and detached. Her grandmother Elsa, and an uncle she'd never met named Alfred, who was Felix's younger brother, sat in the front while Gerty was directly behind Charlie, touching her shoulder periodically for support. Heartbreakingly, Cece was unable to attend.

Afterwards, they traveled to the cemetery, where folks gathered graveside, and another tapestry of words were woven about the life of Felix Kane, and about eternity. The heat and humidity of the day formed droplets of perspiration under Charlie's dress, making her not only want to peel off her clothes but shed her skin as well. The whole experience felt otherworldly, and she didn't hear a single word that was spoken. It felt like she was underwater.

Elsa was quieter than Charlie had ever remembered. In fact, her grandmother barely said two words to her in a day, shutting herself off in her room, or sitting for hours in her late husband's office, just staring. From the time Charlie arrived back home to the day of the funeral, Gerty had been the one to console Charlie, to sit with her, the one who told her the sad details of her grandfather's sudden demise. He'd died instantly from his second heart attack, falling face down at his desk.

She should feel sorry for her grandmother, but Charlie couldn't help but feel the woman had had something to do with his stress. Still, she could almost hear her grandfather saying to her, *"Make your granddad proud, my dear. Be the best version of yourself. Your grandmother means well."* It was hard to find anything redeemable about the woman, but she was her grandmother, and like it or not, they were the only family each of them had at this time.

When the last guest left their house after a largely catered reception, Gerty was helping the waitstaff clean up and Charlie found her grandmother sitting alone in the atrium. She sat surrounded by countless arrangements of flowers with condolence notes attached, including some from Jack, which touched Charlie's heart. He'd wanted to fly out to support her, but Charlie had declined his offer. She'd only fall completely apart if she saw him.

Elsa stared blankly out through the glass into the early evening. The backyard was lit up by strung lights and fireflies dancing in the trees. Her face was slack, her eyes devoid of light, like she was a ghost, a shell of herself. Charlie felt a pang of guilt. Maybe Elsa loved her grandfather more than Charlie gave the woman credit for. She sat down next to her on a rented folding chair brought in for the occasion.

"Forty-eight years we were together," Elsa whispered, still looking out the glass windows of the atrium to the night beyond. "I have no idea what to do without Felix. I've always been his wife. Now…" The end of her sentence hung in the climate-controlled room, suspended until it vanished like a puff of smoke.

Charlie slowly rested a hand over her grandmother's knotted ones, twisted together in her lap. This touch seemed to awaken Elsa, and she turned to look at Charlie. The corners of her mouth strove for a smile but fell short. "The reading of your grandfather's will is this Monday," Elsa said. "Our attorney has requested that you attend. Felix loved you very much, you know."

A fresh batch of tears pooled in Charlie's eyes, threatening to spill over. She nodded her understanding and squeezed her grandmother's hands. "I loved him too." Charlie stood up in her too-tight heels that she knew she'd never wear again. "Is there anything I can do for you?"

Elsa looked her in the eyes and gave a small smile. "Just be here. That's all." Charlie gave a tired smile back, nodding, then turned to leave. Walking away, she heard Elsa say, "And Charlotte?"

She stopped and turned back in question, raising her eyebrows. "I really only wanted what I thought was best…for everyone."

Nodding again, Charlie looked down, still unable to address the weight of what that entailed, but she didn't argue. "I know grandmother." She walked away, too tired for more.

∽

He'd left her everything. All his stocks, his generational wealth of his family's fortune, and even the house, once Elsa passed, were all to be Charlie's. A trust had been set up in her name. She could access some of it immediately, and then more upon her twenty-fifth and thirtieth birthdays. Elsa had her own money he'd set aside for her that would be more than enough to keep her in the lifestyle for which she was accustomed, but she wasn't able to will any of it to anyone else. Cece had her own smaller trust that would definitely give her a higher standard of living, but she had to go to counseling and rehab in order to receive it. Charlie could understand that. As for Gerty, as long as Elsa needed her, she was guaranteed a job, and Felix had also gifted her one hundred thousand dollars. She cried when the attorney read this aloud.

There was a sealed letter Felix had written for Charlie in the event of his death. The attorney handed it to her after the reading, as well as one for Elsa, and one for Cece that she'd receive as soon as she was released from jail. When the driver brought them all home from the attorney's office, Charlie went upstairs to her room to read her letter alone.

With the door closed, she tapped the letter nervously and looked outside at the pool and outdoor entertainment area below. Visions of them swimming for his therapy, her granddad joking, comparing himself to a stork trying to swim like a frog, clouded her vision. More tears welled up as she carefully opened the envelope.

My darling Charlotte,

If you are reading this, then my time has come. I feel immensely blessed to have finally gotten the opportunity to know you and have you come to know a little more about me. My greatest regret is that we didn't spend enough time together sooner. For that, I'm afraid your grandmother and I are to blame. Try not to be too hard on your mother.

Having said that, remember you make your own path in this life. It is in the choices you make with what you are given that alters the course of your life. Choose wisely, my dear. Use both your head and your heart. I trust you to do both.

As for your grandmother, please understand that she only has your very best interests at heart. When she's hard on you or being stubborn, it comes from a place of trying to protect you from the cruel reality that others are always watching and, yes, judging. Do not let this stop you from being who you truly are. I admire your tenacity and your fierce determination.

But remember, my darling, that no one does anything in this life completely alone. Not even me. Although I made a name for myself, my family gave me my start. I am now giving you one too.

With your good heart, talent, and intellect, I've no doubt of your capabilities. A fortune is only worth something if you create something to offer. Be of service, remain humble, and create your art. You are a remarkably gifted artist, Charlotte, and I have every faith you will put your talents to good use.

Please look after your grandmother for me. I fear she will take my leaving hard. She may seem strong on the outside, but she's soft on the inside and will need you to remind her of her own strength. I know you will be up to the task of encouraging her. And your mother Cecelia is my fiery daughter with enormous potential.

Please remind her that second chances are for learning to live a better life. I hope she finds that.

You have brought me great joy in the time we've spent together, and being with you has shined a bright light on this old man's life. Continue to shine, my dear, and always know how very special you are.

With all my love,

Granddad

As she finished reading, tears streamed down her face. Charlie clutched the letter to her chest, brokenhearted that just when she was coming to love the only father figure she'd ever had, he'd left. She reread the letter three times and let his words sink in. He really had faith in her. He'd left her his entire life's fortune. Not to some organization, not to her mother, but to her.

Gathering her strength, her tears drying up, Charlie wrestled with what she could do to make this man proud of her. She would get her degree in both business and art. She knew he would expect her to be the top of her class. But the best feeling of all was that her grandfather had actually seen her. He'd understood her, or at least really tried to. That was a far cry better than what she'd expected given all the stories her mother had shared, although Cece was right on the money about her grandmother. Elsa was a piece of work. But Felix seemed to have learned a hard lesson in losing his daughter and hadn't wanted to repeat the mistake with Charlie.

Charlie got up and walked around the room. She was a millionaire. *A fucking millionaire!* And the strangest thing of all was that she didn't feel different. She stood in her lavish bedroom and lived in a mansion, so of course she was different in what she'd become accustomed to. But on the inside, Charlie was the same person. She might have started to really enjoy the nicer things in life, but she still wasn't about to judge others harshly like her grandmother and her old friends did. Charlie was going to pride herself on staying honest, grounded, and do as her granddad had told her to do. Remain true to herself.

❧

On her last day before flying to California, the paintings she'd made in Paris arrived. Daphne had followed through on her promise, and something in Charlie's chest ached so badly for her friend she could hardly breathe. It seemed all those she loved were beyond reach.

Later, Charlie and her grandmother sat in the light-filled sitting room opposite each other, the same room where Charlie had introduced Jack to her grandparents. A lump formed in her throat, remembering Felix sitting next to where Elsa was now, only he was gone. She got up and went to sit next to her grandmother, feeling the push of her grandfather's spirit.

"Grandmother? You are going to have to be strong while I'm away. You know how I can get. I'll be calling and bossing you around to get your ass out with those auxiliary women to do fundraising and go to fancy hundred-dollar luncheons. If you don't, I'll be forced to leave school, risk being kicked out, and fly home to kick you right in the butt. You know how that would piss granddad off. I'm meant to be the top of my class, so please make sure I don't have to do that." She smiled at her poised, proper grandmother who was learning in the last few weeks to loosen up and indulge Charlie's colorful language. If they were to have any sort of relationship, Elsa was going to have to remove the stick that was up her ass. And now that Charlie knew her grandmother hadn't originally come from money, there was no excuse for Elsa to be snobby. Even if they didn't discuss it openly yet, Charlie planned to wear her down.

Elsa looked up into Charlie's eyes with tears forming and a small smile on her face. "I understand. But watch your language, young lady. I'm still your grandmother." She took Charlie's hands and gave her a playful slap.

With her bags packed, Charlie stood in the foyer, feeling slightly sick to her stomach. She'd always planned to leave, but now that she really was, she found it hard to go. Even knowing all that waited for her in California, leaving the stability of this home and her connection to her grandfather tugged at her heart.

While Charlie tearfully hugged Gerty goodbye, Jason, the driver, took her bags, and Charlie was left standing in front of Elsa, searching for the right thing to say. Just when she opened her mouth to speak, Elsa spoke first.

"I've made a decision." Elsa took her hands and looked up at Charlie's surprised face. "I don't like you always calling me Grandmother. Sounds too stuffy. Afterall, you at least called Felix Granddad. I think I should be Grandma. Is that better?"

Charlie laughed. There might actually be hope for their relationship after all. "Grandma it is. I like that better too. Or I could call ya Granny."

"Don't push it." Elsa hugged her and walked her to the door.

Waving goodbye from the back seat of the black Mercedes, Charlie took a deep breath and watched the house that had seemed ominous when she'd first arrived fade into the tree line. Somewhere along the line it became home, and she knew she'd always return there.

By the time she arrived in San Francisco, the sky was turning pink and lavender. A driver that Gerty had arranged for her picked Charlie up to take her the hour and a half to her old bungalow in Sebastopol, where the light was still on in the window and the memories of a life she used to have felt like someone else's.

Her Volkswagen Beetle was still in the driveway with a film of dust across it. Her mother's red Mazda sat there as if she were inside just waiting for Charlie's return, but upon using her key, there was no one home. The smell of old carpeting and stale air hit her at the door. Their old ratty wingback chair, coffee table with the huge ashtray, and sad, saggy couch reminded her of a movie set or some staged room at a museum depicting her past life. The ancient, yellow-and-orange wallpapered kitchen was clean. The hum of the white refrigerator, the empty dish drainer on the counter, it all seemed like they were from some daydream.

There was a soft knock on the door. Charlie set her bags down in front of her old room and went to look out the window. Their neighbor Joan Taylor stood at the door with a casserole dish.

"I saw the car drop you off and couldn't believe my eyes. You look so beautiful and grown up. Are you home for good now?" Joan half hugged her and held the casserole dish in her other arm.

"Only for a day or two. I'm going to see my mom then drive down to school. I start at UCLA in a week."

Charlie filled her in briefly but promised to come by the next day to tell her more. She was exhausted and ready for bed. Joan obliged and handed her the dinner she'd made of meatloaf and mashed potatoes with green beans, one of Charlie's favorites from when Joan had cooked for her before. It seemed like an eternity ago now, everything that transpired here in this house. Charlie felt older. She certainly was wiser.

With a full belly and dressed in her pj's, Charlie opened her bedroom window and lay on the worn quilt of her double bed inside her childhood room. With the lights off, she lay thinking of all that this house had witnessed over the years. Charlie could hear the echoes from past arguments, the far-off laughter of her mother when things had been good and the screams from when they'd been bad. Once Cece got out of jail, she'd no longer have a use for this place since she'd be able to buy her own house with the inheritance money. These next few nights were the last times Charlie would ever be in this house.

The next day, after running her Bug through a car wash and

filling the tank, Charlie went to the jail and said goodbye to her mom. They shed tears because of Felix, and without giving too much away, she told her mother that their ship had come in. Charlie knew better than to discuss the money in any detail at the jail, but Cece got the hint.

"All those times I told you to get your shit straight and not screw up in school, I knew what I was talking about, didn't I? I told ya your grandparents would take care of ya if you just stuck it out. Maybe I wasn't such a screwed-up mother after all, hey, baby?"

Charlie gave her mother a smirk then took an exaggerated look around the room. "Uh...Mom. Where exactly are we having this discussion?" She was teasing but getting her point across too.

"Yeah, yeah. I know. Maybe I was a slow learner, but I'm better now. Wait til I get outta here. You are gonna see a new and improved Cece."

Charlie could only hope.

The last night at the house where Charlie used to climb out of the window at night to go painting with The Guerrillas, she pulled a long canister out from the back of her closet that held her stencils she used to use on the streets. Her signature girl unraveled out of the cylinder. It was her insignia, her stamp, that let everyone know Star was the one who created the piece. Star, her street name so no one would know her real name. Star, after her favorite wildflower the star lily, or *Leucocrinum montanum*. She rubbed her upper back near her shoulder blade where her tattoo was.

Jack had been so intrigued by it when he'd first realized she had a tattoo. She could remember that conversation like it was yesterday and could still see the light in his eyes at her description of why she loved wildflowers. He'd been fascinated by her answer, and she loved that. She loved that he listened. *She loved Jack.*

Lying in the darkness now, with the soft sound of a hoot owl outside, Charlie contemplated what Los Angeles had in store for her. She had a school to navigate, a grandfather to make proud, a father to find, and Jack to decide about. Was he really going to want her, or was he torn between her and that platinum-blonde Barbie doll? The walls were still up around her heart. She'd put them back as soon as that phone call had come in from Giselle. Now that she was in California, was it too late? Charlie worried her fears would come to fruition, and she'd find that Jack had grown tired of her.

She turned on her side, feeling the frayed edge of the pastel quilt her mother had bought her years ago at a yard sale. How many nights had she cried herself to sleep on it? Her breathing slowed to a soft purr, and like a cloak of velvet, the sweet slumber that she always counted on to quiet her mind pulled her down into a river of peace. The only true freedom she'd ever known was sleep.

CHAPTER THIRTY-ONE

JACK

AS HARD AS he tried to focus on his current work in progress, Jack wondered what the hell Giselle had done to him. It was difficult to know whether she'd been behind *Wildflower* failing to launch or not, but the timing was suspicious. He was curious if Richie would even take a pitch meeting with him now for his new screenplay. Wrapping his hands behind his neck as he sat at his laptop, Jack's focus spun all over the place.

He hadn't been eating or sleeping well either. Between fears about his career and worries about him and Charlie, Jack was beginning to look like a homeless man, unshaven, hair mussed. He lived in the same sweatpants and T-shirt for days at a time.

With weeks passing at a glacial pace, visions of Charlie walking through Paris and kissing other men on moonlit bridges, or beneath the Eiffel Tower, haunted him. Or worse, his nightmares of some Parisian hunk rolling around in the sheets with her, touching her milky skin, tasting her body as he had. Jack's mind was searing hot with frustration.

"What the fuck is up with you, man? Stop letting these women lead you around by your dick!" Zane said, lecturing him a few weeks after the Giselle-Paramount fallout, thinking that was the main culprit of Jack's funk. "Get back out there, man. Whatever happened with Giselle, and then that Sebastopol chick you say you saw in Virginia... *get over it.* You are Jack-fuckin'-Connors! You sold your first screenplay to Paramount Studios, and your best friend is an incredible specimen, a godlike stud, who directs and produces indie films. Your life is golden." Zane smiled brightly, puffing his chest out. "Life is good, my friend. Now go take a shower and put something else on. I can't stand to see you like this anymore. We are going out."

Circulating again on the end-of-summer party circuit in the land of the rich and famous, Jack started to lift his head up. There didn't seem to be any rumors floating around about him, *Wildflower,* or even his breakup with Giselle. Nobody cared. Feeling foolish that he'd spent so much time sulking and fearing the gossip mill of the industry, Jack conceded that Zane was probably right. He had to get his shit together and reclaim his own power. He dove headfirst back into making connections at every party and event he could, saying yes to each invitation he got.

He tried to ignore the fact that Richie Lamont hadn't invited him to his annual Labor Day weekend bash. Everyone was talking about it coming up, and yet Jack hadn't received an e-vite in his emails, nor an actual invitation in the mail. Not that he and Richie had ever been that chummy anyway, but it did sort of make Jack's fear of being an outcast for life bubble up and try to suffocate him. He swallowed it like a bitter pill, tamping it down until he could feign indifference, and moved on to other things to look forward to.

Then Jack was surprised, receiving an invitation to attend the premiere of *Captain America.* It was a red-carpet event for Paramount, and he had no idea how he was on the list. Regardless, he did a happy dance through the apartment after opening the fancy invitation with gold foil. He took his mother, Rita, instead of a date, keeping his vow to stay true to Charlie. His mother was over the moon, squealing with delight at the prospect of seeing movie stars up close.

But once again, while Jack's life was beginning to shine up like a new penny, Charlie's took a spiraling downward turn. She'd text him from Paris to say her grandfather Felix had passed, and she was devastated. Immediately, Jack offered to fly to Virginia to attend his funeral with her, but she promptly said no. Flat out no, and wouldn't discuss it.

Please don't come. I fear I'll fall apart if I see you right now, and there is so much I have to focus on.

She'd text him the day she was flying home, sitting in the airport. He felt like a total shit because deep down his insides were smiling at the thought of her leaving France and coming back to the States. Outwardly, he couldn't even admit to himself that he was feeling this kind of relief. What did that say about him? She'd just lost her grandfather! But knowing Charlie was that much closer to coming back to him felt like subtle champagne bubbles of joy rising through his body. He didn't tell anyone he felt like this. He just secretly acknowledged it, allowing it to lift him up.

He sent flowers to both Charlie and her grandmother Elsa. A tasteful gesture to let Charlie know he was there with her in spirit. Jack took every opportunity to let her know how much he cared about her, hopefully without suffocating her. Giving her space was like trying to split atoms. It felt impossible.

But the movie premier took his mind off Charlie. His mother, Rita, wore a plum-colored Debra Kerr-esque number, with a chiffon top and scarf that was sewn onto the neckline, draping over both shoulders and running down the back. It was floor length and elegant. She looked like a 1950s movie star.

"Mom, you look gorgeous." Jack beamed.

He ordered a limo to pick them up from his mother's house. Jack went all out, taking her to dinner first at Shirley Brasserie's, inside the Hollywood Roosevelt Hotel, then pouring them more champagne in the limo. Their laughter and rapid chatter made them seem like teenagers.

As they approached the theater, Rita grew nervous. "What do we do? Oh my God, is my hair still pinned right?" She fussed, touching her head.

"Relax. No one will care that we've arrived. Once they realize we aren't A-listers, photographers will jump to another limo."

Rita set her hand on Jack's and gave him a pointed look. "Honey, you are important too. You were invited to this incredible evening. That means something."

Jack didn't have the heart to tell his mother that lots of people who weren't well known, or ever would be, attended these things. Still, she was right in that *somebody somewhere* at Paramount thought of inviting him, but who?

Just as he described, photographers swarmed them momentarily as they got out of the limo, then promptly moved onto the next one. His mother was oohing and aahing over seeing Samuel L. Jackson and Stanley Tucci, but when she spotted Tommy Lee Jones, Jack had to hold her up, she was shaking so much. They'd entered the theater and were just inside when Jack found himself standing right next to the iconic actor. Taking a leap of faith, Jack tapped Tommy Lee on the shoulder and told him what a huge fan his mother Rita Connors was. Being ever-gracious, Mr. Jones beamed a smile at her and kissed her hand. It was the highlight of her night.

After the Marvel Comic movie credits rolled and speeches were made, there was an after-party. A hive of actors and their families, along with industry people, buzzed around in flashy clothes, carrying sparkly glasses filled with liquid encouragement. Jack looked up and saw Richie Lamont strolling his way. Jack quickly swallowed his champagne and smoothed his shirt.

"Jack it's great of you to come. Enjoying yourself?"

"Uh, yes. Absolutely. I was surprised by the invitation, but my mother and I are having a fantastic time." Jack raised his glass to Richie. "Oh, Richie Lamont, please meet Rita Connors, my mother."

Richie took her hand in his, and Rita was smiling her pearly whites at the big-time movie exec. "Pleased to meet you, Rita. You must be proud of your son. He's a helluva writer."

She blushed and then turned to Jack. "Oh, yes. I'm so very proud of him. Of course, Jack has always excelled at whatever he sets out to do."

"Well, get used to this sort of thing," Richie chimed. "Because next year you will be attending one of these for his own script."

Jack furrowed his brow, confused. "Pardon me?"

Richie looked perplexed at Jack, smiling oddly. "For *Wildflower*, of course."

His head started spinning. He pulled at his collar. "But uh… what about the email that went out saying filming was going to be delayed, possibly indefinitely?"

"*What?*" Richie spoke a little too loudly. Those nearby turned to look a moment, and then he lowered his voice. "What the hell are you talking about?"

"I got an email a few weeks back saying just that. It was from Paramount. Had the logo and email address from the office. I don't underst…" Then he paused, realizing what had happened.

She couldn't have!

"Look, Jack, I have no idea what the hell you got in your email, but I can assure you *Wildflower* is still scheduled to start filming in the fall. I'd be interested in seeing what you are talking about though." Richie seemed serious now, looking at Jack pointedly, one eyebrow raised. Seeing this email wasn't a request.

"Yes, of course. I'm just glad to hear it." Jack laughed away his nerves and looked at his mother who was shaking her head, confused but smiling at the whole thing.

"Great. I'll call you Monday, and we'll get this all sorted. In the meantime, drink up. Enjoy yourselves. Rita, it was a pleasure. Jack…" Richie nodded at him, conversation tabled, and he floated away.

It had been a hoax. A lie.

It had been Giselle.

That Monday, as promised, Jack got a call from Richie early in the day. After his tech team looked into the email records, it was confirmed that the email had been contrived by none other than Giselle, from her computer, using the company email. They fired her.

"Look, Jack, I don't give a shit what happened between you two. Business is still business. I can't have someone who is that emotionally immature making fake emails and severing ties for the company because she feels jilted. Thomas J. Baker might be her daddy, but there's no nepotism here. This is fucking Hollywood. We make movies. It's a multibillion-dollar industry annually, so we don't stop doing business with people because of breakups. Nobody fucking cares. Anyway, I'm glad you told me. We're still good, so let me know when you've got something new to pitch."

After their conversation, Jack felt lighter than air. His muscles relaxed, and hope for his bright future returned. He'd also found out that the invitations sent out to the *Captain America* premiere had been sent by a different department that Giselle wasn't part of. That was why he'd gotten that invite. But after discovering Jack was sent the fake email, Richie apologized, saying he'd put Giselle in charge of his private Labor Day weekend party invitations too. To right things between them, Richie extended a personal invite to Jack. He was back in the loop.

With his career back online, he was energized again with his writing, selling multiple freelance articles to big magazines, and his first draft of the new screenplay was nearly complete. Then the best news of all came from Chalie. She was back in California.

"I can't imagine how hard that must have been," Jack said to her on the phone about her leaving Virginia and saying goodbye to her grandfather at the funeral.

"I'm still numb, I think. Like, my mind is swimming. Then seeing my mother again was like a reality check. She's almost done serving her time, but no telling what she's gonna do when she gets out and finds out about the money."

Jack sat up straighter in his bed. They were talking late at night, and she was planning to drive down the next day. He was trying his hardest to disguise his excitement for her arrival because he knew she was still grieving. "Did your grandfather leave her money?"

"Well, yeah. I just hope she doesn't piss it all away on something stupid. She needs to buy a house, move away from here, someplace where Greg can't find her, and start fresh. He'll get out one day and come looking for her, I'm sure."

Jack felt a twist in his gut thinking about this asshole possibly looking for Charlie too. "Well, I'm glad you're getting far away from there. If he came anywhere near you again, I'd kill him. You have good things to look forward to, baby. LA is waiting. I'm waiting." There was a long pause, and Jack furrowed his brow. "Charlie?"

"Hmm. Yeah. I'm here. Just thinking. I'm actually going to miss some of this. Teri and Michael, Retrograde, I think I'm even going to feel weird driving away from this house, even though it's a shithole and falling apart. I lived here for a long time." She sounded far away in her thoughts.

"Goodbyes are hard. We can go back together sometime and visit my uncle, and then you'll see Teri and Michael too. I promise, all the good stuff won't get washed away."

She promised to text him before she left Sebastopol. A smile spread across Jack's face, his insides filling with anticipation of her arrival. He went to bed that night feeling like the world was his oyster. All his ducks were lining up in a perfect row. But things don't always work out like you planned, and he was about to find that out.

❧

CHAPTER THIRTY-TWO

FALL 2011-WINTER 2012
CHARLIE

WITH ALL THE money she'd ever need, Charlie could have bought herself a new car of any model she desired, but the kinship and familiarity of her Bug gave her the security that not everything had to change. Her car was more like a friend, a confidant, than a machine, and it was the perfect companion to attend college with.

On a hot, late August afternoon, Charlie arrived in Los Angeles and felt like she was a character in a movie. The palm-tree-lined Sunset Boulevard with its historic buildings and neon signage left Charlie feeling tingly all over with possibilities. The campus of UCLA continued the feeling, where the Roman-like, redbrick buildings loomed above her, steeped in history. Echoes from the past were everywhere, from speeches by the likes of Martin Luther King Jr. and Maya Angelou to the fact that Bradbury wrote his *Fahrenheit 451* in the Powell Library.

Since she arrived late, the kind woman at the student services desk gave her a very abbreviated orientation, loading Charlie up with brochures, a packet of papers—complete with websites for more information—and a map of the four-hundred-acre campus, including her freshman dormitory area. She could move in as early as the next day if she chose to.

For the first two days though, Charlie got a room at the Plaza la Reina down the street. She wanted a few days to decompress in the Spanish-style suite and sit on her balcony with the terracotta-tiled deck and stucco surround that overlooked the city. *Why the hell not? She could afford it.* She used this time to contemplate her next move and acclimate to her new life in Los Angeles. To have no responsibilities for just a few days.

Turning down Jack's offer to stay with him in Culver City meant risking hurting his feelings, but once he came to see her at the hotel, he conceded that her choice was better. When they met in the lobby, sleek with dark wood and tropical plants, their eyes locked onto one another. Her connection to Jack was just as strong as ever. He kissed her in the midst of other travelers checking in, and the warmth of his mouth and the fierce strength of his embrace dissolved her surroundings until all she was aware of was the two of them. Her fears about Giselle vaporized and were replaced with overwhelming exhilaration for this chance with Jack.

They made love, talked, ate, and slept on a repeating cycle. In all of their conversations, Charlie never discussed the magnitude of wealth she was sitting on. She kept money out of the conversation, although she wasn't sure why. After two days of bliss, she had to come to grips with reality again. She was here to start a life. She was here to be a college student.

In the following months, Charlie dove headfirst into her education, taking seventeen units and volunteering her time to paint sets for the Performing Arts Center. Her business classes made her think of her grandfather, and the familiar pang of loss would wash over her whenever she had something of interest she wished she could share with him. Overall, Charlie was enjoying herself immensely, getting acquainted with her roommate Mindy, another business major, and all the amenities of campus living. She practically lived in the library, a place of worship as far as she was concerned, and the cathedral-like building seemed appropriate.

But her heightened fascination with her studies and her homework load put Jack on the back burner. Slowly, a wedge grew between them, and Jack's patience seemed to be wearing thin. She had turned him down for multiple invites to parties, outings, and staying over. Charlie simply didn't feel that she had the time. Traffic in Los Angeles was murderous, and just the time it took to cross town and back alone could eat up an entire afternoon. Their intimate time together was dwindling, and she could feel the tension in their short conversations building.

"I don't know what to say, Jack. I have midterms coming up, and I have to study. I can't just cut out of here to go to some fancy party. There will be others, I'm sure. Just let me study this weekend, and next weekend, I promise I'll come stay with you."

"That's the same shit you said last week, Charlie. You've got tunnel vision. You know, there is more to life than getting straight As. Your degree will be just as good if you got a few Bs now and then."

This pissed her off so much she could feel her blood pressure in her ears. *Did he know nothing about her?* She never just dialed it in. She did her best, or she fucking didn't do it at all! Besides, she had made a commitment to her grandfather, a vow she'd pledged herself when he'd left her his entire fortune that she'd work her ass off and graduate top of her class. Period. Jack needed to respect that about her, or it wasn't going to work between them.

"Jack, I'm not interested in getting fucking Bs! If you can't understand that, then we have bigger problems than whether I can go to a party or not."

And so it went, Jack clinging and requesting her time, and Charlie feeling guilty and pressured to split herself in two. Sometimes the ugly monster of fear would surface and bring visions of Jack falling for Giselle again because Charlie was too busy for him, but she shoved the thoughts away. She needed to stick to her priorities, but it was proving to be more difficult than she'd ever imagined. She rarely had time to paint outside of class but knew if she were going to use her skills and improve on them, she'd have to learn to balance her time so that art was just as much a priority as her business classes. Clearly, her first semester was turning out to be learning time management.

In mid-October, Cece was released from jail and was flown to Virginia to go over her new trust. Charlie felt badly that she couldn't fly back to be a buffer between her mother and grandmother, but the timing was bad for her to leave school. It was good her grandmother would have Cece to focus on to keep her mind from drowning in grief. Charlie also felt a sense of relief knowing her mother would have money to buy a house now and start over someplace new.

"I think I'll move near you," Cece said on the phone from her childhood bedroom in Virginia. "I'll get a realtor to help me find a small cottage near the beach and maybe work at a salon doing hair. What do you think, Charlotte?"

Charlie agreed and encouraged her mother, but after that call, each subsequent conversation they'd have, Cece changed her mind as to where she wanted to live. She wound up flying back to Sebastopol without a plan and decided to live off her money a few months until she could decide. Typical fickle Cece.

With all she was adjusting to, Charlie had put Dwight Ledger on the farthest back burner. Her father, who had no idea of her existence, would have to wait a little longer to find out he had a daughter, at least until Charlie gave herself a moment to breathe. She hadn't even allowed herself to look him up online again since moving to LA. She'd waited almost nineteen years, so she figured waiting a little longer wouldn't hurt. Besides, the idea of one more loss, should he reject her, wasn't something she could stomach yet.

Between Halloween and Thanksgiving, Charlie got tickets for her and Jack to see the play *Something Wicked This Way Comes* on campus. She'd helped paint the sets, so she got free admission, and for once, they spent time together immersed in her new world, taking Jack back to his old roots and softening his mood about her obsessing so much.

"God, I remember this campus like the back of my hand. So much happened for me here. I'm sorry I've been so impatient. I know it's a lot to adjust to," Jack said, holding her hand as they strolled outside Royce Hall, the Performing Arts Center. Their connection that night brought them closer again while they meandered in the moonlight, rekindling the magic.

They spent Thanksgiving at Jack's mother's house, and his uncle Rob—her old high school principal—arrived with a wildly surprised look on his face to see her. The cat was out of the bag, and before Rob, or *Mr. Hill* as she was accustomed to calling him, could say much, Jack took him aside and explained that they'd just texted and been friendly until after Charlie had graduated from high school. It was close enough to the truth, and Rob understood. They had a lovely time, reminiscing about Jack's youth, and Charlie really liked his mom. Rita was the kind of mom Charlie always wished Cece could have been—a homemaker and a nurturer. Still, Charlie worried in the back of her mind about her mother during the holidays. But over the phone, Cece assured Charlie she was celebrating at her friend's house, still living in Sebastopol, and her new AA friends were very supportive. She remained sober.

With only weeks until the winter break, an opportunity came up that Charlie couldn't refuse. Her advanced painting class was offering students pursuing an MFA in visual arts a chance to create for submission a painting for an exhibition that would raise money for a women's shelter in the city. This exhibition would allow students to showcase their work and gain recognition while doing something good to give back to the community. Charlie loved this idea. The question was, what did she want to paint? What message did she want to share?

She worked countless hours on an oil canvas painting of a girl sitting on the edge of a cliff overlooking the ocean. Seen only from the back, the girl was surrounded by wildflowers while she sat on a rocky ledge, where the warm light seemed to touch the land and highlight her hair in a haloed glow from the fading sunset over the Pacific. She entitled it *Hope*. It was the best work she'd done using a technique she'd learned in Paris, called *chiaroscuro*, where using darkness to create more drama with the light is achieved. This was popular with Renaissance artists such as Rembrandt and Caravaggio. Her teachers praised her, and her classmates were inspired. With a feeling of accomplishment, Charlie signed the lower right corner, Charlotte Kane. No more C.K. and hiding out. She'd been using her full name since France, with much encouragement from Daphne, the friend she missed so much she ached.

Local news covered the expedition. It was held in a nearby gallery in Santa Monica, the third week of December, where KTLA, NBC Los Angeles, and ABC7 News crews arrived with cameras and journalists all talking about the special fundraiser and helping women in need. Throngs of local newspaper and magazine journalists arrived as well, taking pictures and interviewing some of the collaborators for the event. The art pieces were to be sold as a silent auction with the highest bidder winning at the end of the event.

Charlie fidgeted awkwardly in her dressy slacks, silk blouse, and designer slingback heels. Her grandmother would be so proud. Jack attended with Charlie, holding her hand steady while she stood anxiously chewing her bottom lip. He ran into several people he knew from different magazines, chatting up reporters from *Above the Fold Larchmont*, *Los Angeles Magazine*, and *Entertainment Weekly*. He introduced Charlie, and each time, they'd ask her which piece was hers. Upon seeing her painting, they'd take pictures, sing her praises, and ask if she had other pieces for sale anywhere. Her painting brought in the most money of all, selling at a shocking twenty thousand dollars. It was Christmas after all, and the donation was someone's tax write-off for the end of the year, but it got her name in the papers, magazines, and on the news. Suddenly, everyone was curious about the "up-and-coming, new artist."

They went out to celebrate, and Jack took Charlie to The Four Seasons in Beverly Hills. Gigantic Christmas trees, white poinsettias, and shimmering lights filled the lobby. There was much to celebrate, especially since her winter break was here, and Charlie promised Jack she'd let loose a bit and spend more time with him, starting at the hotel. They soaked in the Jacuzzi tub, had champagne, and made love in the softest sheets Charlie had ever felt. When they returned from a lobster dinner, their bed had been turned down, mints waited for them on their pillows, and swans made out of the fluffy towels sat on the edge of the tub.

"Your dreams are coming true, Charlie. We won't stop until we have everything we want, and I'm going to be right there beside you making sure you get the life you deserve." Jack lay beside her, playing with her hair in the king-sized bed.

She wanted to pinch herself. How could she be living this life? An avalanche of sorrow used to follow her around, so naturally this was all too good to be true, wasn't it? She struggled to enjoy it all without letting fear strip it away. Looking into Jack's loving eyes helped.

She moved into Jack's apartment for winter break and painted three new pieces while on his balcony as he clicked away on the keyboard of his laptop. Jack was finishing his edits on a screenplay he hoped to pitch to Richie Lamont, nearly one year after selling *Wildflower*. She'd never read *Wildflower*, but Jack toyed with her, saying his infatuation with her had been the catalyst for writing it. They fell into sync, his writing, her painting, them reading books aloud to one another in bed. It felt natural. His roommate, Zane, gave them all the space they needed. He was hardly ever home. Living with

Jack became so easy that she worried about moving back to campus and how it would affect their relationship again. Freshmen year, it was mandatory to live on campus, and for her studies, it worked best for her. Charlie knew she would dive headlong back into the deep end of education. She had to. She only hoped her relationship would survive.

Then January arrived, and with it was a new year and a new semester. Jack bought her a ruby necklace for her nineteenth birthday…and Charlie's period was two weeks late.

With a sick stomach and paralyzing fear that her world was about to burst into flames, Charlie kept her terror to herself. She drove to a drugstore away from campus and bought a home pregnancy test. She didn't want to risk her roommate, Mindy, finding out she might be in trouble. They didn't have that sort of relationship. If only Daphne were here, she'd hold Charlie's hand and come up with some witty British bullshit to make her feel better. But Charlie was alone, and more scared than she could ever remember being.

Leaving Walgreens, Charlie drove into the parking lot of a Holiday Inn and strode through the lobby like she belonged there. She swiftly found the ladies' room and locked herself into a stall. The walls closing in on her and her breathing labored, she pulled the test out of the bag and sat staring at it in the tight enclosure. She peed on the stick and waited there, frozen in place, her jeans remaining around her ankles as she set a timer on her phone, her heartbeat hammering like a bass drum.

She couldn't remember if she prayed or what she asked for, but her fear was a slithering thing inside of her gut, moving into her throat, threatening to close her airway. The timer went off, and she forced herself to check. A deep breath, and an exhale, she looked into the little window. Inside was a small pink plus sign. She shoved the test into the hanging trash bin and turned around to vomit into the toilet.

∽

CHAPTER THIRTY-THREE
FALL 2011-WINTER 2012
JACK

JACK DRIFTED THROUGH his days like an overfilled balloon when Charlie first arrived in Los Angeles. She was the missing piece to his puzzle, the spice to his life. He was completely enamored with her. The wit she brought to every conversation, the way she nibbled her bottom lip while taking notes for school... Jack could just sit and watch her mind spin, and it gave him a hard-on.

But soon, Charlie seemed to have less and less time for him, and slowly, his overfilled balloon was starting to deflate. The old demon of desperation poked its ugly head back up, and Jack hated how it made him feel. Hated how he behaved when his clingy side unfurled unexpectantly like one of those pop-up snakes from the peanut can. Once the demon was out, it was embarrassing and hard to put away discreetly. He knew it made him unattractive, and the last thing he wanted to be was a burden to Charlie. Still, he was tired of being last on her list of priorities.

He gave her space though and filled his time finishing his screenplay. He went with Zane to check out filming locations, helped his mother with some odd repairs around her house, and attended a few parties…alone.

Then he ran into Giselle.

He was at a house party, walking around the corner to the bar in the Mulholland Estate home of the infamous film composer Samuel Christy, when Jack literally ran into Giselle. She was holding a pink cocktail, and it sloshed just over the rim of her glass, barely missing her clingy white designer dress. Her breasts were pushed up to a rhinestone-encrusted plunging neckline. Jack was momentarily stunned. Seeing her crystal-blue eyes, he started to apologize, then anger flipped his switch, and he tried to dart around her to continue on his mission for a drink. Her slim hand with light-pink fingernails wrapped around his bicep like tenacles, catching hold of him with a soft squeeze. He stopped long enough to glare daggers at her, cautioning her to leave him alone.

"Let go, Giselle. I've nothing to say to you."

"Just for a minute, Jack. I want to explain."

"What the hell could you possibly explain about trying to sabotage my relationship with the studio? I think it's a bit too late for any explanations." He yanked his arm away from her, steam rising from his head. If only Charlie were with him.

He continued to the bar, and Giselle followed, keeping pace with his steps in her tiny high heels across the polished stone floors. "I'll admit I was jealous. I was wrong, but I was mad. I'm sorry… Jack. Jack."

"What?!" He looked around, hoping they weren't making a scene.

They were near a large potted ficus that partially blocked them from view. She moved in closer to him and whispered, "I just said I was wrong. I've lost my fucking job over it, so of course I'm sorry. But I just…I don't know. I was hurt and angry, so I was vengeful, I guess. When I called you, and that girl answered…I sort of lost it. You can understand, can't you?" She put her hand on his chest, looked up into his face with those electric eyes of hers, and parted her glossed lips.

Jack swallowed as something stirring inside of him, then he looked away from her. He couldn't get pulled into her gravity. He wasn't about to be snared in her net. "*That girl*...is my girlfriend. I'm with someone else now, Giselle. You and I had our chance. It didn't work out."

"Oh...I see. Who is she? I mean, how'd you meet?" She pulled back and held her glass with both hands.

"Nobody you know. Anyway, I'm happy now, so..."

"Where is she? This girl. Why isn't she here if it's so serious?"

Jack's cheeks burned with anger again, and his face pinched. "That's none of your business, Giselle. Look, I've moved on, and so should you. Have a good evening."

He turned to leave, then she raised her voice. "I did a lot for you, Jack. Without me, you wouldn't have sold that screenplay, and you know it."

The fact that she gave him his break in the business burned his ass. But it was true. He knew it, and she knew it. Jack turned around. "Yes, Giselle. I know, and I'm grateful. But just because you did something nice doesn't mean you get to own me. I won't be indebted to you for life." He turned to leave then and, instead of heading for the bar, went straight to the door.

The frustration Jack felt at seeing Giselle and not being with Charlie at a very important party made him shrink into himself again. He went back to wearing sweatpants and never leaving the apartment.

But then Charlie invited him to an event on campus, a play, and somehow the light started to shine again in their relationship. They were connecting, talking more, and intimacy grew. They spent time with his mother during the holidays, and the icing on the cake was watching Charlie light up when she began making her own art again. Her piece for the expedition to raise money for the women's shelter gave her the needed recognition to get started in the local art community. Jack was happy to introduce her to all his connections, and Charlie expressed her gratitude in a most generous way.

Living together over her winter break had given him a glimpse into how beautiful their lives could be. The fairy tale of two artists under one roof. They'd been living a dream, but it was short-lived.

After the night he'd run into Giselle, she continued to try to push herself back into Jack's life, sending him text messages in the middle of the night. It frazzled his nerves, leaving him jumpy that his perfect, celestial existence with Charlie could be burned to the ground should she get wind of his ex-girlfriend contacting him.

Jack blocked Giselle's number from his phone, making it impossible for her to call or text him any further. He thought that would finally be the end of it. But when Charlie had to move back to UCLA campus for the next semester, the boat of their potential dream life was rocked again.

Charlie became moodier than usual. Her short temper left Jack's nerves irritated like she'd rubbed them with sandpaper with each conversation. He was tired of fighting her, so the only thing he could do was dive deeper into his own life and hope she'd come around.

Then, in February, he had his pitch meeting with Richie at Paramount for his new screenplay, a rom-com that was like *Hangover* meets *You've Got Mail*. It went so well that Richie wanted Jack to send the script over immediately. Feeling high on life and distracted by the intoxication of success, Jack hopped into an elevator at Paramount, glued to his phone while he shot a text off to Charlie with his good news, hoping to lift her spirits. She'd still been distant and down lately. He pushed the button before looking to see who was on the elevator. As the door started to close, he saw Giselle standing in the back corner staring at him.

His heart slammed against his chest wall. *Hadn't she been fired from this place?* Before he knew what was happening, she slinked up to him like a sleek panther about to pounce. He moved back, but she moved closer.

"What the hell are you doing here, Giselle?"

"I'm asking Richie for a second chance, trying to get back in his good graces. Listen, Jack…"

The floors were illuminating 12, 11, 10…going down but not fast enough. Jack prayed someone else would hop on.

"Just stop, Giselle. I'm not interested in anything…"

She reached under his shirt, her warm fingers rubbing his stomach and up his chest. The sensation was unsettling because it wasn't unpleasant. Rather somewhat familiar. It set all kinds of alarms off in his mind. *No. This was not good.*

"Say you still want me, Jack. I know I want you."

Floor 8, 7, 6. Jack was pressed as far at the back of the elevator as he could be. He pulled at her hand, then Giselle gripped at him, scratching down his front with her manicured nails, pulling some hair as she went. Jack's muscles clenched at the stinging pain.

"Are you crazy! What the fuck?" He held both of her wrists to keep her from touching him further.

She tried to smile but had a hurt look on her face and pain in her eyes. She looked pleadingly and stopped moving. Giselle just stood there and let him hold her wrists. Floor 3, 2, 1.

"I'm in love with you, Jack. I've always loved you."

They'd never said those words the entire time they dated, and Jack had never been compelled to do so, but he had to admit, it felt really good to hear them even now. It seemed like he'd been waiting forever to hear Charlie say it back to him, and yet she still hadn't, no matter how much she appeared to feel it. He longed to hear her say the words and continued to wait. Now, the entirely wrong woman was pledging her love for him, and he felt incredibly vulnerable.

The elevator dinged, and just before the doors opened, Giselle leaned up and kissed him full on the mouth. For a split second, he kissed her back, then the doors started to open. Jack dropped her wrists like they were burning his hands and bolted towards the door, nearly knocking Giselle over.

"Jack, wait." She tried to follow, pushing through the doors after him.

"Let it go, Giselle. Whatever you feel, it will pass. You were quick enough to burn me with Richie. You obviously don't know what you feel." He walked as fast as he could to the huge glass doors that would lead him out to the sprawling metropolis and safely away from her begging eyes and the smell of her perfume.

What had he done? He loved Charlie. Charlie was the one.

When he got into his car, Jack pulled his shirt up and studied the scratch marks on his chest and stomach. Three bright-red lines. *NO, no, no!* He hoped to God they would fade, but they were already starting to pucker, screaming proof of an entanglement. His mind raced. How the hell was he going to explain them to Charlie?

Two days later, it was Friday, and Charlie had promised to stay with him for the weekend. For once, he hoped she'd break her promise. That morning, the scabs on his chest and stomach had darkened, not faded. His nerves twisted him into a knot, and dark circles under his eyes attested to his lack of sleep. Exhausted, Jack decided to come clean and tell Charlie about his encounters with Giselle as soon as he saw her, minus the kiss.

But when Charlie arrived with a sour look on her face, Jack lost his nerve. Her skin was pale, and her eyes were dark with worry. Jack suggested she take a break, maybe drop a class. The beautiful creature he adored erupted into tears and spit venom at him.

"I'm not going to fucking quit just because something is hard, *Jack*! Christ, I thought you knew that about me by now. I can't just give in. I thought you'd be a little more supportive, but I can't even count on you to understand. NOBODY seems to understand. My mother would tell me to just go to the parties with you and *live a little*. That's something I would expect *from her*. NOT from you. I thought you knew how important all this was to me. If all you want is some girlfriend to give you a piece of ass and hang out at parties with, then maybe you've got the wrong girl."

She started for the door. Jack moved in front of it, blocking her exit, and put his hands on her shoulders. "Whoa. What the hell is going on? I'm *worried* about you, Charlie! I don't give a shit about parties, although, yeah, it would be nice to see my girlfriend once in a while. It would also be nice to see you feeling better and smiling again. You're fucking miserable, babe! Have you looked in a mirror lately? What is going on? I mean, if this is what you want so badly, then why the hell are you so goddamned upset all the time? Talk to me."

For a split second, he saw something in her eyes. The doelike onyx pools bored into his soul with some kind of silent pleading, but then, in a flash, it was gone, replaced with fire and anger. "You wouldn't understand. I just gotta go."

"No. Not like this." He pulled her into a hug, and she sank into him, crying and gripping a fistful of his shirt, shaking. Then she slipped her hands under his shirt, and for a moment, he forgot about the scratches. Something was wrong with Charlie, but she was so unreachable he had no idea how to navigate the situation. She was slipping away again like sand through his fingers.

"Please," she said into his chest. "Just let me go. I need time to think." She grazed her fingers across the welted marks on his stomach and looked up at him with a furrowed brow. "What's wrong with…?"

Alarms went off in his head. He yanked his shirt down and held her hands. "It's nothing. I scratched myself."

Luckily Charlie was far too preoccupied and dismissed them. He pulled her away from him, looking at her face for answers. "What do you need to think about, Charlie? You've been acting crazy. Tell me what's wrong. Stop shutting me out." He held her chin and made her look up at him as huge wet tears clumped her dark lashes together.

"I'm pregnant."

He dropped her chin.

They stood there in front of the door, staring at each other, saying nothing. Shock rippled through his body, and confusion melted his mind. *Pregnant. Pregnant.* The odd word that suddenly shifted their entire universe. It would either minimize their options or open up new possibilities. Still, he hadn't pictured himself as a father yet. He was only twenty-five. But he loved her.

"You are sure?" he asked.

"Yes. Completely sure."

He took both of her hands and smiled down at her, trying to compose himself and pretend to be steady. "I love you, Charlie. I'm here for the long haul. This wasn't in the plan, but let's get married. I wanted a family with you anyway. We're just starting a bit sooner, that's all. Maybe this will be a big adventure."

She stared blankly at him. "You don't get it, do you? If I have this baby, that's all I'll ever do. I'll be a mom, and everything I wanted for my life will be over. The years of struggle to get out on my own and make something of myself, all I endured to get here, will be for nothing! I can't bring a baby into this world like my mom did with me. Look how fucking great *that* turned out! I don't know if I would be any good at it, and I certainly won't put some poor defenseless child through living with a mom who has no fucking clue. *I've lived that!* You...you had Rita, a Stepford Wife in comparison to my mom. Fucking June Cleaver. My mother is a train wreck, and I have no skills."

He wasn't prepared for this. Blindsided and without an aptitude for talking her off a cliff, he grasped at whatever he could. "But you're not your mom, and you won't do it alone. We'll raise this kid together. Me and you, a mom and a dad, and I know you, Charlie. You have so much love and compassion that you will be an amazing mom."

"YOU AREN'T LISTENING! I'm not having this baby, Jack.

I'm not having it, and there isn't anything you can say to make me change my mind."

Stunned, he blinked and stepped back from her vehement outburst, the slap of her words blasting him like an explosion, ringing in his ears and shaking his resolve. She pushed past him, opened the door, and left him standing there. Before he realized what happened, she was in her VW and driving away.

She'd made up her mind without him. What he wanted didn't matter to her. Not that he'd even had a minute to so much as think about it. She hadn't even discussed it.

Suddenly, the weeks of her foul mood and distance started to make sense, and the floor dropped out from under him. Jack might have kept Giselle's unwanted advances a secret, but what Charlie hid from him was far worse. She was carrying his child and obviously cared so little for Jack that she couldn't even have a conversation about it. Wracked with emotion, he wept. Then he chastised himself for being so surprised that she would leave him out of the equation. Of course she had. She'd never even said she loved him.

CHAPTER THIRTY-FOUR

CHARLIE

DRIVING AROUND TINSELTOWN with no direction and in debilitating fear, Charlie felt rudderless. Night fell, and the city lights mocked her, making everything glitter and shine in contrast to her emotions. *How could she just leave Jack standing there after dropping such a bomb on him?* She felt like a monster.

She had no idea where she was going. After driving around for hours through the ghettos of Hollywood, where prostitutes and gangsters were like confetti in the streets, to the hills in Bel-Air, which were sprinkled with affluent homes of the rich and famous, she finally wound up in front of The Waldorf Astoria Beverly Hills nearly out of gas. Tired, buzzing from anxiety, and knowing she couldn't sleep at her dorm with Mindy, Charlie valeted her car and checked into a suite without a departure date.

Her room was plush in white, black, cream, and gold, complete with a full living room, an enormous flat-screen television, and a white-marble bathroom fit for a queen. The thick carpet felt so soft on her bare feet it was like walking on velvet. With all the opulence and lavishness around her, all she wanted to do was lie on the bed and cry. In the fetal position, Charlie lay in her blue jeans and UCLA sweatshirt, shuddering with both hands over her belly and her heart shattered in a million pieces.

Who did she have to blame for her pain this time? No one. Herself. Life had given her everything she thought she'd ever want, and she was more miserable than ever. This time she wasn't fearing for her life. Greg was locked away and couldn't hurt her. Her mother was doing well in AA, sober, and out of trouble—something of a miracle. And she not only had all the money in the world, but the love of the best guy she'd ever known, and what did she do? She fucked it all up.

How could she even consider keeping this child? She'd have to drop out of UCLA and disappoint her grandfather by neglecting his one wish for her to have a successful life. She'd shame her family as her mother had and probably win the award for *Most Clueless Mother Alive*. She had no idea how to take care of a baby.

Then there was the burning truth and shame about her own selfishness. For *once* in her life, Charlie wanted her future to be about her. What *she wanted*. She'd fucking earned it after all the years struggling to care for her crazy mother and living in fear all the time. She'd dreamed of a triumphant future where she became a screaming success in the art world, equipped with enough knowledge to start an empire, maybe internationally. She'd barely started following her dream. Drowning in a sea of tears, Charlie felt it all ripping away, vaporizing into thin air.

The worst part of it was that her dream hadn't really materialized until she met Jack. He'd encouraged her and made her believe in a life outside of her shadowy existence. He brought light, filled her with hope and wonder. He himself was a dreamer and making his dreams come true, and that was one of the biggest reasons she loved him. His unfaltering belief. He was why she'd moved here.

She loved him.

Why couldn't she ever tell him? Say how much she needed him. Being without Jack would be like living without oxygen. Her world would go dark again. But somewhere in the back of her scared and twisted mind, Charlie felt like needing and loving were weaknesses. The very last upper hand she'd ever have would be gone in saying those three words. She'd be vulnerable forever then, without defenses.

She rolled onto her back, hugging a down pillow to her chest. Or maybe saying those words would be the bravest thing she could ever do. It truly was something that scared the shit out of her. It scared her almost as much as the thought of being a mother.

She pulled out her phone to text the one person who she trusted to tell her exactly what to do without pulling any punches or sugarcoating it with any bullshit. She only hoped it wasn't too early in London.

⤟

Two days at the Waldorf Astoria and all Charlie had eaten was a few bowls of fruit and two slices of pizza that she eventually threw up in the fabulously extravagant bathroom that rivaled Julia Robert's in *Pretty Woman*. She was living on room service tea and 7UP, her body rejecting everything because of nerves and insomnia. When Daphne arrived from the airport via taxi, Charlie met her downstairs.

"Chuck, you look bloody awful. You use a fucking eggbeater to do that hair? Thank God I'm here. Nice sweatshirt though. Think I could get one while I'm here?"

They spent the day wrapped in fluffy hotel robes on the sun-drenched balcony of her suite, lounging on her silky sofa, or curled up on her bed against the padded, linen headboard. They talked about everything that plagued Charlie's mind, and Daphne made her eat some oatmeal she called porridge. The calming effect her friend had on her took the sting out of her buzzing nerve endings, and for once, Charlie kept the food down. But her body felt like a truck had run her over.

"Has Jack called you since?"

She heaved a sigh, and tears started to pool in her eyes again. "Just a text yesterday and today. He wanted to know if I was still set on my decision, and I said yes. Then he insisted that we need to talk. I text back that I wasn't ready, but soon."

Daphne grabbed her hands as they sat with the duvet over their laps. "You know I'll support whatever decision you make, love. I'm on your side one hundred percent. Just make sure you are sure, ya know? Because if you do this without him, there will be no going back. And I know ya love the bloke because ya turned away from Prince Long-Dong-McSexy-Pants in Paris because of him. He has no idea how much you love him! God knows I wouldn't have had the willpower to turn down that Parisian hunk."

Charlie laughed so hard a snot bubble nearly burst from her stuffed nose. Daphne was just the support she needed. But she was right. It was a life-changing decision, and she just might lose Jack in the process.

After emailing her instructors that she was too sick to attend class, Charlie was given her assignments online. Then, knowing Mindy's schedule, she snuck into their dorm room while it was vacant and grabbed clothes, then lied, sending her a text that she didn't feel well and was staying at Jack's in case she was contagious. Once she was cleaned up in fresh clothes, Daphne and Charlie left for the women's clinic where she'd made an appointment two days ago to end her pregnancy and kill any dream she had of a life with Jack.

The exam room was cold and smelled of rubbing alcohol and disinfectant. Her body shook involuntarily after she left her urine specimen in the cup in the bathroom. Now, sitting on the crinkly papered table in the flimsy gown, she looked around the room at posters on the walls of a uterus, of information about doing breast exams, and of tracking your menstrual cycle. Bile crept up her esoph-agus as the shaking continued. Sounds from down the hallway were muffled as she looked at a calendar that hung on the wall by the sink.

The picture for the month of February was a field of early wild-flowers from Chino Hills State Park. The Arroyo lupine, covering the Santa Ana foothills, grew without any tending or nurturing from anyone. It flourished, creating a beautiful blanket of blue blossoms, seeking the sun and never comparing itself to other flowers. It never asked permission where it could grow and didn't feel threatened by the environment. It simply persevered each year, blooming with-out fail wherever the wind blew its seeds. Charlie reached back and touched the tattoo on her shoulder, her reminder of strength, endurance, and finding beauty in resilience.

She stood up and ripped off the stupid robe, dressed, and opened the exam room door. She stormed through the hallway, passing a confused nurse, and bolted into the waiting room, finding Daphne sitting with a magazine. Upon seeing Charlie, she tossed it aside, and they flew out the door and into the parking lot, not stopping until they reached her Bug.

"So? I guess we're having a baby, huh?" Daphne smirked.

"I couldn't do it." Charlie sobbed. "She deserves a chance to grow. I'll probably fuck it all up, but I'll love her. I can't give up just because I'm scared out of my mind. Maybe Jack is right. Maybe having a kid will be a big adventure."

Daphne reached for her hand. "So then…you need to tell him, right?"

She dropped Daphne off at the hotel and drove to Jack's apart-ment in Culver City. She had rehearsed so many things in her mind about how she was going to apologize and say how wrong she was. She would beg his forgiveness and tell him she wanted to have his baby. She'd finally tell him about the money. She'd tell him she loved him.

She reached the parking lot in front of his place and hopped out of the car, trembling with fear but propelled by sheer adrenaline. As she was walking on the sidewalk, she looked up at his door, and it opened. A blonde woman came out wearing a pink skirt and fluffy blouse. For a moment, Charlie thought one of Zane's girls was leaving, and she paused, worried about having the baby conversation with an audience. Then the door opened again, and Jack stood on the landing. She stopped behind a huge banana tree and heard him speak to the blonde.

"Giselle...your purse."

The blonde with the perfect hair and pearls around her neck walked back to Jack and took the bag from him, standing and speaking softly for a moment.

Charlie's world started to spin. Her body turned icy, and her heart hammered in her chest as she ran back to her car and started the engine. Glancing up again at his open apartment door, she saw Jack looking at her car and waving his arms wildly, running down the stairs past Giselle. She threw the car in reverse, gasping, desperate to flee. Leaving the parking lot, she ran over a curb before racing down the street and flying towards the freeway, running from heartbreak and yet another devastating blow.

CHAPTER THIRTY-FIVE

CHARLIE

JACK CALLED HER so many times she had to turn her phone off. She drove back to the Waldorf on autopilot. She was completely oblivious as to how she arrived when she robotically handed her keys to the valet.

Daphne tried her best to comfort her, bringing her hot tea, drawing her a bath, and listening with pained eyes as Charlie ranted on inconsolably about the cliché of a blonde bimbo slinking out of his apartment.

How long had Jack been seeing Giselle? Had he ever stopped? Had all this been happening right under her nose all along, and she'd been too busy wrapped up in her studies to notice? Guilt for neglecting Jack twisted her guts while rage bloomed in her chest for his infidelity.

By nightfall, Charlie was done with her tirade, and a dark silence took hold of her, closing her off like an iron door. Inside her body, the shock and trauma had wrecked her intricate systems, and she felt as if everything was off. She withdrew to a place inside of herself so far away she barely recalled where she was or that Daphne was even there. Her caring friend with her soup, pep talks, and pink dyed hair tried her best to reassure Charlie that it would all work out, but all she wanted to do was sleep and escape into the beautiful abyss of nothingness. The peaceful void where there was nothing. She was nothing.

⁓

Something woke her. In the darkness, Charlie didn't remember where she was. Something sickening and sharp. Her stomach was nauseated, and her groin cramped. Moaning came from somewhere in the room. It was her. Chills wracked her body. Then a stabbing pain, intense and biting, doubled her up in bed on her side. Blinding light illuminated the room as Daphne's face appeared swimming near her own.

"Charlie? Charlie, what is it?"

Unable to talk, she held her low belly, then a warm wetness came from between her legs. She reached down to feel the sticky mess. She squinted her eyes at the dark redness on her fingers, unable to process what was happening.

"Oh, no, no, no. We have to get you help. Jesus, Charlie! Hang on, love. I'm calling an ambulance."

The pain was blinding. She rocked her head back and forth, crying and moaning, "My baby. My baby."

Paramedics. She was lifted onto a gurney. Overhead lights in her suite whizzed by. Daphne's voice, like she was miles away, speaking underwater. The elevator. More overhead lights. She squeezed her eyes shut, picturing her child attached to her womb, and prayed she'd hang on. Tears leaked from her eyes and ran into her ears as she heard Daphne insist on riding with her. A siren pierced the night, and as it whaled on, she was jostled through bumps and turns in the city. Daphne's hand squeezed hers. Her voice still muffled, promising not to leave her.

Somewhere along the way, Charlie passed out. Slipped into the darkness again, and in it, there was nothing. Quiet. Then far away and slowly approaching was the smallest pinpoint of light. She strained to see it. It floated nearer, a soft humming sound at first. It flickered, like a star pulsing slightly as it grew larger and brighter. The humming sound turned into a vibrating musical tone like a flute or the held note of an organ. It was soothing. Reassuring.

She woke up. Sitting next to her was Daphne flipping through a magazine, her pink pixie haircut out of control and dark circles under her eyes.

"Daph?"

Her friend slapped the magazine shut and popped up to the side of her bed. There were monitors all over with tubes like an octopus, an IV in her arm, and beeping sounds filling the room. Their eyes locked as Charlie searched Daphne's for any sign of hope, too afraid to ask.

"Well, you are one fucking tough bird, Chuck. Stubborn, but tough. So's your little one."

A gasp escaped her throat, and tears burned her eyes. "I didn't lose her?"

"You are so sure it's a girl, aren't you? No. She's still there, although it was very close."

"So...no miscarriage?" Her chin trembled.

"No. You have toxic shock syndrome. The infection hit fast and hard. You've been out for three days. The doctors were able to slow the infection, and it seems the baby is okay so far. Looks like we got you here just in time. But I'm told you're going to have to be on bed rest for a while."

Bed rest. Not exactly conducive to college life. So much was about to change, but as long as she didn't lose the baby, she'd be okay. The floating light dream, if that's what it was, had felt like a promise that something better and brighter was coming, even though she'd thought she had died. But then a sinking feeling came over her. She was about to embark on this parenthood journey alone. Jack was with another woman. She'd have to be strong and make the baby a priority now. Maybe one day she'd get back to her own dreams, but for now, her child was more important, and she'd almost lost her.

"Listen, Chuck. You're not going to be very happy with me, but I did something. In a few minutes, you are gonna be really mad, but just remember, it came from the heart, and I only have your best interests in mind."

Charlie furrowed her brow at Daphne's remarks when around the corner, carrying two cups of coffee, came her mother, Cece.

"This shit tastes like mud, but if you put enough cream in it, it's not so…Oh, thank God you're awake!"

Daphne looked at Charlie, shrugging her shoulders. "I used your phone and called. I figured you'd need your mum."

Under normal circumstances, Charlie would have wanted Cece to be as far away as possible, but now, seeing her mother's clear sober eyes, bright skin and smile, she welcomed the thought of letting Cece actually be her mother for a change. Charlie's heartache came bubbling to the surface, and when Cece touched her face, all her emotions spilled over again.

"Oh, baby, it's the hormones. You are going to cry, be pissed, want to punch people, then hug them. It's natural. You've got a war going on inside of you with those hormones, but they are building you a beautiful baby, so try to relax. Doc says the infection was caught just in time, so you are both going to be okay. Still, I'll teach you some of the meditations I've been learning. They work wonders."

Cece looked renewed and years younger, and if there was hope for her after all this time, then maybe Charlie could build a good life, even if it didn't look anything like the one she'd planned.

So many questions were filling her head, and she was about to ask them when doctors and nurses started to fill her room. They checked her vitals, asked how she was feeling, took blood, and asked if she wanted to have the catheter removed so she could walk. Her mind was on overload. Then it was just her mom and Daphne again, and for a moment, there was an awkward silence. Where to begin?

She'd never even talked about Jack to her mom, and now here she was, pregnant.

Just as she was about to speak, Charlie saw someone in the doorway, and her breath caught. Jack stood with dark stubble on his face, his blue-green eyes shadowed with dark circles, and he was carrying a bouquet of wildflowers in his hand. At first, she was overjoyed to see him, then she remembered Giselle, and her heart broke all over again. She turned away from the door and looked out the window, anger and pain building a wall.

Cece stepped over to her and whispered in her ear. "Baby, just hear him out. He's been here every day, and I think he really loves you. Besides, with those eyes and that face, you are going to have one gorgeous kid. We'll give you two a minute." She kissed her cheek, and Cece and Daphne left the room.

Charlie refused to look at him. If she did, she'd cave immediately, and all her defenses would be gone. Beneath her bedsheets, her body quaked. She ached from her illness, and she ached for Jack. She wanted him, a life with him, but he'd ruined it. How could he possibly fix this?

"When I saw you that day, I chased you," he said from just inside the doorway. "I got in my car and tried to follow you, but you disappeared into the city before I could track you down. I drove for hours. Called you. Left you messages. Giselle came by on her own. I didn't invite her. She actually just walked right into the apartment, begging me to take her back. I told her I was in love with someone else and that there was nobody I could ever love as much. She finally got the hint. Actually, Charlie, she'd been begging to get back with me since Virginia, but I didn't tell you because I was scared out of my fucking mind that you'd read too much into it and bolt. Your faith in us, I'm afraid, isn't as strong as mine, and before you told me about the baby…well, I thought you were going to break up with me or something. You seemed so upset and angry all the time."

She glanced at him as Jack walked towards her bed, then she looked to the floor, afraid to look him in the eyes.

He continued on. "Then when I found out you were going to terminate the pregnancy, I thought my life was over. Of course, I wasn't ready to be a dad. Who the hell is ever ready? But I am already in love with this child because we made it. You and me. Our love made that baby, and if you just give us a chance to be a family, I will move heaven and earth to make you and our kid happy."

"Her. Make *her* happy." She turned towards him, her heart softening, and tears wetting her face. "And I have faith in us. I'm just so damned scared, and that's my own fault. My past experiences haven't been full of many supporting cast members. You surprised me, Dog Man. You came into my life when I was pretty much at my lowest… It got lower for a while, but you were like this guiding light with your text messages and encouragement. I found myself in Virginia—who I am—and you showed up like this knight in shining armor. But then Giselle brought up old tapes in my mind, of how people aren't usually what they seem. My experience was that they lie and make false promises. That's why I put up my guard again, until I got back here. You say she's your past, and I want to believe you. God knows I *need* to believe you." Her tears streamed down now uncontrollably.

He moved closer and placed the wildflowers in her lap, then took her hands in his. "You remember the day in Retrograde when you described to me why you had wildflowers tattooed on your back shoulder? You said they were resilient and grew in places where nobody expected, without any nurturing from anyone. That they could thrive in the harshest conditions and didn't need anyone to tell them they were beautiful in order to grow. Well, what if they actually got that nurturing and support and admiration from someone? Wouldn't those resilient flowers thrive even better and stronger? I know you don't need me, Charlie, but I hope you want me. If you choose us, nobody will love you more. And I promise you, our daughter—since you say it's a girl—will want for nothing when it comes to love, support, and a family. Please, lean on me. You can stop carrying the weight of the world on your own. Let me be there for you. I love you."

The ice melted inside of her, and her walls crumbled down. Charlie took Jack's face in her hands and placed a warm, soft kiss on his mouth, shaking and crying as she did. "I love you, Dog Man. I've loved you from the first moment we met on the street when Henry brought us together. It's not easy for me to admit, but I do want you. More than anything. I want us, and God help me, I want this baby, even though I'm scared out of my mind!"

"We can be scared together," he gushed. His smile pierced her heart. "And I'll find us a house, wherever you want. I'll even leave LA. I can write from wherever. We might be on a budget, but I think I've sold my second screenplay, so I just might be making a name for myself that could bring us some good money. Our dreams don't have to die because we start a family. Your talent is going to take you places. I know you want a fancy degree, but you can still go to school online and at night. I'll stay with the baby. I promise your career will be just as important as mine. Only, love me, Charlie. Don't shut me out anymore. I can't bear it. I can't survive without you."

In that hospital room, something inside of Charlie flipped like a switch, and she realized how heavy the load was that she'd been carrying all of her life. She could finally put it down. At first, she didn't know who she was without the metaphorical luggage. Her pain, suffering, anger, and disappointment all rolled into her bag of pride, suffocating her. With Jack, she could breathe, and there finally was lightness, hope, and mostly love.

∽

CHAPTER THIRTY-SIX

SPRING 2012-FALL 2012
CHARLIE

IN THE MONTHS that followed, Charlie made a full recovery, and her little girl grew healthy and strong in her womb. Daphne was back in London, texting every day or so with funny anecdotes and pictures of potential men she'd like to date. Cece finally moved out of their old bungalow and bought a house in nearby Santa Rosa, cutting hair in a new salon. She was too afraid to move very far from her AA sponsor, having made a good connection with her. Cece didn't trust herself yet to leave her routine, but she had made great progress.

Charlie told Jack about her inheritance. All of it. In true Jack fashion, he was happy but seemed unfazed otherwise. He'd loved her before the money. Charlie refused to marry him until she could walk down the aisle without looking like a balloon in a dress, but she agreed to living together.

In May, they bought a house in the Point Dume area of Malibu that had a view of the ocean that gave her a sense of déjà vu. The inside was luxurious with freshly remodeled finishes in light colors and a sleek style, but that wasn't what drew Charlie to the house.

As Jack spoke with the realtor, the view magnetically pulled Charlie to the accordion glass doors and outside to the patio. Still on bed rest, she moved her wheelchair for a better look. The terrain of the hills, the way the light hit the landscape covered in wildflowers with the turquoise ocean below, it was the painting she'd created for the fundraiser for the women's shelter. She'd painted this place before she'd even seen it in person. She belonged here.

In her third trimester, Charlie bloomed like a flower, bright and soft with a peaceful demeanor. She spent days in the baby's room, supervising, as Jack did all the painting of the walls and building of furniture. She created art from a sitting position, producing one canvas painting after another, her creativity flowing like downloads from the universe. Charlie set up her easel outside on their patio, or in her studio where the light was golden and magical.

They were happy. At ease. For the first time in her life, Charlie felt like she was exactly where she was supposed to be, doing exactly what she was supposed to be doing. She invested in a start-up at a local studio that taught art to kids in need. Kids like her, who had talent but no resources and no place to go. She hoped it would keep them off the streets and give them a sense of belonging. Like her grandfather said, **"It is in the choices you make with what you are given that alters the course of your life."** She was using both her head and her heart, as he'd told her to do. She hoped she made him proud.

In October, the premiere for *Wildflower* was like a Hollywood fairy tale. Charlie dressed in a sapphire-blue satin evening gown by Versace, her basketball bump protruding in her lap as she sat in the wheelchair. She was getting so close to her due date that her doctor agreed she could go, providing Jack wheeled her about.

She'd never attended school dances or her prom, so all the fussing with hair, nails, and makeup made her feel slightly squeamish. But at Jack's insistence, Cece and his mother, Rita, came to help and attended with them, along with his uncle Rob. Sitting among the famous actors and Hollywood elite in the theater, they watched on-screen all of Jack's genius unfold, bringing Charlie to tears with his portrayal of a girl who was inspired by her. The tragic ending with the death of her lover brought the whole house down. But the strength and resilience of the young girl gave hope, which was the point of the whole movie.

That night at their home overlooking the ocean, Charlie lay in bed with Jack softly snoring, and she rubbed her belly, feeling so much gratitude. Her heart was full. And knowing her mother was sound asleep in the guest bedroom down the hall made her feel complete. Charlie's life had turned into a dream. What she'd always wanted had somehow miraculously manifested, even if it had arrived in a way she'd never imagined.

But there was one thing, one person actually, who was the last missing piece of her puzzle, and she couldn't put off finding him much longer. Until she located and told Dwight Ledger he was her father, there would be a void and uncertainty inside of her. She still stalked him on social media, following the progress of his band, Warning Signs, finding no indication of a family but that he'd been divorced. She had to find him soon. He was going to be a grandfather.

With the moonlight shining off the Pacific, she continued rubbing her protruding belly, feeling her child softly move inside of her. As she rolled over in bed, stroking Jack's hair from his forehead, her water broke.

CHAPTER THIRTY-SEVEN

FALL 2012- WINTER 2013
JACK

ON A WINDY day in October, Avalon Iris Connors arrived in the world with a full head of hair and bright-pink lips. Her first name meant magical fruitfulness and long life, while her middle name signified a vibrant flower or rainbow. Looking at her, Jack knew it suited their daughter perfectly. Her mother lay resting while Jack sat in the nearby recliner in the quiet morning hours of the serene hospital room. He cradled his sleeping little bundle of joy in his arms, heart so full he thought it might explode, and whispered to his daughter about all she could become in this wild and wonderous world.

In the raised hospital bed, Charlie stirred, arms stretching above her head. Droopy-eyed and long locks pulled to one side, she'd never looked more beautiful than she did at that very moment. Everything he would ever want or need was right there in the room with him. As Charlie sleepily looked over at the two of them, tears filled the corners of Jack's eyes. His life was complete.

Their little family fell into a sort of routine that seemed to work, and although Jack was sure he was going to screw things up somehow along the parental path, Charlie seemed to take to being a mom like a fish to water. She was a natural, and each time he watched the two of them as she rocked Avalon in her nursery, his heart would break wide open with so much love it made him ache. Never did he imagine this kind of all-consuming, powerful feeling he had for his family. All he wanted to do was protect them and keep them safe forever. They were in this love bubble together, and when his eyes connected to Charlie's as she held their precious gem, he knew he'd die for them without question.

Within a month of Avalon's birth, they all flew back to Virginia and were married in the atrium of Charlie's grandparents' home, with his mother, uncle, and Charlie's mom and grandmother in attendance. Zane was his best man, and Daphne was kind enough to fly over from London to be Charlie's maid of honor. Gerty was all too happy to be the one to plan the food and decorations for their intimate occasion. The fall leaves in gold, crimson, and orange were a glorious tapestry outside the floor-to-ceiling windows, the perfect backdrop to the day he finally put a ring of diamonds around Charlie's finger, promising her forever.

Their life in LA was full as they took turns working and being with Avalon. Jack was writing a new screenplay, while Charlie was starting to expand on her art and had an idea for giving back to the community where it all started.

Sebastopol.

Her investment in the art studio for kids in need worked so well in Los Angeles she wanted to do it for Sonoma County as well, partnering with her former art teacher, Mr. Ingle. Jack was so proud of her for opening her heart so much since it had never been easy for her to do as a student. Kids apparently hadn't always been nice to Charlie, but having the baby changed something in her. His wife had softened. She smiled more and was less quick to anger. Jack could see the gleam in her eyes and felt the energy she exuded whenever she spoke of the project.

One day in December, Jack walked with Avalon asleep in his arms into Charlie's art studio that faced the ocean. The huge windows let in so much light that her hair seemed to become a halo around her. Magical swishes of her brush created colorful forms that started out as random strokes and developed into works of genius. She was growing her collection of canvases for her first art show, all signed Charlotte Kane, sticking with her maiden name for all things business.

As he watched her, pride filled every space inside of Jack. That first painting he bought of hers still hung in his office. He'd never part with it.

By February 2013, filming was about to begin on Jack's second screenplay, and Charlie was ready for her first exhibition at a swanky space they'd rented in the Downtown Los Angeles Arts District. The DTLA's eastern side was known for its loft workspaces, lively wine bars, quirky shops, and art galleries. It drew in millions of people a year, so Jack thought it was the perfect location for her show.

Each evening of the three-night event, the loft buzzed with lively conversations over small plates, wine, and piped-in jazz music. Charlie's twenty-five-piece collection called *Exposures and Enlightenment* received rave reviews and sold almost every piece before the weekend was up. His wife was a huge success!

Within months, Charlie's art career was on a fast track to national recognition like a speeding locomotive. Her philanthropy of helping underprivileged children was also being recognized, and soon invitations to appear on morning news shows were pouring in. Jack's guarded, camera-shy bride never anticipated this, and just discussing the idea while they lay in bed made her stammer nervously. He reassured her that she was up for the challenge. With Cece as Charlie's personal stylist, the interviews went swimmingly.

Days were filled with raising Avalon alongside both of their blossoming careers, and Jack's new screenplay about parenthood seemed to write itself. When Charlie had to fly back to Sebastopol for a meeting about The Chrysalis House, her nonprofit art center in Sonoma County she was opening with Mr. Ingle, an idea popped into Jack's head while he sat on the floor with Avalon as she chewed her toe.

There was something he wanted to do to help make Charlie's life complete. But knowing his wife like he did, Jack realized that without a little push, she might never risk making the leap. Still, he couldn't do it alone. He'd have to consult with Cece, and although she and Charlie were finally building a new relationship, going behind her back might backfire on him. It was a chance he needed to take though. Handing Avalon a toy, Jack placed a call to his mother-in-law, hoping for cooperation in locating the missing link from Charlie's life.

ॐ

CHAPTER THIRTY-EIGHT

SPRING 2013

CHARLIE

EVERY DAY CHARLIE woke up feeling like she was living someone else's life. A perfect life. The best possible life she could ever imagine. She was intoxicated most days by sheer gratitude.

Being a mother was the greatest gift of her life. Avalon was more beautiful each day. The funny faces she'd make, the way she looked around with wonder and curiosity with her bright blue eyes, made Charlie cringe at the thought that she'd almost lost her. That they *both* had nearly missed this chance. Becoming a mother had almost not happened for her, and it was a miracle they were both alive. Charlie vowed to cherish each milestone. She knew she couldn't have survived without Jack.

His undying love had been the glue in her life. They were one hundred percent a team in both their marriage and raising their daughter. And even though she knew they'd screw some stuff up, they would come through anything life threw at them as long as they were together.

Their wedding in Virginia was just as she wanted. Small and

with only those she truly loved. Her grandmother had softened after the loss of her grandfather. And even though they still sparred periodically, Cece had finally made peace with her mother. Someday, Charlie wanted to move back to Virginia, but for now, their businesses were in California.

Dropping out of UCLA had felt like saying goodbye to a dear friend, as she'd adored being in the college, but she felt blessed to have had the experience at all. One day, she'd continue her business degree online, but for now, she was blissfully floating on a cloud being Mrs. Jack Connors.

The Chrysalis House was becoming Charlie's main focus outside of her homelife. She and Mr. Ingle were working nonstop on filing the proper paperwork to create the nonprofit, securing a building, designing a logo, and creating buzz about the opening. Her involvement in the nonprofit in Los Angeles involved merely showing up periodically to teach art and provide financial donations. But The Chrysalis House was her baby. There was much to learn, and she was diving in headfirst with the enthusiasm of a bright-eyed child at Christmas. It thrilled her so much she had trouble sleeping at night from the excitement.

Her personal art show had sold nearly every piece, and she thought of creative ways to use her profits. She put half of it into starting a trust for Avalon, and with the other half, she wanted to start a charity called Wildflower. The charity would house, educate, and support homeless single mothers and their children, while allowing space and time within the housing complex for art classes as well as a library full of books. She also worked with a financial advisor that her grandparents had known for years, making investments that would grow her existing money. Charlie visualized a bunch of Wildflower housing units to be set up nationwide someday. That was the dream.

Her mind was on fire with ideas. She felt so alive and electric with energy it was almost like she never required sleep. When she did finally unwind at night and Avalon was tucked into her bed across the hall, Jack appreciated Charlie's energy in bed. Their lovemaking was more passionate and exploratory than ever. Her insatiable appetite for his body surprised even her, and sometimes Jack, her loving husband, would just stare at her with so much appreciation it was enough to make her cry. *How could this be her life?*

By early May of 2013, Mr. Ingle, whom she had been coaxed into calling by his first name, Doug, had set up a press conference for the ribbon cutting in Sebastopol for the opening of The Chrysalis House. The news spread like wildfire to local radio and television stations as well as newspapers. Charlotte Kane was becoming a household name.

The day of the opening, a pack of news vans and reporters gathered around the leased Willow Street, Victorian house like teenagers storming the gates of a concert venue. The mob of reporters and their camera crews stood on the sidewalk in front of The Chrysalis House along with the mayor of Sebastopol, some folks from the Chamber of Commerce, and Charlie's support system. Jack, her mother, Teri and Michael, and of course her partner in crime, Doug Ingle, all surrounded her as the mayor stood by Charlie's side with oversized scissors the likes of something Edward Scissorhands would have used. Avalon was with her grandma Rita in LA, but at that moment, Charlie was thinking of Avalon, hoping to build a life where her daughter would be proud of her. She and the mayor cut the yellow ribbon in front of the entry to the art center together as the crowd cheered on, applauding with the enthusiasm of a game show audience.

Doug, who came dressed in khakis and his signature tweed jacket with elbow patches, like some Ivy League college professor, was clearly amazed. "Everything you touch lately has turned to gold. People are curious what's next for Charlotte Kane. My friend, you are becoming famous."

With a beaming smile, Charlie stood outside the door, shaking people's hands and thanking them for coming while Doug escorted a group inside to poke around at what they'd created. While chatting with a female reporter from the *Press Democrat* who resembled a young Katie Couric, Charlie looked down the sidewalk at a man approaching about fifty yards away. The incessant questioning from the bob-haired reporter faded into the background as Charlie's heart started thumping like a racing Clydesdale. She recognized the man. He appeared to be in his mid-forties with long, curly hair, and he wore a leather jacket and dark jeans. Dwight Ledger stopped walking when he spotted Charlie looking at him. Charlie felt Jack's hand move to her lower back, pulling her away from the reporter as he asked if they could have just a minute.

With several people still mingling outside near the flower beds, Charlie felt herself float away, like she was having an out-of-body experience, somehow magnetically pulled and separated from the group. She stood staring, disbelieving, at the man who she'd avoided talking to for fear of rejection, and he stared right back, a dumbfounded look on his face.

Cece appeared, having made her way back out of the house, and stood by Charlie. "I knew you'd be too scared, so I contacted Dwight myself. Believe me, he was just as angry with me as you were. But he's here now, baby. Jack made me realize it wasn't your responsibility to tell Dwight he was a father. It was mine all along. I called him, and even though I'm not sure how this will go moving forward, he's here now. He seemed genuinely interested in what you've been doing with your life. I'm sorry I robbed you both of so much time. But this is part of what I am supposed to do in my recovery—take responsibility for my actions. I'm so very sorry, Charlotte. I told your father I'm sorry too. Anyway, I hope you get to know each other. Maybe even have a relationship."

With all Cece's rambling, Charlie said nothing. Her father started to move closer, and as he closed the gap between them, a huge smile spread across his bronze, sun-kissed face. Charlie smiled in relief.

His eyes resembled her own, and he was tall, with long legs and a thin build, just like her. As he came nearer, she noticed a lotus tattoo on the back of his hand. Just a black outline, but knowing flowers, Charlie recognized its meaning of rebirth, strength, and spirituality. A lotus grew in the mud, overcoming adversity to become something beautiful. To her, this was a good sign.

When he was close enough to speak to her, somewhere to her right, coming from across the street, a man started yelling. His voice, gravely and deep, startled Charlie, distracting her from the dream-like connection she was having with Dwight Ledger. The man's ranting sent cold shivers up her spine as horror strangled her, and her stomach lurched towards her throat.

"You fucking Kane women think you are such hotshots! All over the news, parading around like you own the fucking town! You ain't any better than a couple of whores."

With all eyes diverting away from The Chrysalis House to the bedraggled man across the street, those outside the building seemed to pull together like a school of fish, deciding which direction to move in unison. Cece moved in front of her, more protective in her sobriety than she'd been during the days of her addiction.

"You keep away, Greg! I mean it. This has nothing to do with you. We've moved on. You need to do the same," her mother bellowed.

Greg White, the greasy fireplug of a man who'd nearly killed Charlie was now standing in the middle of the street with both his hands inside a wrinkly, dirty brown coat. His hair was overgrown, hanging across one eye. His jeans were smeared with grime, and he staggered slowly towards them. With his every step, Charlie's terror gripped her throat tighter, and she shook, grabbing at Jack's arm for support.

"Get inside, both of you," Jack said to her and her mother. "All of you"—he spoke to the crowd on the sidewalk and stairs of the house—"get inside quickly. I'm calling the police." But few took heed, frozen in place. Teri and Michael pushed closer to Charlie, standing right next to her and Jack.

"Go ahead and call 'em, Hoss! Bring on the fuckin' po-po. See if I give a shit. These women already fucked up my life. I can't get a job, I lost my house, and they seem to be sitting high on the hog. Seems to me you gals owe me."

Greg pulled out a pistol from his coat and stumbled closer as the crowd gasped. Cameramen were filming it live, but Charlie still felt paralyzed.

"We don't owe you a damn thing, Greg. You did this to yourself. You are lucky all you got was time in the pen. If it were up to me, I'd have killed you myself for what you did to my little girl." Cece pushed Charlie back farther and stood directly in front of her.

Jack was pulling Charlie back towards the small front lawn, but the camera crews and a few others remained right behind Cece and Dwight, who stood their ground on the sidewalk.

"You really think you could have killed me, you little bitch? I'll be the one with the last word today, baby. Fuck you, and fuck your little whore daughter too. I ain't letting you breathe one more disrespectful word to me."

Greg rushed forward, and Jack threw Charlie to the lawn as two loud bangs sounded off and screams filled the air from those around her. She lay there, the moisture of the ground wicking into her blouse and the smell of earth penetrating her nose as the commotion nearby grew chaotic.

"Call an ambulance," a man hollered.

"He's still breathing," another person said.

"This one's dead," someone else yelled.

Jack pulled up Charlie, and he frantically examined her all over, looking for injuries. He took her face in his hands, searching her eyes. "My God! Baby, are you okay? Charlie, are you alright?"

All she could do was nod. Her eyes felt wild, and she launched herself to her feet as fear tightened her chest. "MOM!" she screamed.

Cece was down on the sidewalk holding Dwight's head in her lap and stroking his hair from his face. Michael leaned over him while using a phone. Dwight's white shirt was bloodstained underneath the leather jacket, and his beautiful brown eyes were closed.

"Is he dead? What happened?" Charlie screeched, her voice not sounding like her own. Her father, not her mother, had been shot, stepping in front of Cece to protect her, and Charlie hadn't even gotten a chance to say a single word to him.

Her old boss had his phone on speaker now and held a compression to Dwight's wound. He told the dispatcher the patient was still breathing but shallowly and was losing blood. He gave them the address and told them to hurry. Charlie locked eyes with Michael for a split second, begging him silently for hope, but he looked away quickly and continued to address Dwight.

A few yards away lay Greg White, shot dead in the head. Confusion spun her mind, and Charlie sat on her knees with her mother, Jack at her side, as they waited for the arrival of the ambulance that would take her father away.

CHAPTER THIRTY-NINE

CHARLIE

THE PAPERS AND *The Ten O'Clock News,* said an off-duty Sonoma County Sheriff Deputy, who had attended The Chrysalis House Grand Opening with his wife, had shot and killed Greg White. Apparently when the commotion broke out, he was near the entrance and came outside, witnessing Greg pull out the stolen 9mm handgun. Sadly, he wasn't quick enough to stop Greg from firing, shooting Dwight in the upper chest.

Doctors worked quickly at Santa Rosa's Providence Hospital, rolling Dwight into surgery and later telling the group in the waiting room how lucky he'd been that the bullet had missed all his vital organs. They'd been successful removing the bullet, and other than a blood transfusion, he only required time for healing. Dwight would make a full recovery.

The tightly wound support group all sighed in relief at the good news. Jack pulled Charlie into a long hug where she melted into his chest. Her mother dropped her head onto Charlie's shoulder as Jack embraced them both. Michael and Teri were next to hug her and said they were headed home but to call them later. Mr. Ingle, who Charlie still had trouble calling Doug, offered to take any calls for interviews about the incident so Charlie could focus her attention on her family.

When Dwight woke up, a nurse came to tell them they could come back a few at a time but only for a few minutes. He needed his rest. Jack told Charlie to go back with her mother.

"Go. I'll wait for you." He kissed her forehead, and Charlie felt torn between wanting to rush to Dwight's bedside and being scared shitless about speaking her first words to a father she'd never met.

Squeezing Cece's hand, Charlie walked to Dwight's room, the sterile smell of the hospital ward stinging her senses. Their footsteps echoed as they meandered down the long corridor towards the ICU. When they arrived at his room, a nurse was in there, looking over his monitors, and she smiled when she saw the two of them, motioning for them to come inside.

"He's awake and ready to see you." The chipper woman looked about Cece's age with smiling bright-blue eyes. "I'm a huge fan of your dad's, going way back to the '90s. You're a lucky girl to have such a talented father. He's doing great." She winked and stepped outside the room.

In the doorway, Charlie stopped, and Cece gave her a knowing look. "Just say hello," she whispered.

His groggy eyes came to attention upon seeing Charlie and Cece. A faint smile curled his lips, and he reached out a hand towards Charlie, indicating she take it. Slowly, she approached him, staring at the offered hand. She took it in her own, feeling his callused fingertips, surely from years of playing guitar.

"This wasn't exactly the way I'd pictured our meeting," he said in a raspy voice.

Tears started to form in the corners of her eyes, threatening to spill over. She sniffed. "Me neither."

"Dwight, I don't even know what to say. You saved my life," Cece said. "I don't know what crazy notion possessed you to step in front of me, but if the bullet hit me any differently than it did you, I wouldn't be here. Thank you." She stepped over to the opposite side of the bed from where Charlie stood and kissed Dwight on his cheek.

"Cece, you have made me crazy in the past, and I said some awful things when I first found out you kept our daughter from me all these years, but you are her mother, and once upon a time, I was crazy in love with you. When I saw the two of you standing there with that lunatic screaming at you both… Anyway, I'm glad I didn't check out. I wanna stick around." He smiled then winced with pain. Charlie looked at him with concern. He just smiled with adoration in his eyes. "I'm okay, kiddo. I'll be alright."

And he was. Dwight couldn't wait to meet his granddaughter. It turned out, they only lived ten miles apart in Los Angeles.

When it was time to return home and back to Avalon, Charlie found it harder to leave her mother than usual.

"I'm only a plane ride away, or day's drive. I love my job and my new friends." Cece beamed. "And, babygirl, you will be back a lot for The Chrysalis House. I knew you couldn't stay that far away from home."

Finally, Charlie was crying happy tears. Cece must have been reading her mind because she said, "No more looking over our shoulders. He's gone. From now on, we only look forward. And Charlotte…*Charlie*," she said, her voice cracking. "I'm so sorry. For everything." It was Cece's turn to cry, which pulled at Charlie's heartstrings, and she hugged her mother goodbye.

Jack was waiting outside in the rental car, and Charlie left Cece's downtown Santa Rosa home feeling grateful they finally were in a place of healing.

Before leaving for the San Francisco Airport, Charlie had Jack drive through Sebastopol to see her old neighbors Joan and Randy Taylor. When they drove into the driveway and stepped outside of their car, Randy opened the door before she could even knock.

"I see all that goes on outside, and when I didn't recognize this gray sedan, I pulled the curtains back. When I saw this gorgeous young woman step out of it though, I knew it was our own Charlie Kane."

Joan quickly came to the door and squealed with delight. Charlie waved Jack closer to say hello and introduced them, declaring Joan the best cook she'd ever known. When the Taylors invited them in, she sadly declined, saying they had a plane to catch and had to get back to their daughter, but she told them about The Chrysalis House and promised she'd be back to visit soon. They left with baggies of home-baked cowboy cookies for their flight home.

✧

Back in SoCal, they drove the winding road to their ocean home to find Rita playing on the floor with Avalon in the great room of their dream house. HOME! Charlie felt a sense of relief and gratitude that she had never known before. She knew exactly where she belonged and the exact people she belonged with. And now she could add her father into the mix. No more pushing people away and closing herself off.

That night after arriving back home, as her husband slept beside her, and with their daughter and Rita both fast asleep in the next room, Charlie lay awake listening to the silence of the house and the far-off roar of the Pacific Ocean.

She'd once read a book by an author named Oriah, that spoke of trying to trade pieces of yourself for the promise of safety. Charlie knew now that she no longer needed to sacrifice being true to herself in order to be safe. She was bolder, braver, and knew that whatever life threw her way, she was strong enough now to endure. She had stopped betraying herself because of fear and insecurity and started honoring herself by chasing her deepest desires, regardless of the possibility of failure or disappointment. She was learning that pain in life was certain, but she got to choose how long she'd suffer. And right now, she was living the best possible version of her life, and she didn't plan to miss a moment of it.

With the moonlight shining across the sea, shimmering like

diamonds in the night, Charlie drew the sheets up closer to her chin and listened to the soft breathing of the man who had saved her. Jack was truly a knight in shining armor, not because he came to her rescue, but because he showed her the way to rescue herself.

Acknowledgements

This book came to me from the love of story, and the love of music. That's why when I was driving and listening to the 1972 song, "Wild-flower," by Skylark, I clearly saw who Charlie Kane was. Having said that, I need to thank my father, Carl, for his love of music and how it played a huge part in our lives growing up. Great songs share a story. My dad taught me that. I miss you every day, Dad.

Thanks to my early reader friends, who gave honest feedback and support where I needed it. Sonya Murch, I can't tell you how grateful I felt when you agreed to dive into my very early, very rough draft. Thank you for helping me to really see Jack. And to Maryann LoRusso, and Courtney Schrieve, my besties from Kick-Ass Writers. Thanks for going line-by-line with me and questioning me when I needed to rethink a scene, or help me to know when I'd gone off course. You two made me a better writer and held me accountable. Also, my lovely friend April Strait, thank you for answering those crazy text messages when the words didn't sound right and I needed your brainpower. Thanks for always believing in me.

To my editor, Tamara Hughes, I have to say that without your guidance and expertise, I'd have gone down a totally different path with this book. You helped me to excavate the gems and tell the best story possible. Thank you for seeing me through.

I marvel at how supportive and encouraging the writing community has been to me. At how inspiring other authors and editors are, and how generous with their time they have been over the years. To Jennifer Lynn Alvarez, Brenda Novak, J.Lynn Bailey, and Jennifer Graybeal, you all have lifted me up and often, without knowing it, paved the way for others to follow their dreams. I know that's what you've done for me. Thank you.

I'd be nowhere without the love of my friends and family. My support system of friends is abundant, and I will always be grateful for how blessed I am that there are so many of you. Too many to name here, but you know who you are. My cheerleaders. My rocks. I love you all.

My beloved family is the cornerstone of everything I do. To my daughters, Fallon and Emma, you both inspire me with your zest for life and many talents. Remember, there's nothing you can't do, no matter how old you get. Keep striving to reach for that next higher branch. My awesome niece, Kacie Drew, thank you for talking books with me, and listening to my ideas. Follow your heart my love, and keep being you. To my wonderful husband, Charlie, I know you often have no idea what it is that I do in my office all day long, but I adore how you still ask if I had a good day. Thank you for loving me all these years and encouraging me to do whatever makes me happy.

But it's you, the readers, that I want to thank the most. I'm ever grateful that you read my books, share them with your friends, and talk about them at book clubs. To those new readers, I'm so happy you picked my book! It's all of you who make me want to keep writing. To keep telling stories. And as long as I'm here, that's what I'm going to do. There's nothing in this world I enjoy doing more. Thank you all.

XOXO PATTI

Patti Diener is the author of *After the Fire*. She lives in Lake County, California with her husband Charles, and their hound, Lily. She's mom to two lovely, grown daughters. Patti loves to be near the ocean, and you can find her often on writing retreats in one of the coastal California towns of Bodega Bay, or Mendocino. Connect with her on social media using @pattidiener for Facebook, Instagram, and X. Websites are both pattidienerwrites.com and pattidiener.com.

www.ingramcontent.com/pod-product-compliance
Lightning Source LLC
Chambersburg PA
CBHW031156020726
47499CB00002B/393